CARMEN
SANDIEGO™

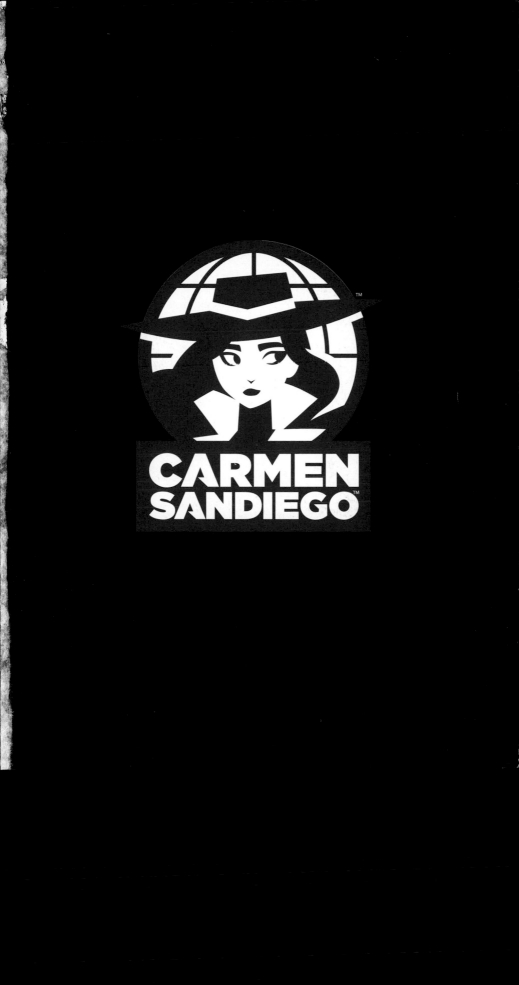

Based on the Netflix original series
teleplay by Rebecca Tinker

hmhbooks.com

Designed by Jenny Goldstick and Sarah Boecher
The type was set in Proxima Nova.
The sound effect type was created by Jenny Goldstick.

ISBN: 978-1-328-49579-2 (paper over board)
ISBN: 978-1-328-49507-5 (paperback)

Manufactured in Malaysia
TWP 10 9 8 7 6 5 4 3 2 1
4500764576

CARMEN SANDIEGO™

THE FISHY TREASURE CAPER

A GRAPHIC NOVEL

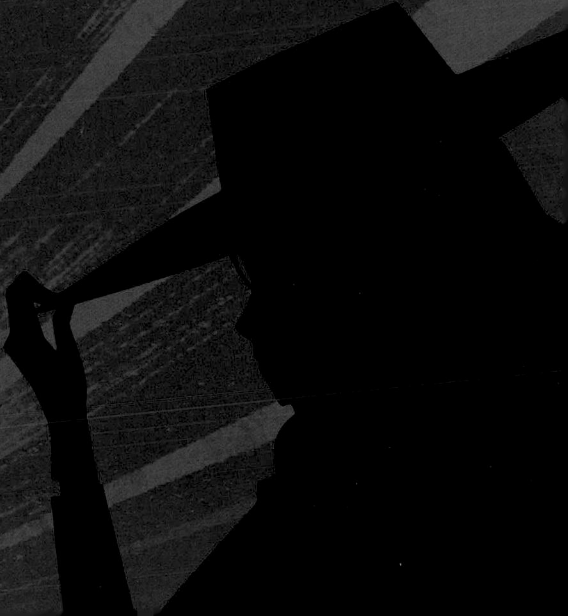

HOUGHTON MIFFLIN HARCOURT

BOSTON NEW YORK

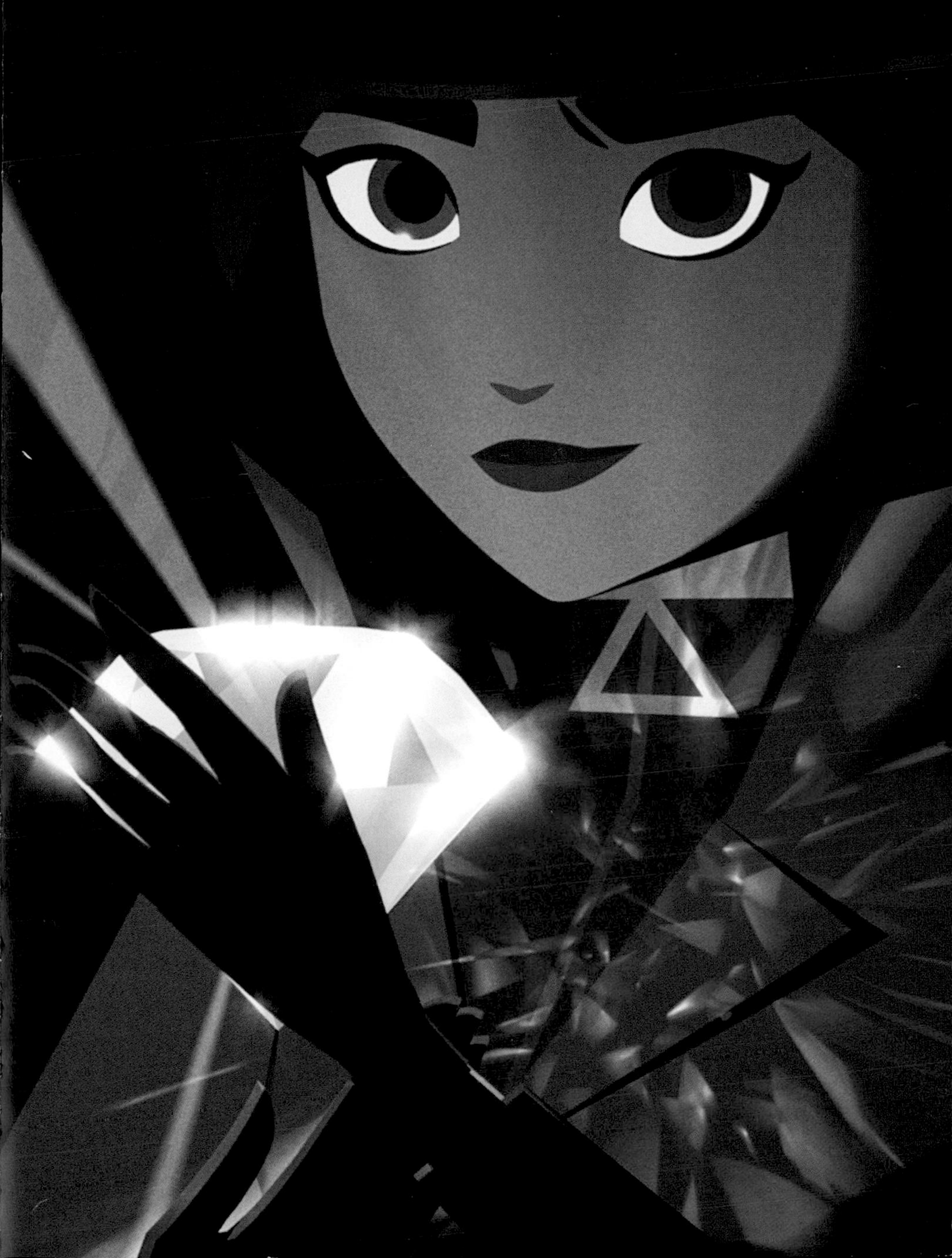

WHO IN THE WORLD IS
CARMEN
SANDIEGO?

FORMERLY KNOWN AS:

Black Sheep

OCCUPATION:

International super thief

ORIGIN:

Buenos Aires, Argentina

LAST SEEN:

Jakarta, Indonesia

I was found as a baby in Argentina and raised as an orphan on Vile Island. But I longed to set out and see the world.

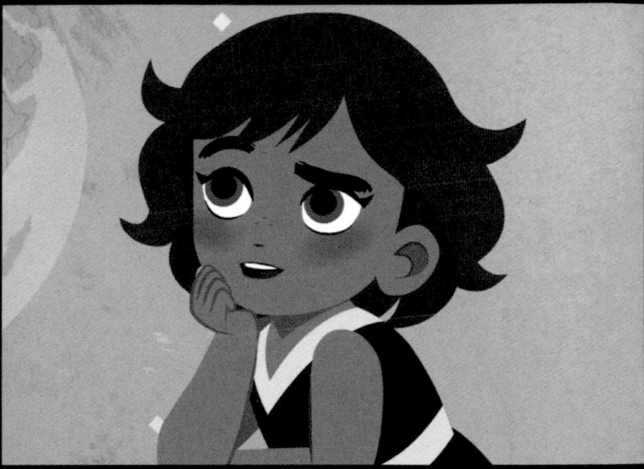

I couldn't wait to train at VILE's school for thieves. I wanted to become a VILE operative, traveling the world to steal precious goods.

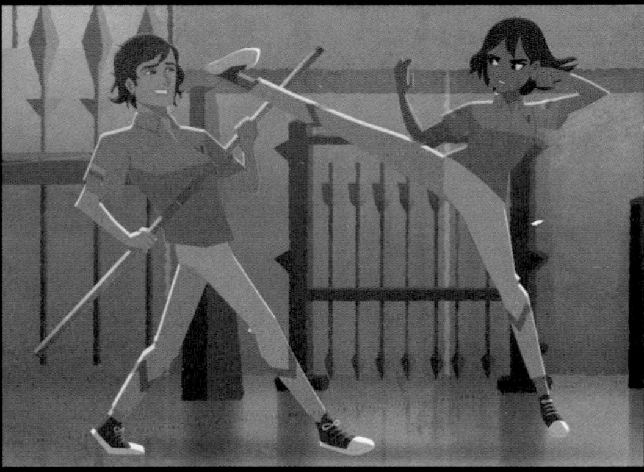

But I knew I had to get out after discovering what VILE really stands for: Villains' International League of Evil!

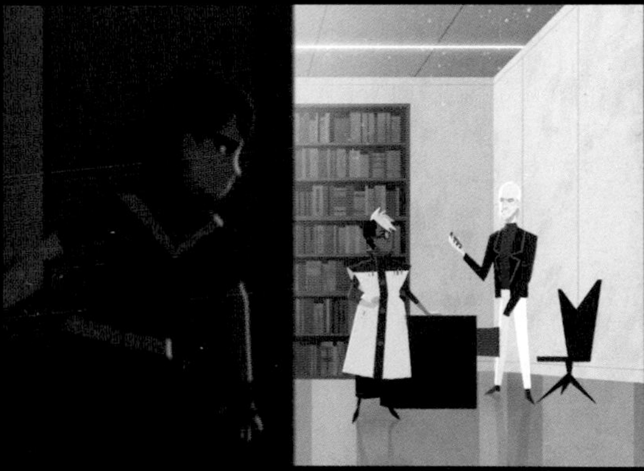

My new mission: take VILE down by stealing from them to give back to their victims.

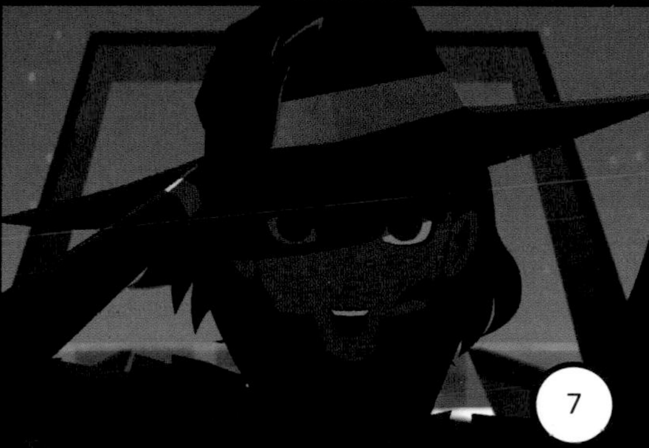

CARMEN'S SKILLS

Super sneak, expert fighter, gadget guru, mistress of disguise

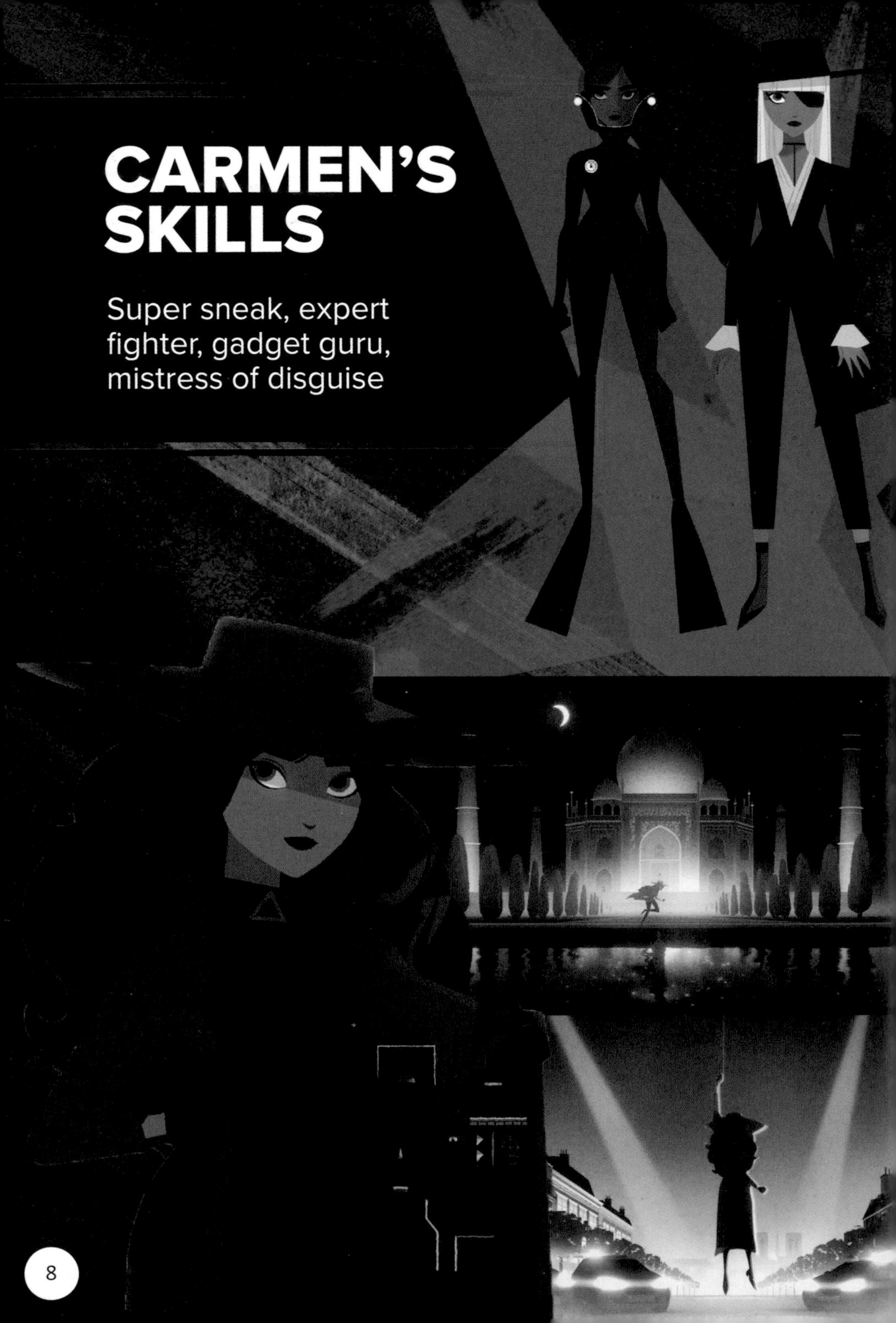

TOOLS FOR A THIEF

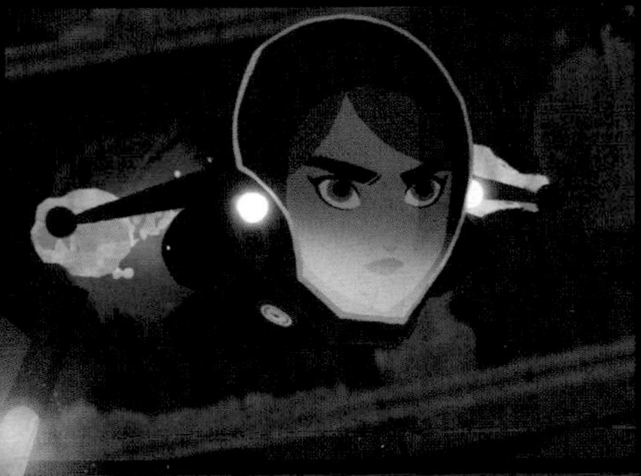

Scubajet

Carmen's scubajet blasts her through the water -- or flips around when she needs to go in reverse.

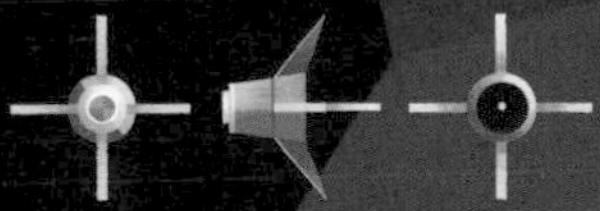

Tracker Dart

This electronic dart attaches to anything, and then Carmen can follow it anywhere.

TOOLS FOR A THIEF

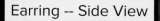

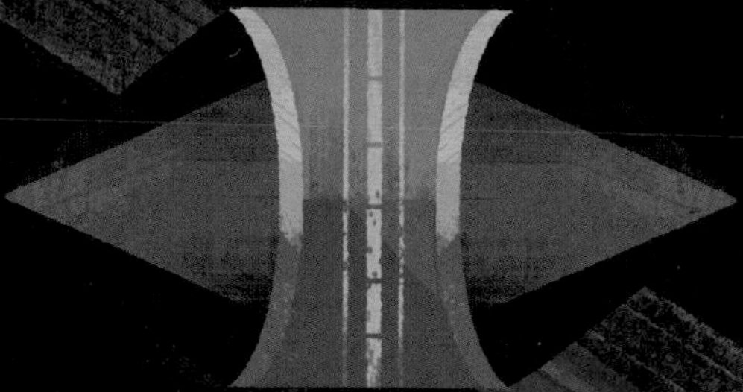

Earring -- Side View    Earring -- Front View

Comm-Link Earrings

Carmen's earrings hide an advanced two-way communications device, which she uses to stay in touch with Player through every mission.

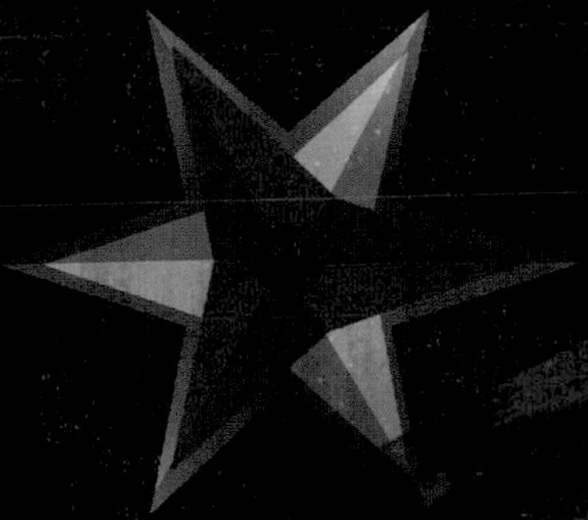

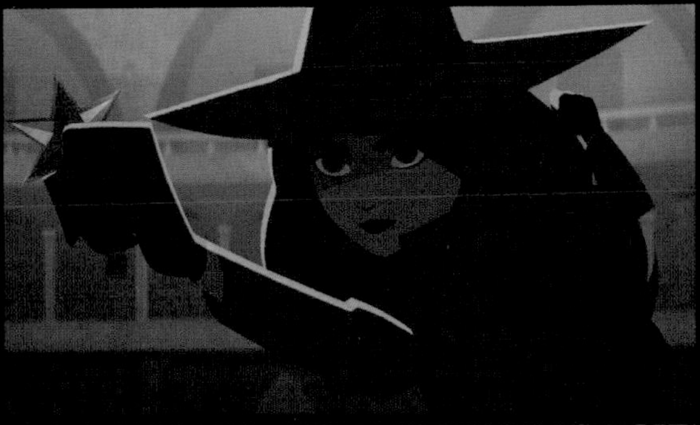

Throwing Stars

Easy to carry. Quick to strike.

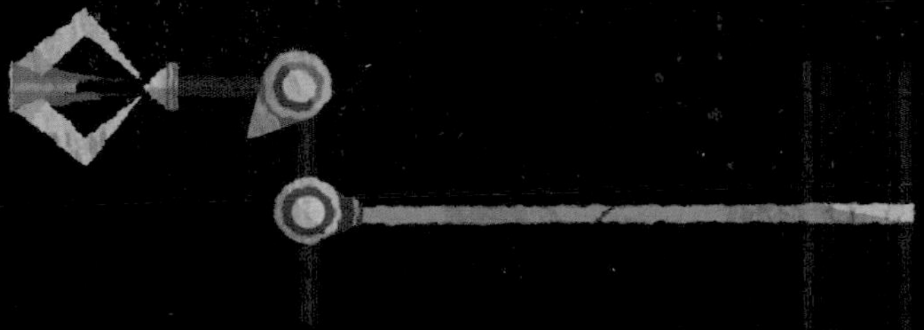

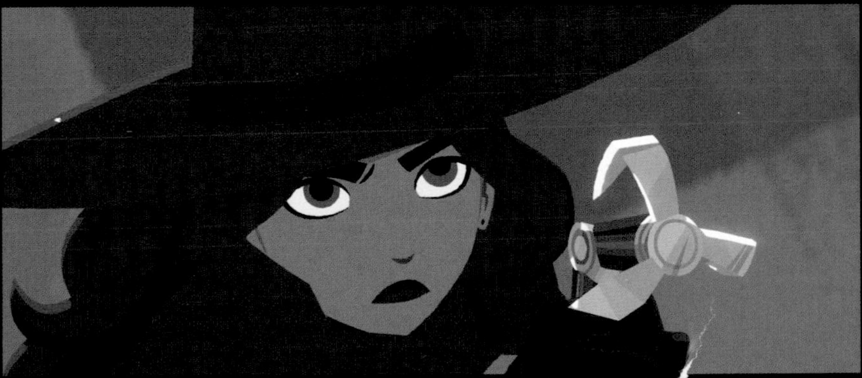

Grappling Hook

A hook on a rope that Carmen shoots from her wrist to reach high places.

CARMEN'S CREW

Player

White-hat hacker

BACKGROUND:

Player is a teenager from Niagara Falls, Canada. He met Carmen by hacking into her phone while she was still at VILE.

SKILLS:

- Learns everything about every place that Carmen goes to help guide her on capers
- Remotely deactivates security systems
- Scours the web for secret signs, coded messages, and hidden clues about VILE's next moves

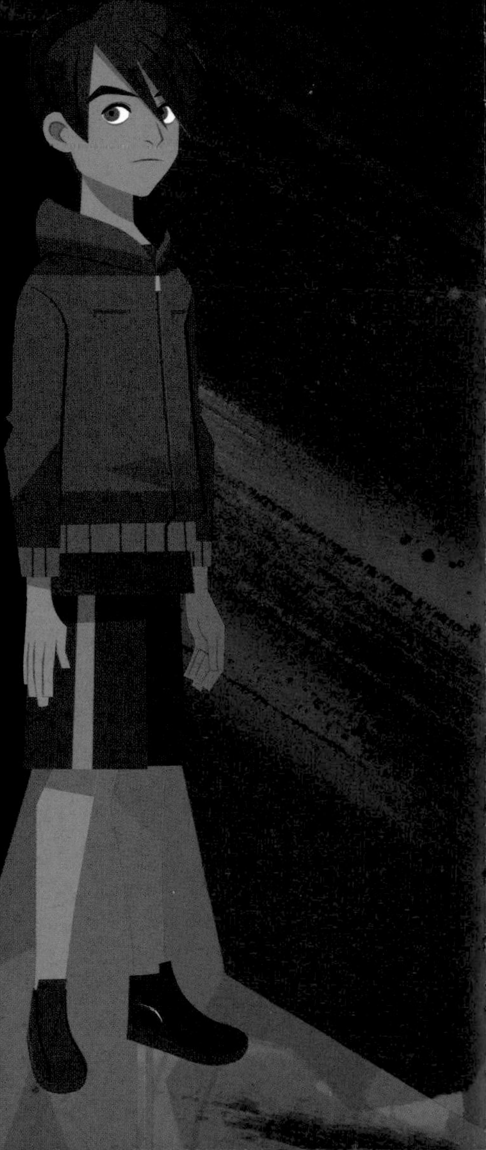

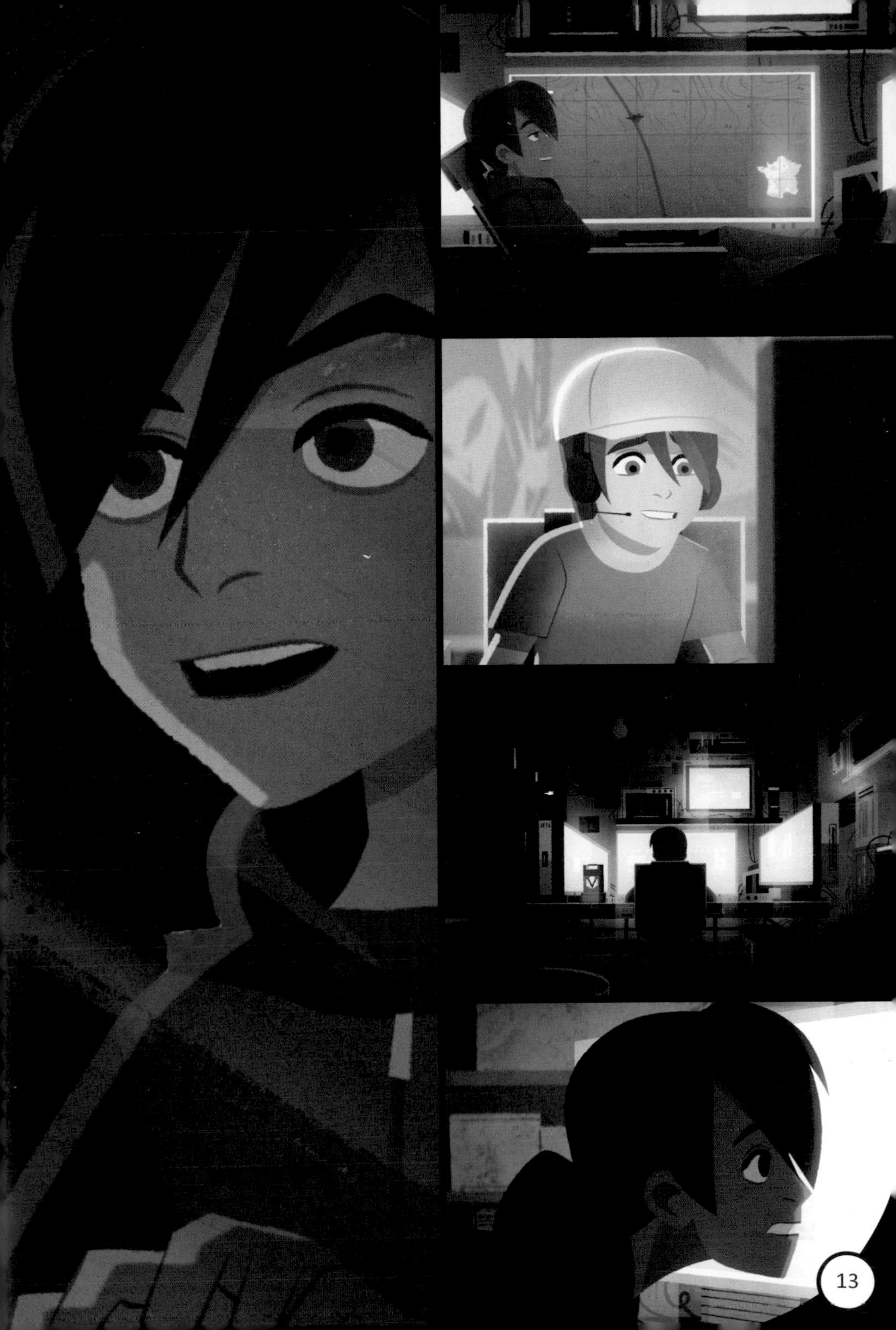

Ivy

Mechanic and tinkerer

SKILLS:

- Operates Carmen's gadgets, like the metal detector
- Great at fixing and making things
- Always has Carmen's back

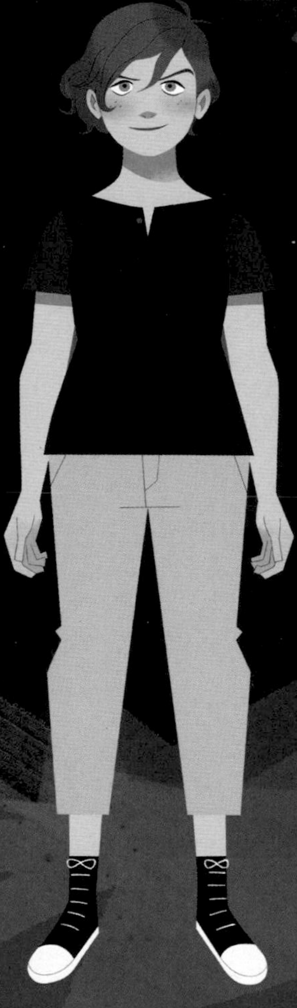

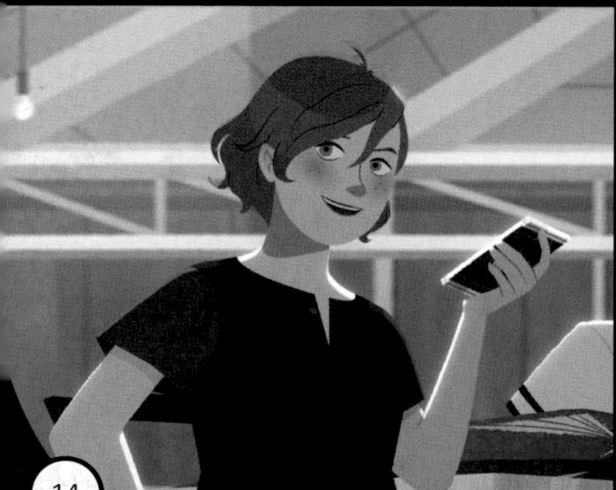

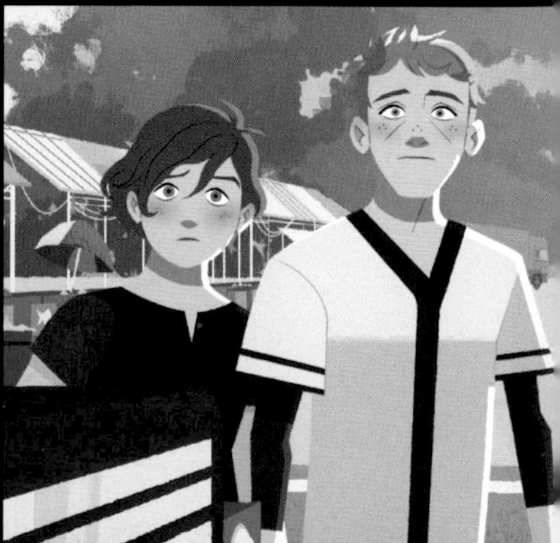

Zack

Driver

SKILLS:

- Great with cars, trucks, motorcycles, speedboats -- anything that goes fast
- Knows how to make a quick getaway
- Always hungry and eats almost anything...except for fish. BLECH!

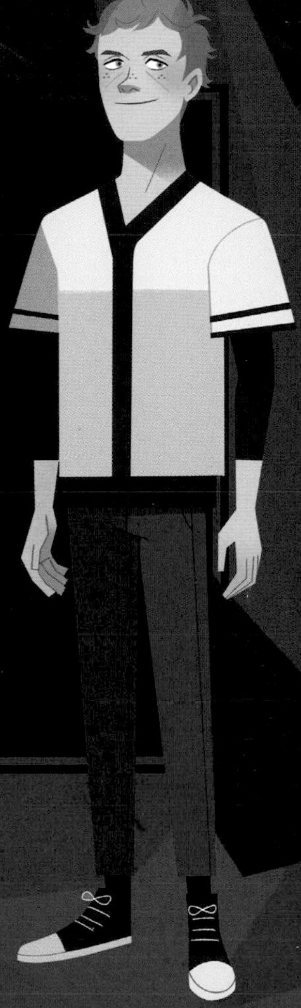

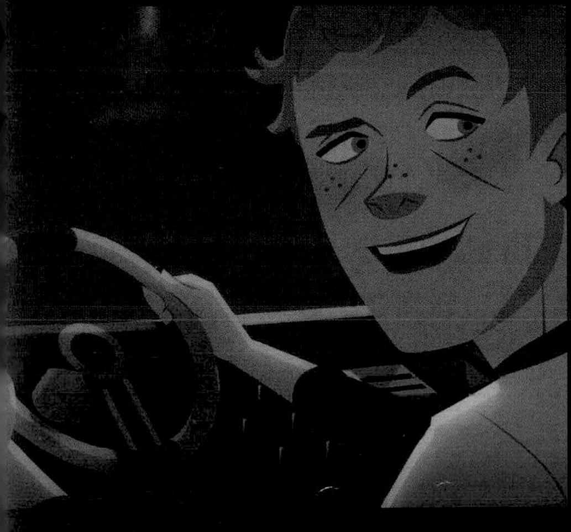

BACKGROUND:

Ivy and Zack are street-kid siblings from Boston, Massachusetts, USA. They met Carmen when they were robbing the same donut shop, which was owned by VILE.

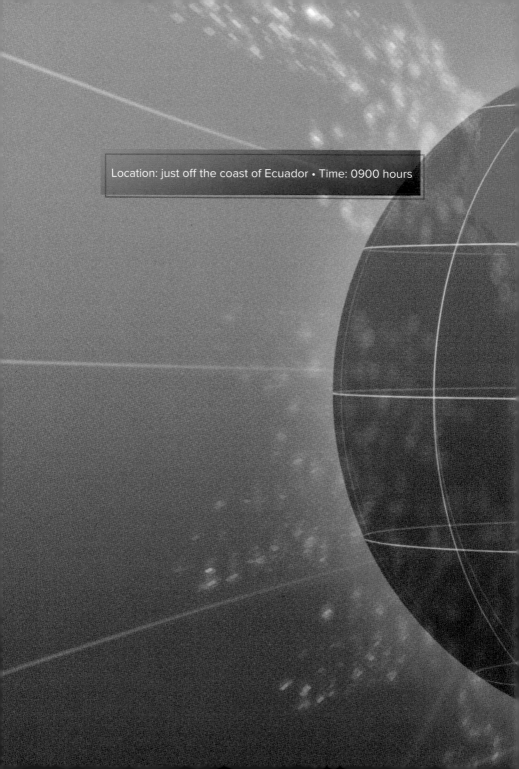

Location: just off the coast of Ecuador • Time: 0900 hours

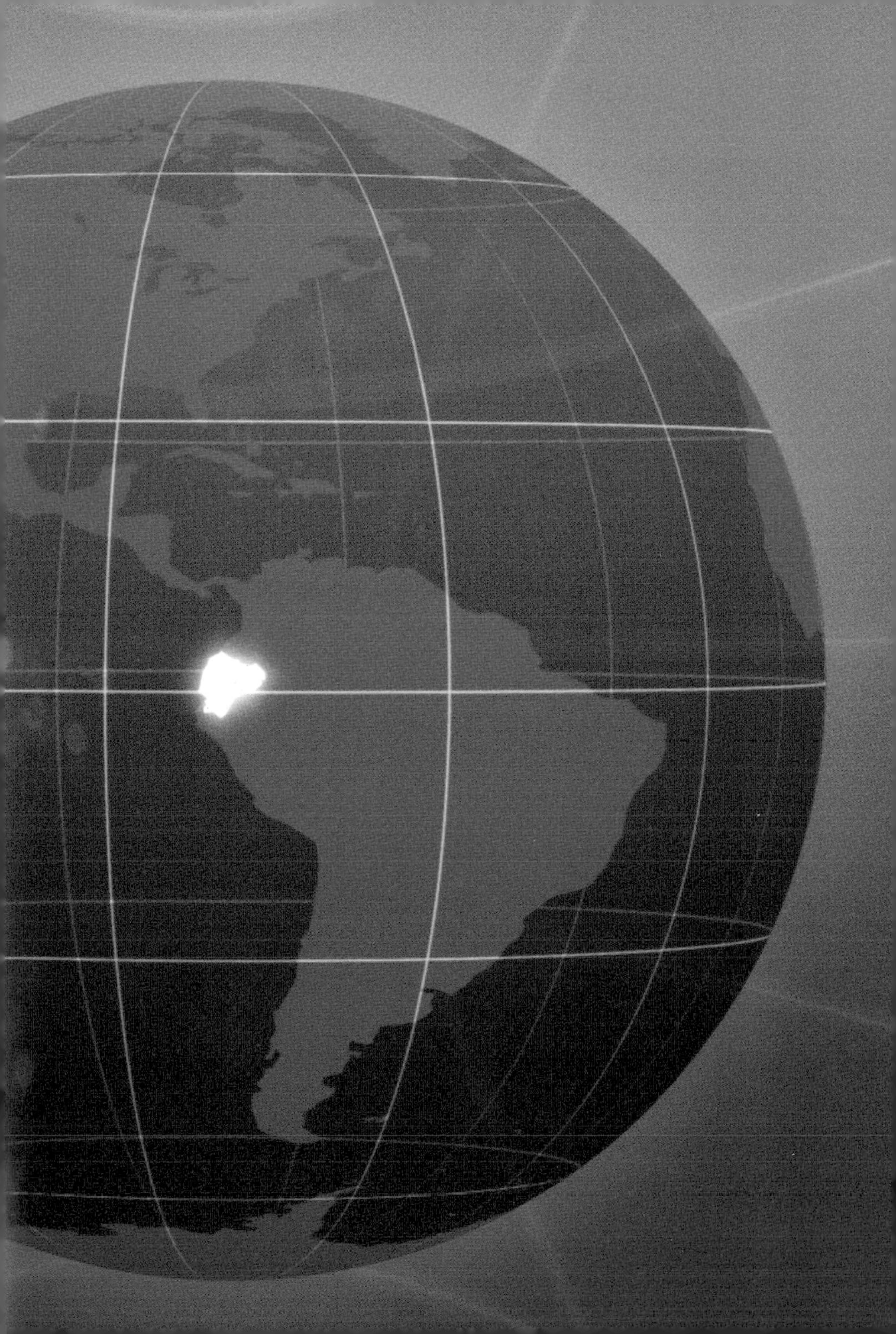

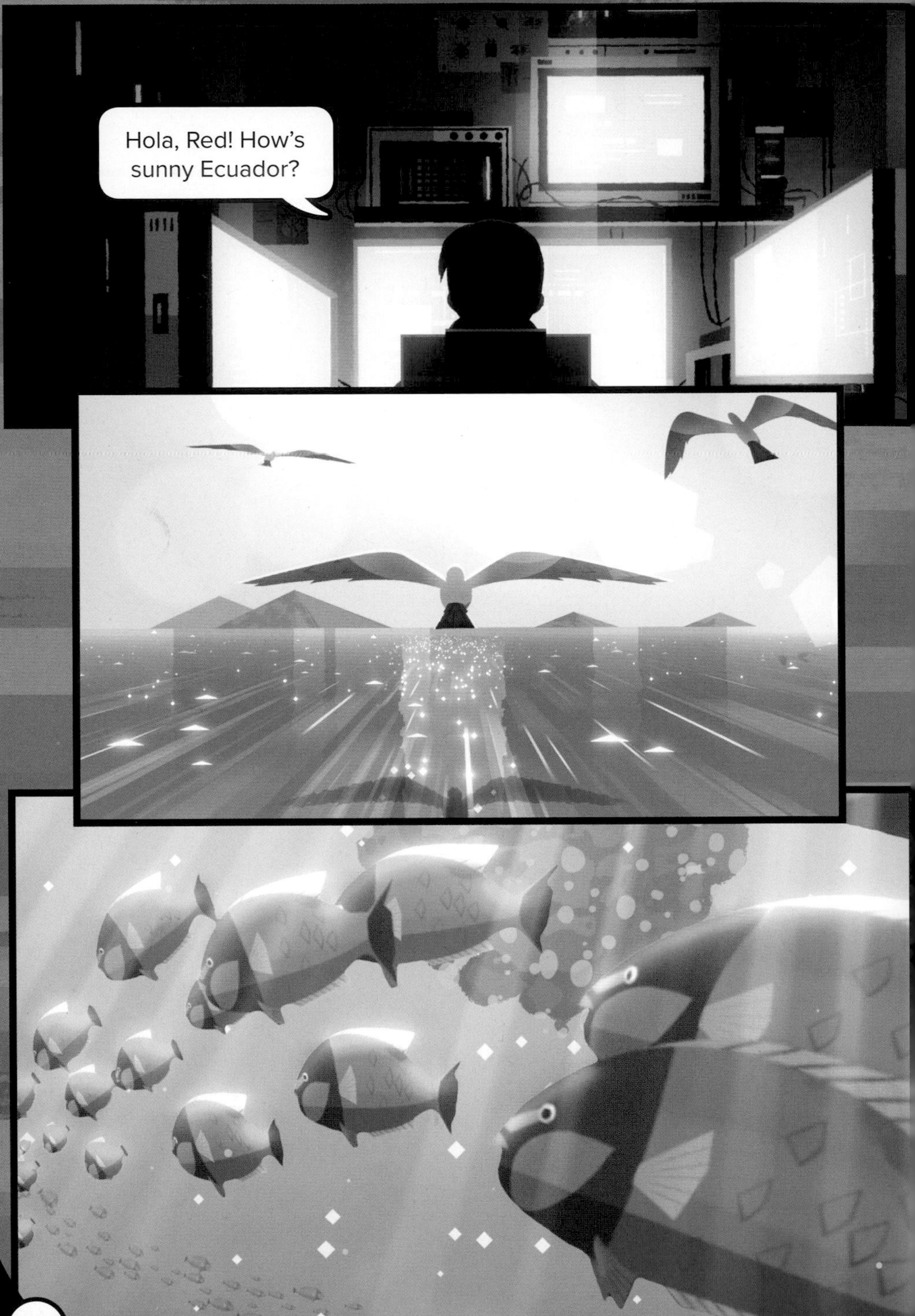
Hola, Red! How's sunny Ecuador?

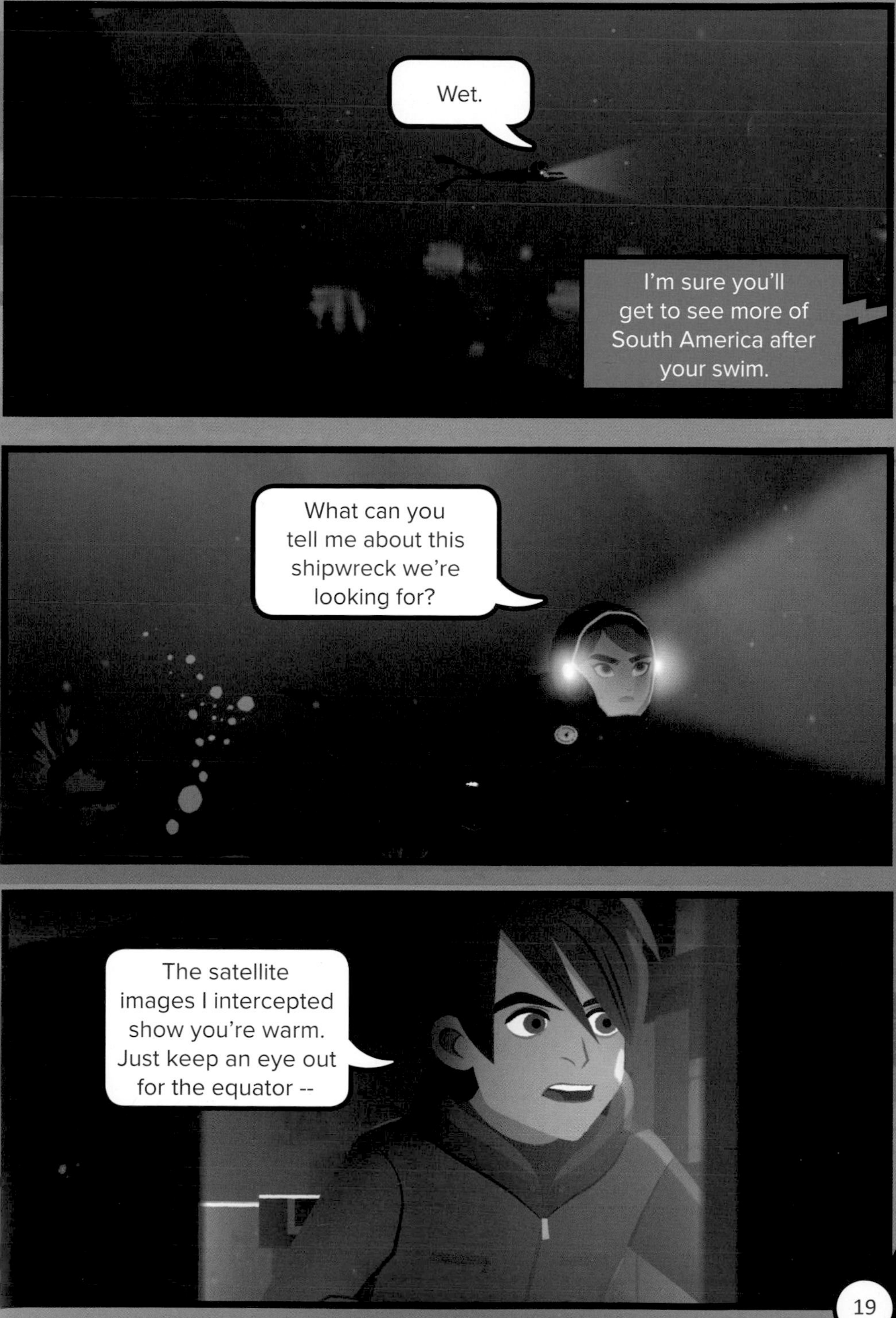

Wet.
I'm sure you'll get to see more of South America after your swim.
What can you tell me about this shipwreck we're looking for?
The satellite images I intercepted show you're warm. Just keep an eye out for the equator --

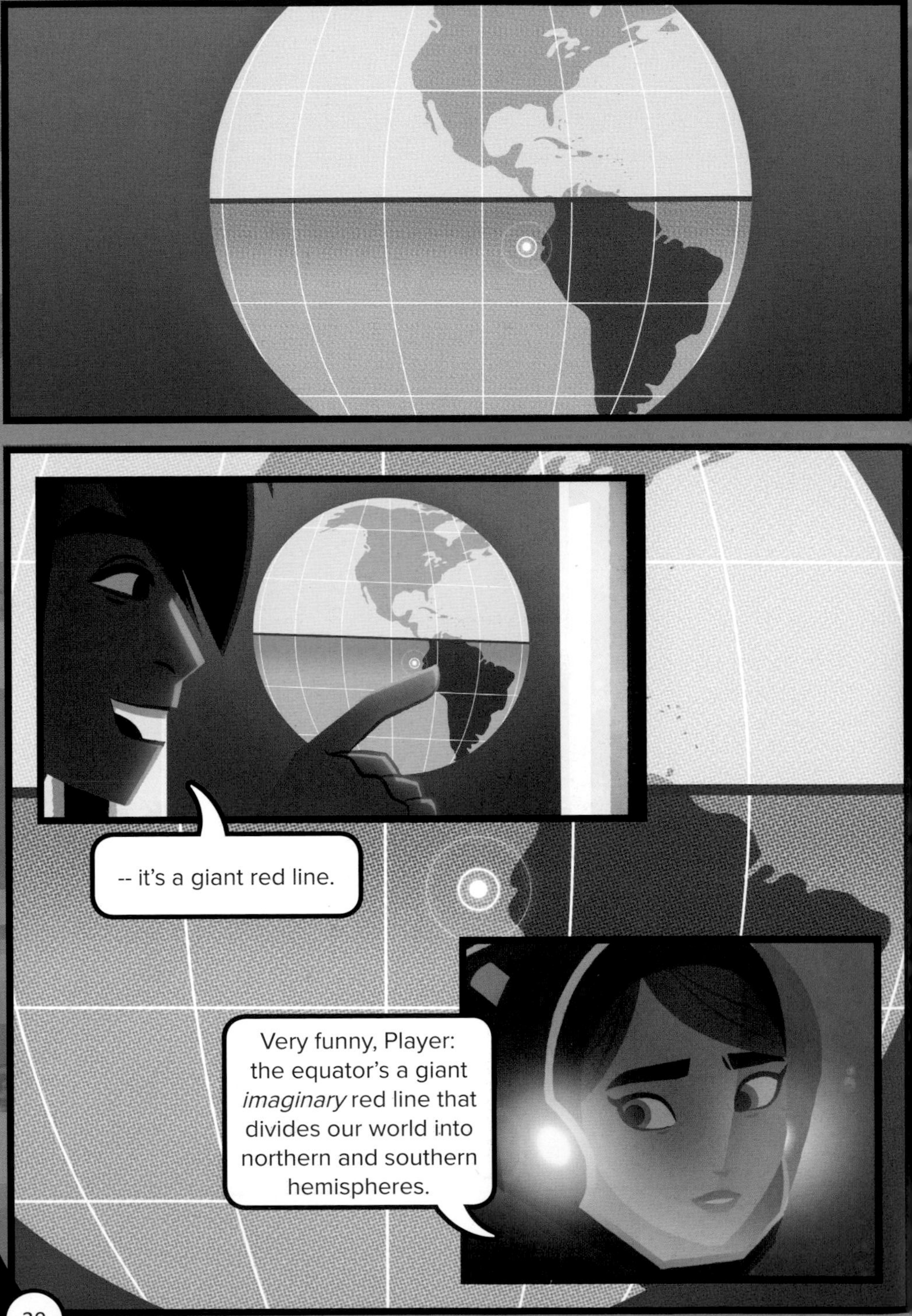
-- it's a giant red line.
Very funny, Player: the equator's a giant *imaginary* red line that divides our world into northern and southern hemispheres.

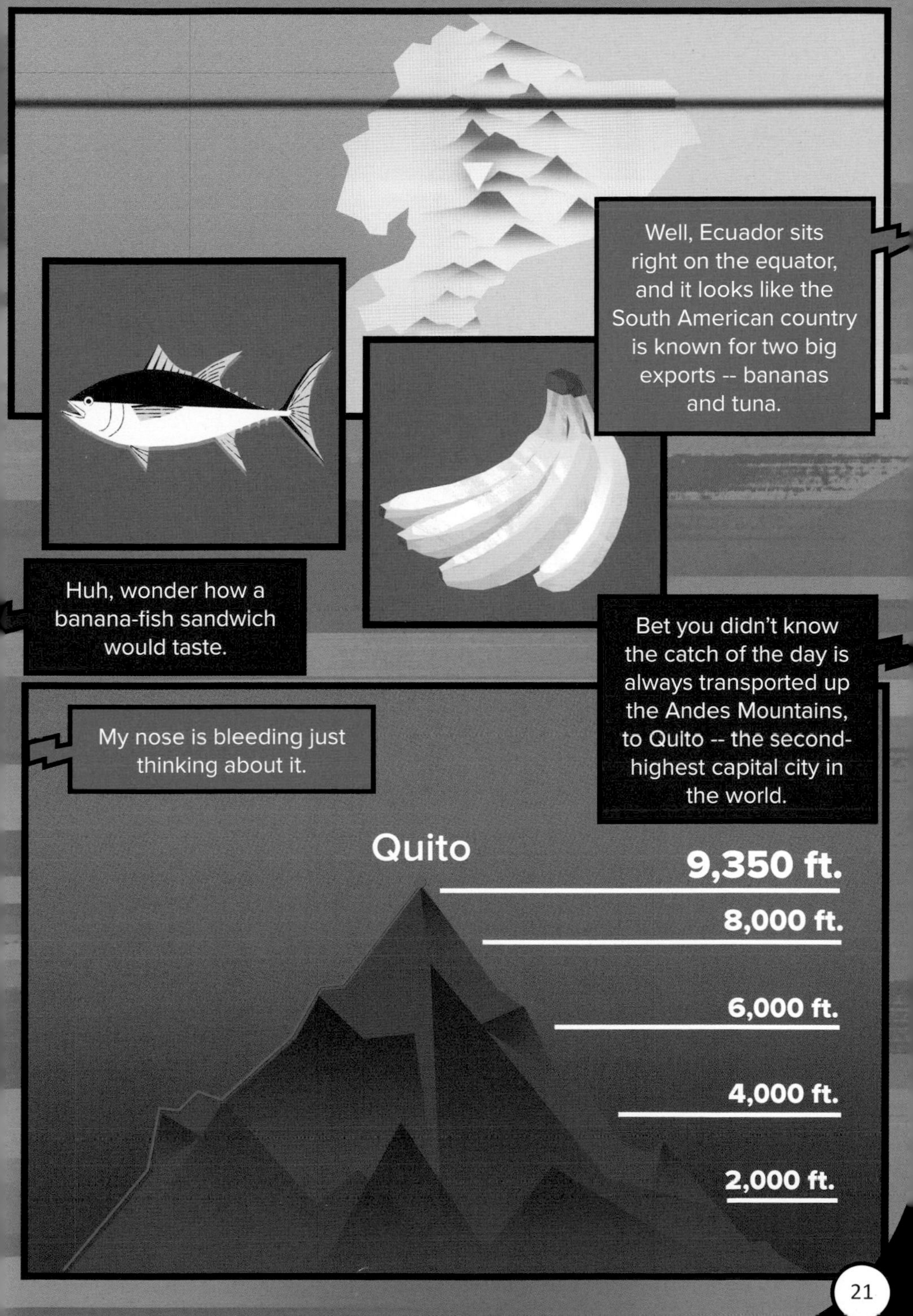
Well, Ecuador sits right on the equator, and it looks like the South American country is known for two big exports -- bananas and tuna.
Huh, wonder how a banana-fish sandwich would taste.
Bet you didn't know the catch of the day is always transported up the Andes Mountains, to Quito -- the second-highest capital city in the world.
My nose is bleeding just thinking about it.
Quito
9,350 ft.
8,000 ft.
6,000 ft.
4,000 ft.
2,000 ft.

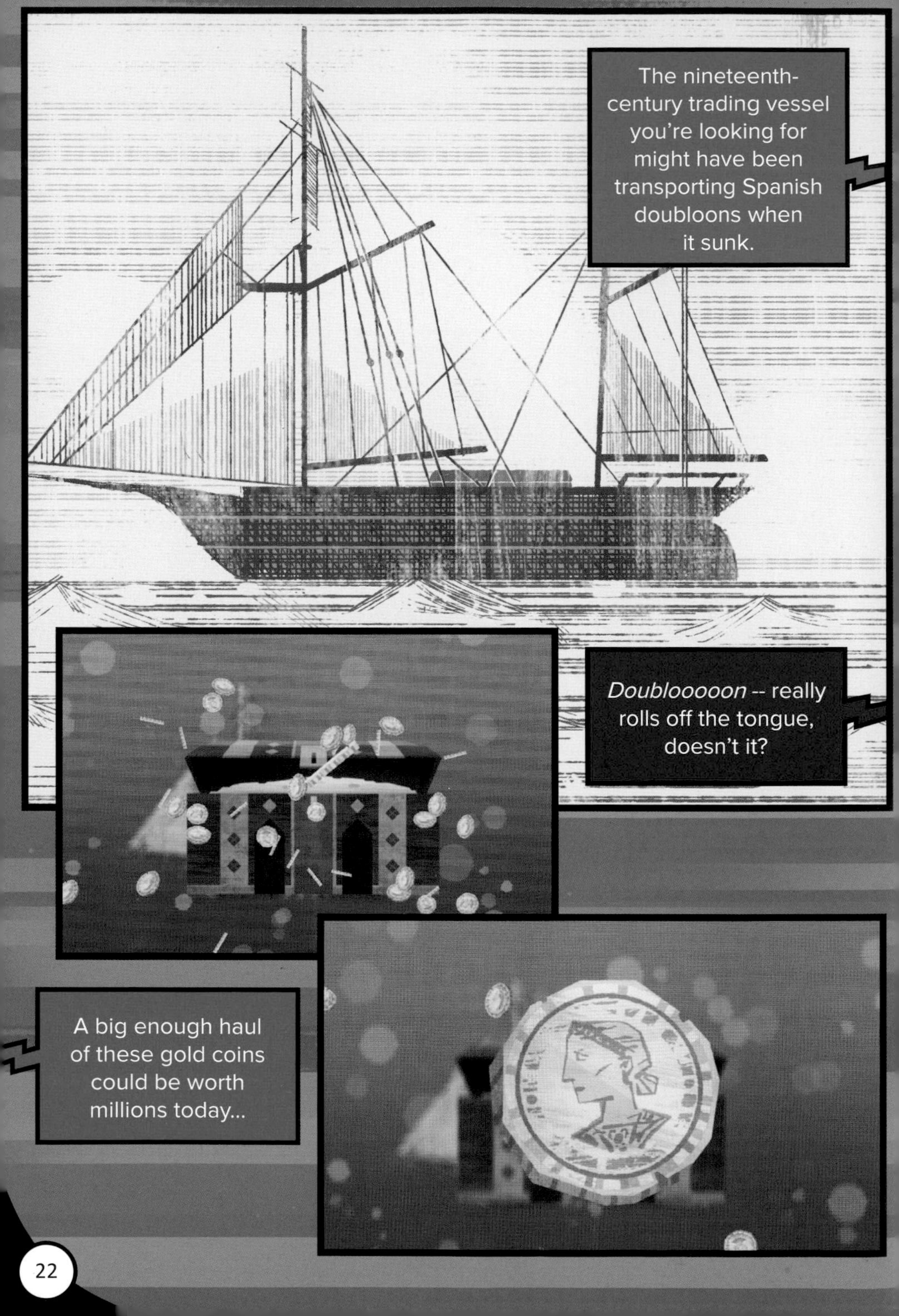

The nineteenth-century trading vessel you're looking for might have been transporting Spanish doubloons when it sunk.
Doublooooon -- really rolls off the tongue, doesn't it?
A big enough haul of these gold coins could be worth millions today...

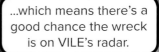
...which means there's a good chance the wreck is on VILE's radar.

With luck, I'll secure any valuable artifacts before VILE can scavenge them. Are all hands on deck?

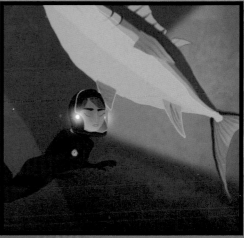

Surface Crew is on high alert.

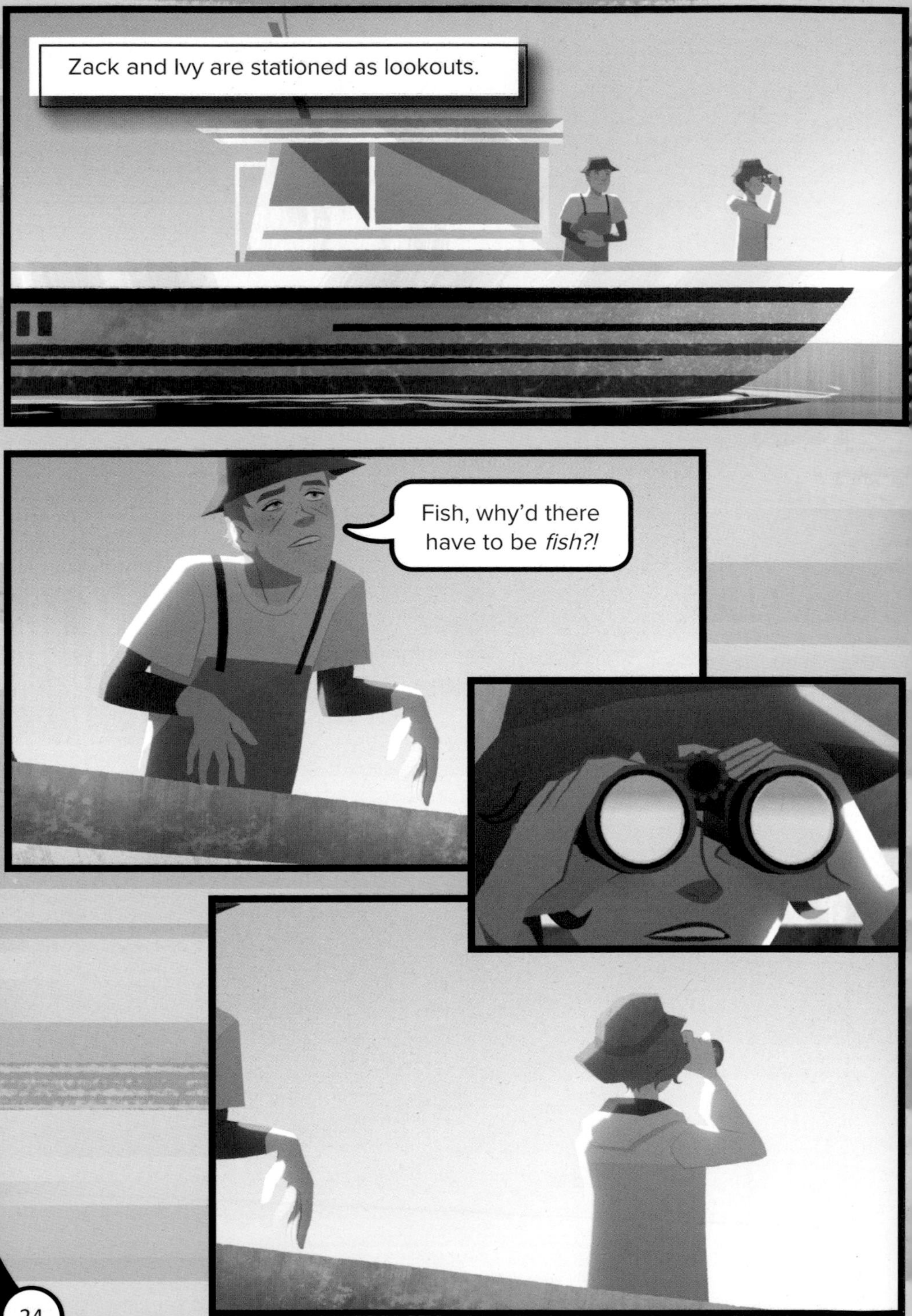
Zack and Ivy are stationed as lookouts.
Fish, why'd there have to be *fish?!*

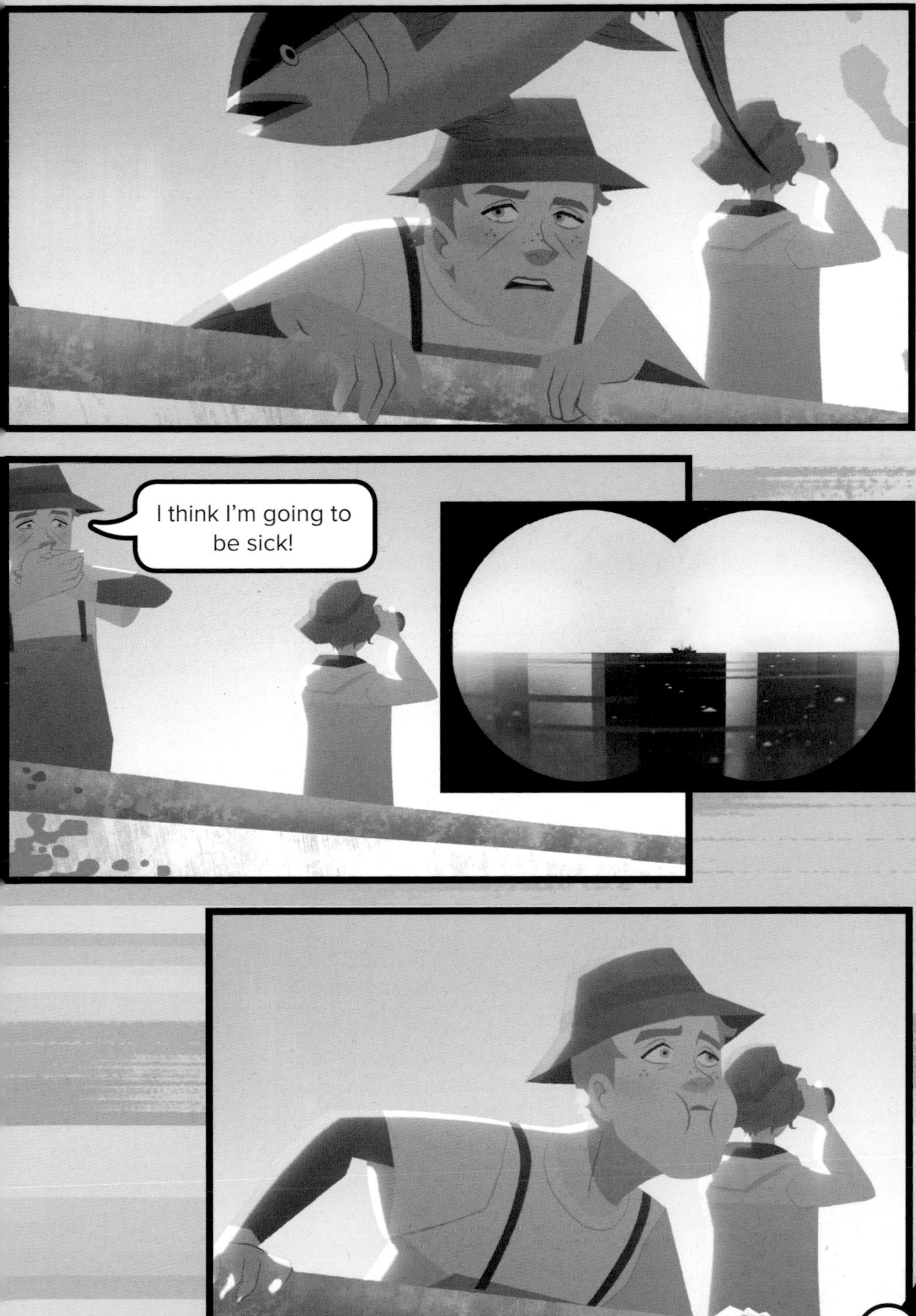
I think I'm going to be sick!

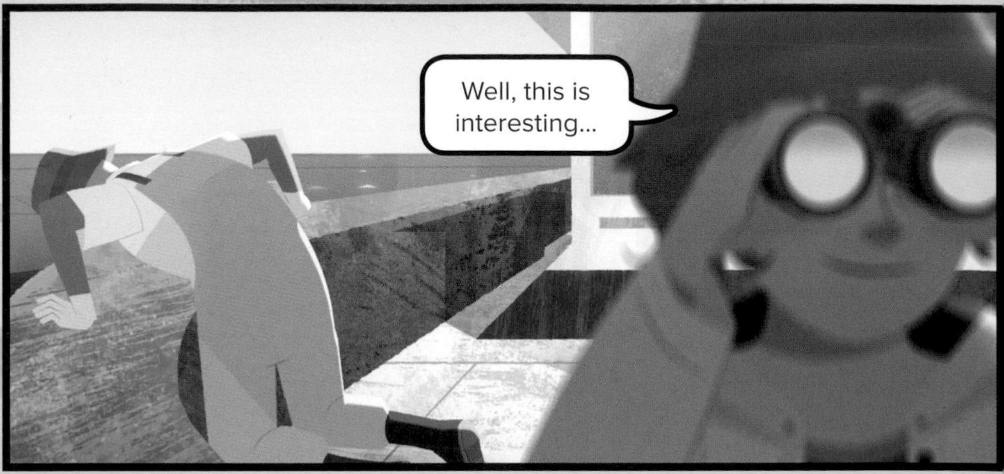
Well, this is interesting...

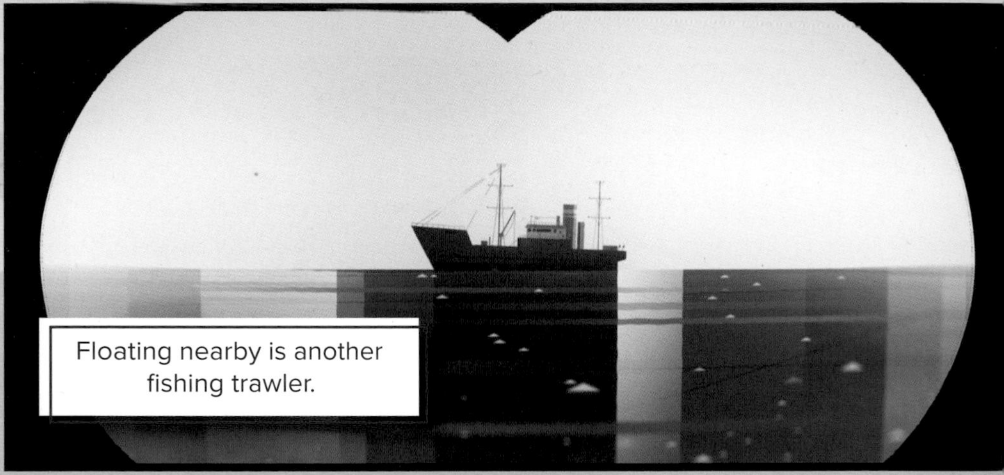
Floating nearby is another fishing trawler.

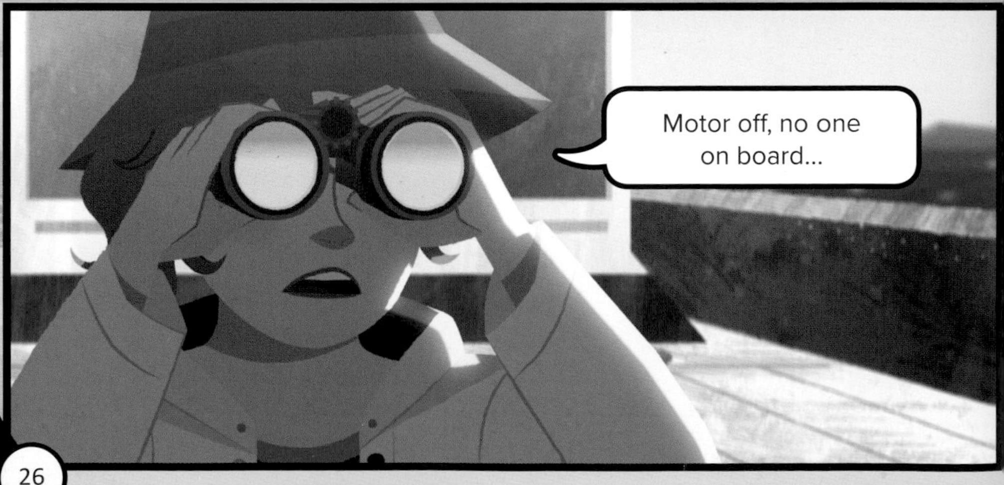
Motor off, no one on board...

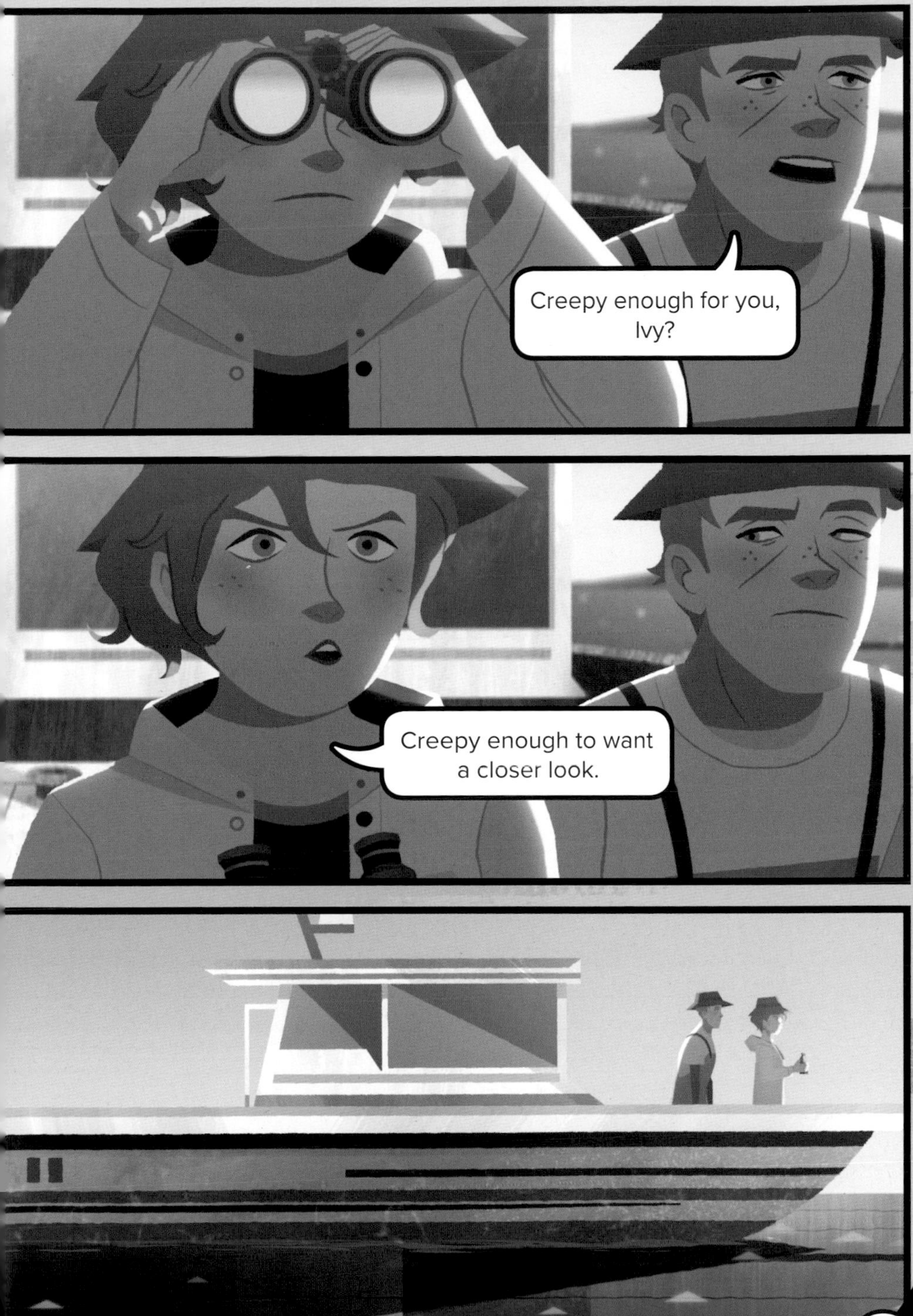
Creepy enough for you, Ivy?
Creepy enough to want a closer look.

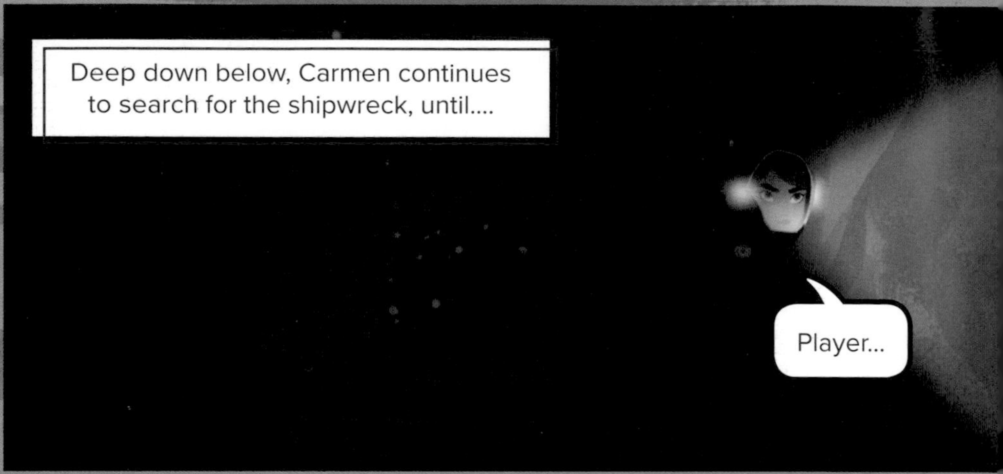
Deep down below, Carmen continues to search for the shipwreck, until....
Player...

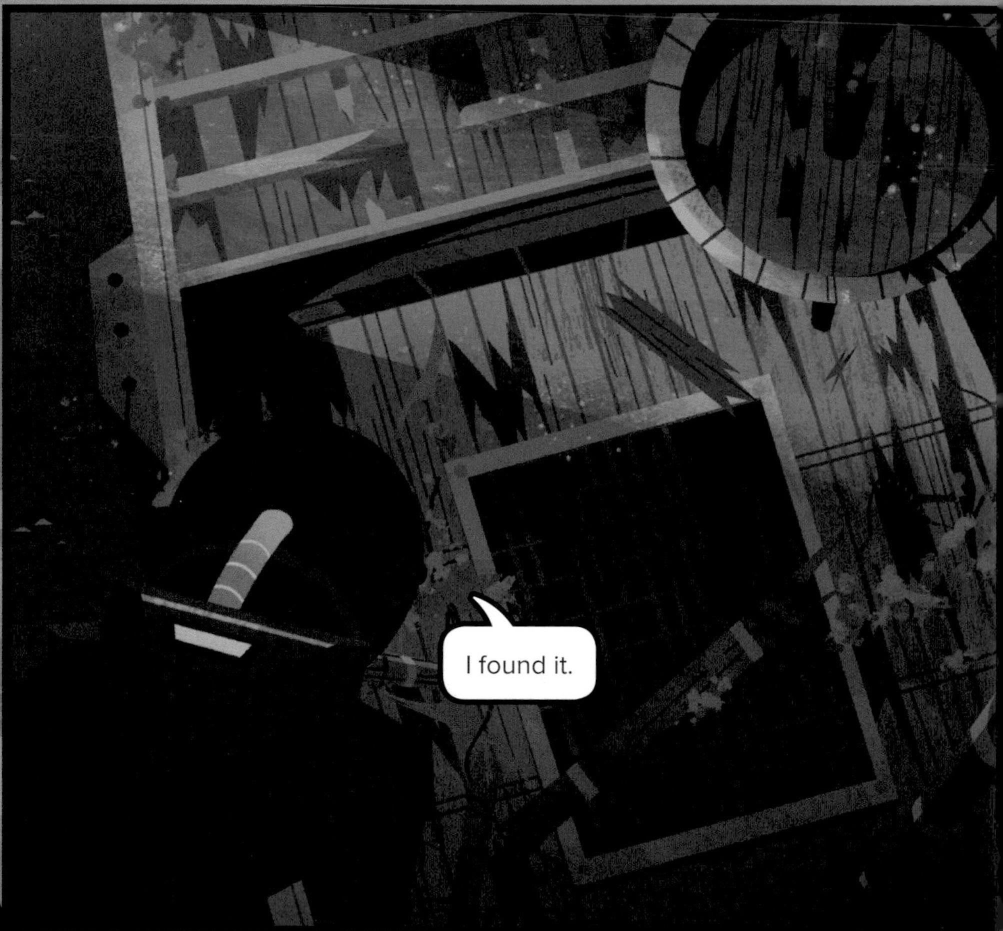
I found it.

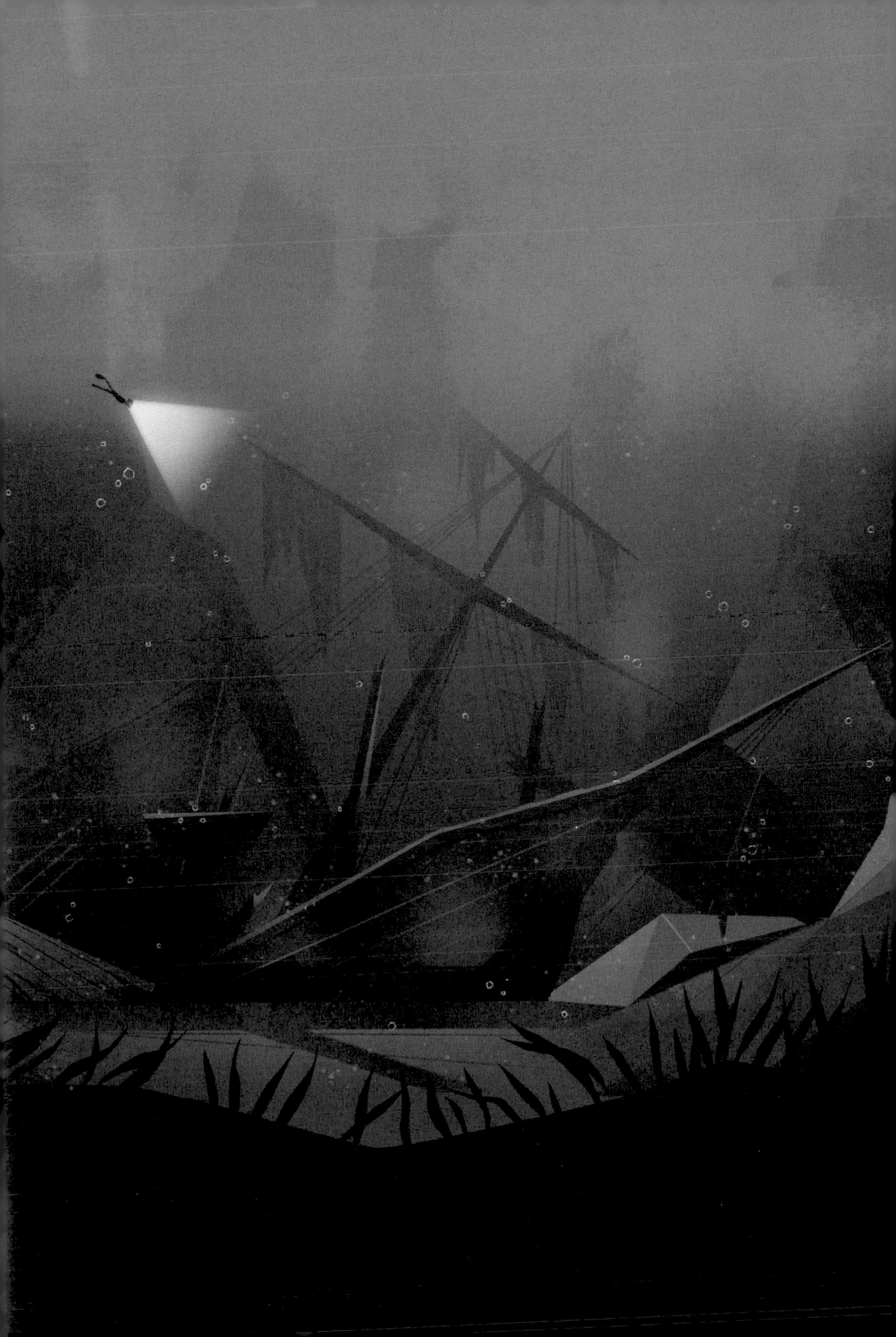

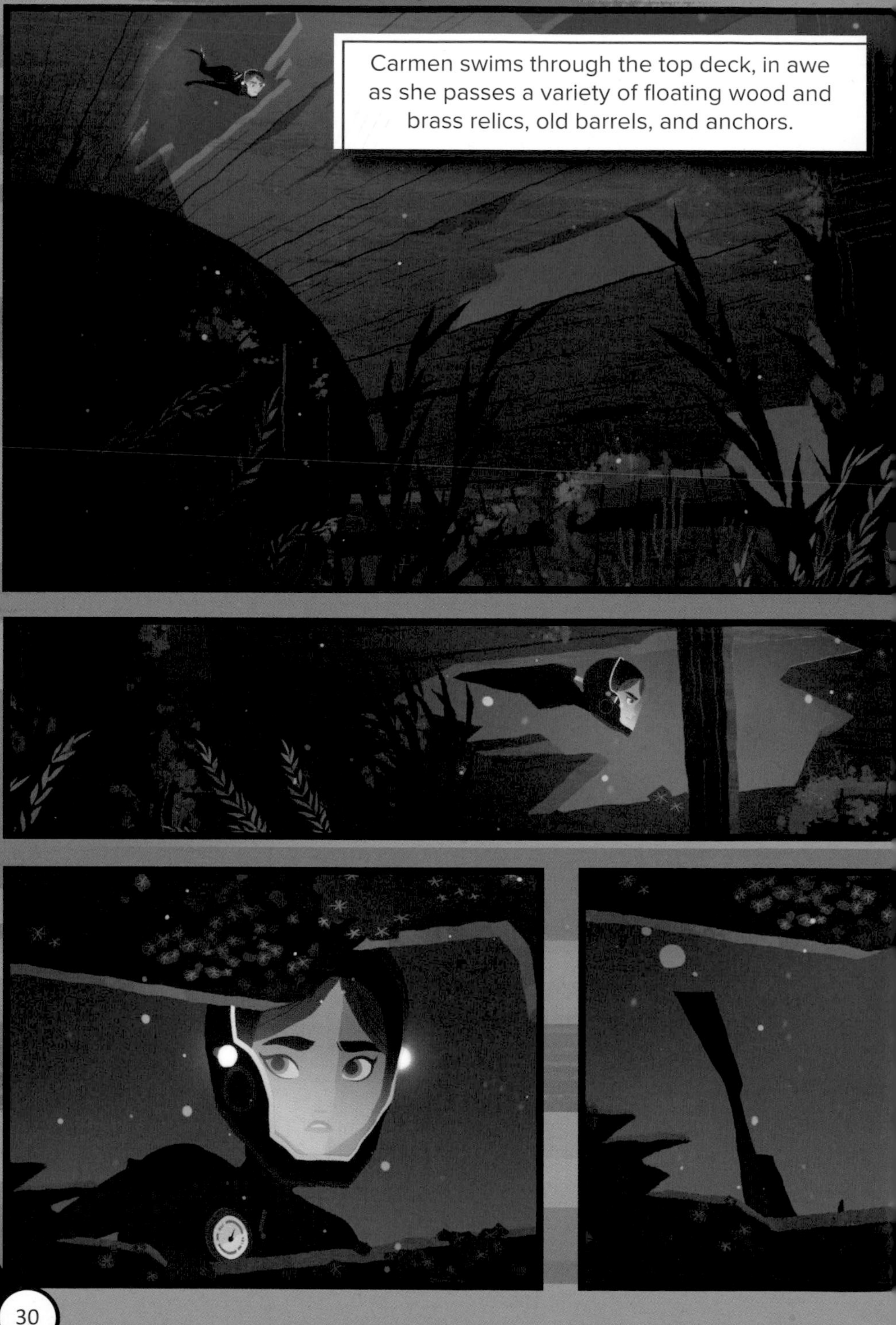
Carmen swims through the top deck, in awe as she passes a variety of floating wood and brass relics, old barrels, and anchors.

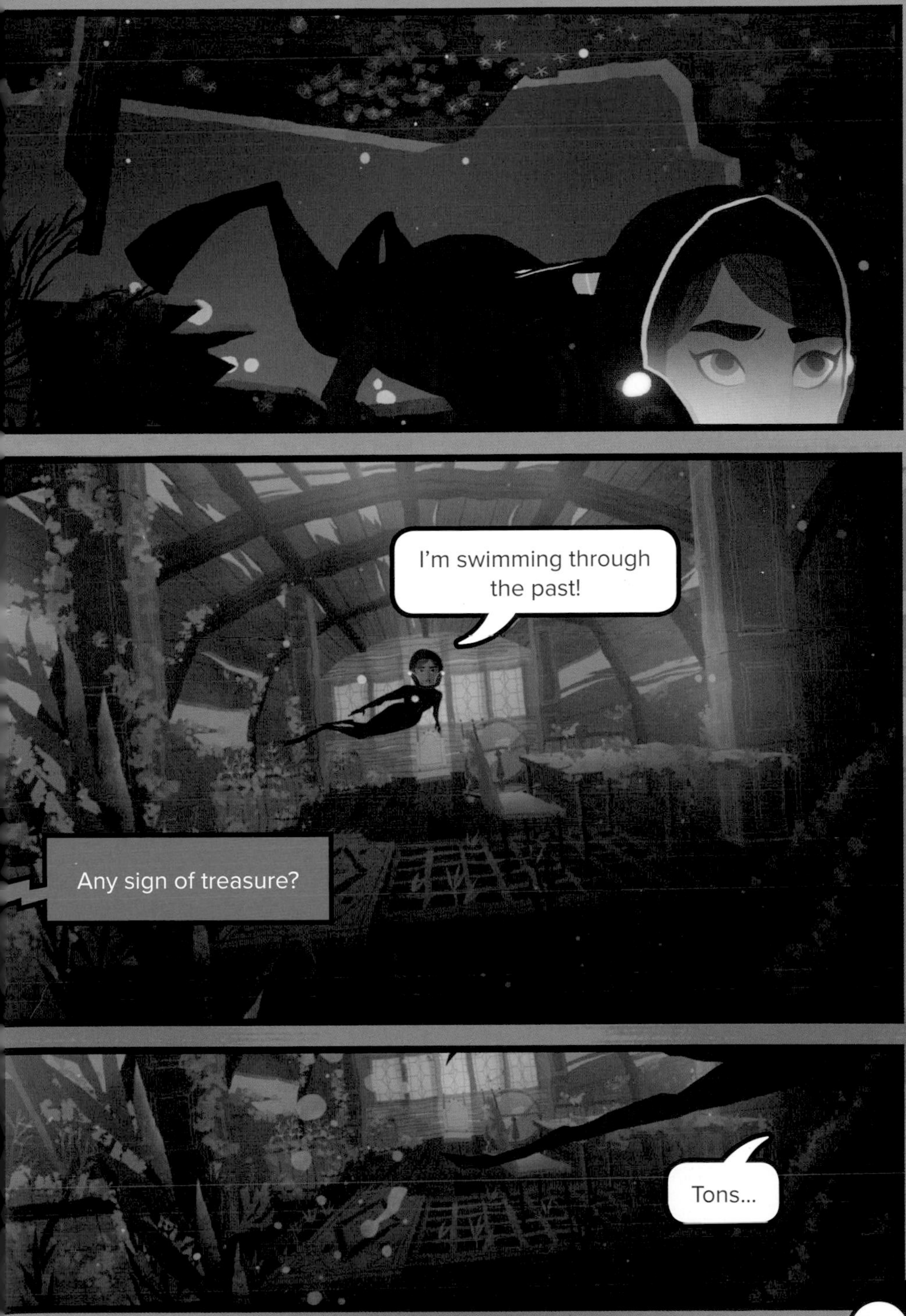
I'm swimming through the past!
Any sign of treasure?
Tons...

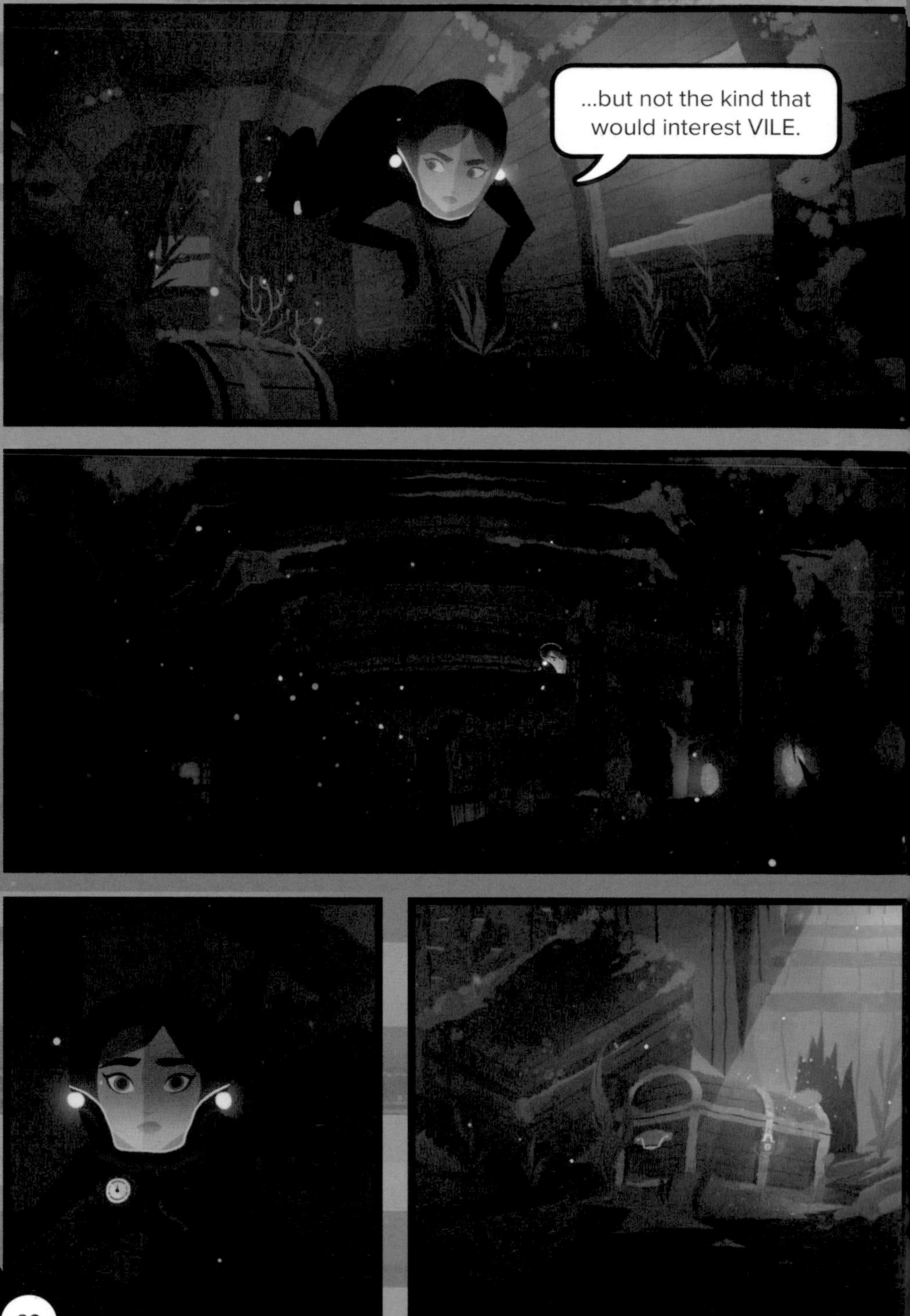
...but not the kind that would interest VILE.

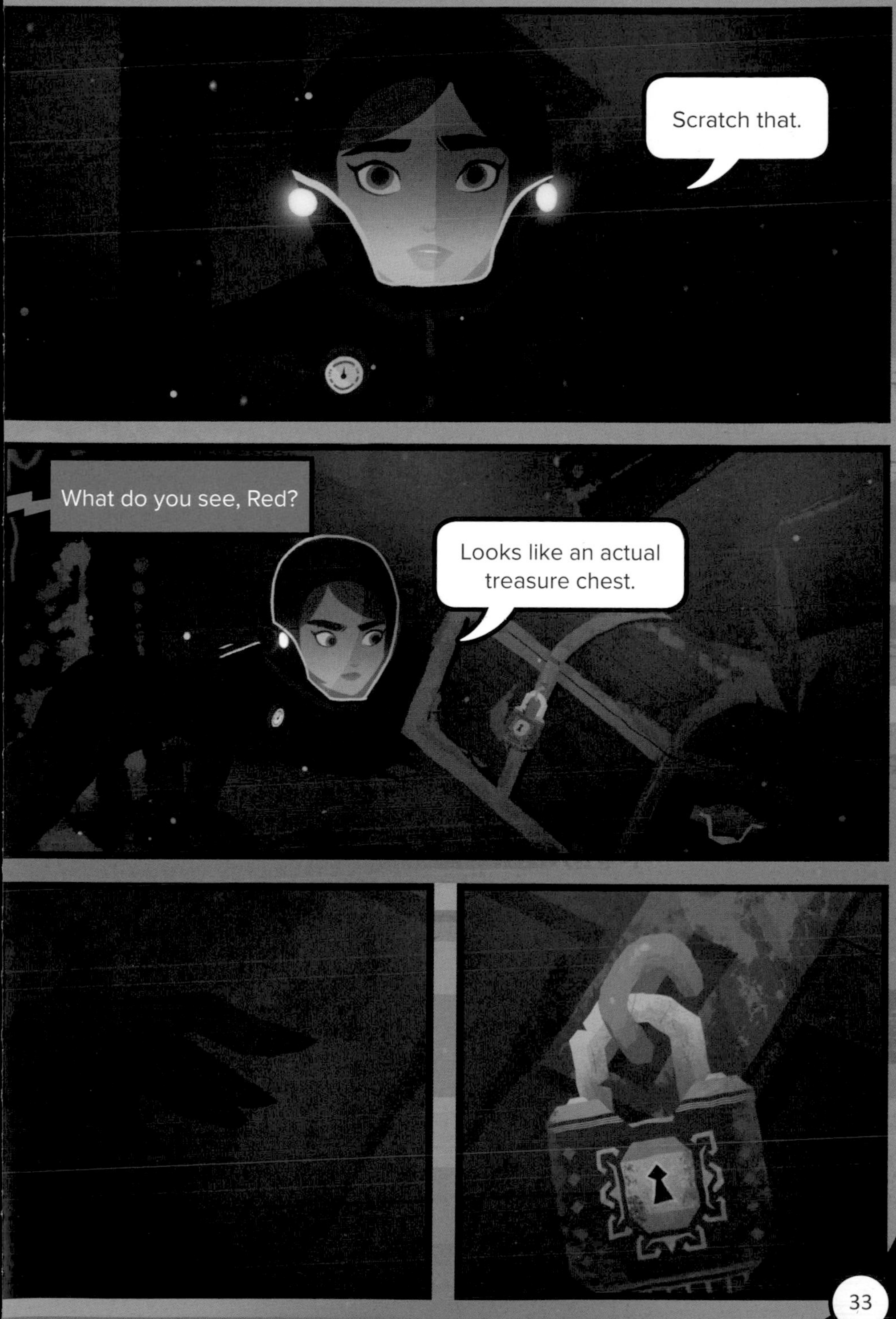
Scratch that.
What do you see, Red?
Looks like an actual treasure chest.

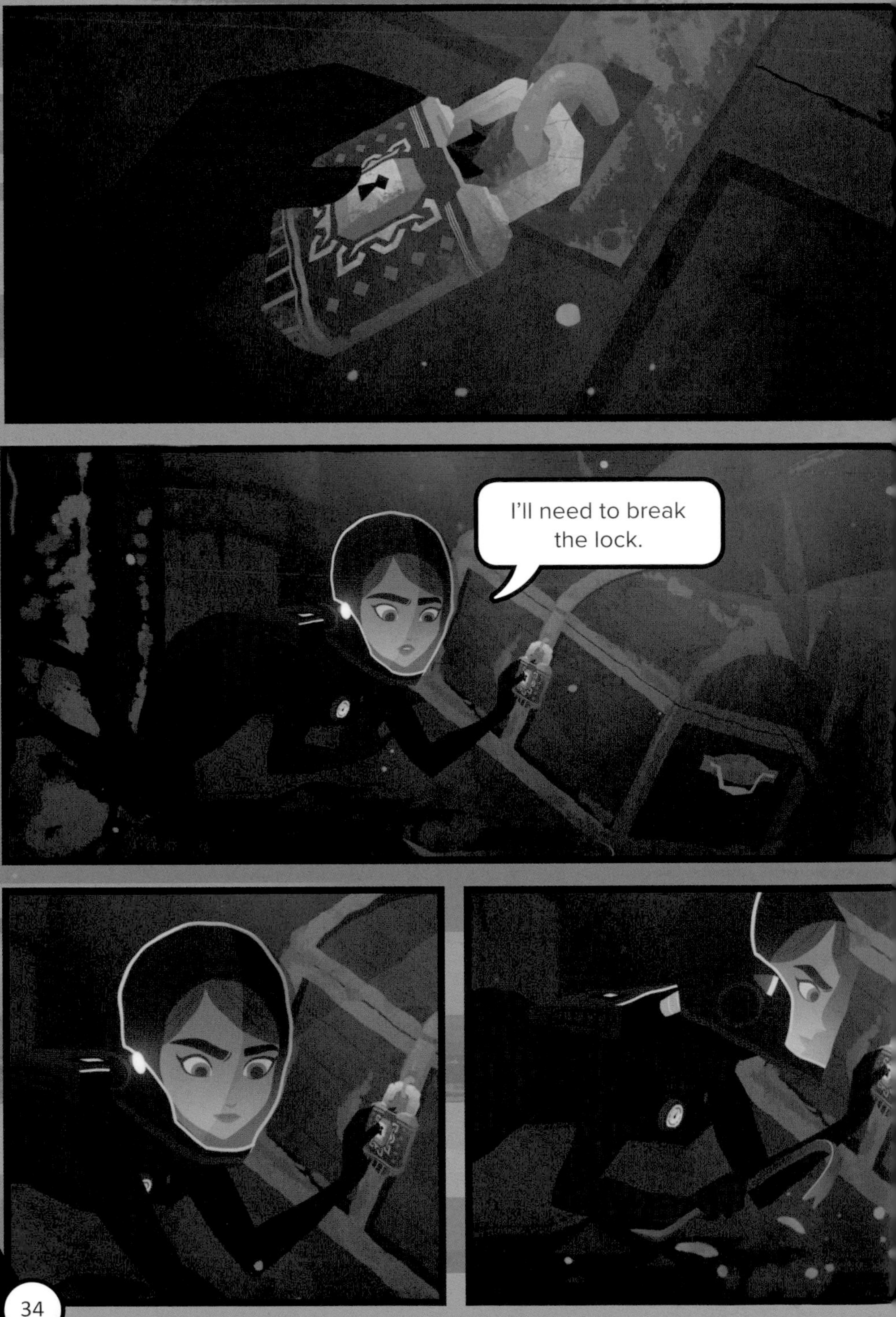
I'll need to break the lock.

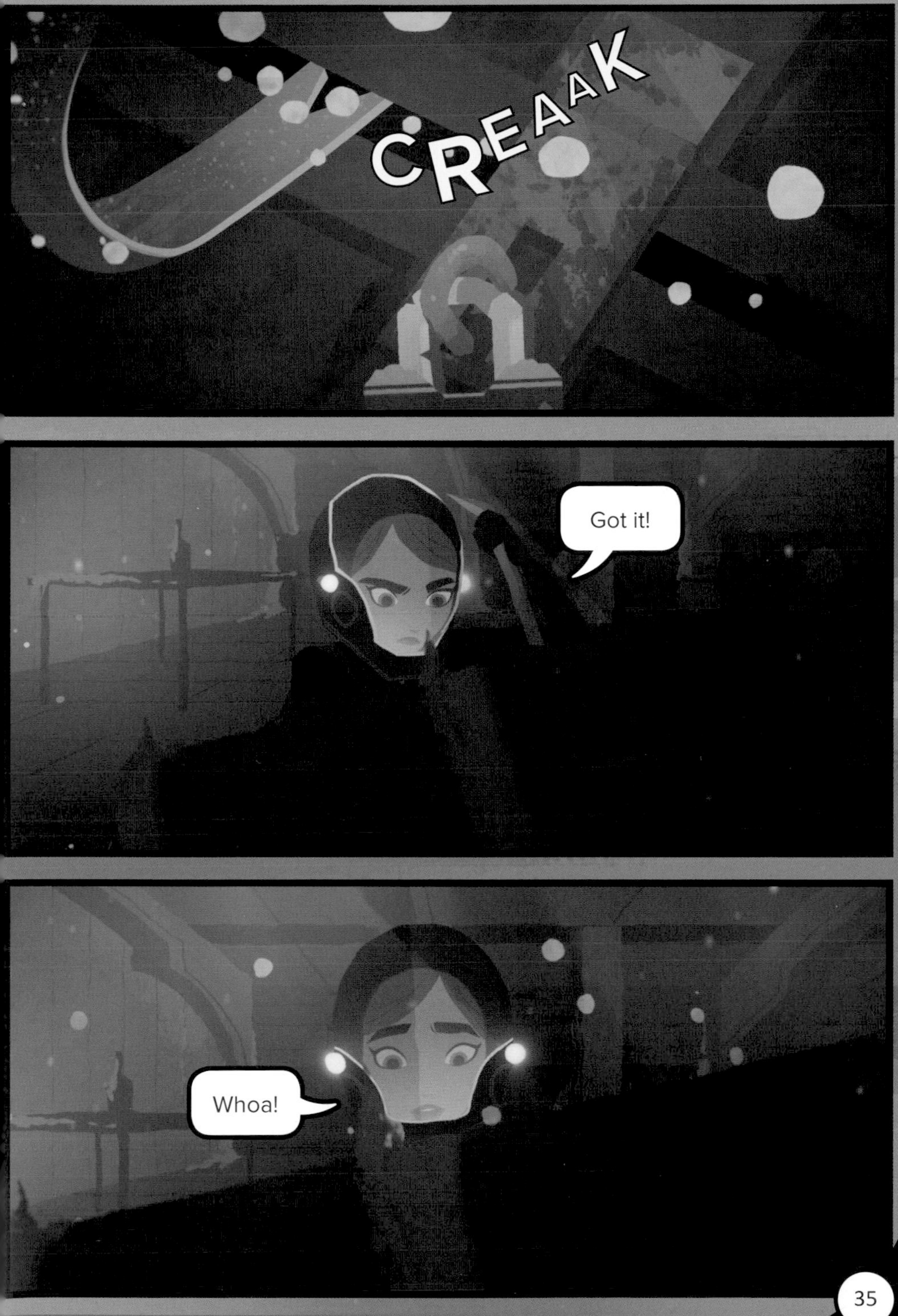
CREAAK
Got it!
Whoa!

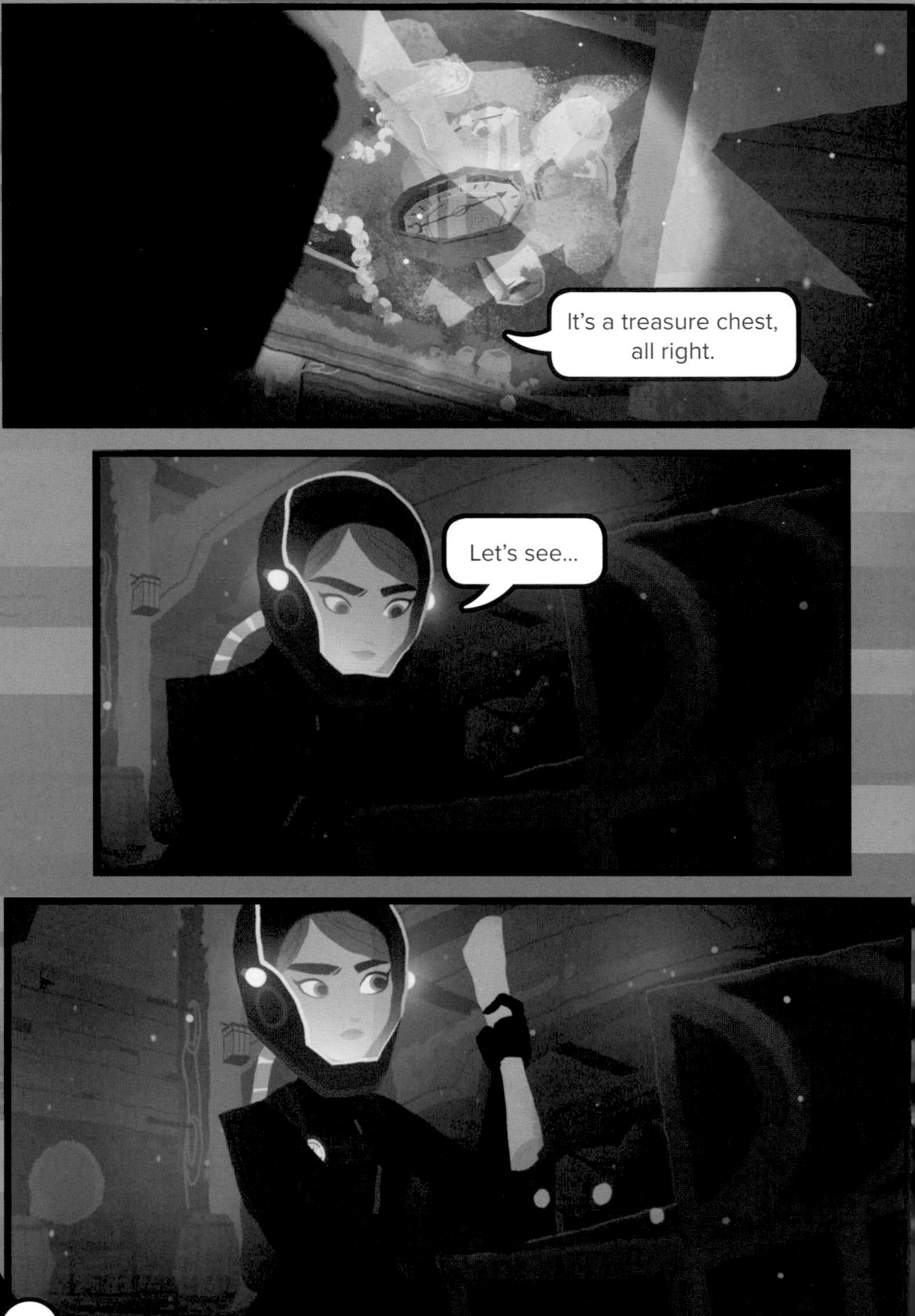
It's a treasure chest, all right.
Let's see...

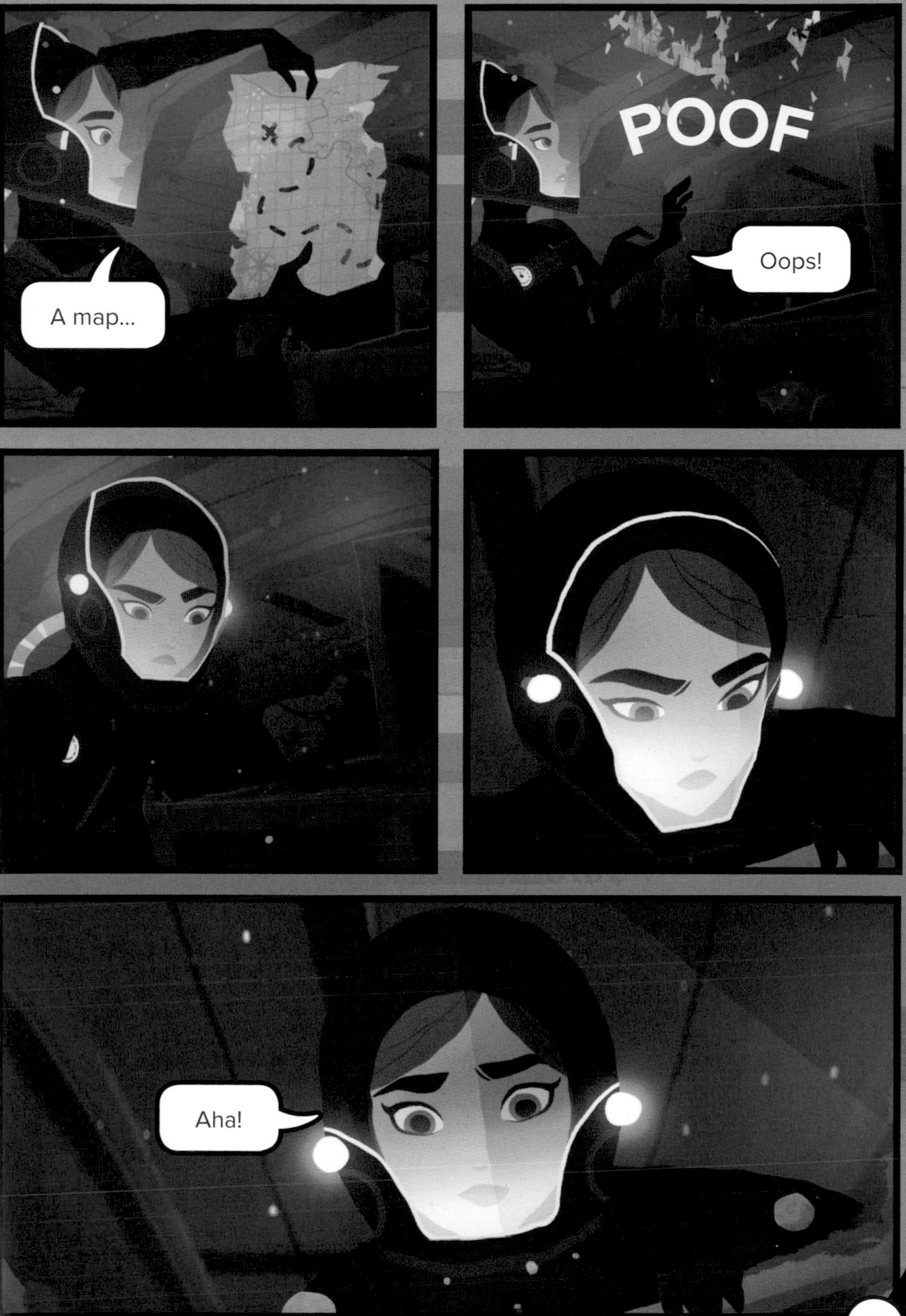
A map...
POOF
Oops!
Aha!

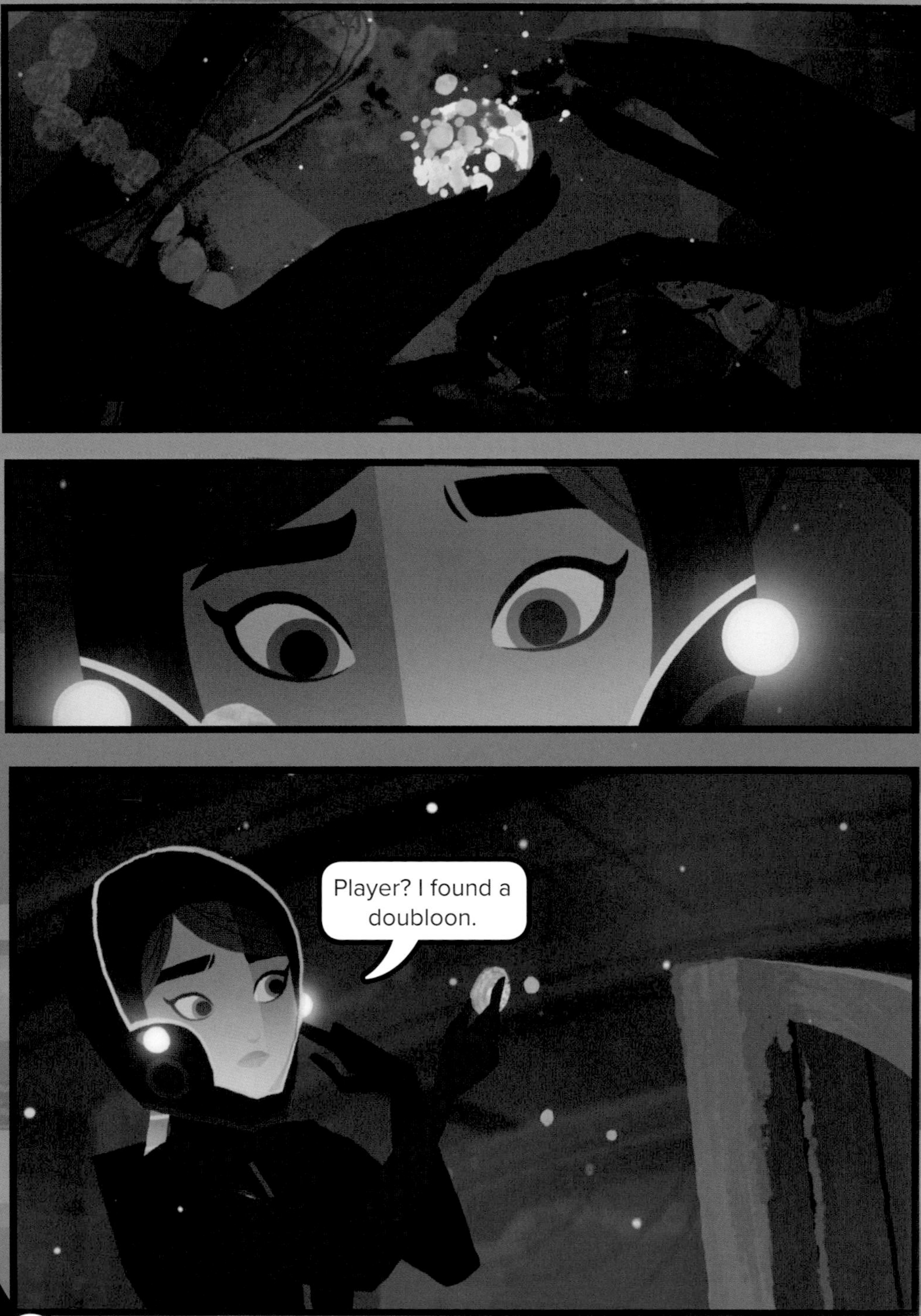
Player? I found a doubloon.

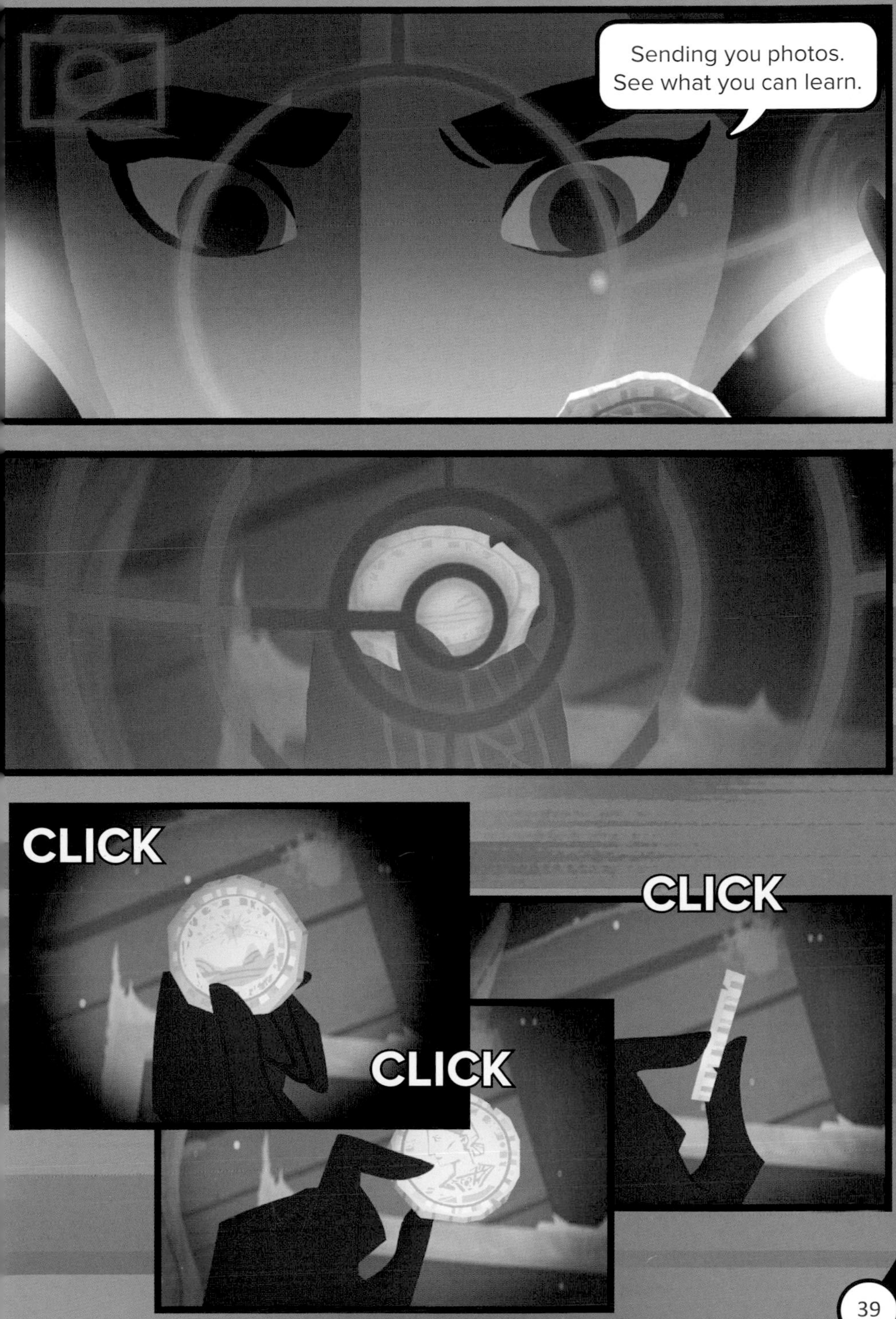
Sending you photos. See what you can learn.
CLICK
CLICK
CLICK

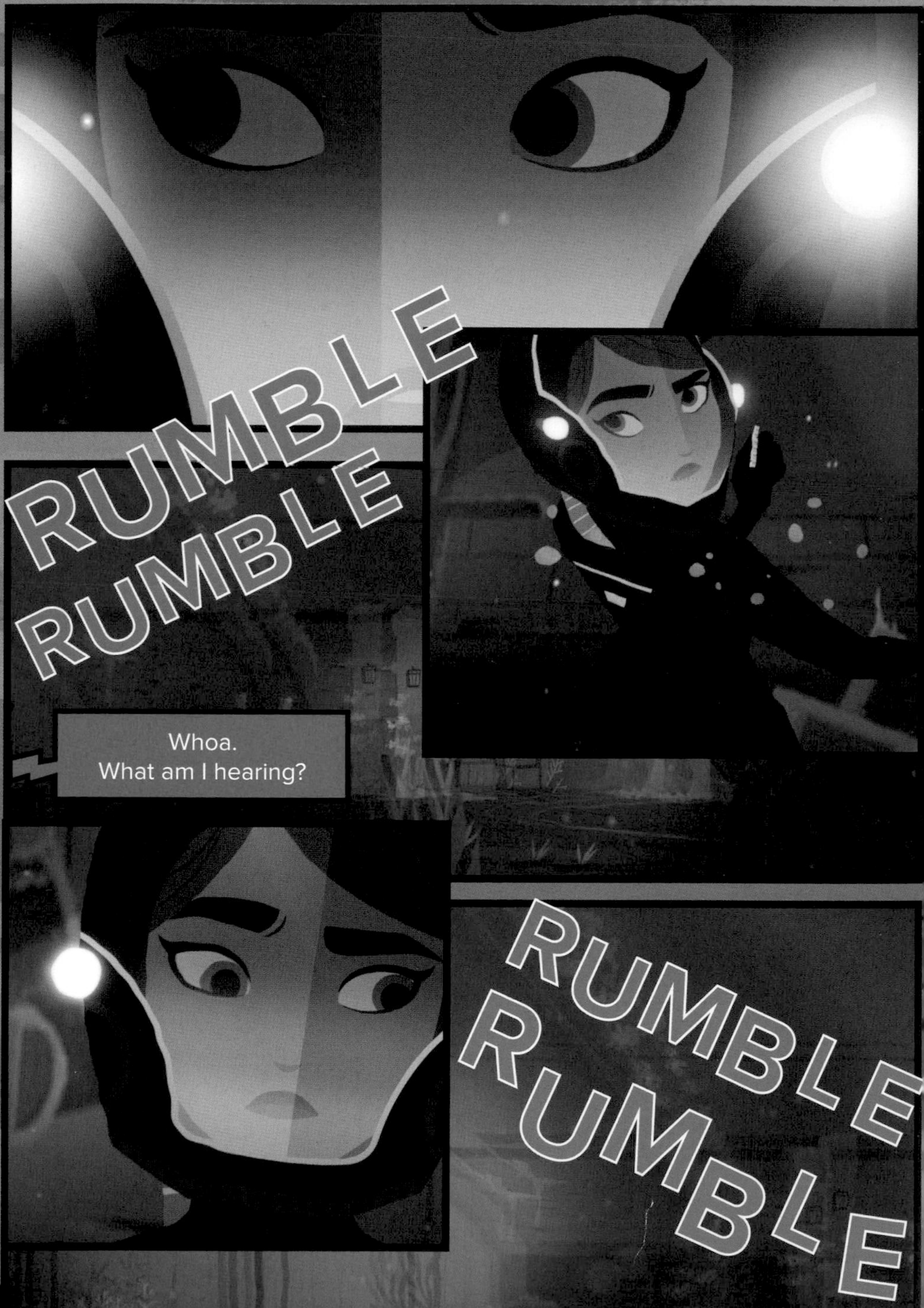
RUMBLE
RUMBLE
Whoa.
What am I hearing?
RUMBLE
RUMBLE

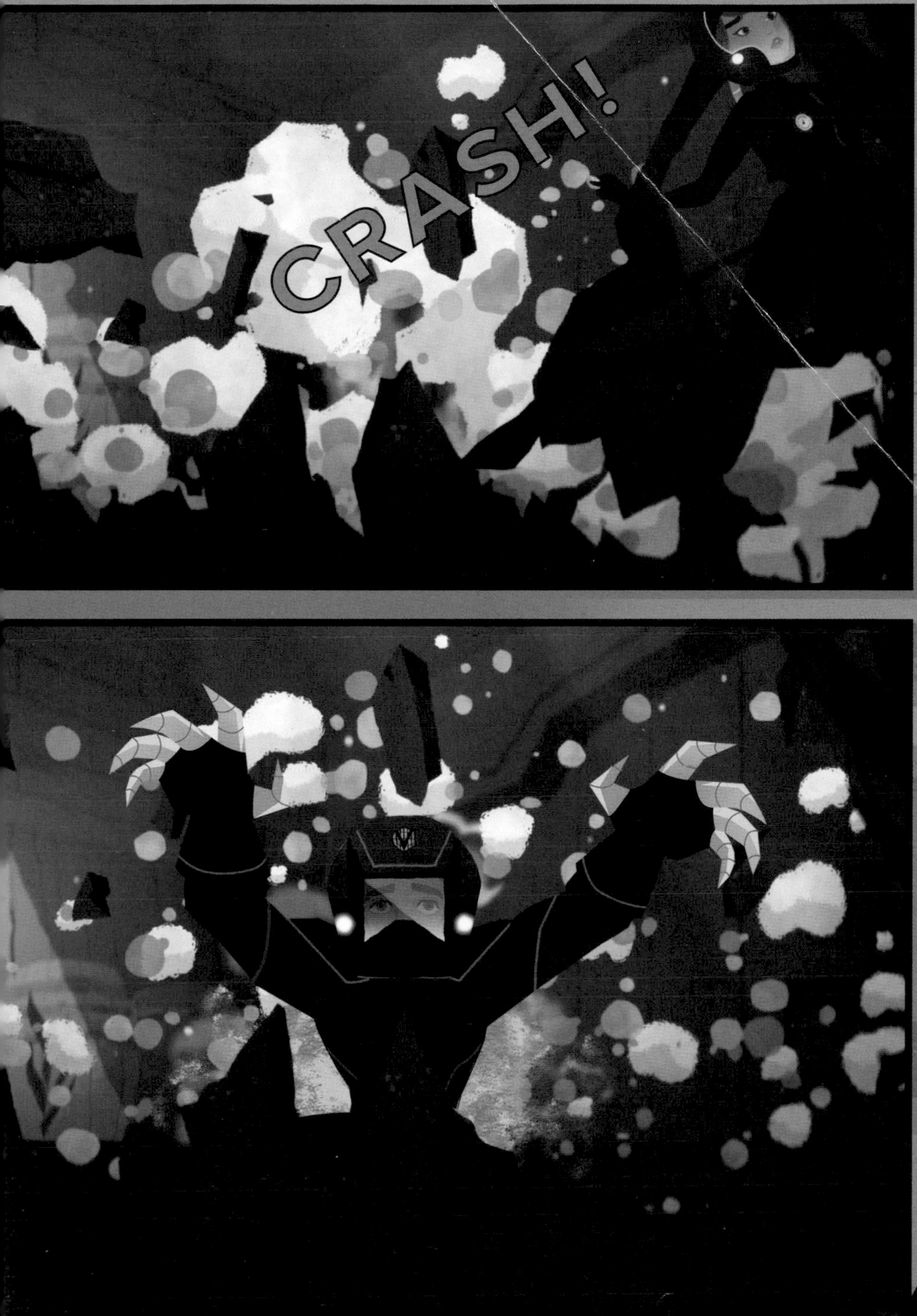
CRASH!

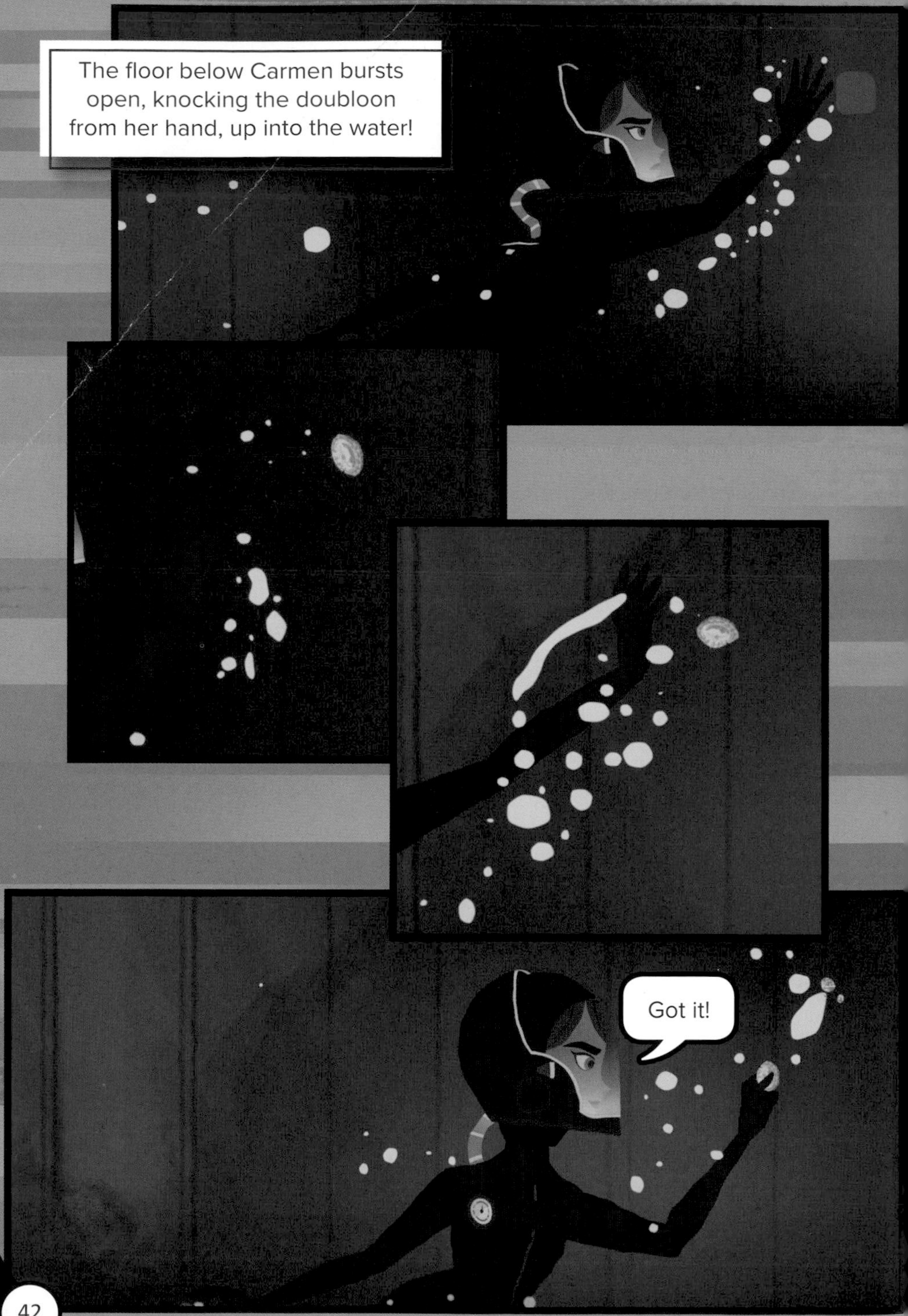
The floor below Carmen bursts open, knocking the doubloon from her hand, up into the water!
Got it!

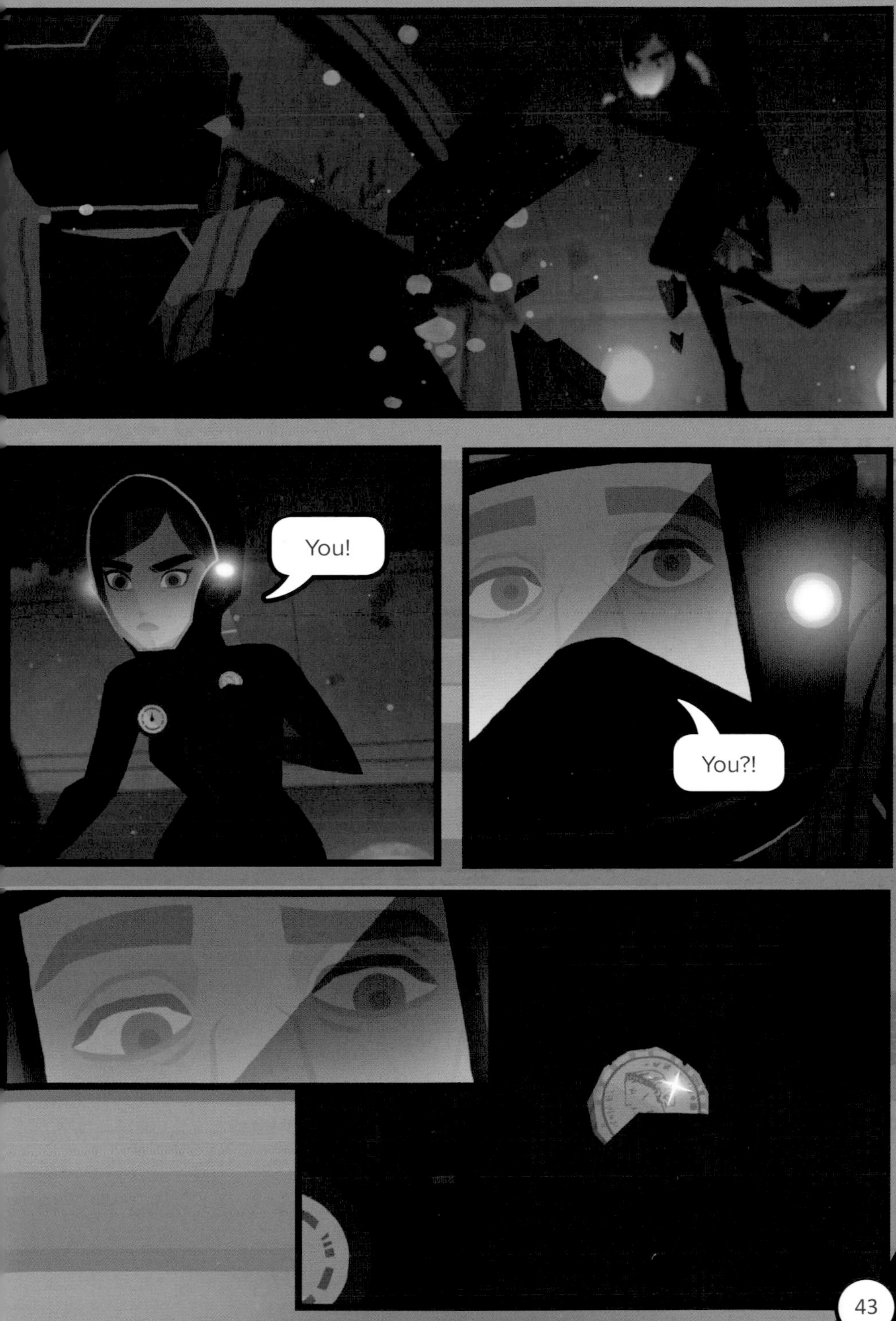
You!
You?!

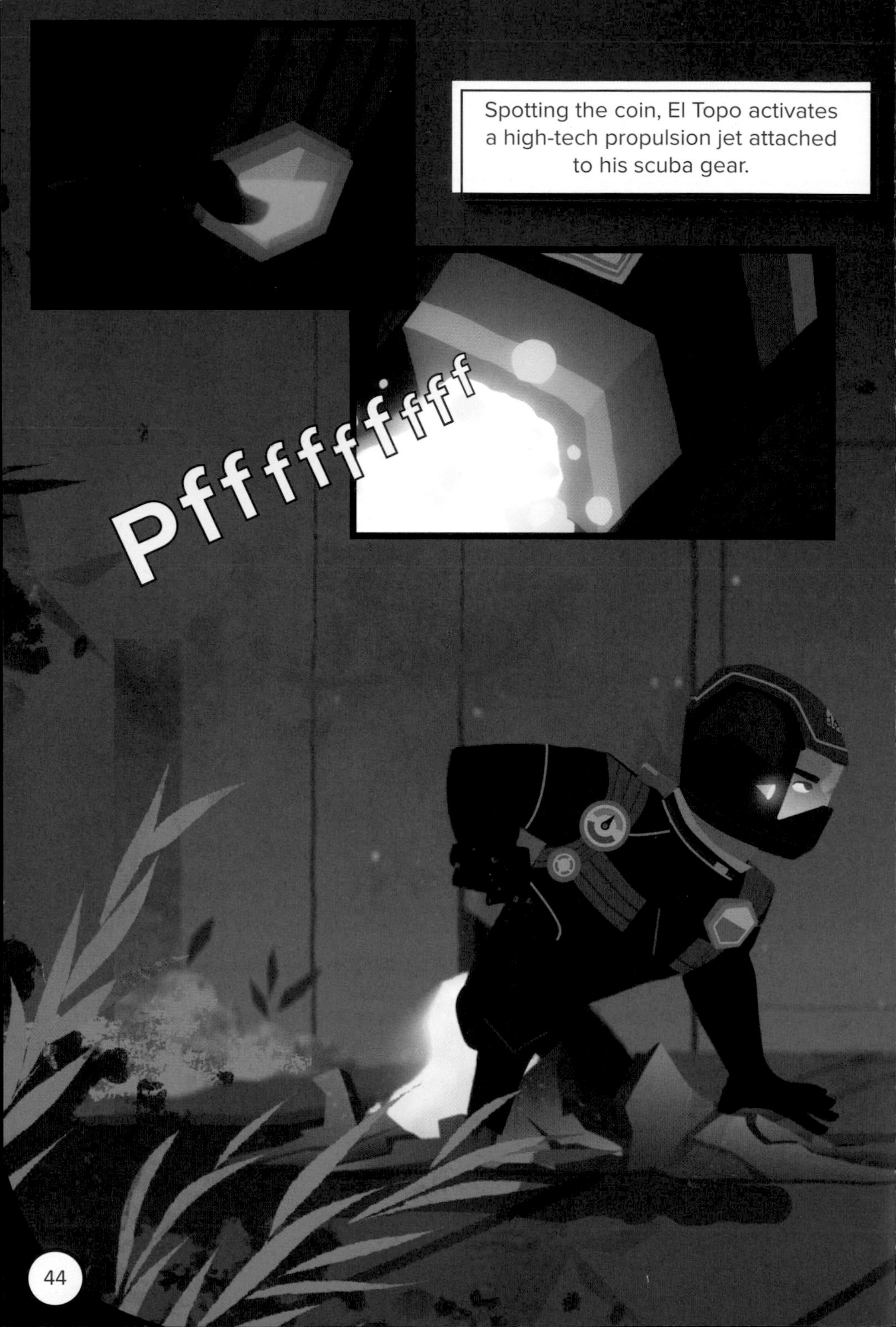
Spotting the coin, El Topo activates a high-tech propulsion jet attached to his scuba gear.
Pffffffffff

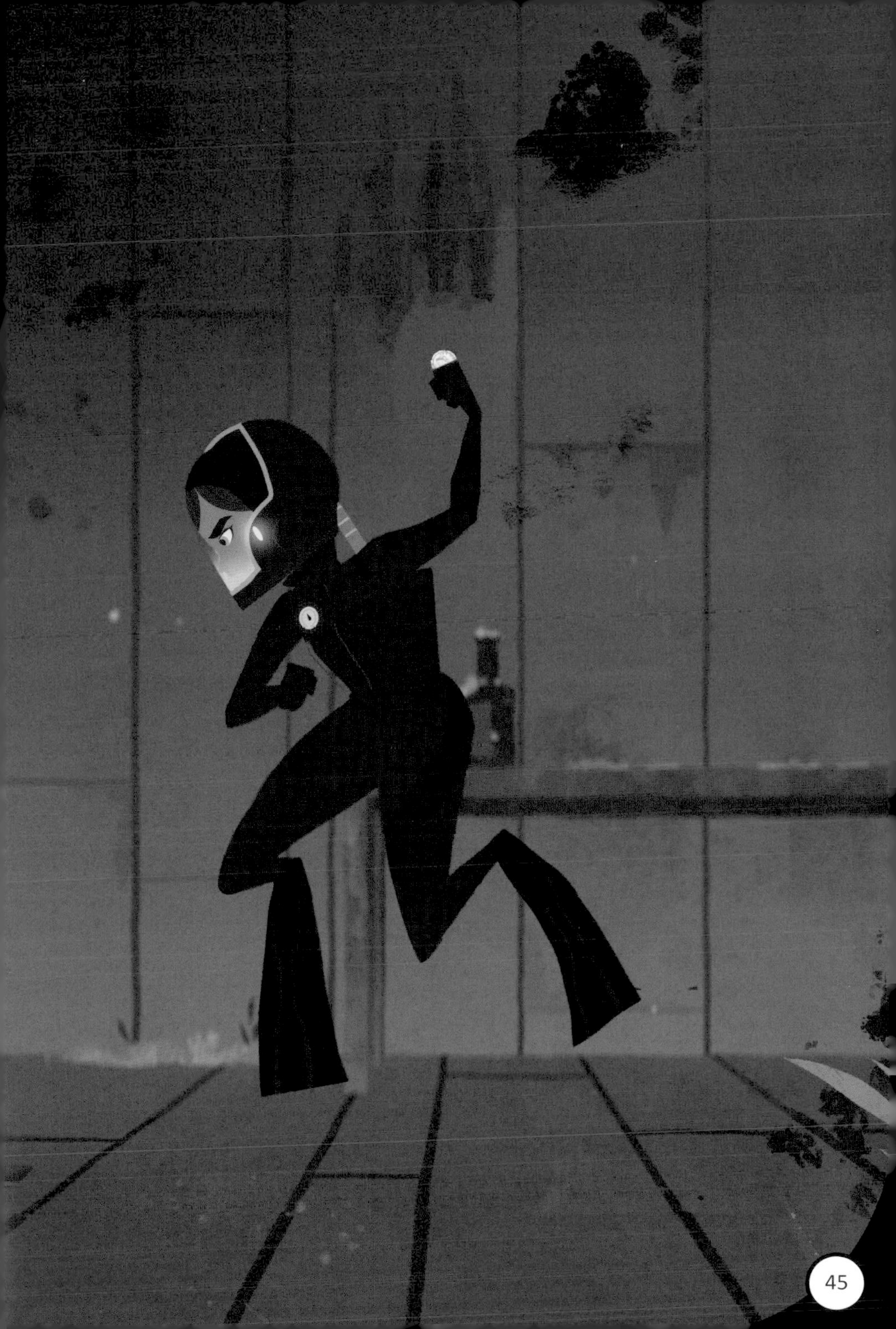

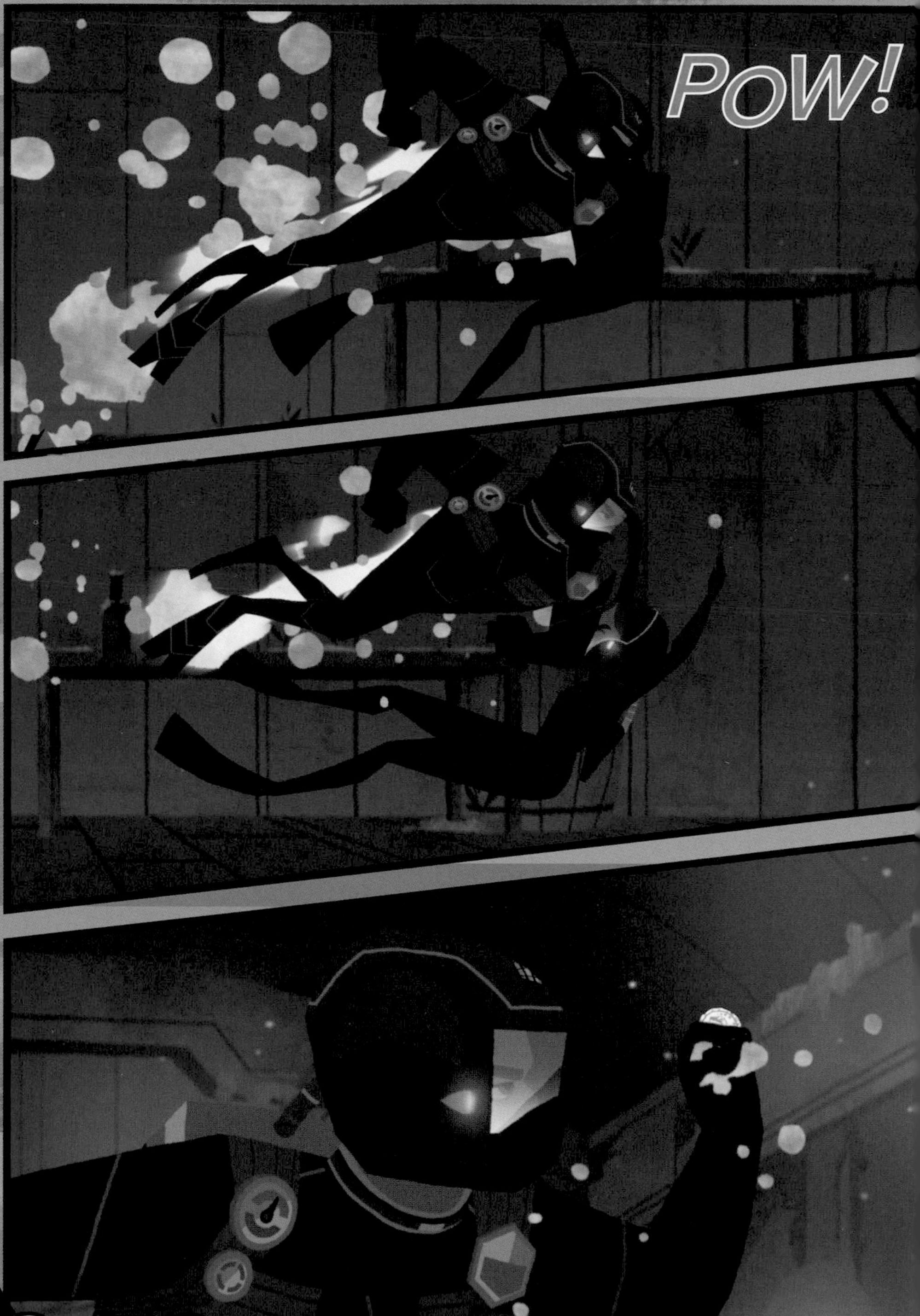
POW!

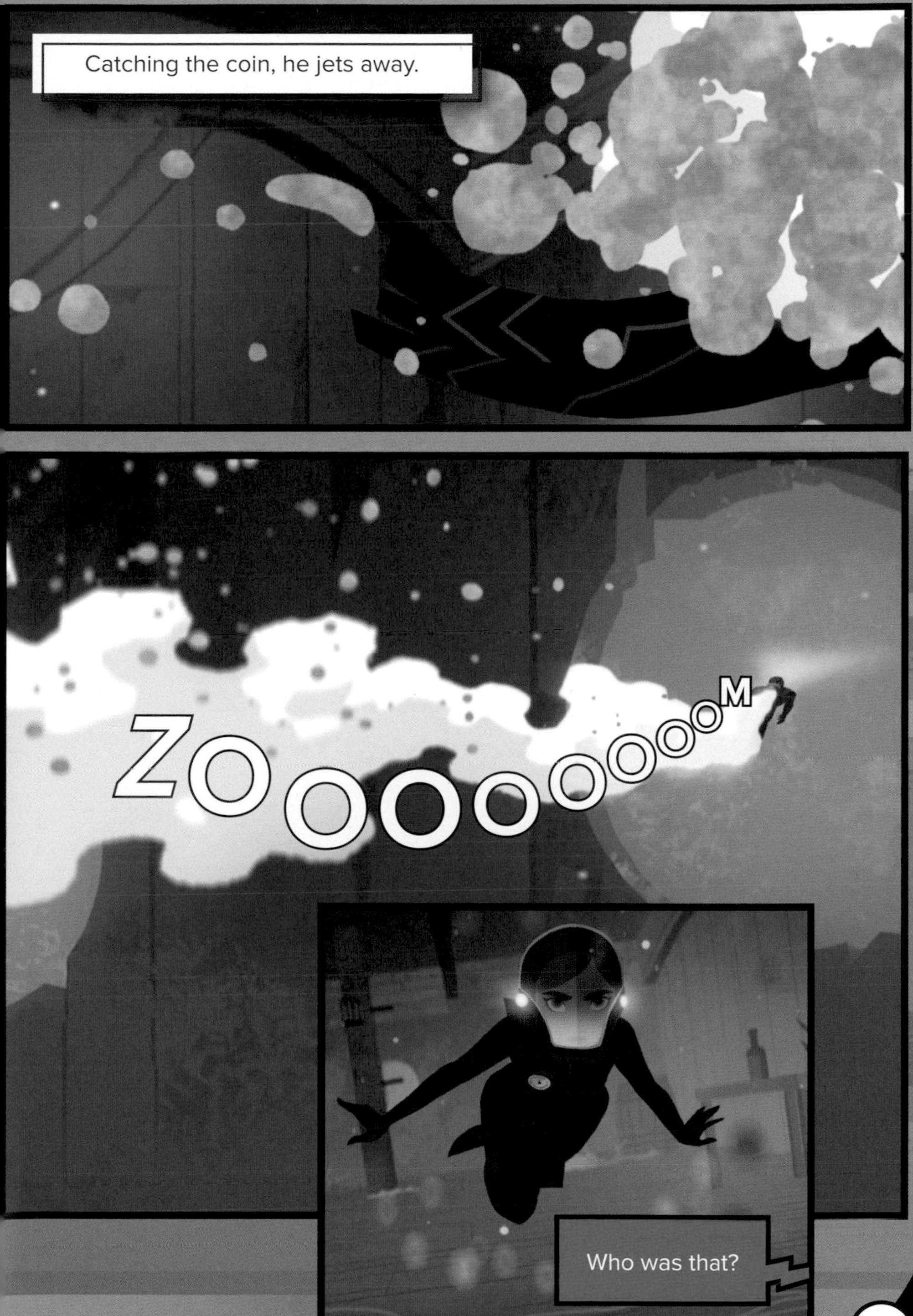
Catching the coin, he jets away.
ZOOOOOOOOOM
Who was that?

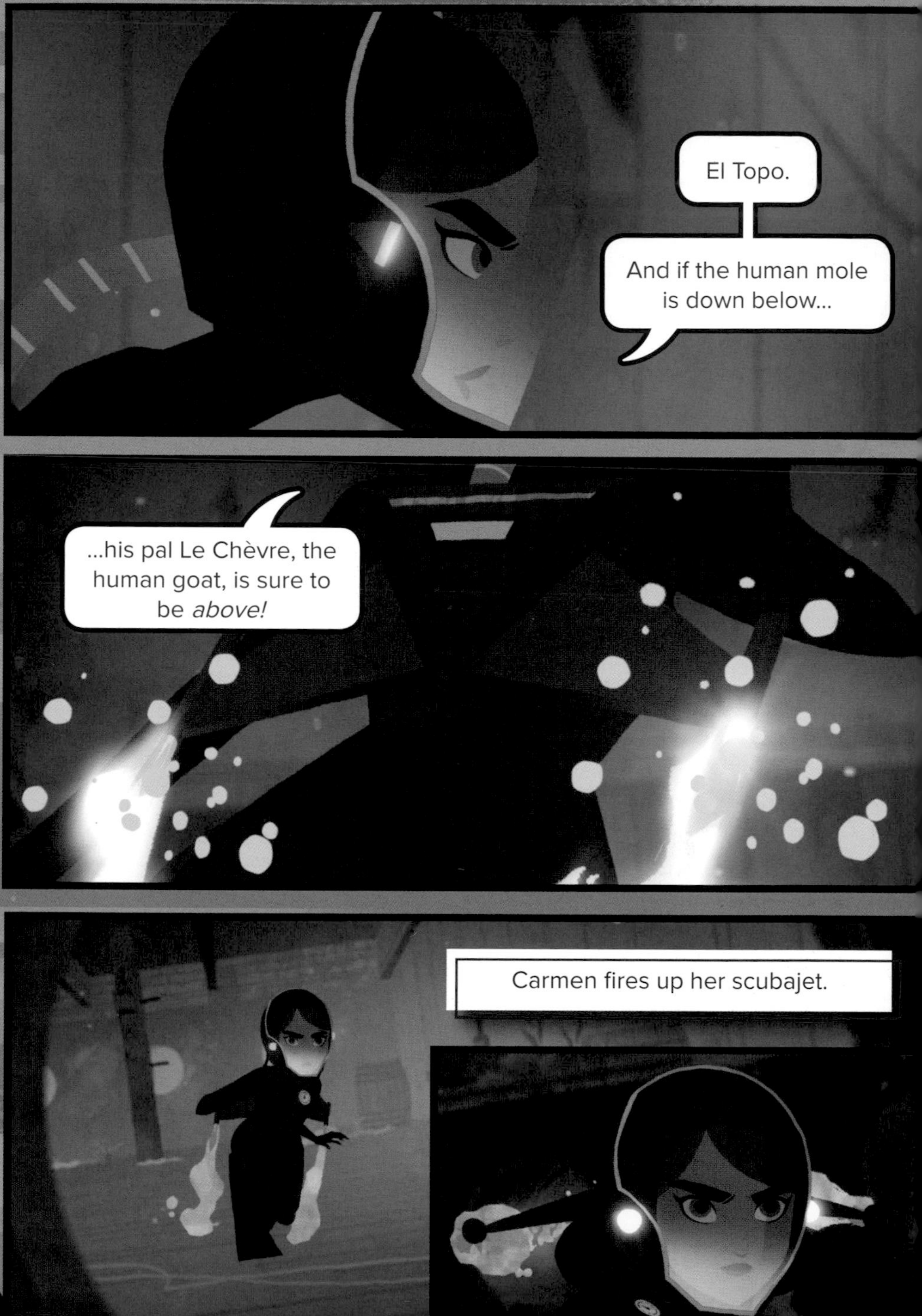
El Topo.
And if the human mole is down below...
...his pal Le Chèvre, the human goat, is sure to be *above!*
Carmen fires up her scubajet.

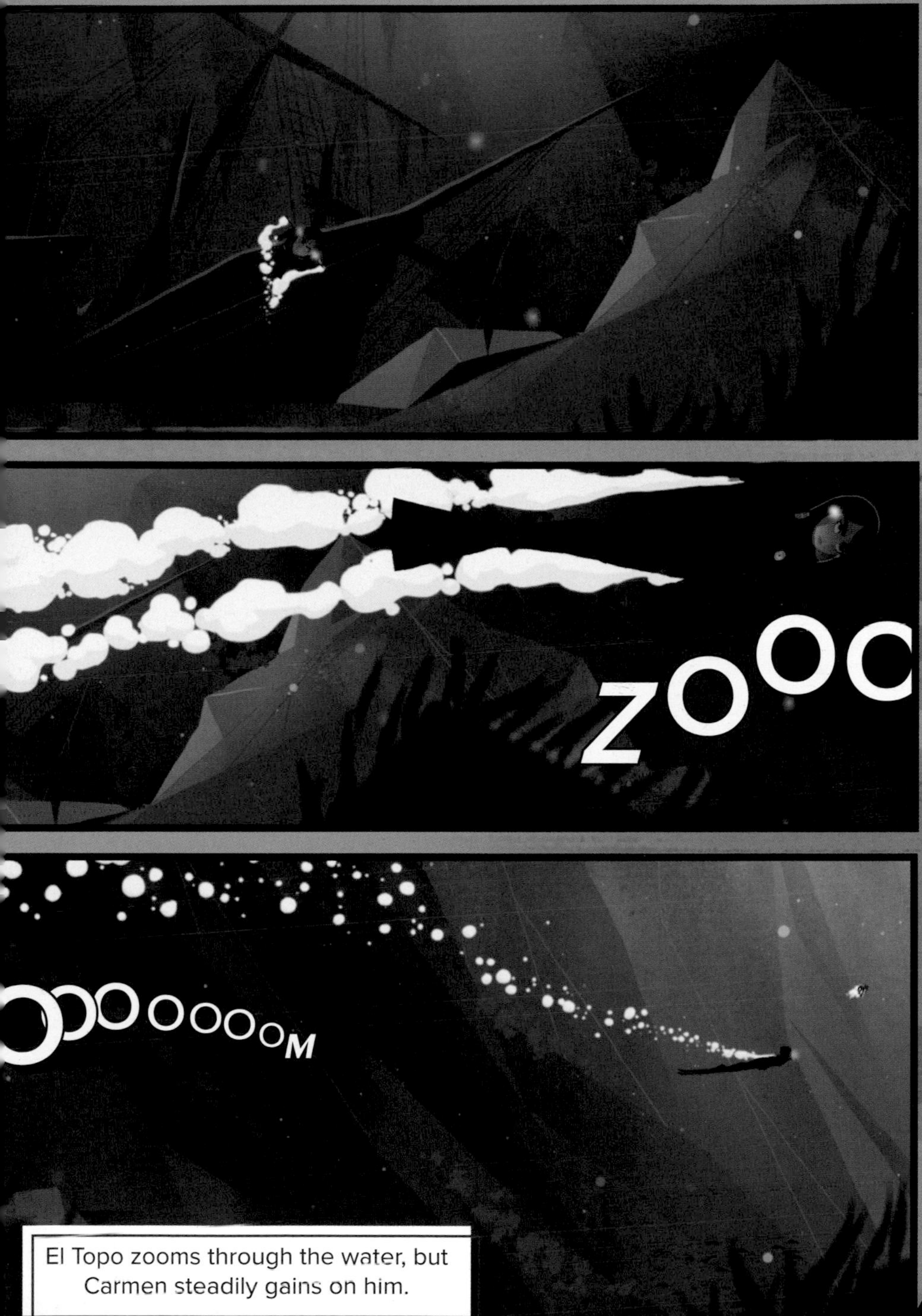
ZOOO
OOOOOOOM
El Topo zooms through the water, but Carmen steadily gains on him.

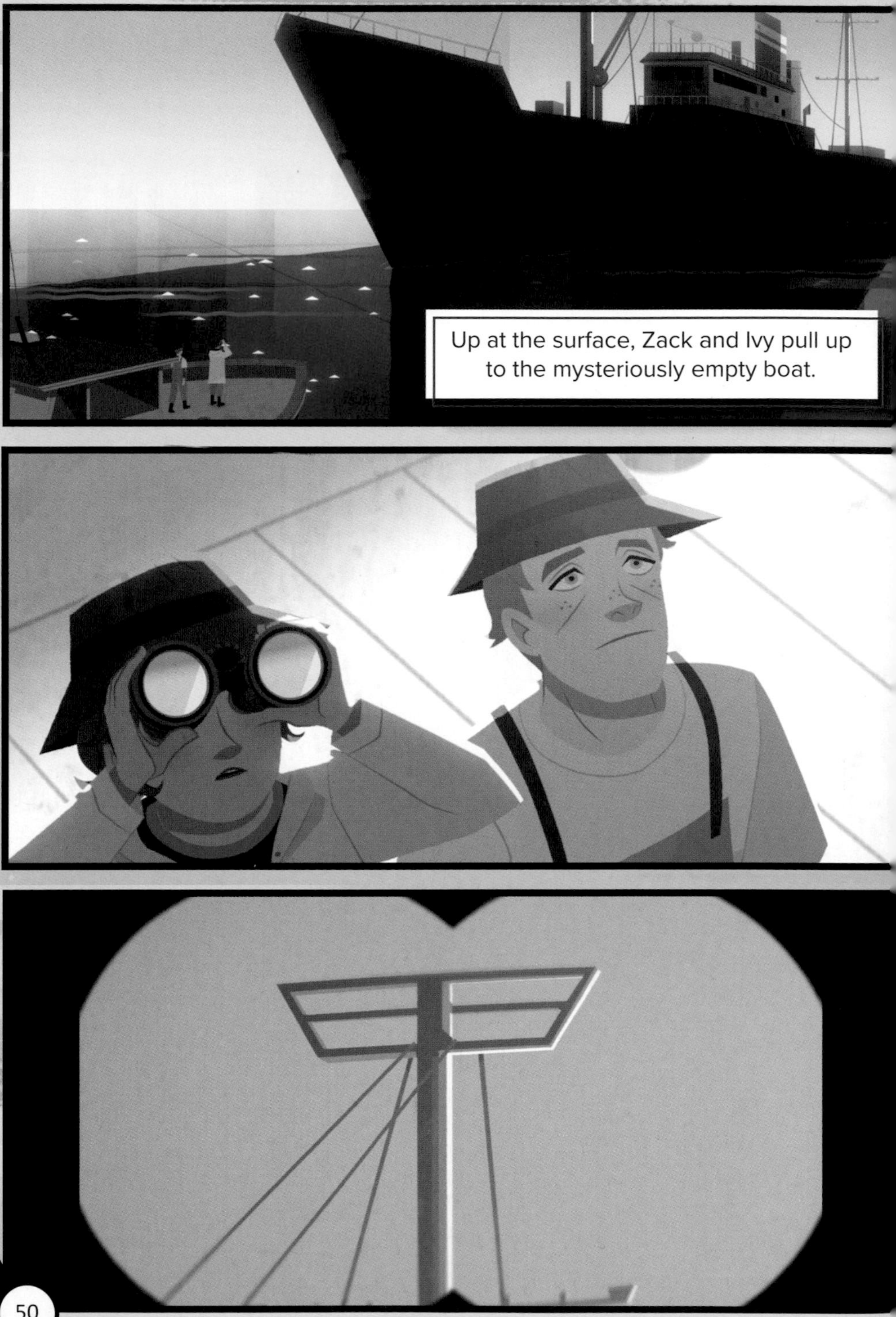
Up at the surface, Zack and Ivy pull up to the mysteriously empty boat.

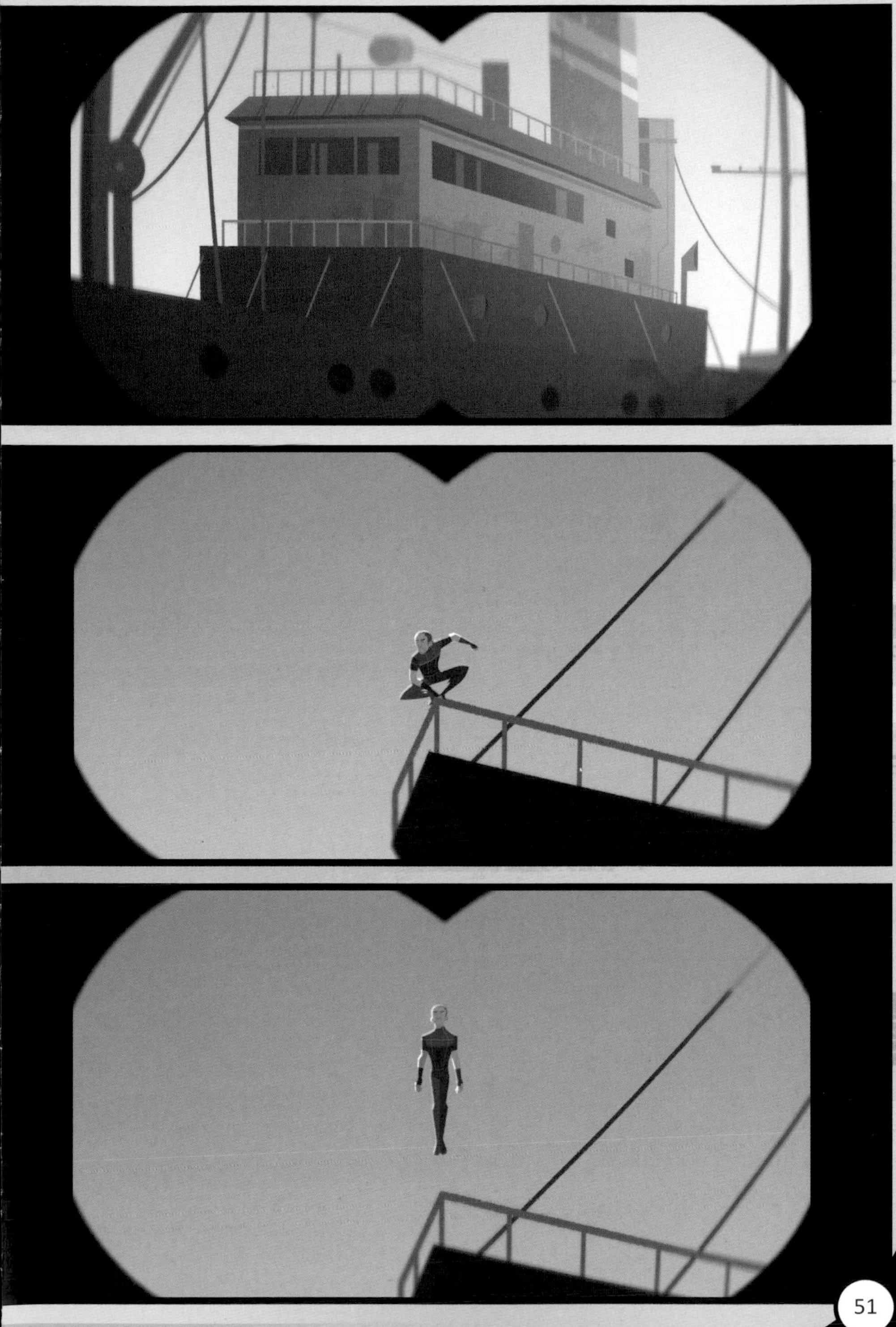

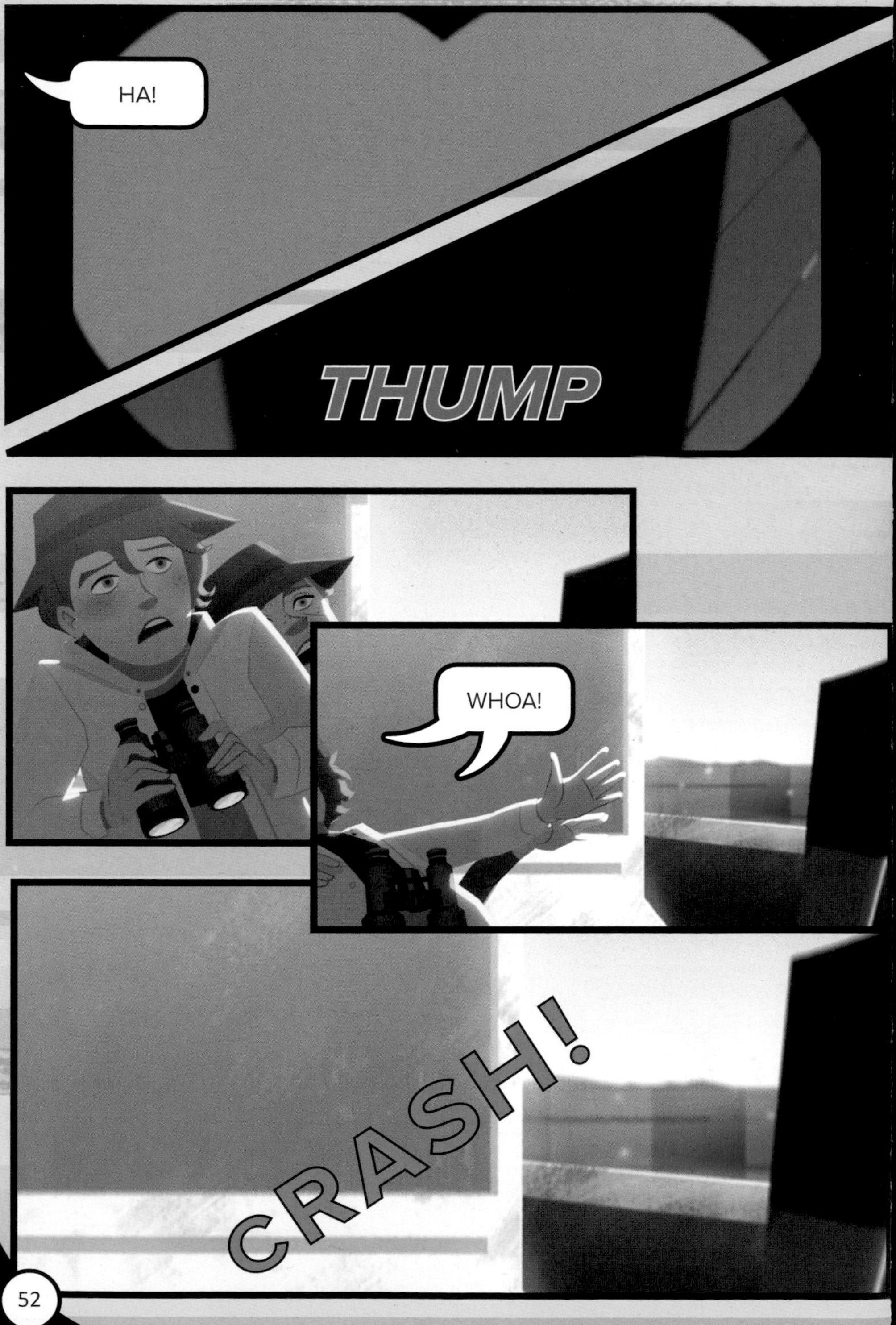
HA!
THUMP
WHOA!
CRASH!

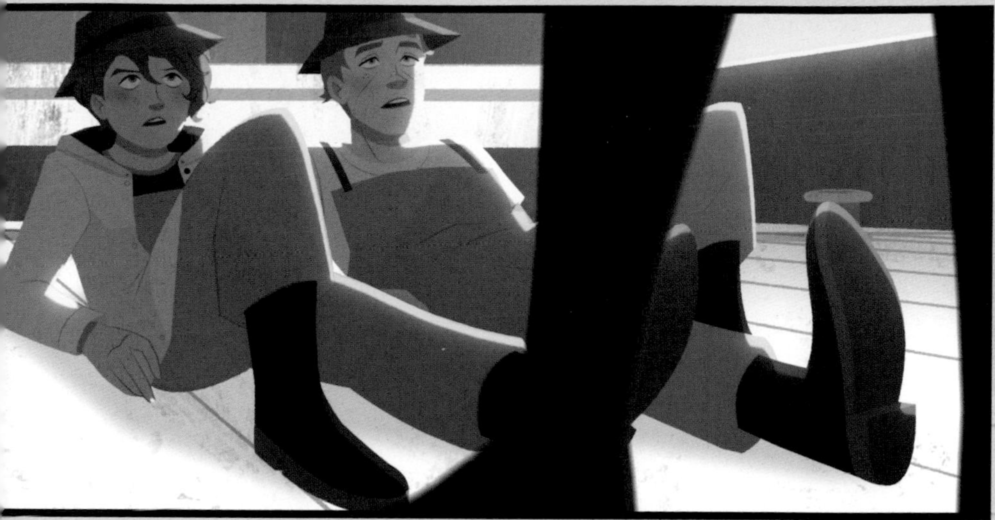

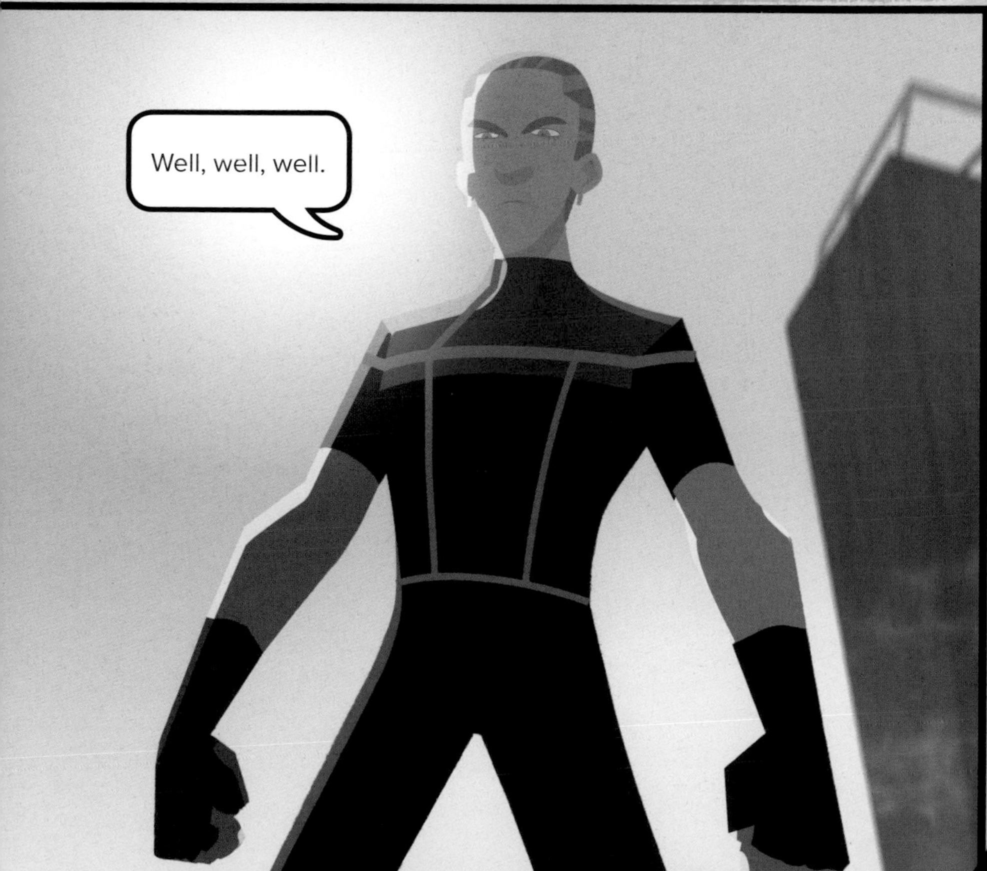
Well, well, well.

El Topo

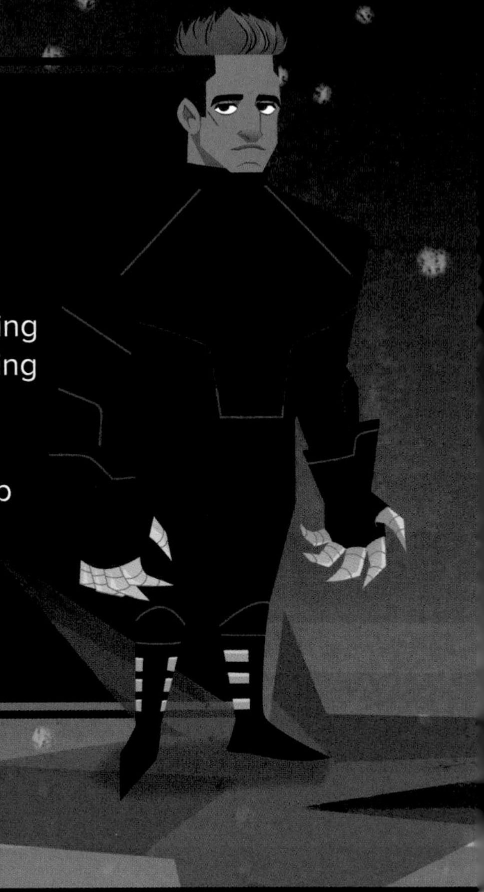

- Real name: Antonio
- Master of the underground, using tunnels and sewers, or burrowing through dirt like a mole
- Metal claws on his uniform help him dig at incredible speeds
- You never know where he will "pop up."

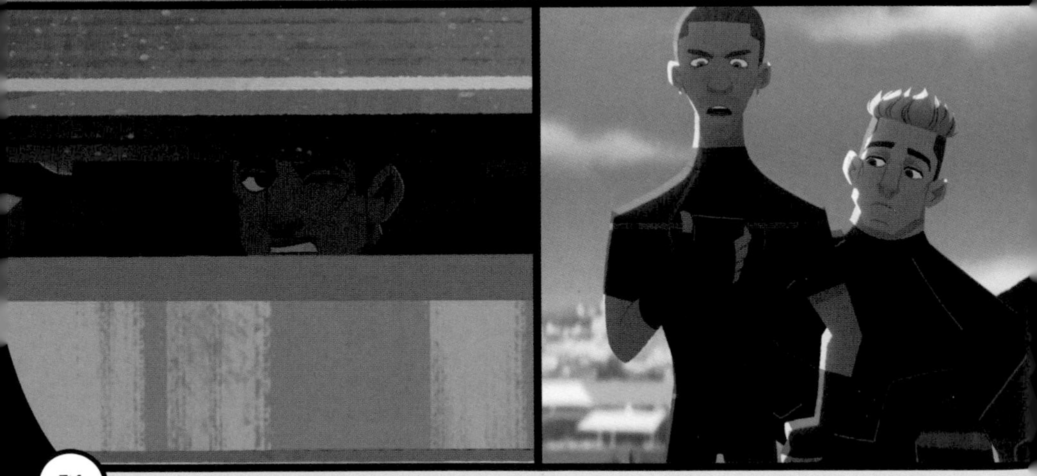

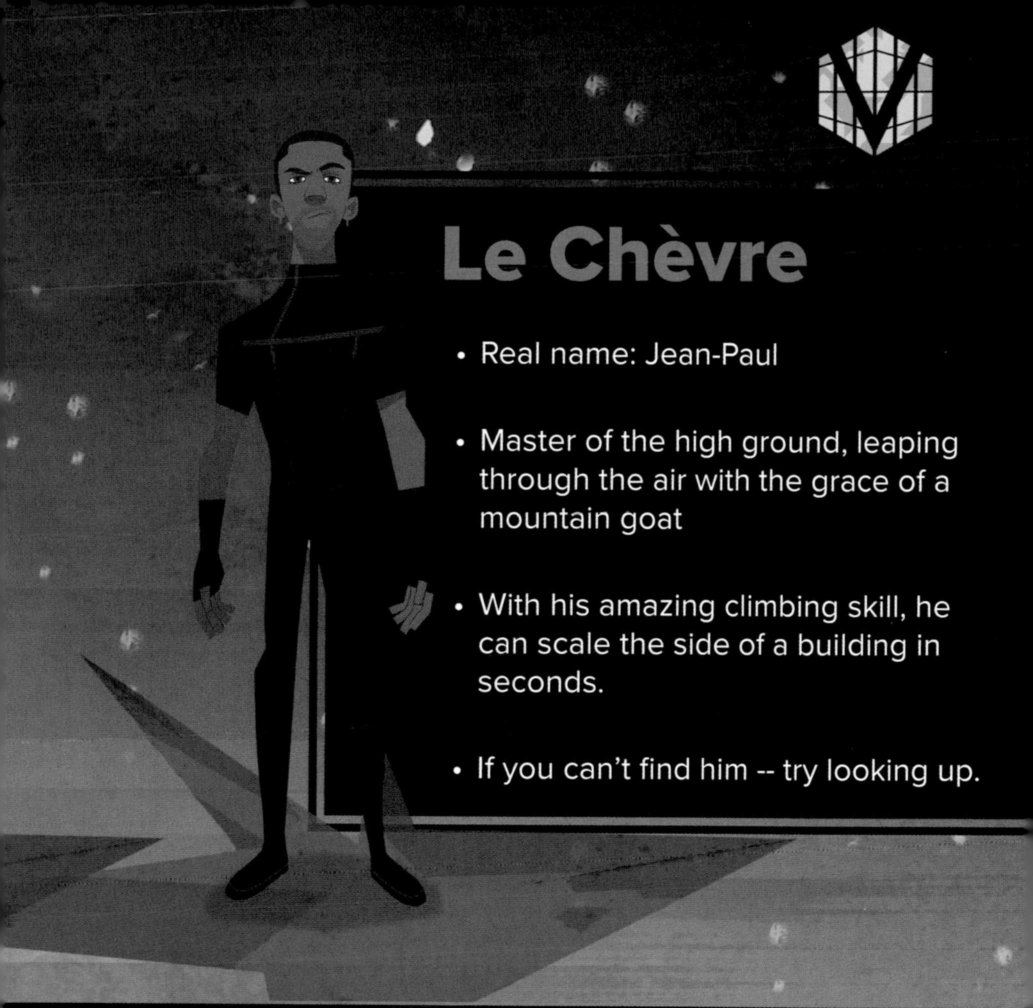

Le Chèvre

- Real name: Jean-Paul
- Master of the high ground, leaping through the air with the grace of a mountain goat
- With his amazing climbing skill, he can scale the side of a building in seconds.
- If you can't find him -- try looking up.

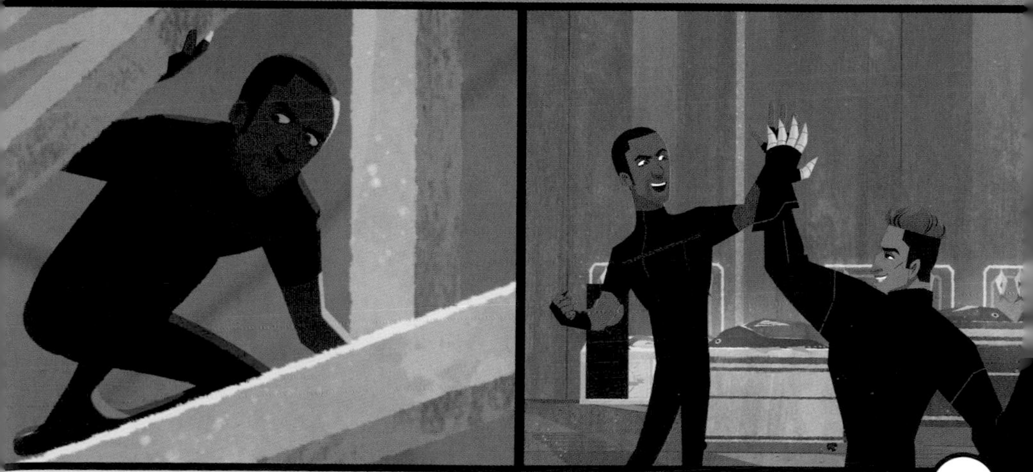

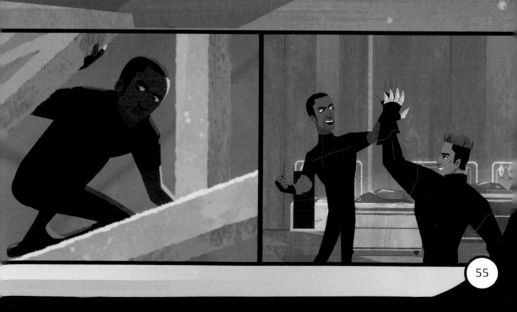

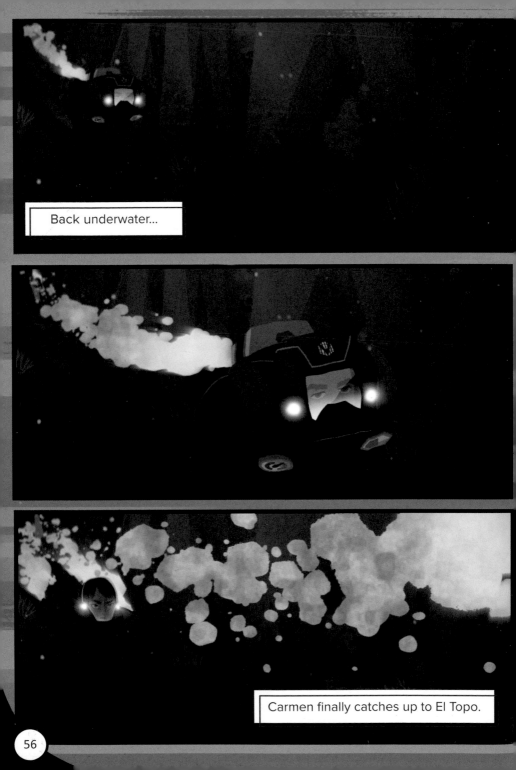

Back underwater...

Carmen finally catches up to El Topo.

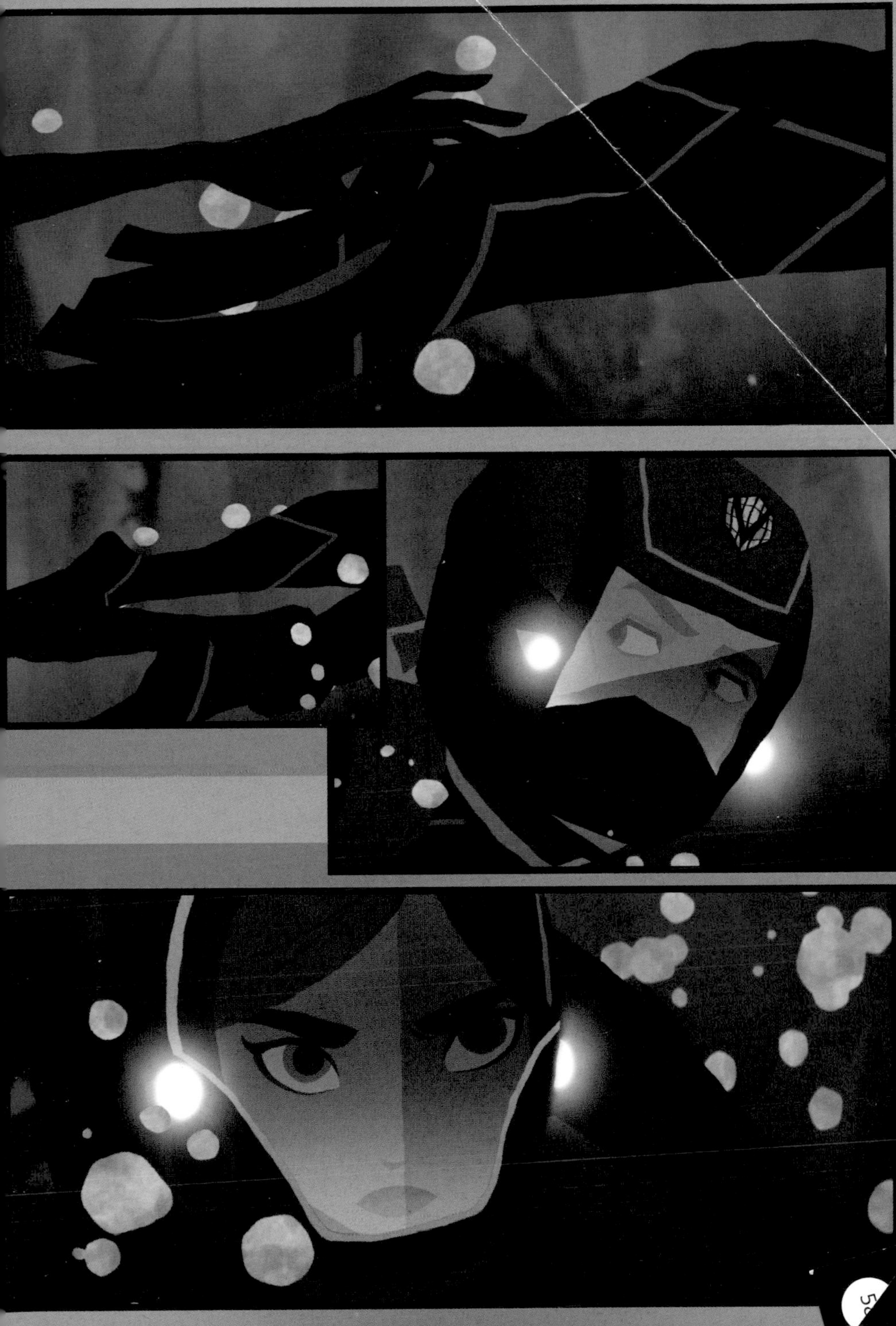

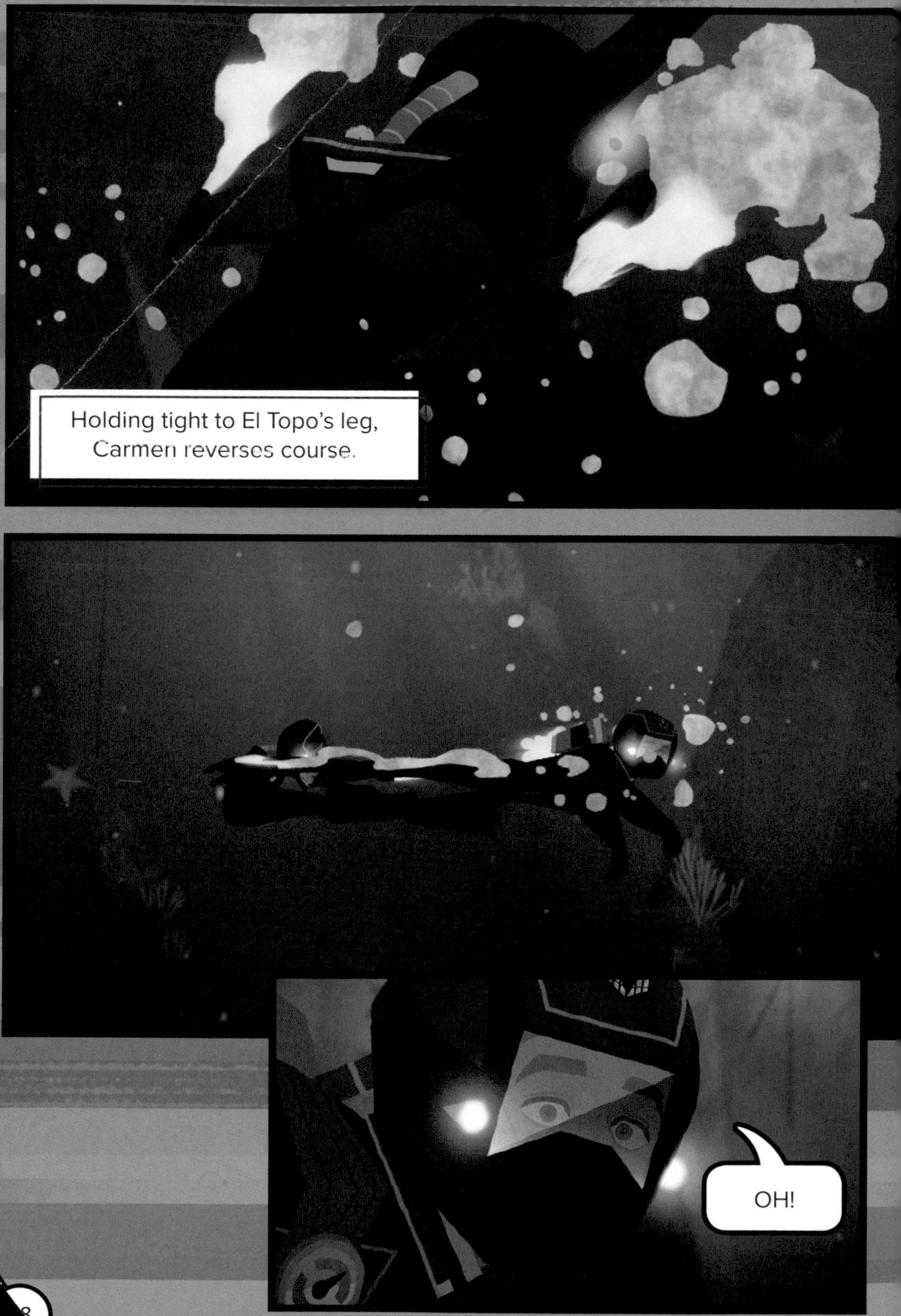
Holding tight to El Topo's leg, Carmen reverses course.
OH!

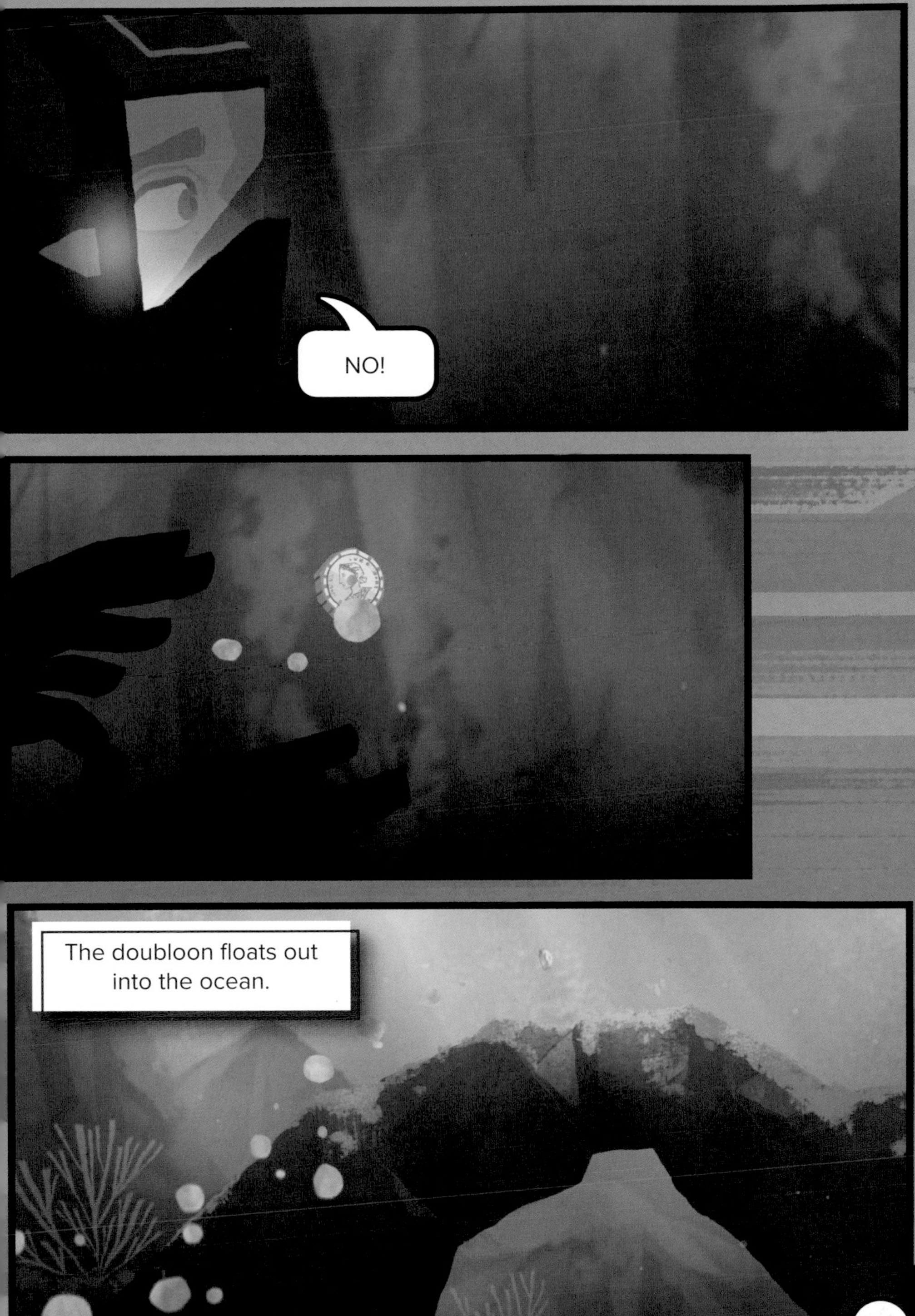
NO!
The doubloon floats out into the ocean.

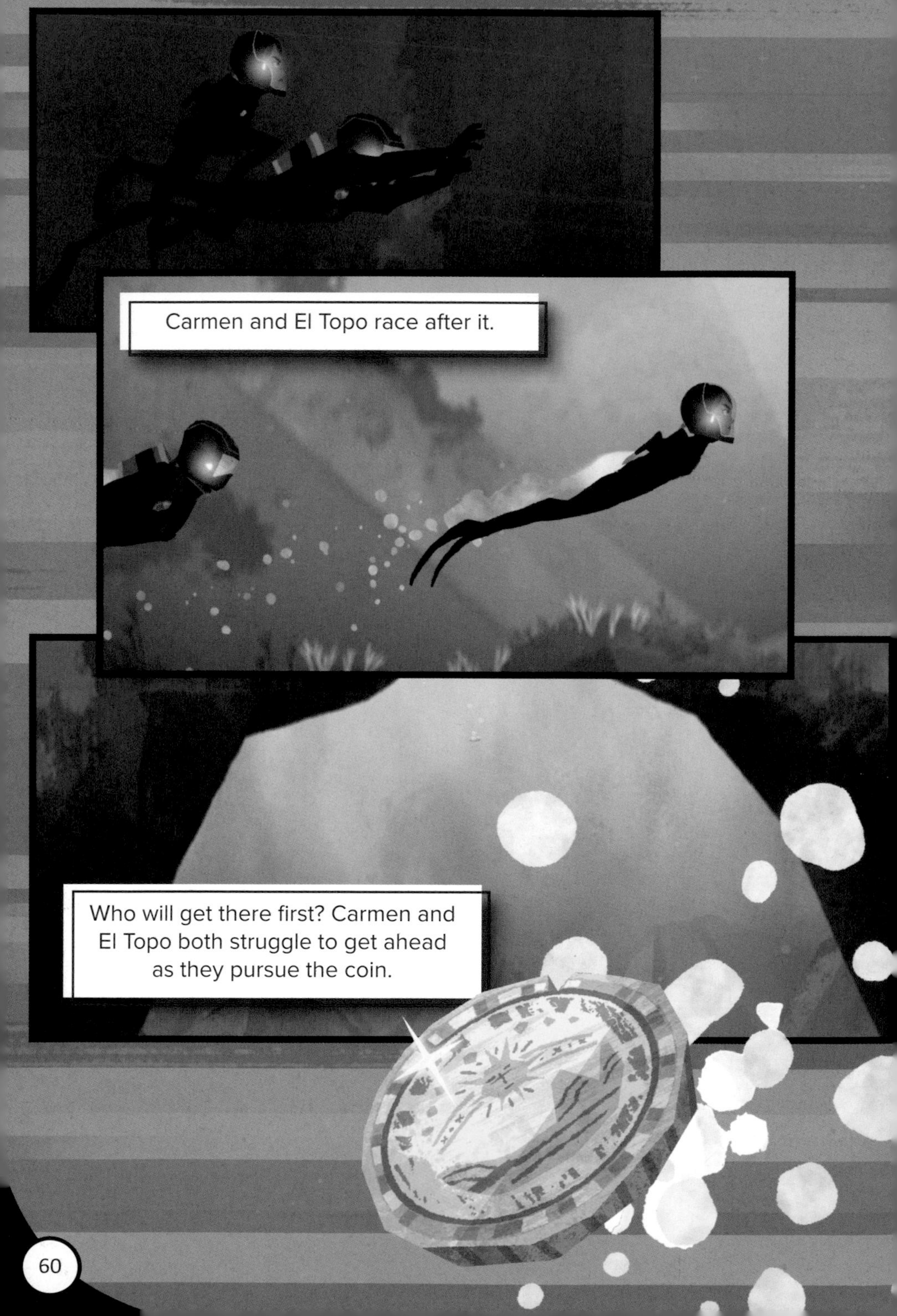
Carmen and El Topo race after it.
Who will get there first? Carmen and El Topo both struggle to get ahead as they pursue the coin.

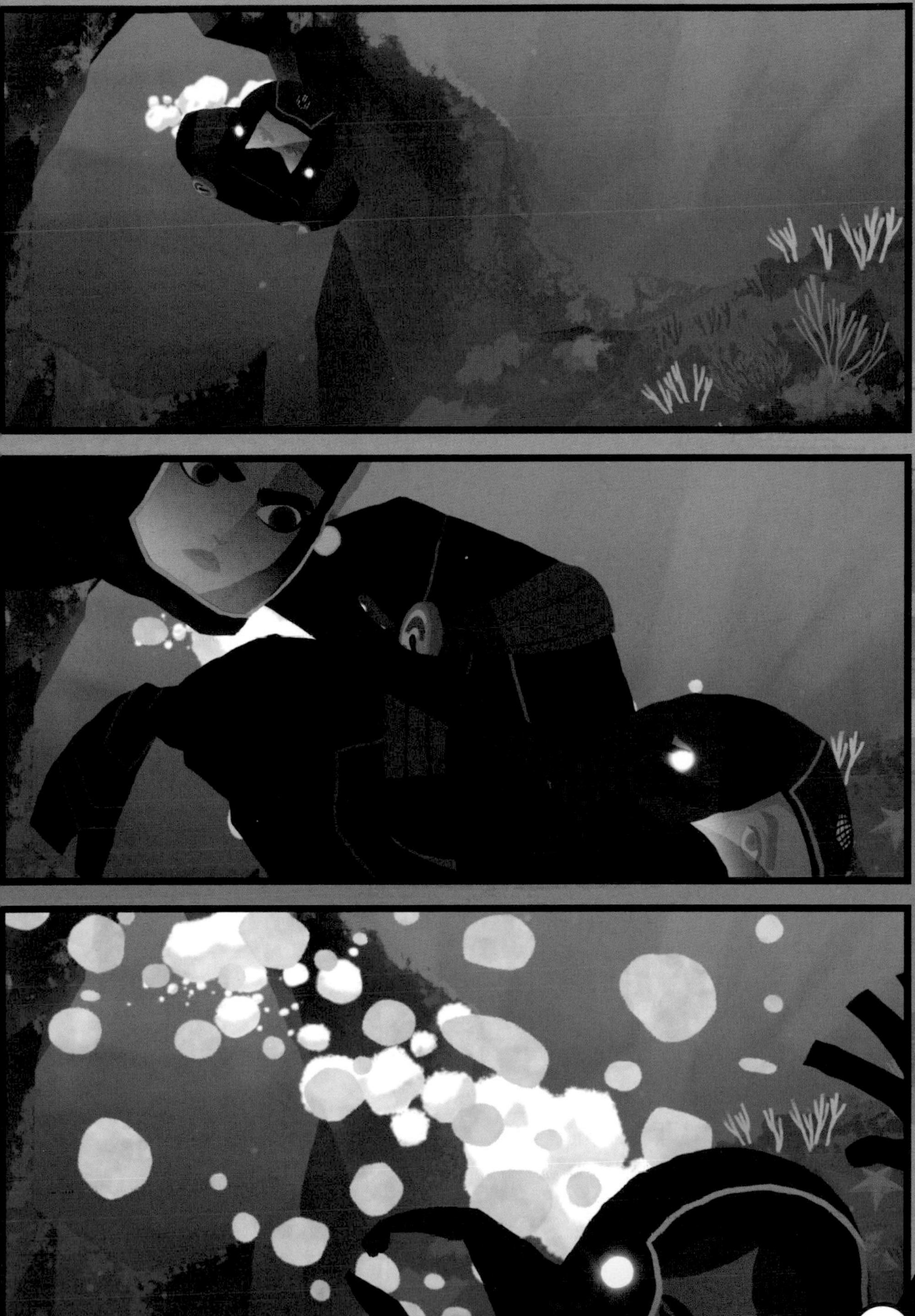

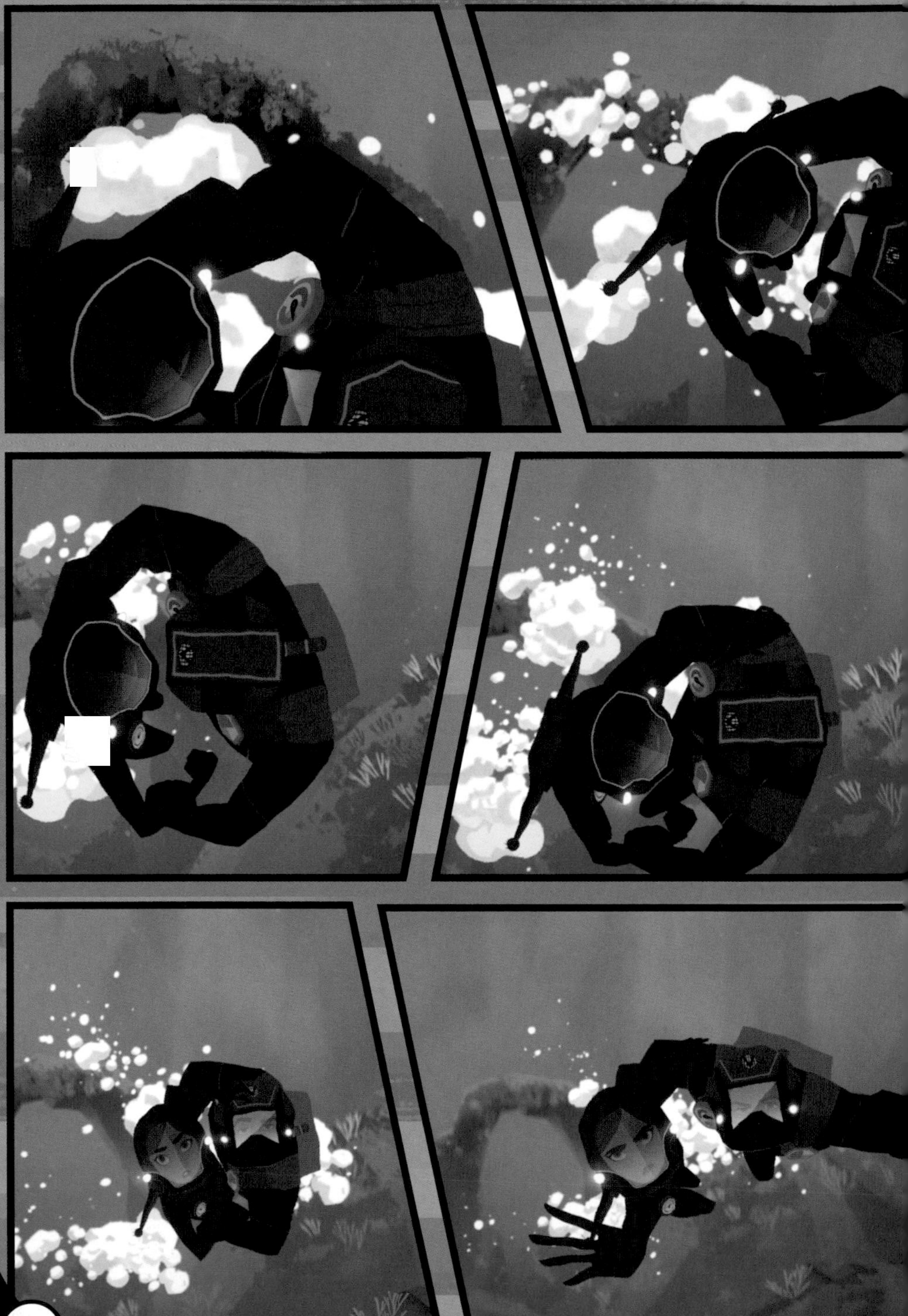

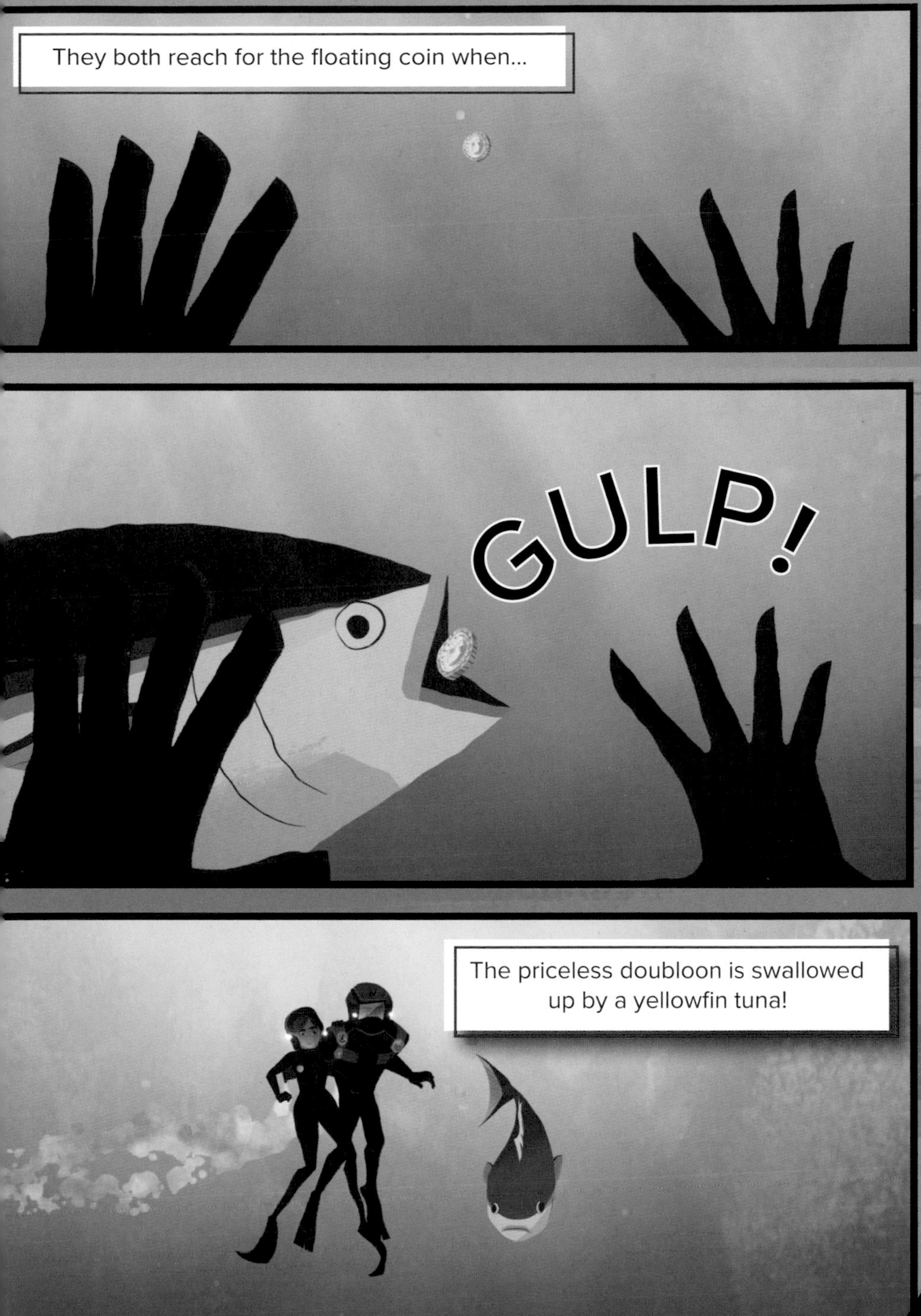
They both reach for the floating coin when...
GULP!
The priceless doubloon is swallowed up by a yellowfin tuna!

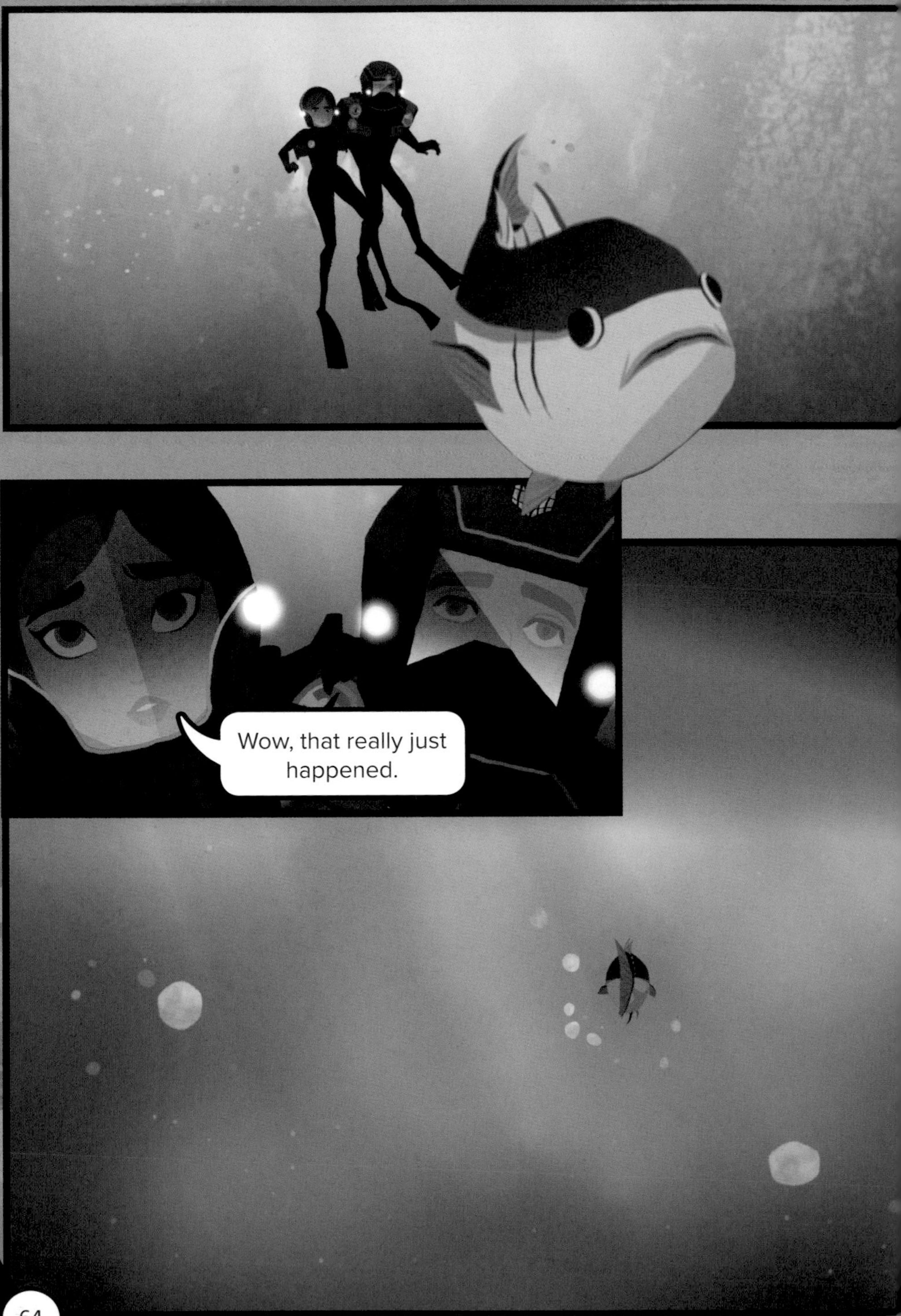
Wow, that really just happened.

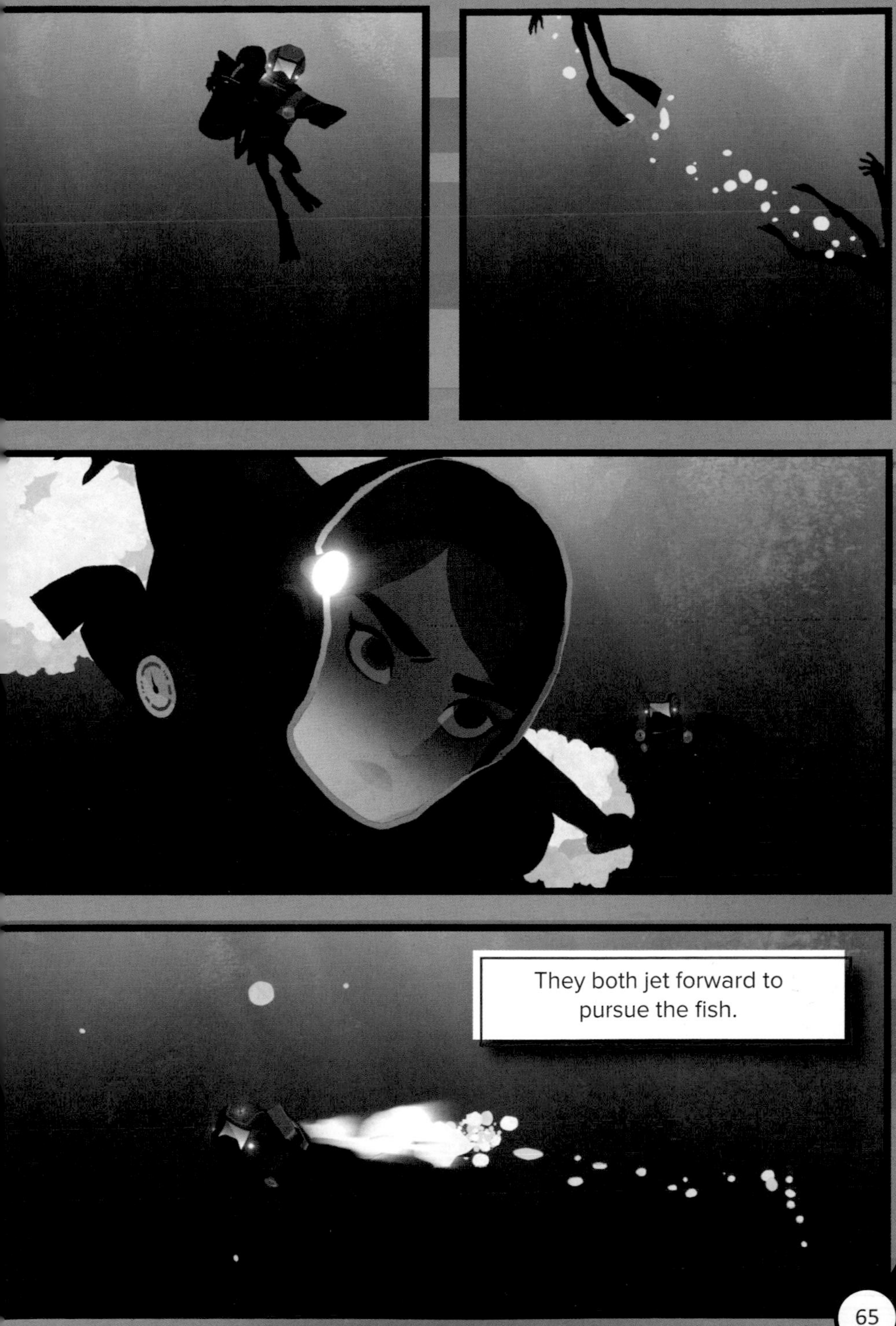
They both jet forward to pursue the fish.

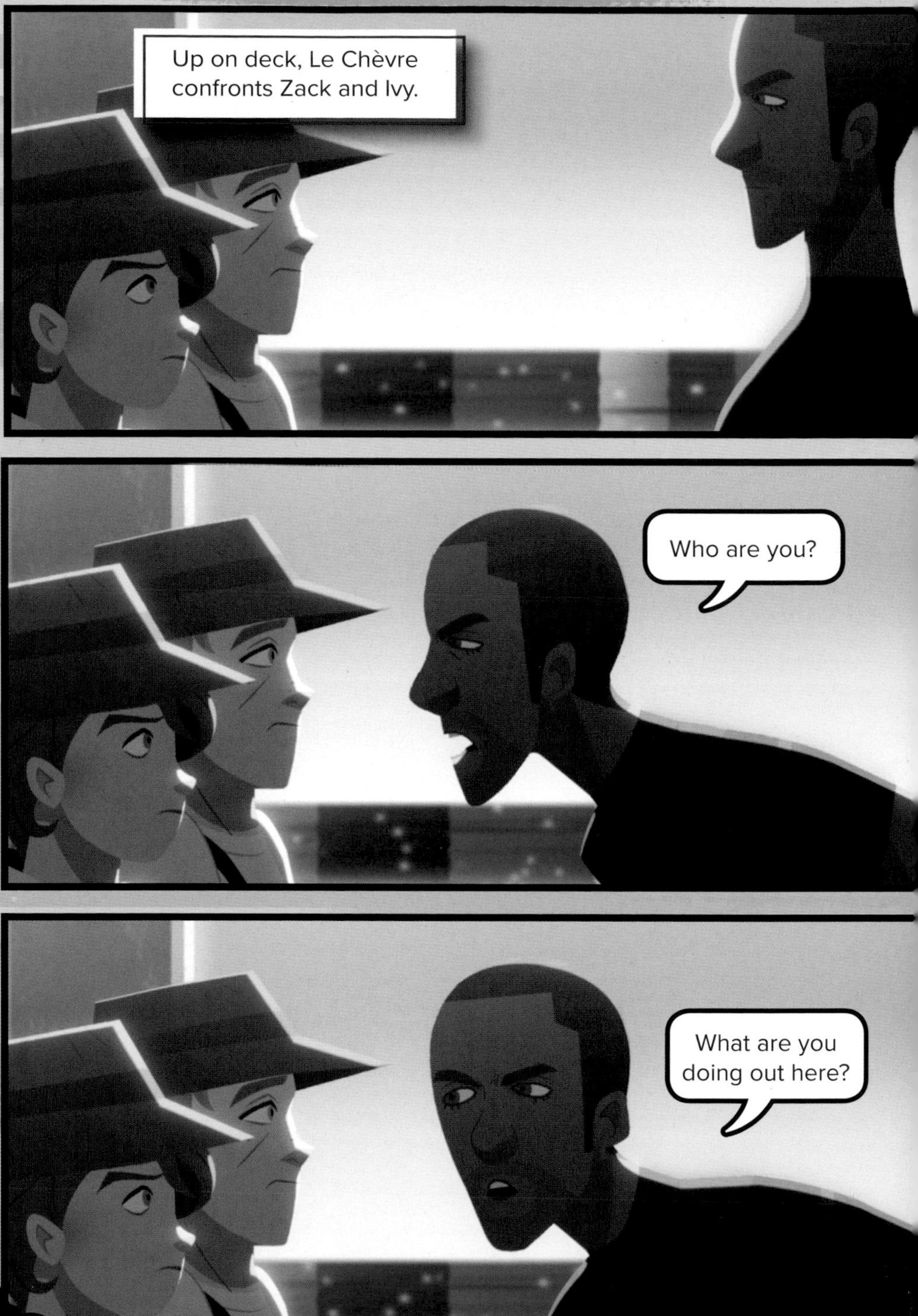
Up on deck, Le Chèvre confronts Zack and Ivy.
Who are you?
What are you doing out here?

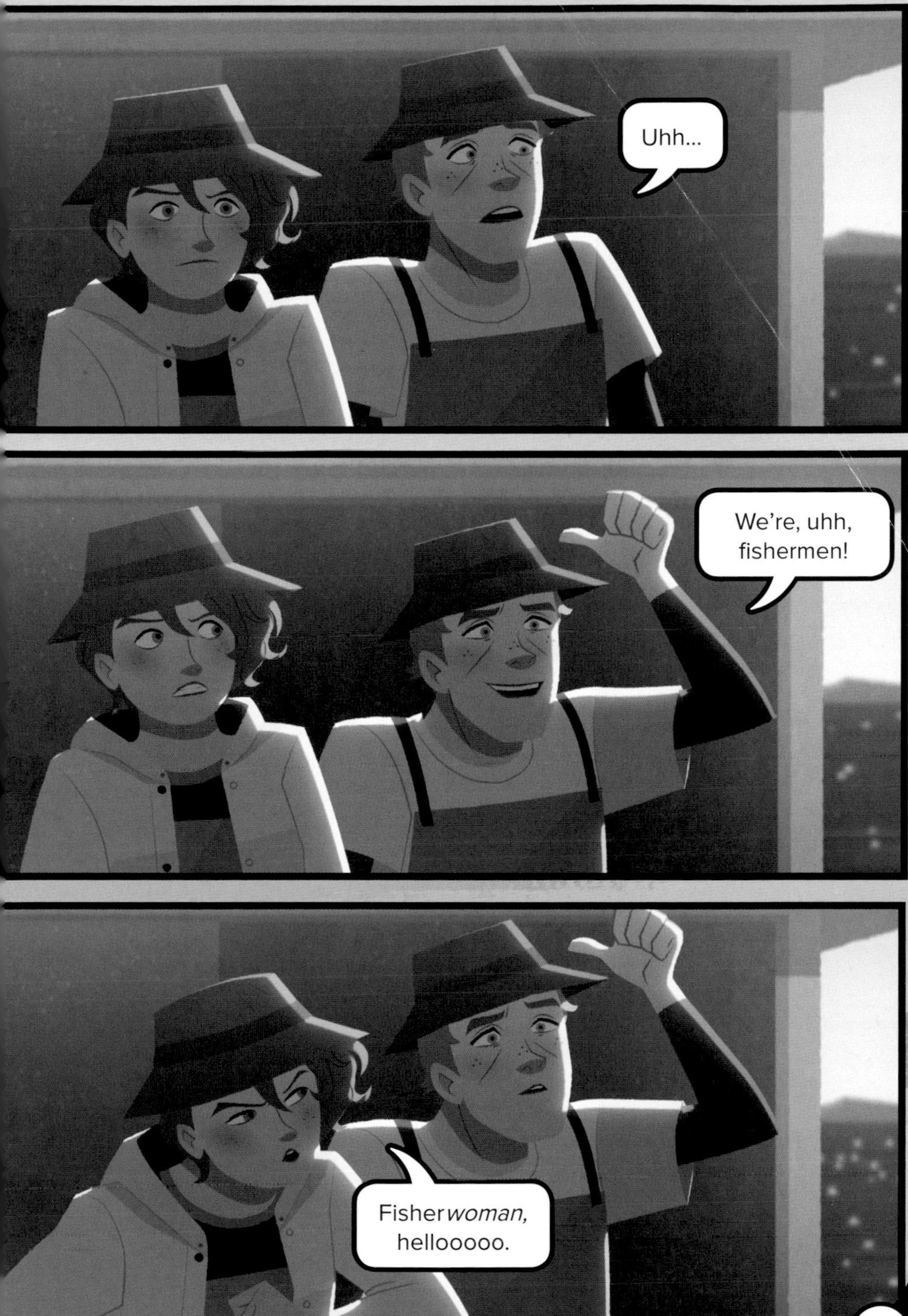
Uhh...
We're, uhh, fishermen!
Fisher*woman,* hellooooo.

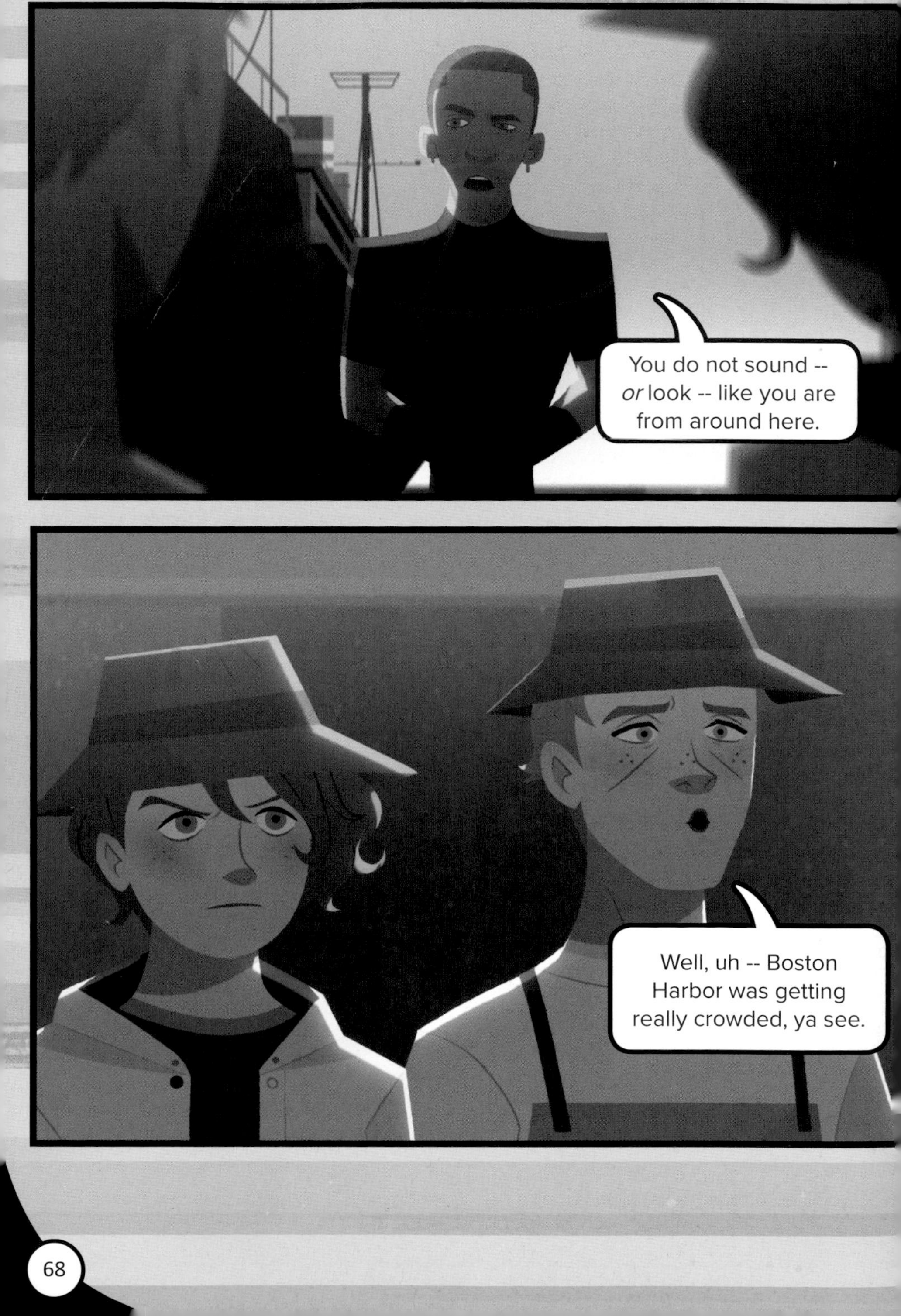
You do not sound -- *or* look -- like you are from around here.
Well, uh -- Boston Harbor was getting really crowded, ya see.

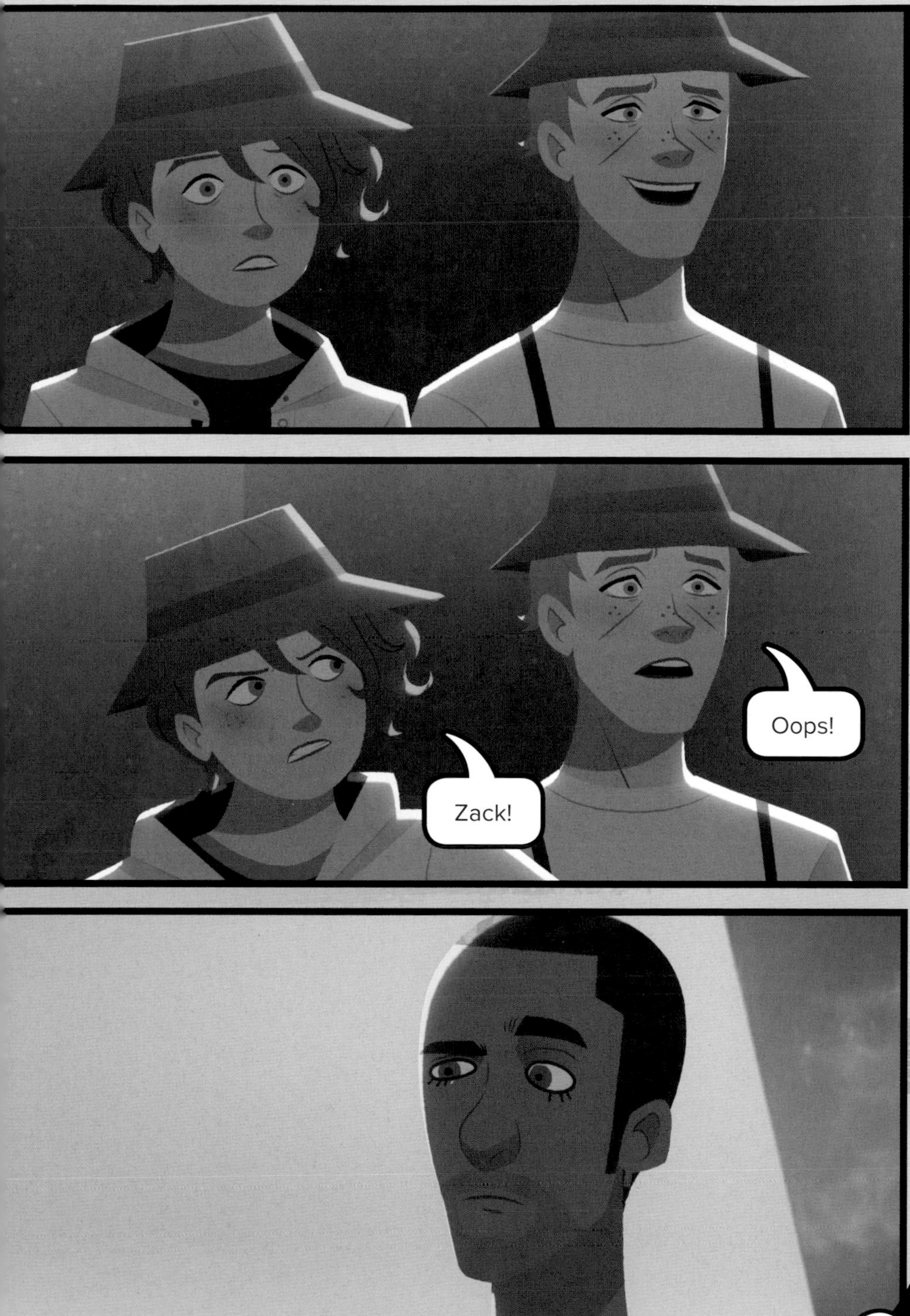
Zack!
Oops!

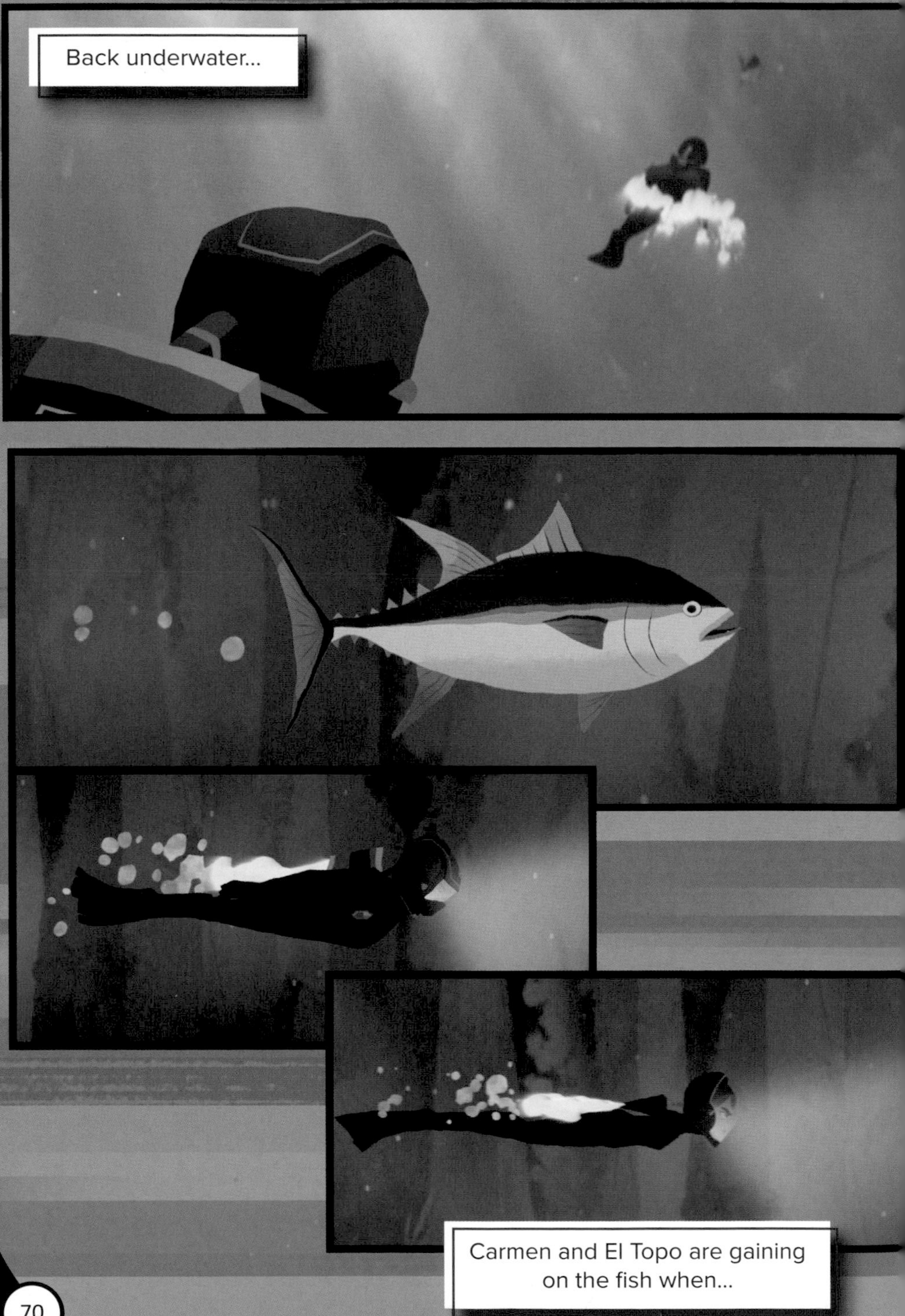
Back underwater...
Carmen and El Topo are gaining on the fish when...

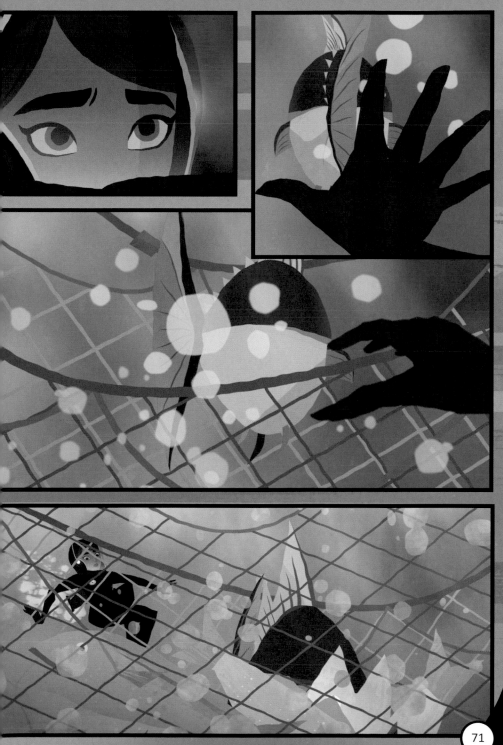

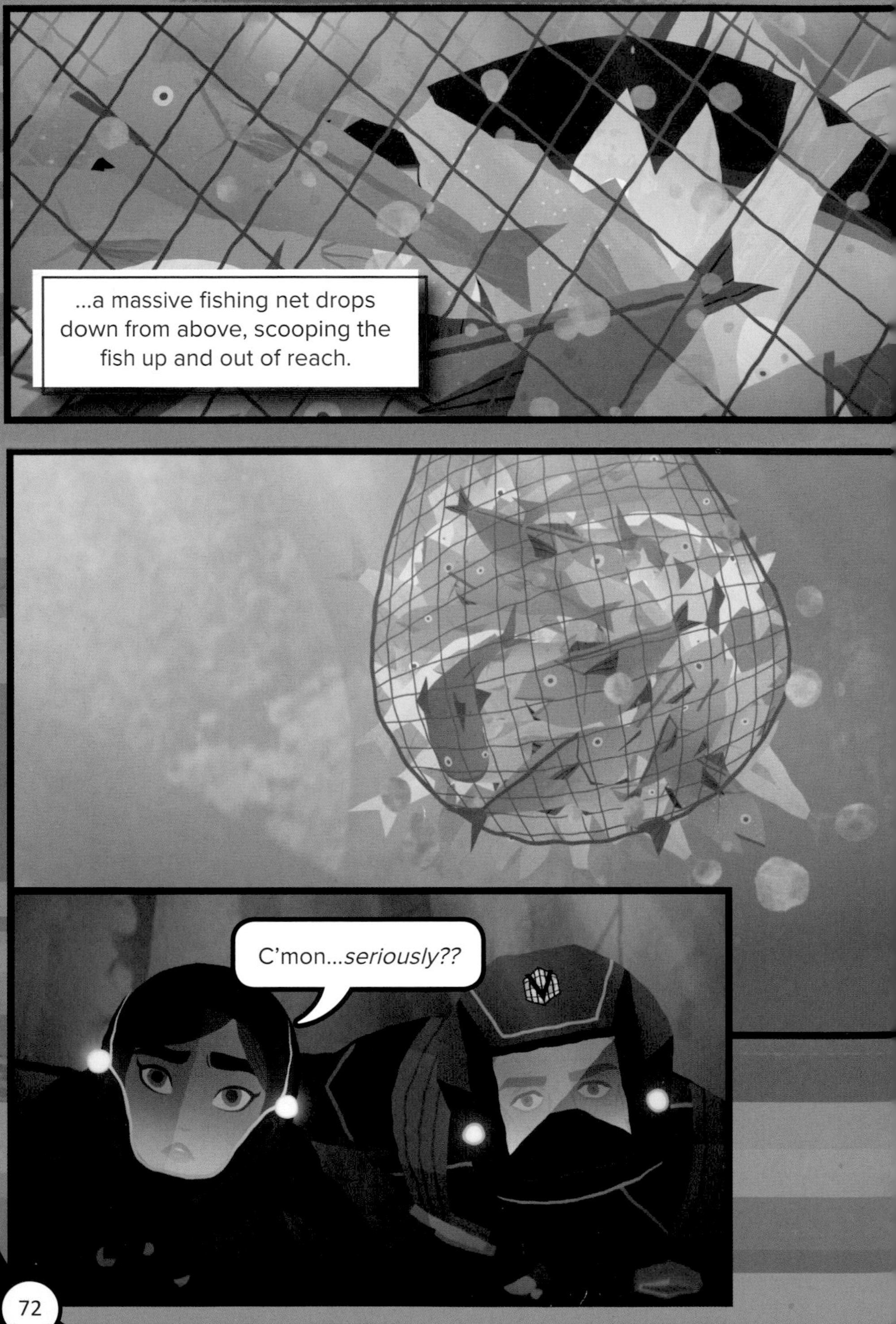

...a massive fishing net drops down from above, scooping the fish up and out of reach.
C'mon...*seriously??*

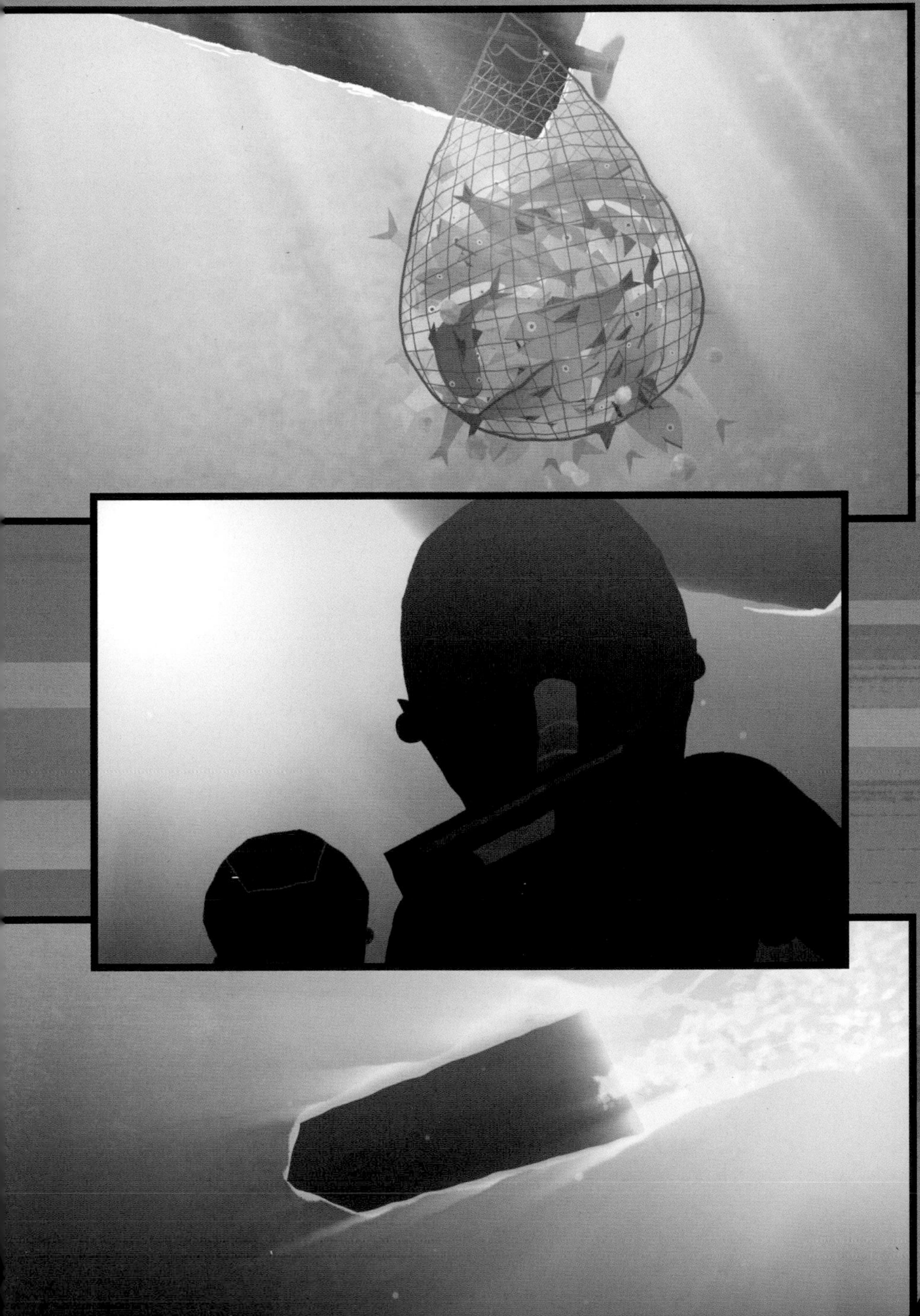

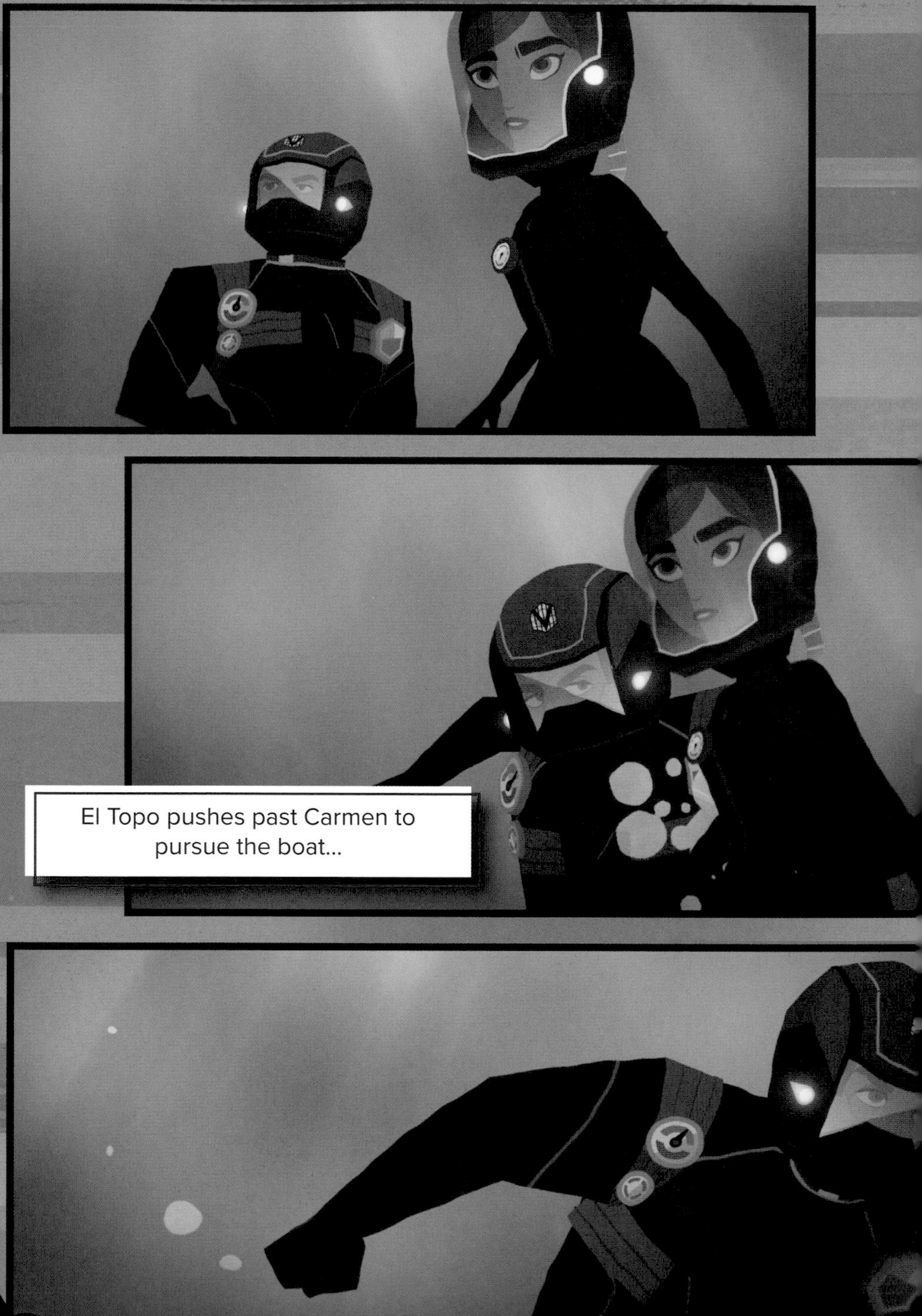
El Topo pushes past Carmen to pursue the boat...

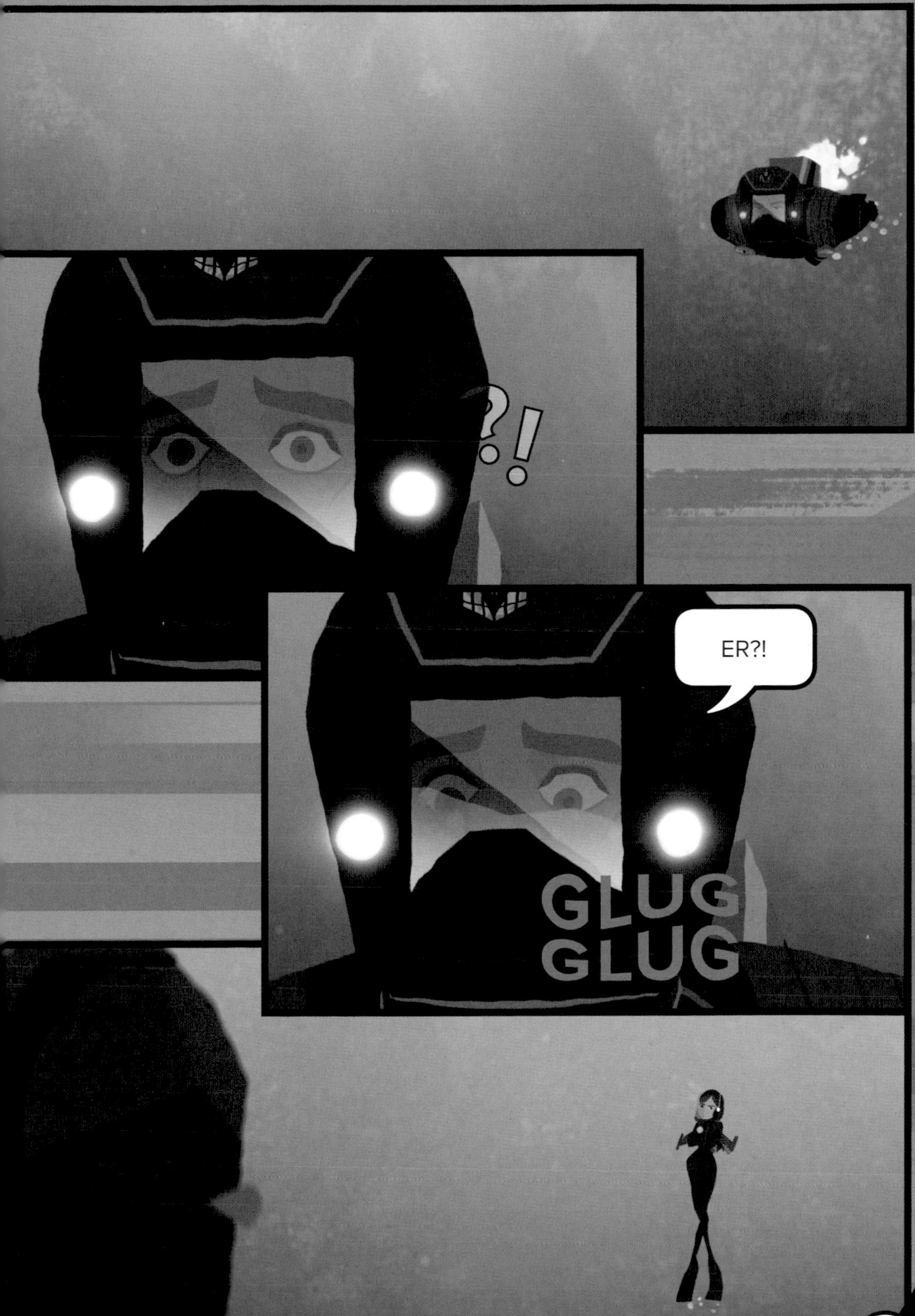
?!
ER?!
GLUG
GLUG

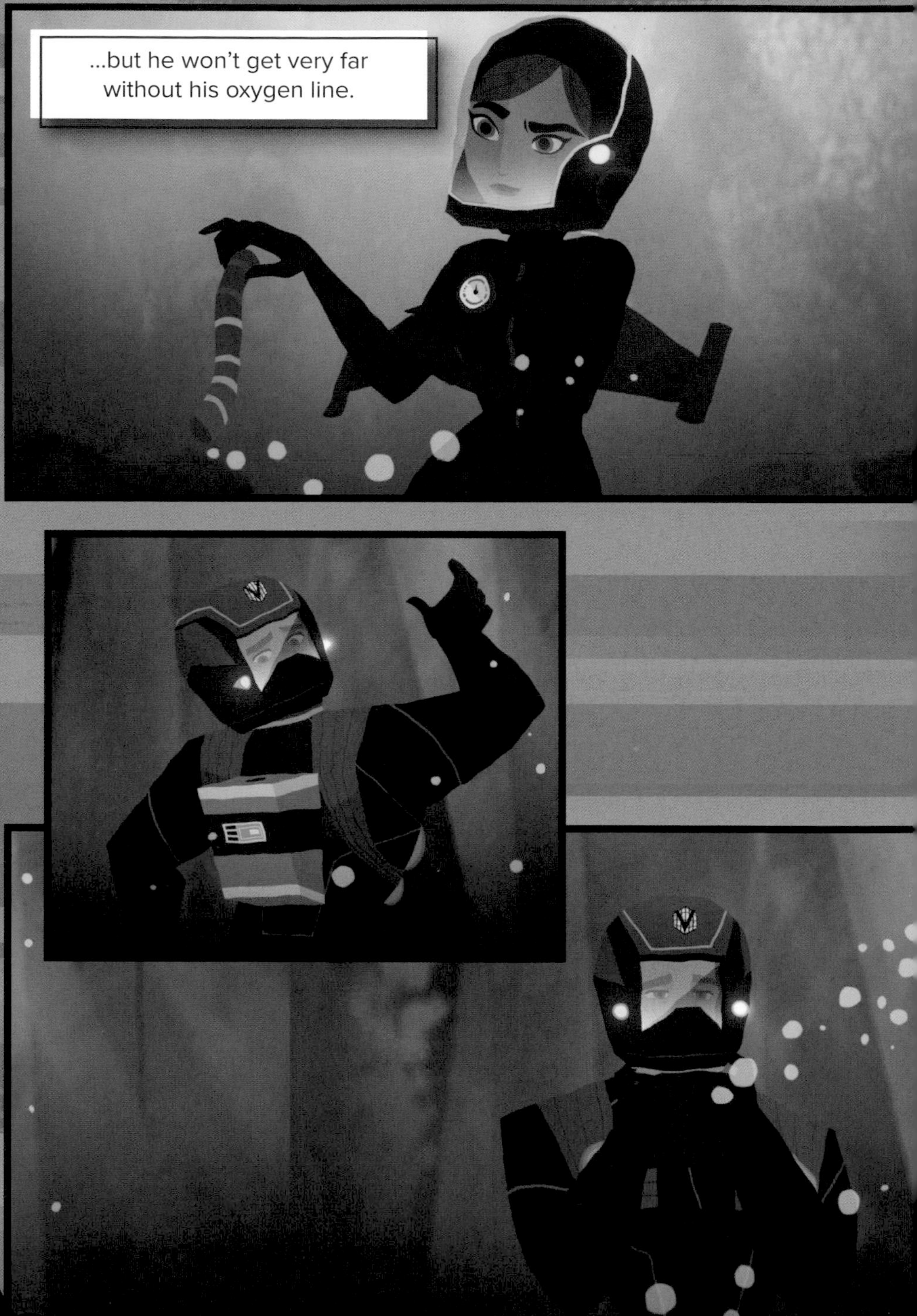
...but he won't get very far
without his oxygen line.

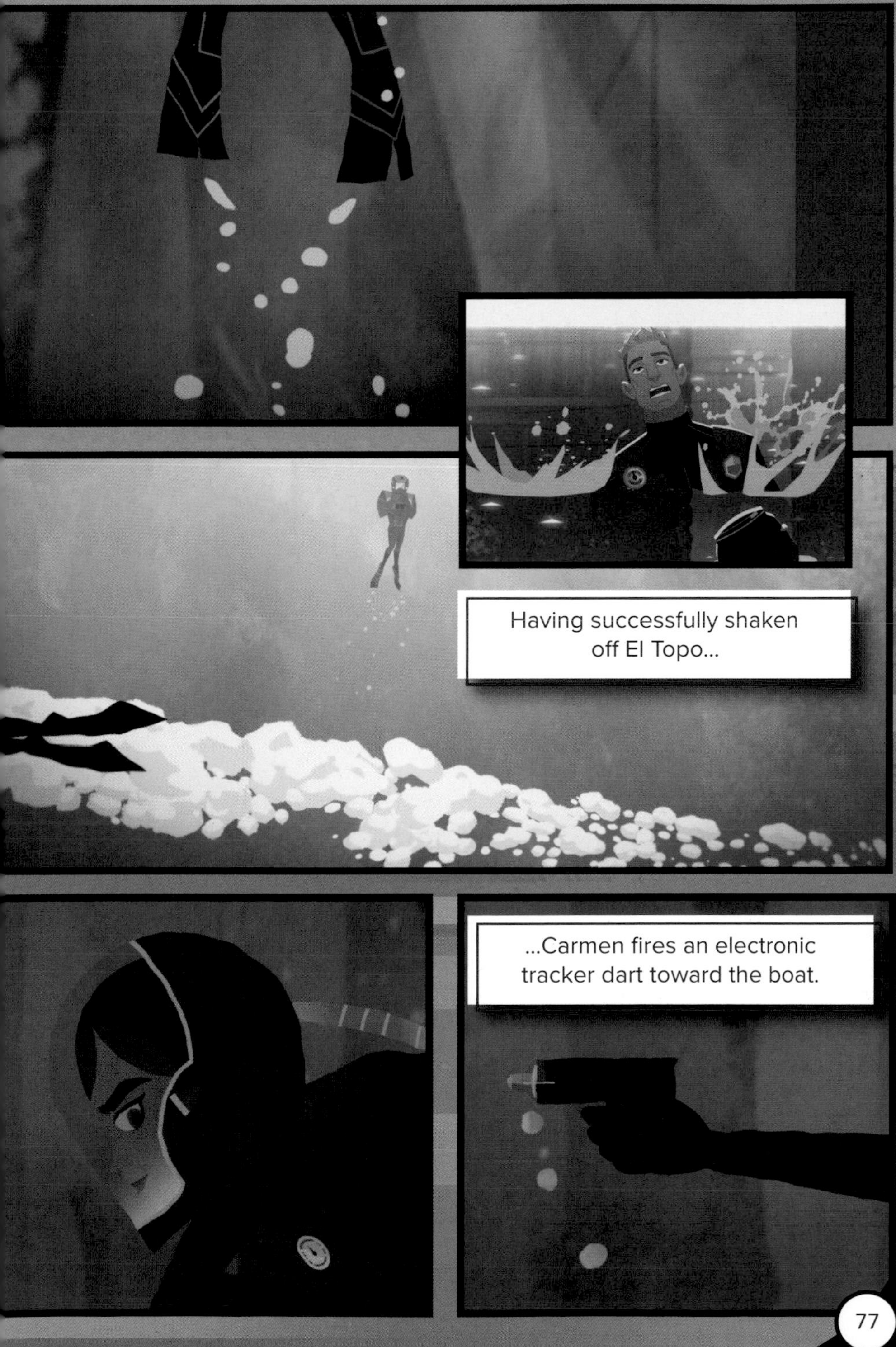
Having successfully shaken off El Topo...
...Carmen fires an electronic tracker dart toward the boat.

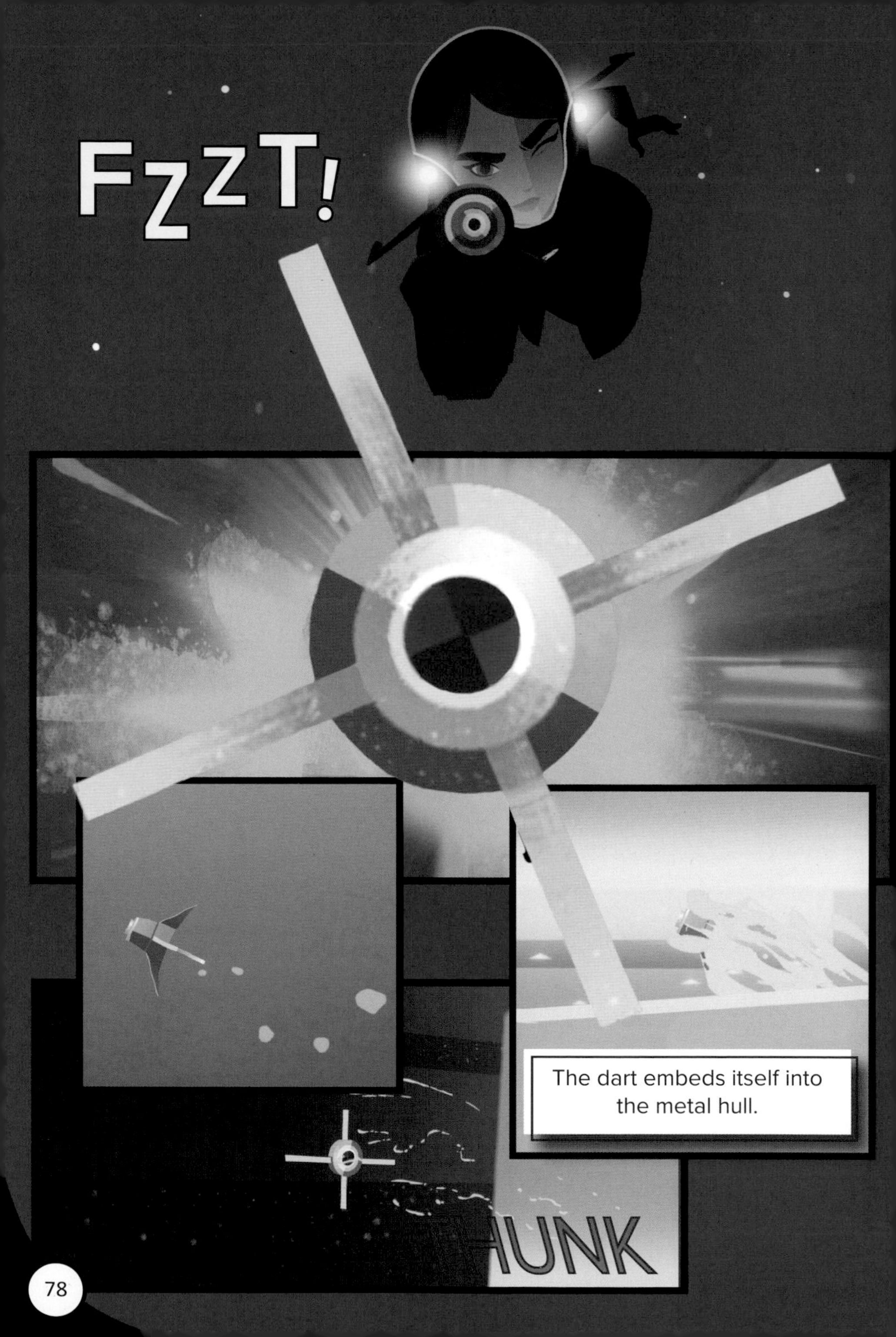
FZZT!
The dart embeds itself into the metal hull.
HUNK

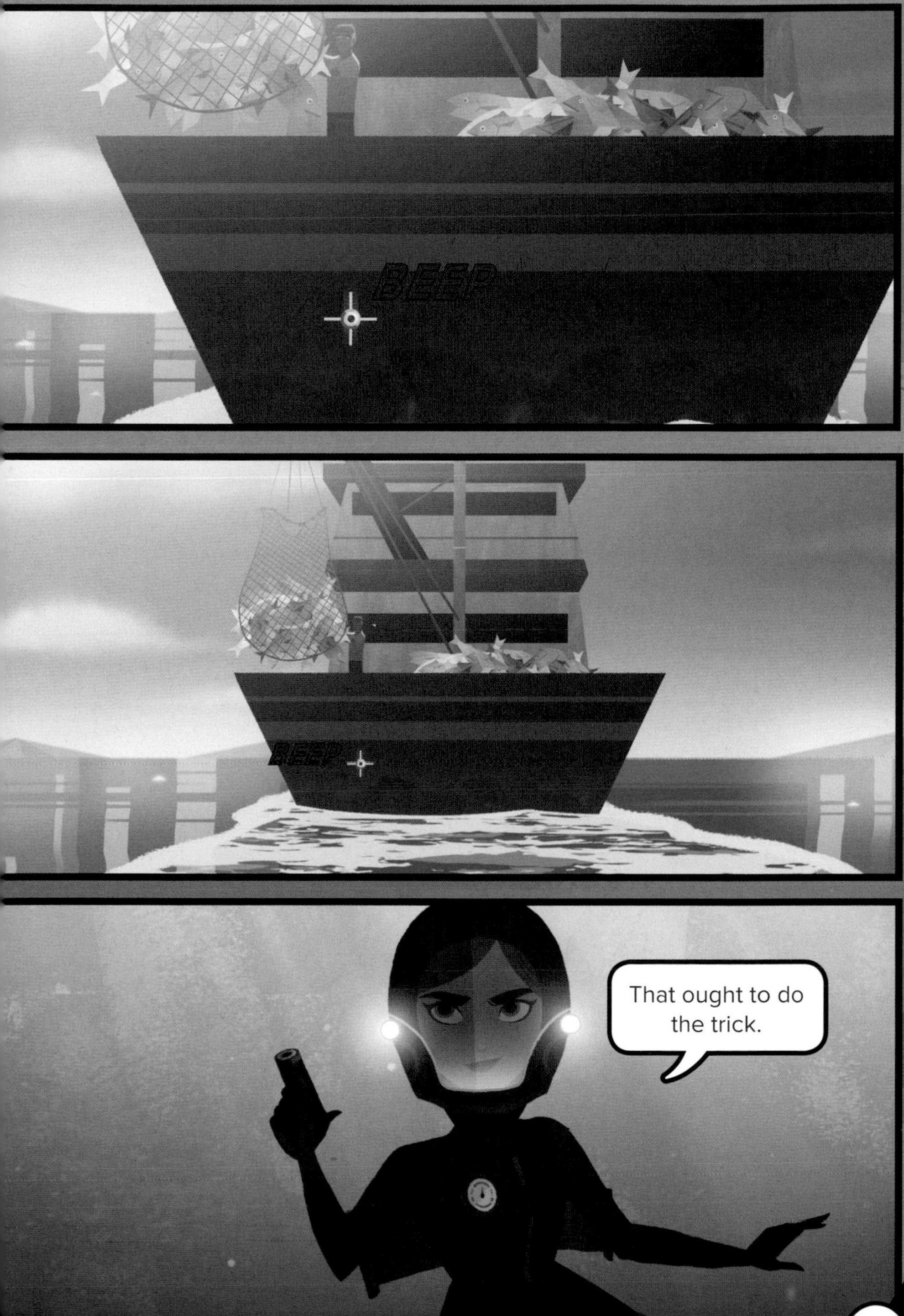
BEEP
BEEP
That ought to do the trick.

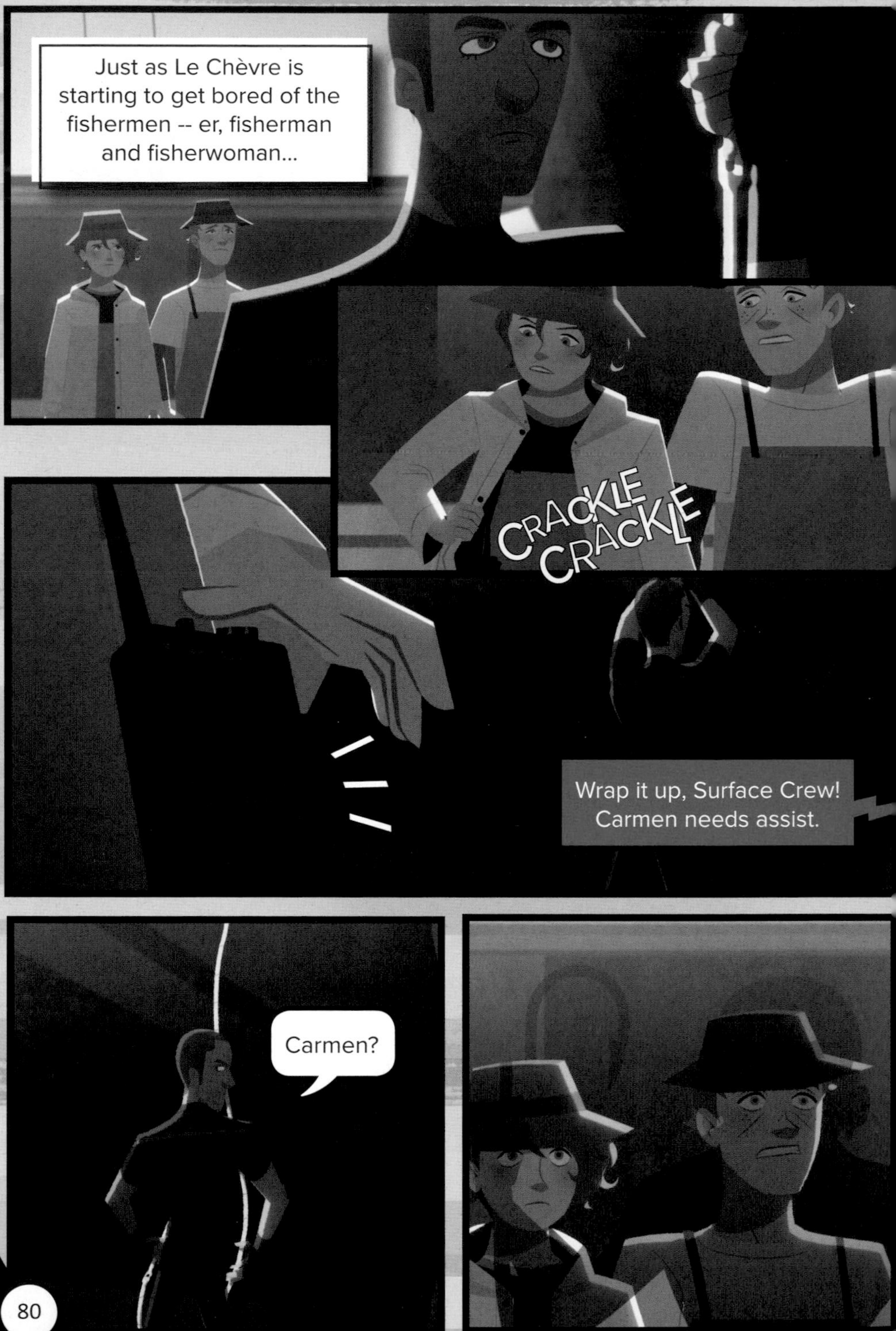

Just as Le Chèvre is starting to get bored of the fishermen -- er, fisherman and fisherwoman...
CRACKLE CRACKLE
Wrap it up, Surface Crew! Carmen needs assist.
Carmen?

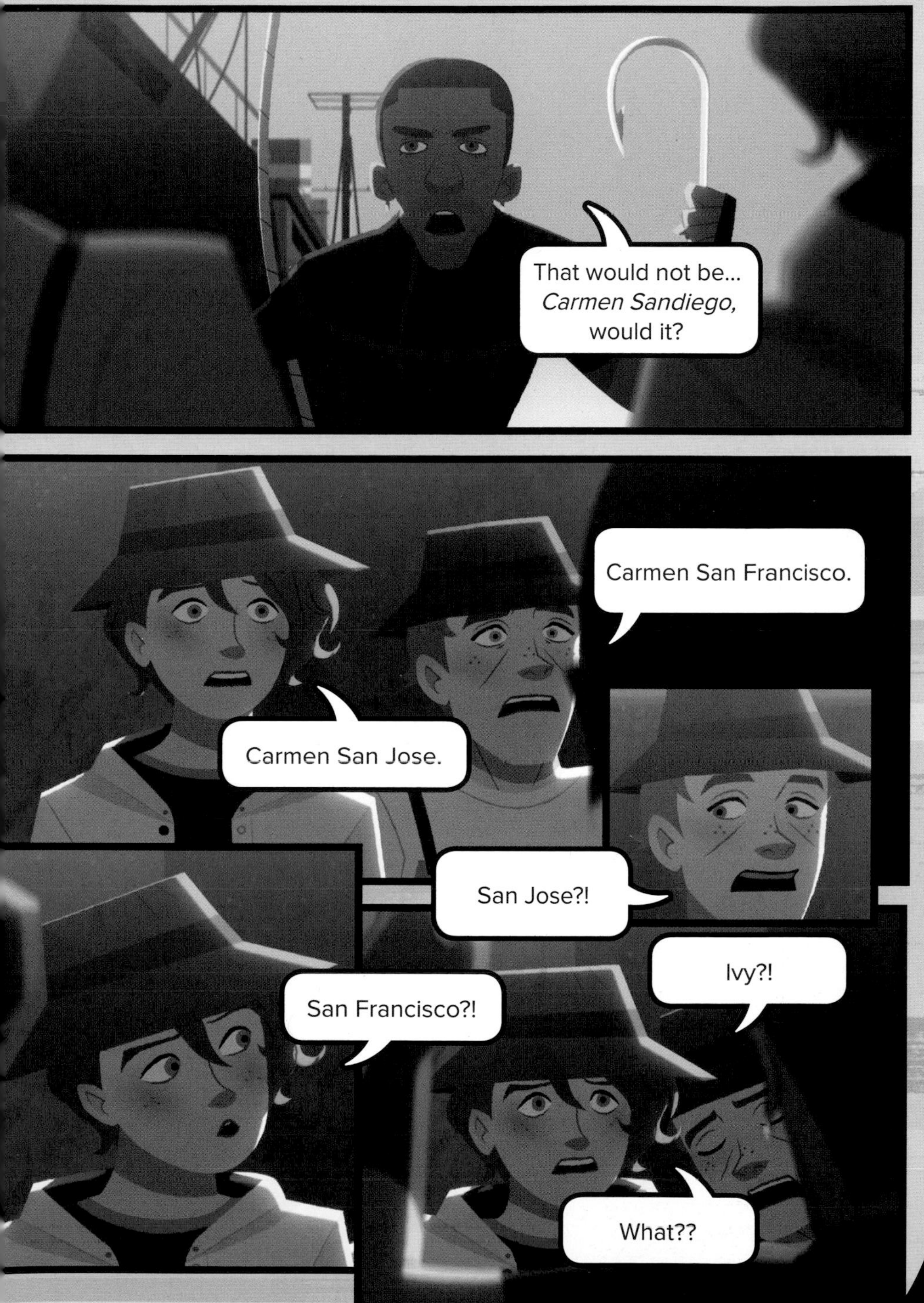
That would not be... *Carmen Sandiego,* would it?
Carmen San Francisco.
Carmen San Jose.
San Jose?!
San Francisco?!
Ivy?!
What??

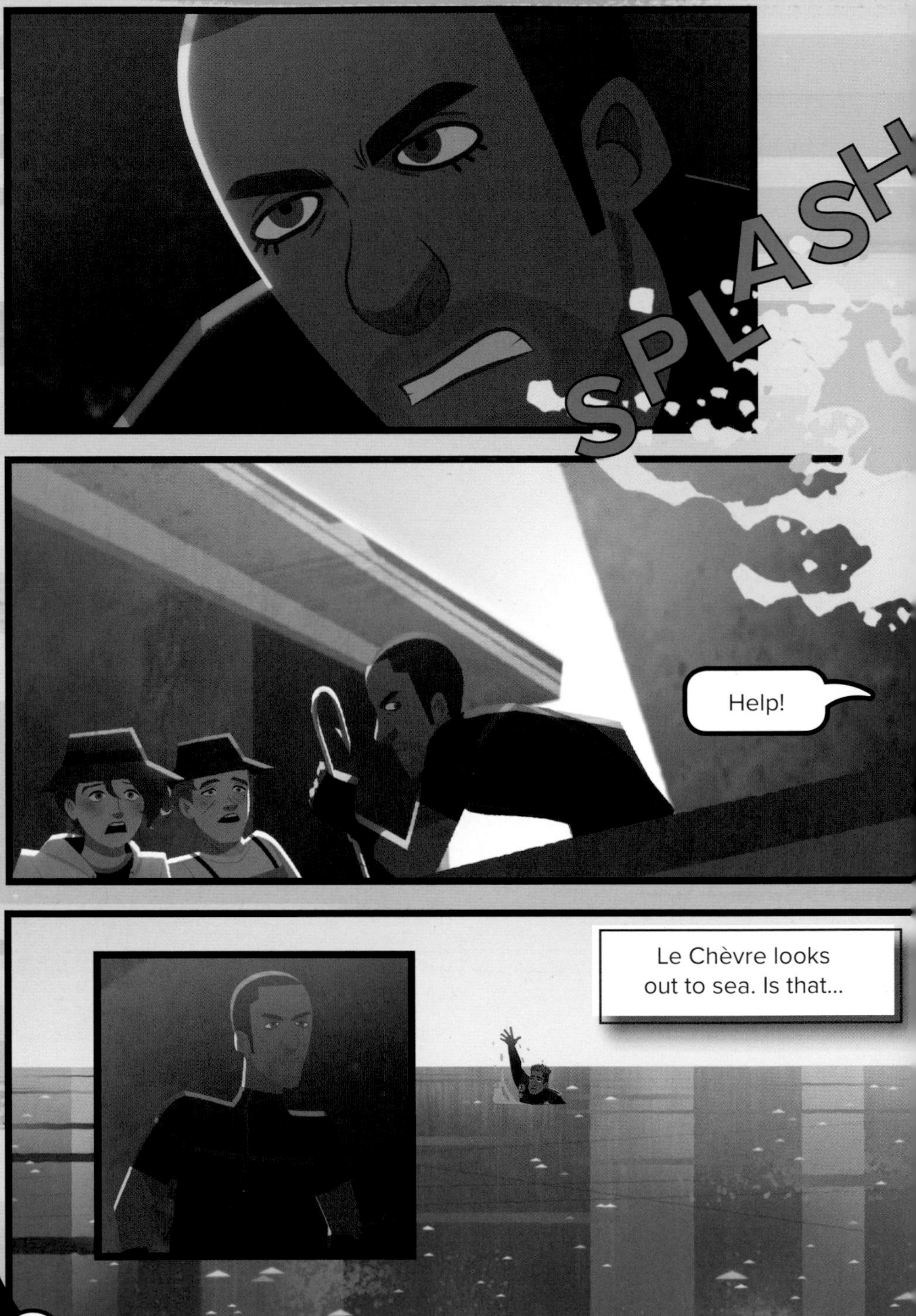
SPLASH
Help!
Le Chèvre looks out to sea. Is that...

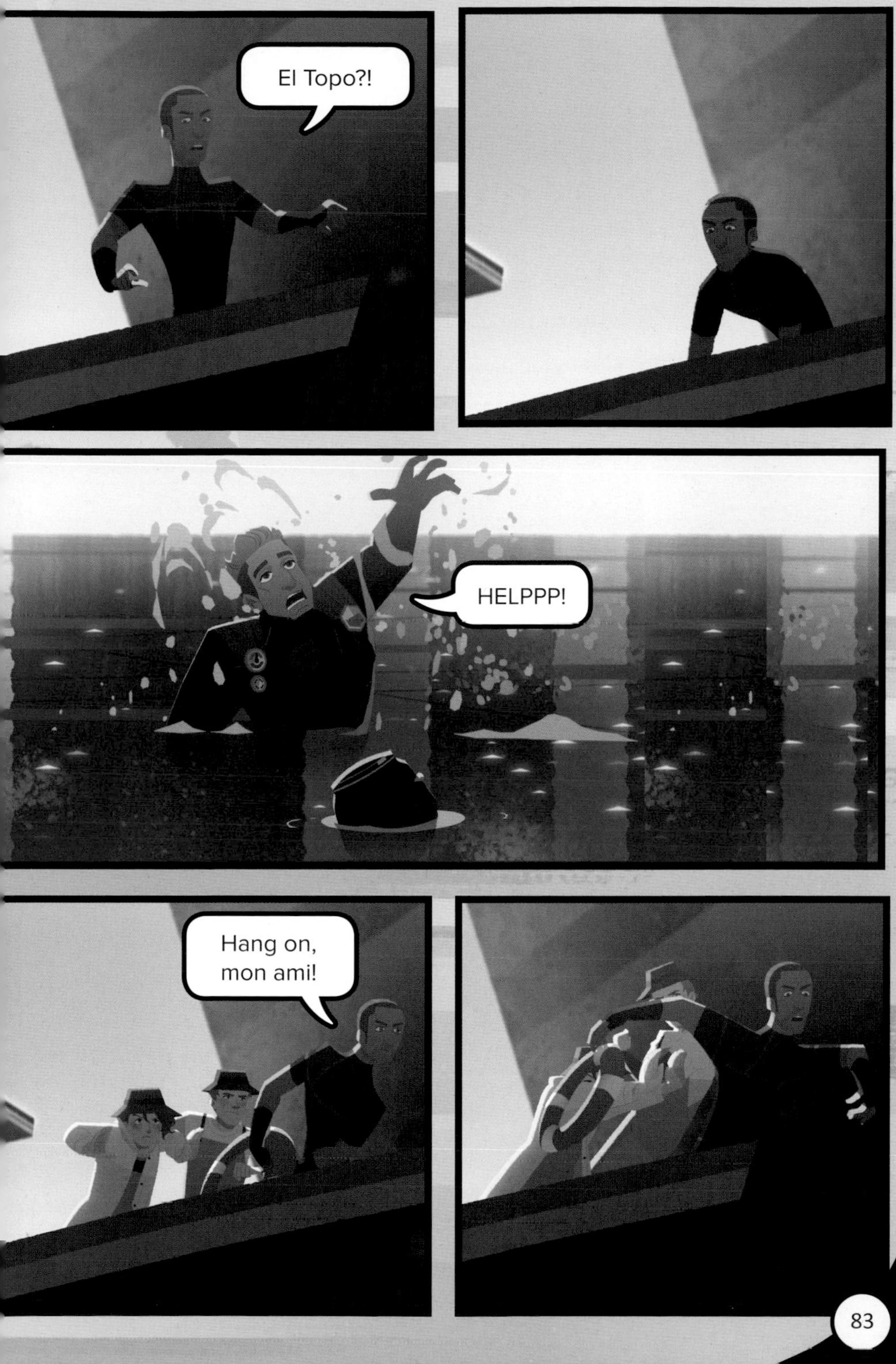
El Topo?!
HELPPP!
Hang on, mon ami!

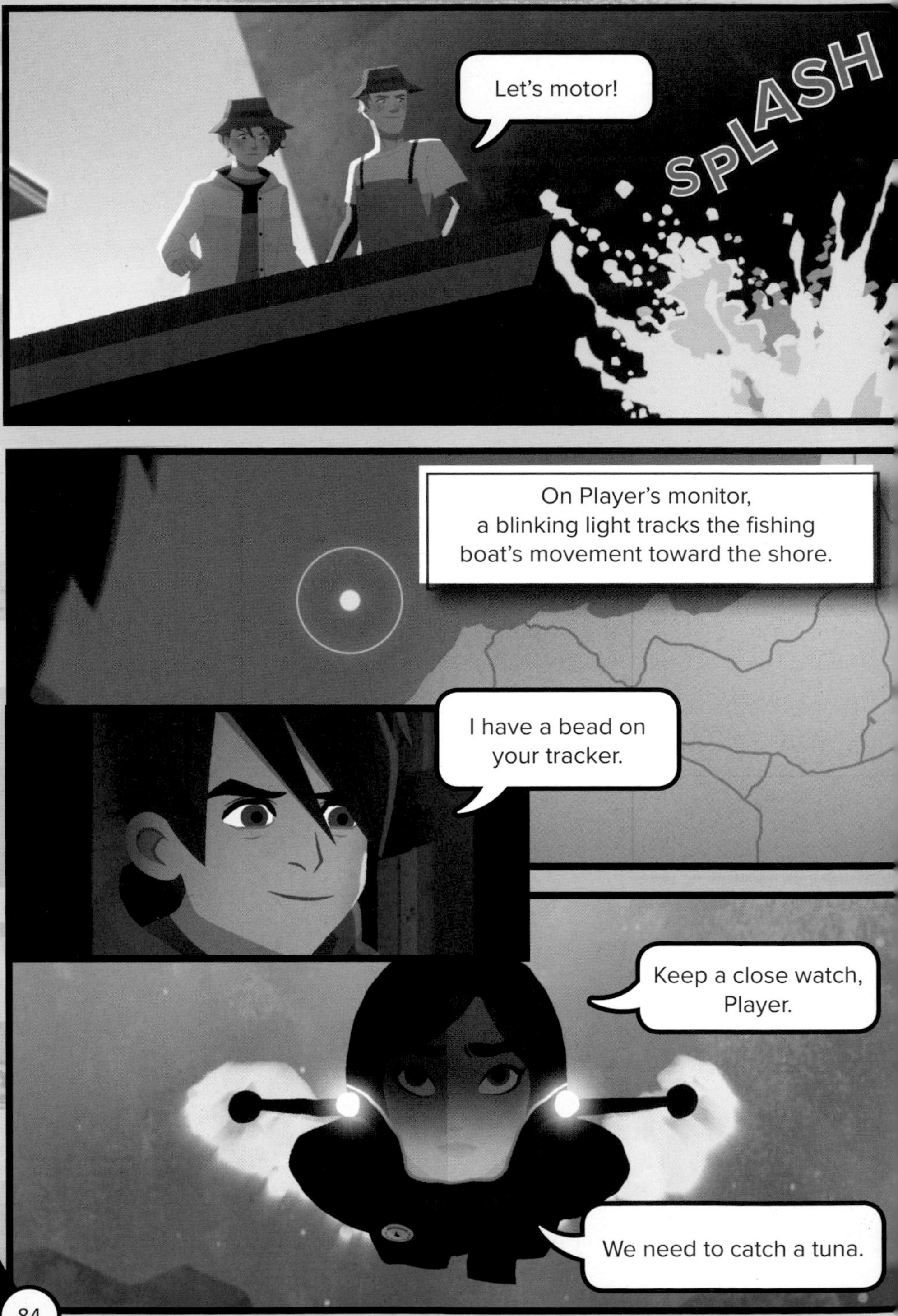
Let's motor!
SPLASH
On Player's monitor, a blinking light tracks the fishing boat's movement toward the shore.
I have a bead on your tracker.
Keep a close watch, Player.
We need to catch a tuna.

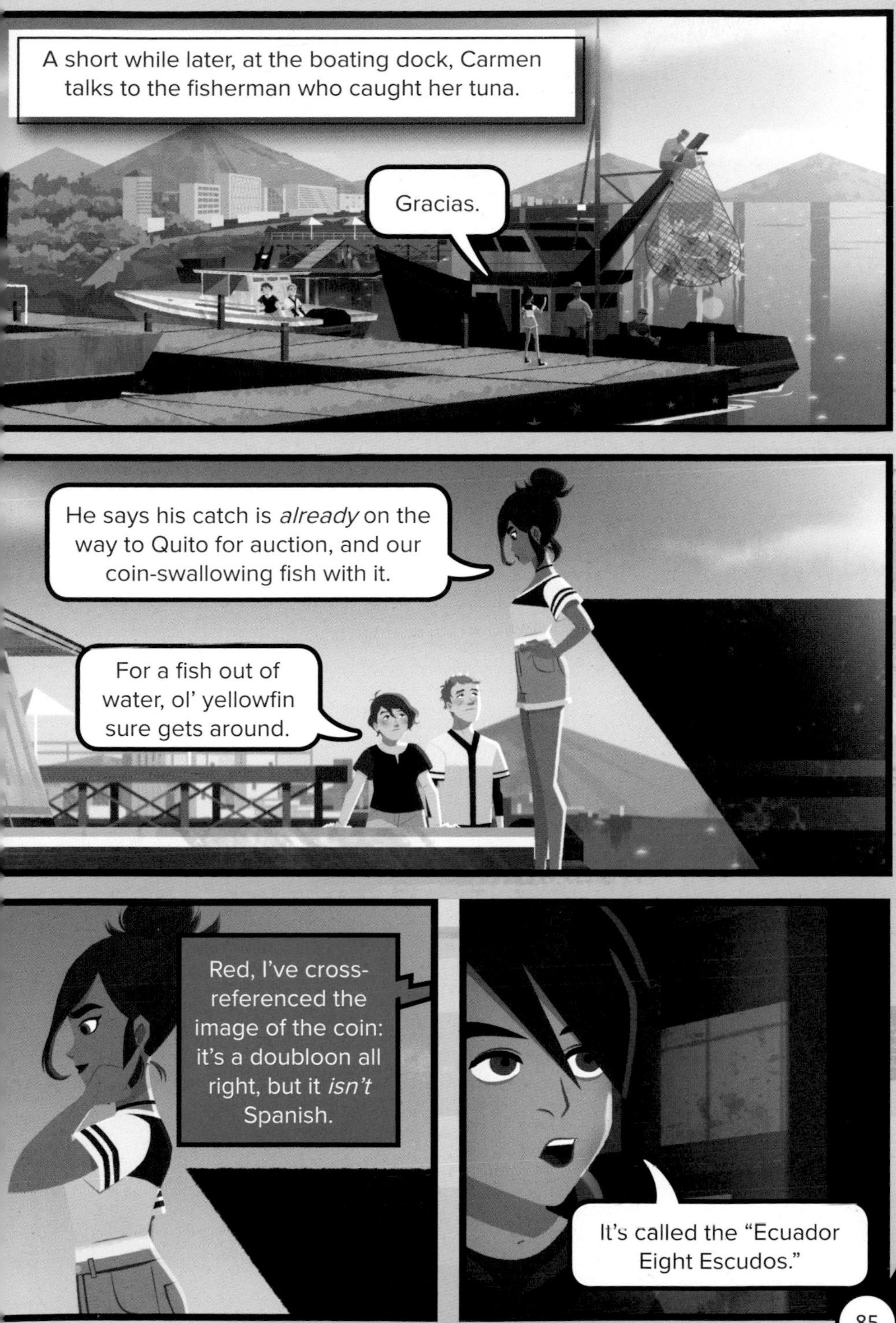
A short while later, at the boating dock, Carmen talks to the fisherman who caught her tuna.
Gracias.
He says his catch is *already* on the way to Quito for auction, and our coin-swallowing fish with it.
For a fish out of water, ol' yellowfin sure gets around.
Red, I've cross-referenced the image of the coin: it's a doubloon all right, but it *isn't* Spanish.
It's called the "Ecuador Eight Escudos."

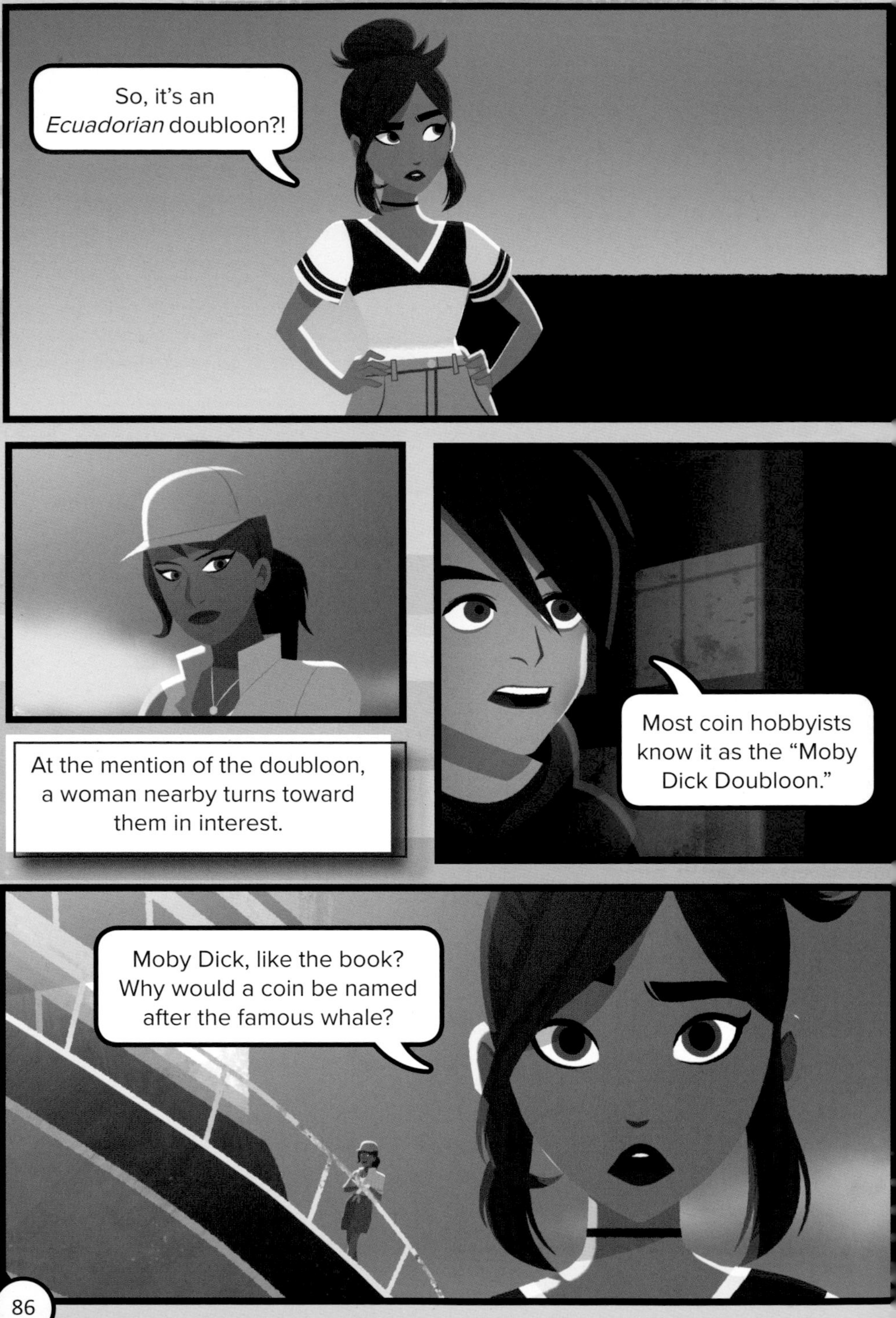
So, it's an *Ecuadorian* doubloon?!
At the mention of the doubloon, a woman nearby turns toward them in interest.
Most coin hobbyists know it as the "Moby Dick Doubloon."
Moby Dick, like the book? Why would a coin be named after the famous whale?

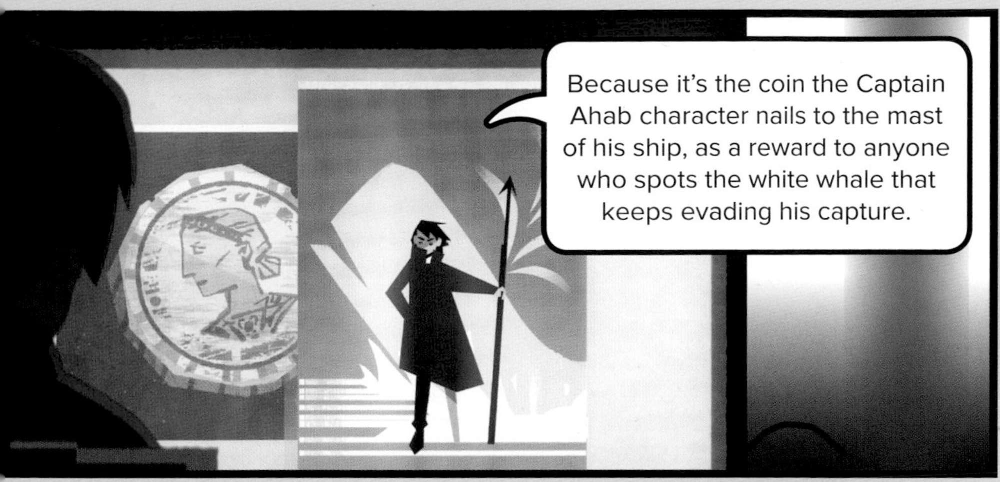
Because it's the coin the Captain Ahab character nails to the mast of his ship, as a reward to anyone who spots the white whale that keeps evading his capture.

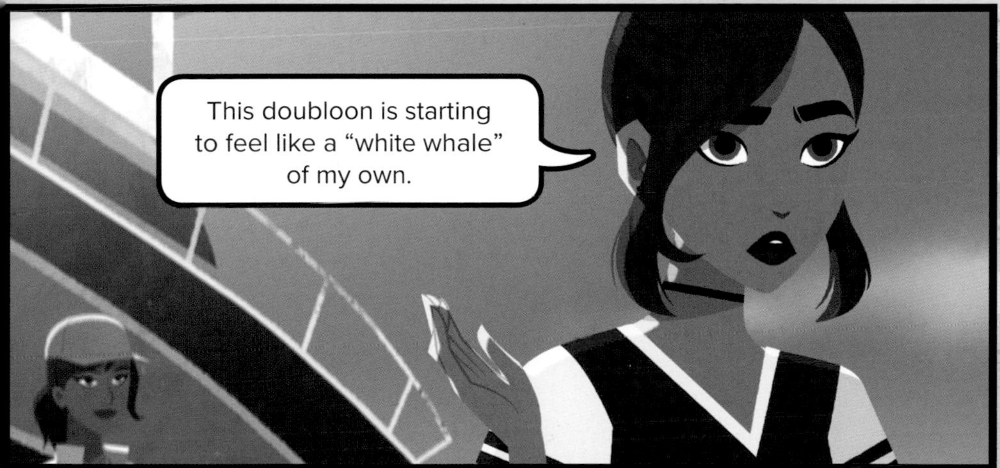
This doubloon is starting to feel like a "white whale" of my own.

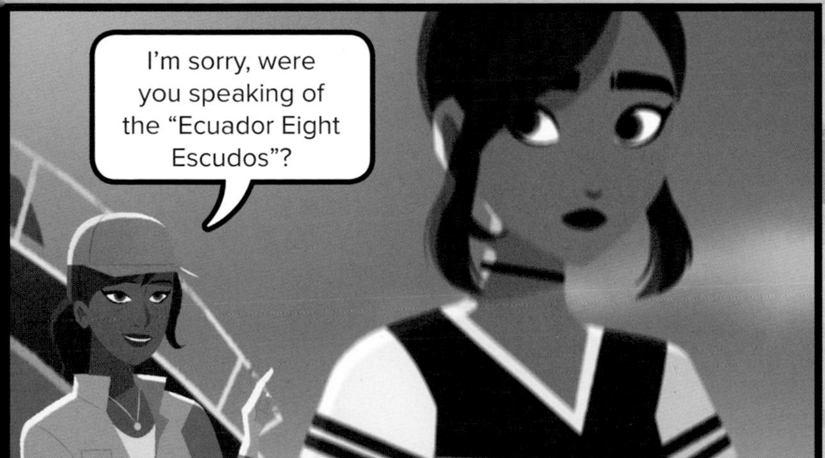
I'm sorry, were you speaking of the "Ecuador Eight Escudos"?

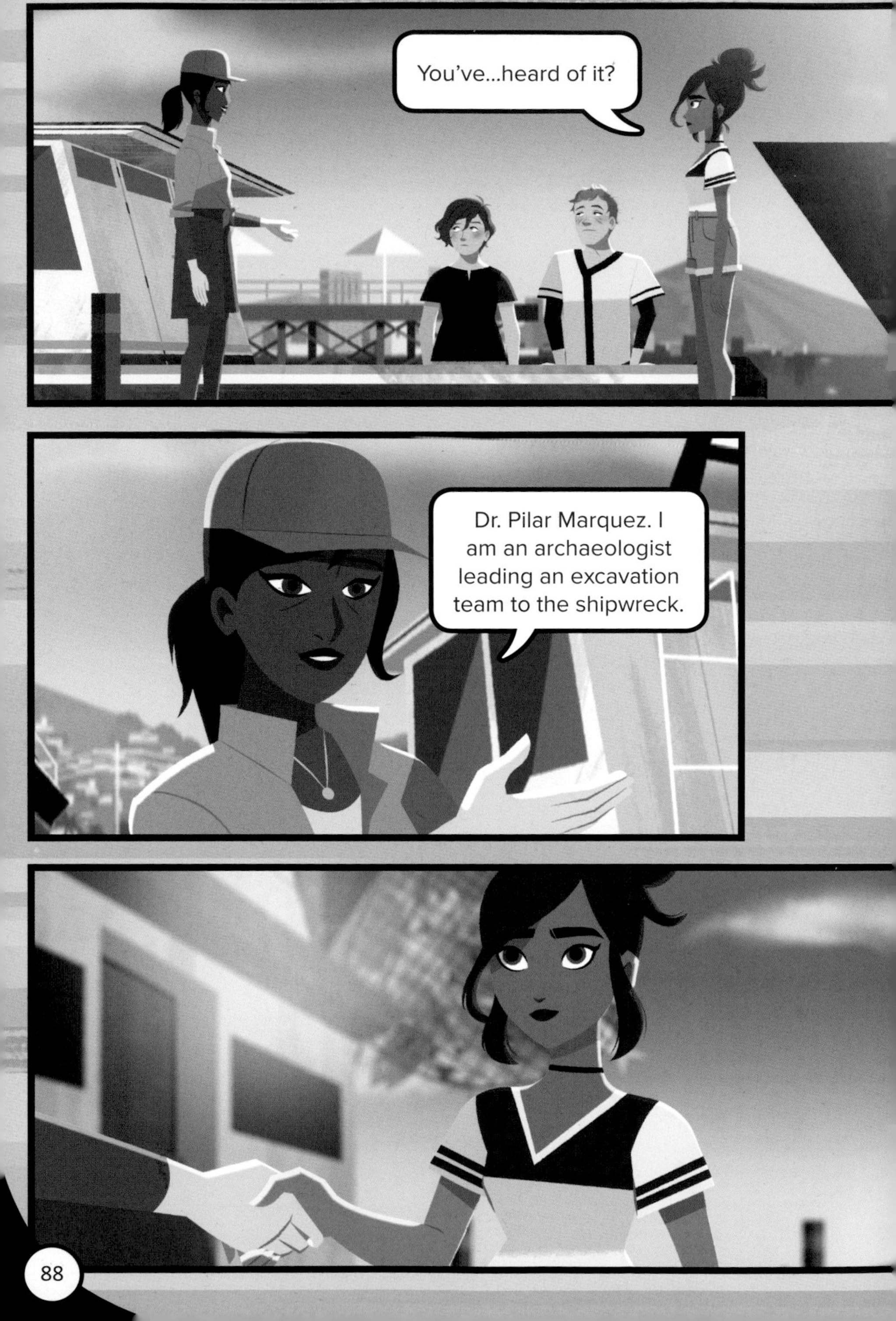
You've...heard of it?
Dr. Pilar Marquez. I am an archaeologist leading an excavation team to the shipwreck.

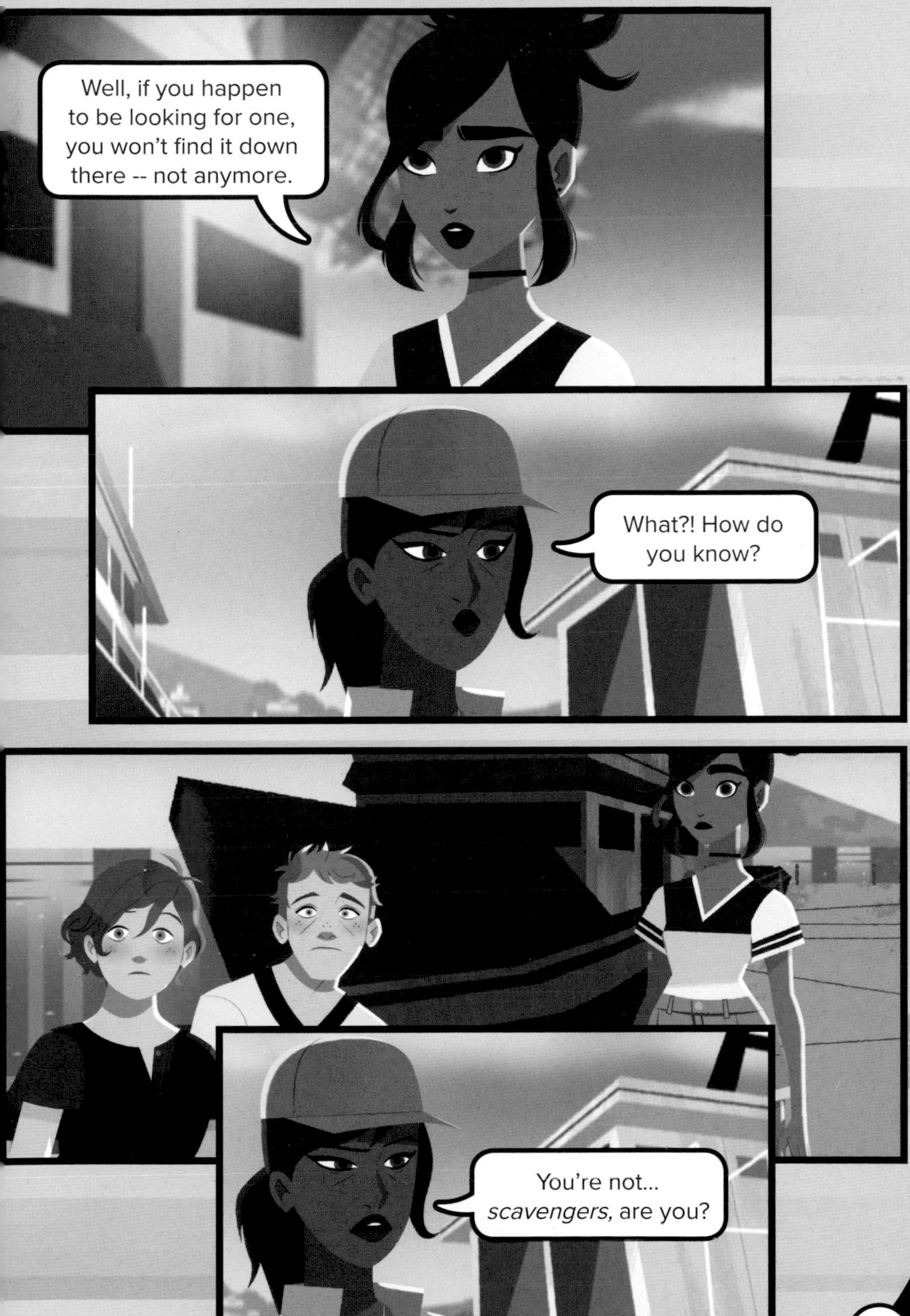
Well, if you happen to be looking for one, you won't find it down there -- not anymore.
What?! How do you know?
You're not... *scavengers,* are you?

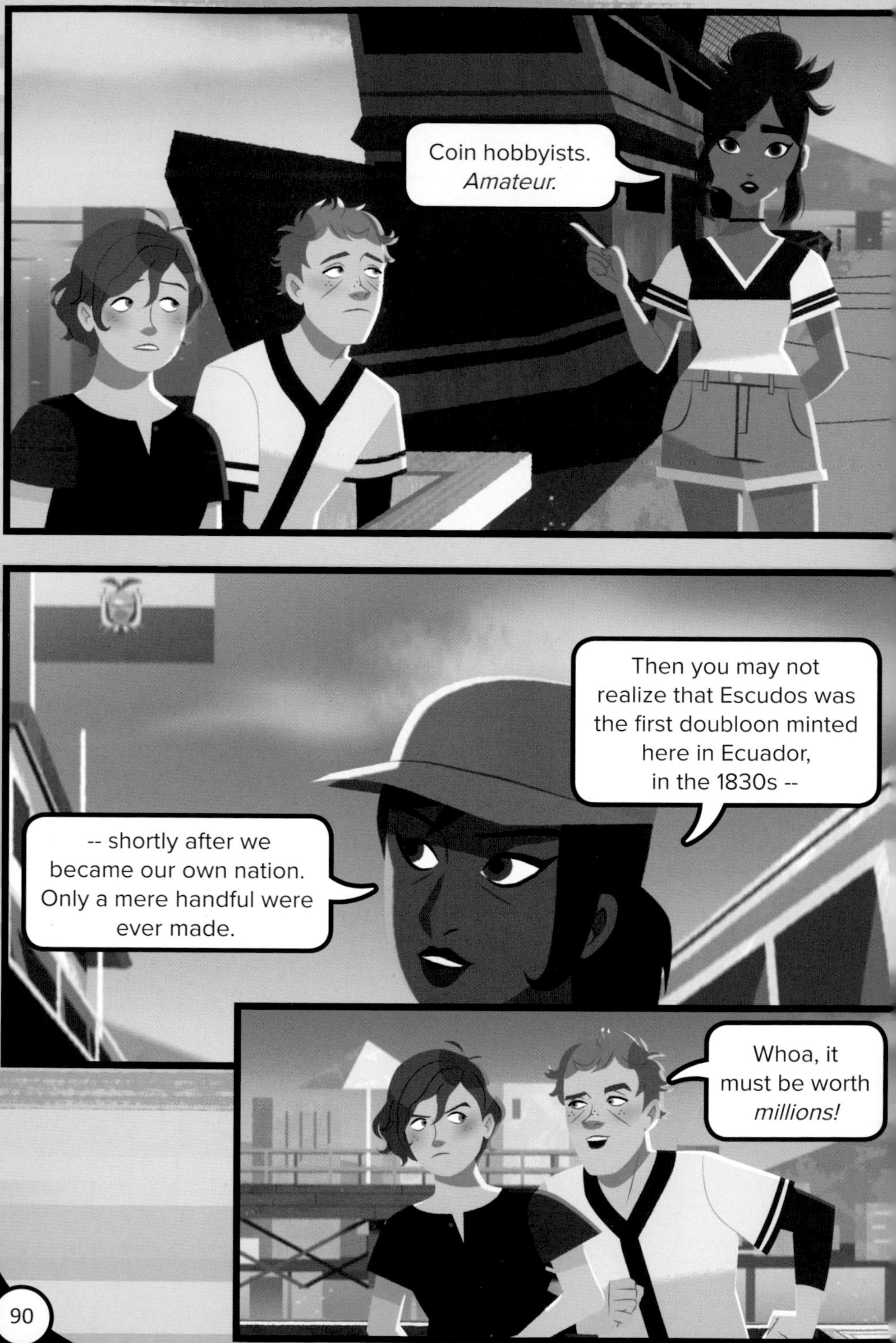

Coin hobbyists. *Amateur.*
Then you may not realize that Escudos was the first doubloon minted here in Ecuador, in the 1830s --
-- shortly after we became our own nation. Only a mere handful were ever made.
Whoa, it must be worth *millions!*

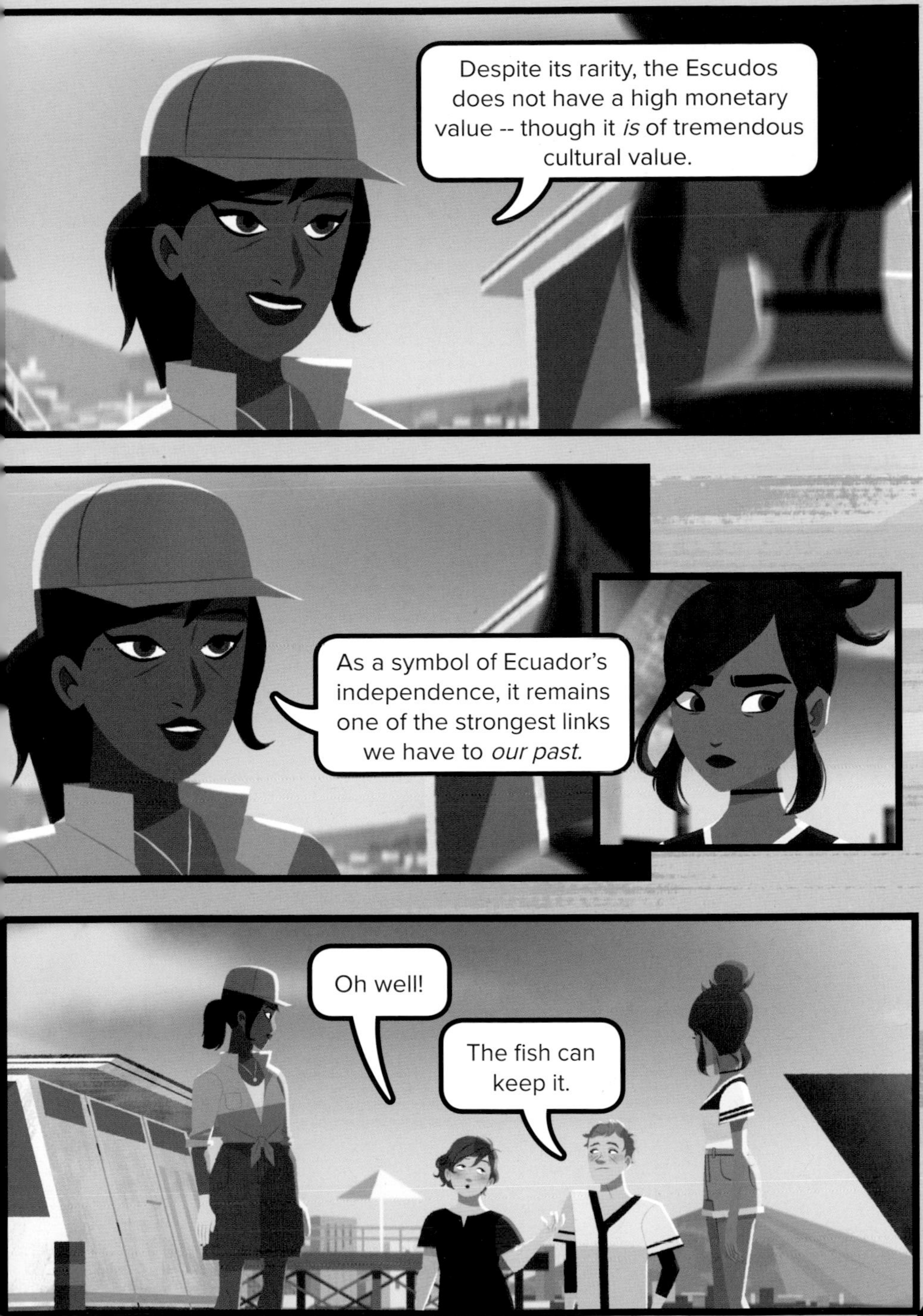
Despite its rarity, the Escudos does not have a high monetary value -- though it *is* of tremendous cultural value.
As a symbol of Ecuador's independence, it remains one of the strongest links we have to *our past.*
Oh well!
The fish can keep it.

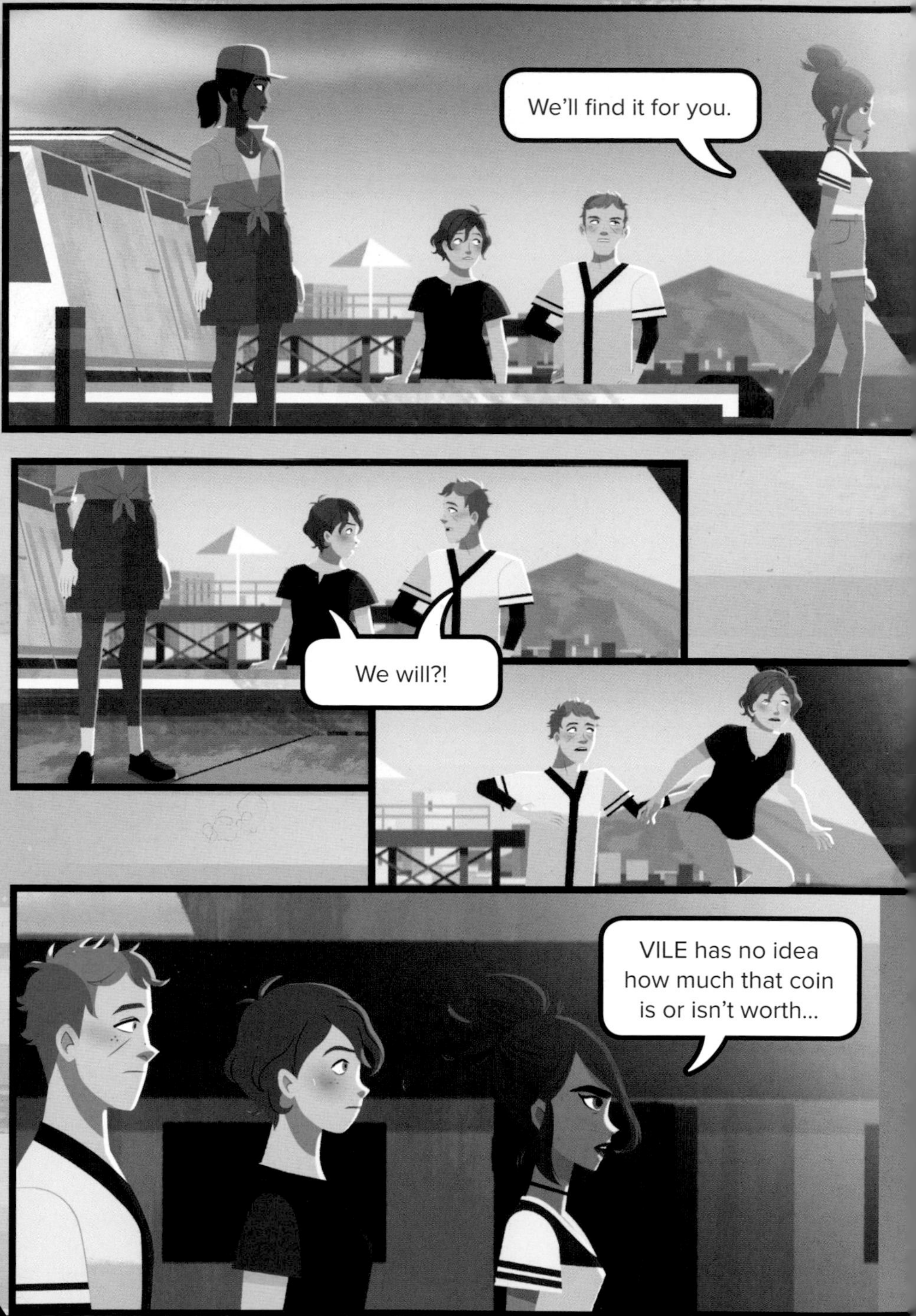
We'll find it for you.
We will?!
VILE has no idea how much that coin is or isn't worth...

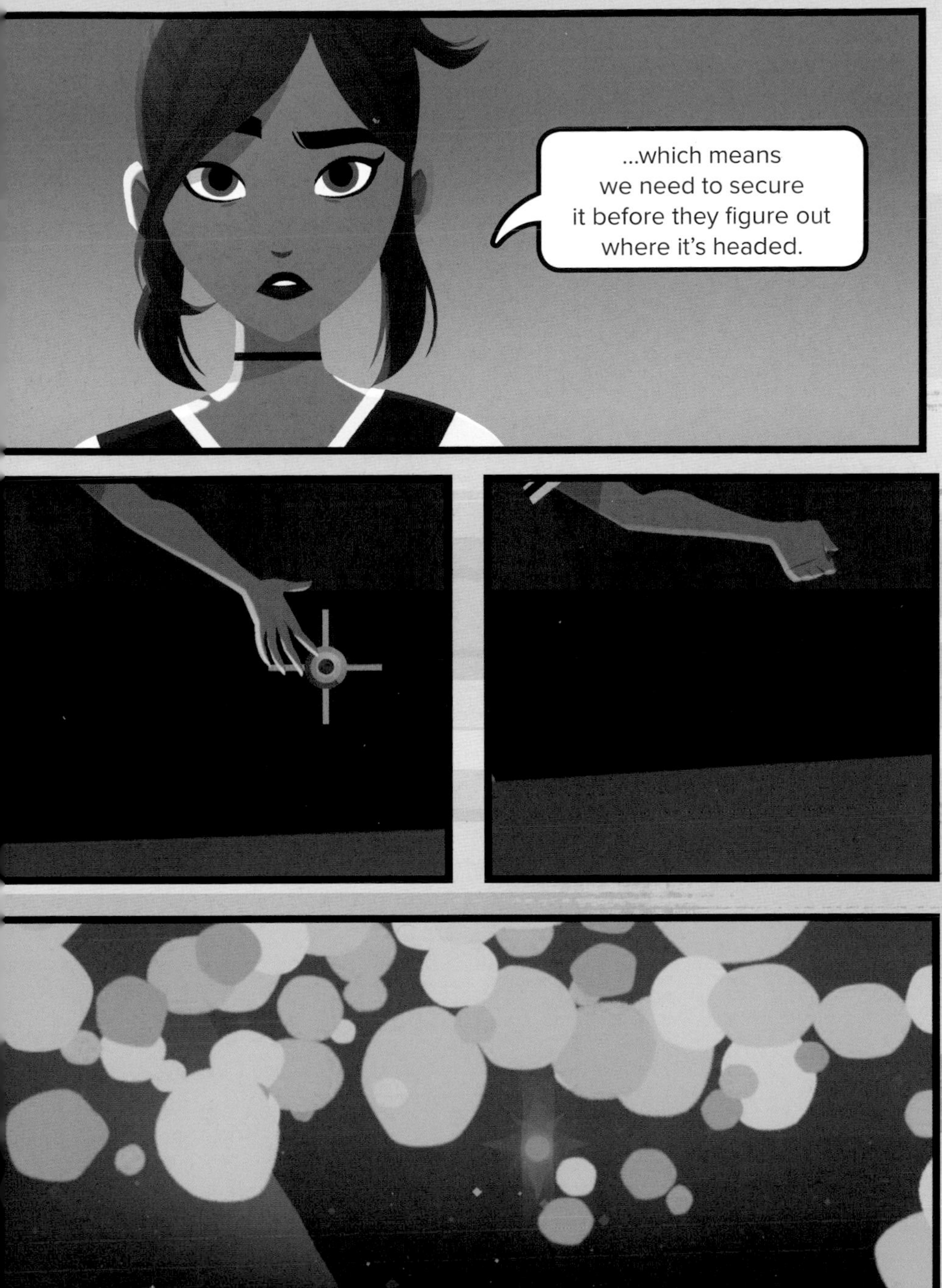
...which means we need to secure it before they figure out where it's headed.

VILE
Academy Professors

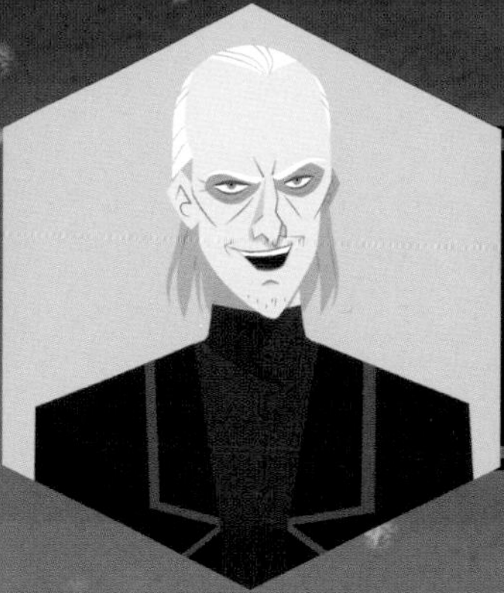

Gunnar Maelstrom

A psychological genius, Maelstrom learns your weaknesses and twists your mind.

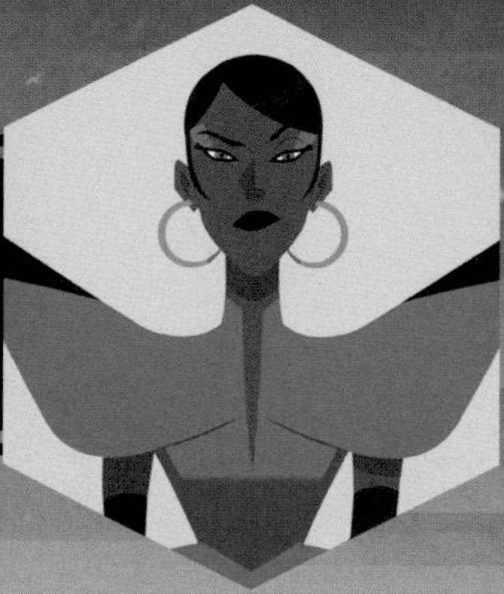

Countess Cleo

Cleo believes that ultimate wealth is ultimate power. She adores expensive everything.

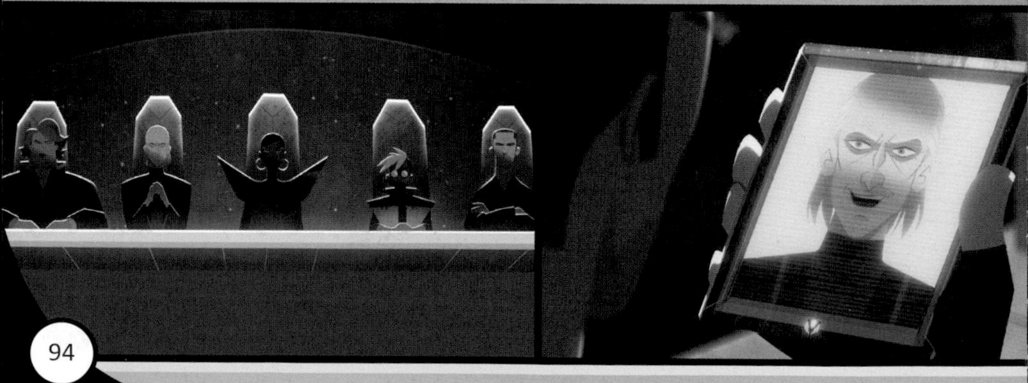

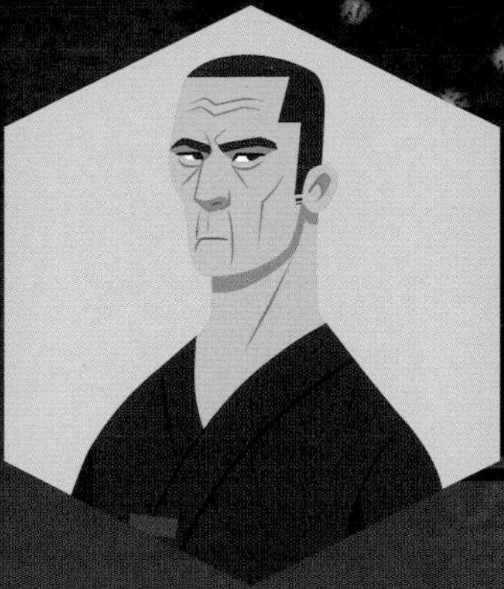

Shadowsan

A real-life modern ninja, Shadowsan teaches the criminal power of stealth and discipline.

Dr. Saira Bellum

Death rays, invisibility fabric, brain-wiping machines -- these are Bellum's favorite things.

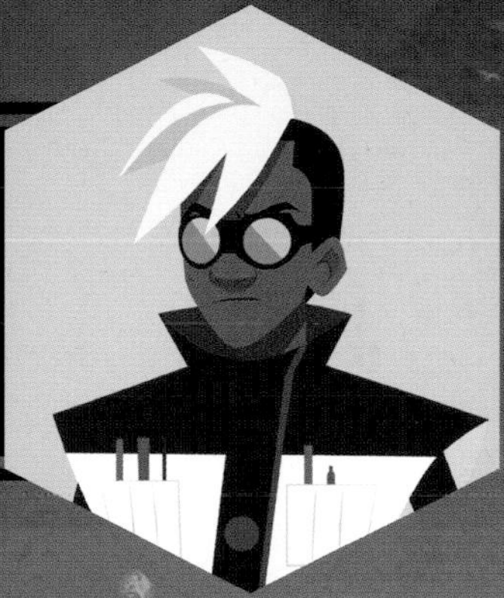

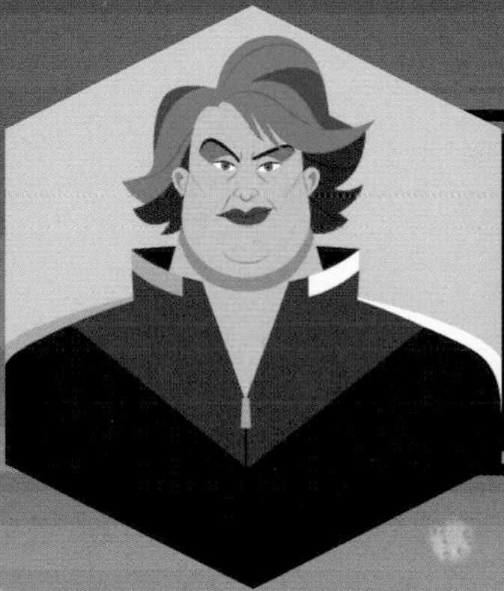

Coach Brunt

Master of hand-to-hand combat, Brunt believes a butt-whooping is the solution to everything.

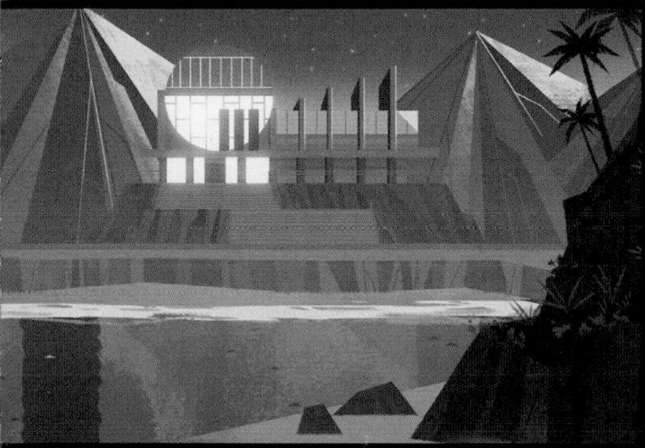

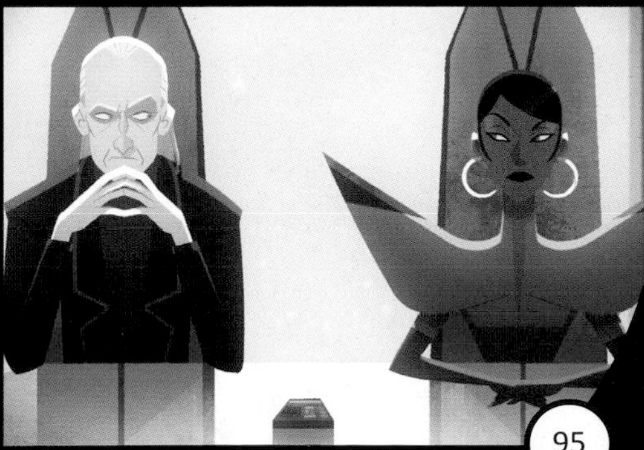

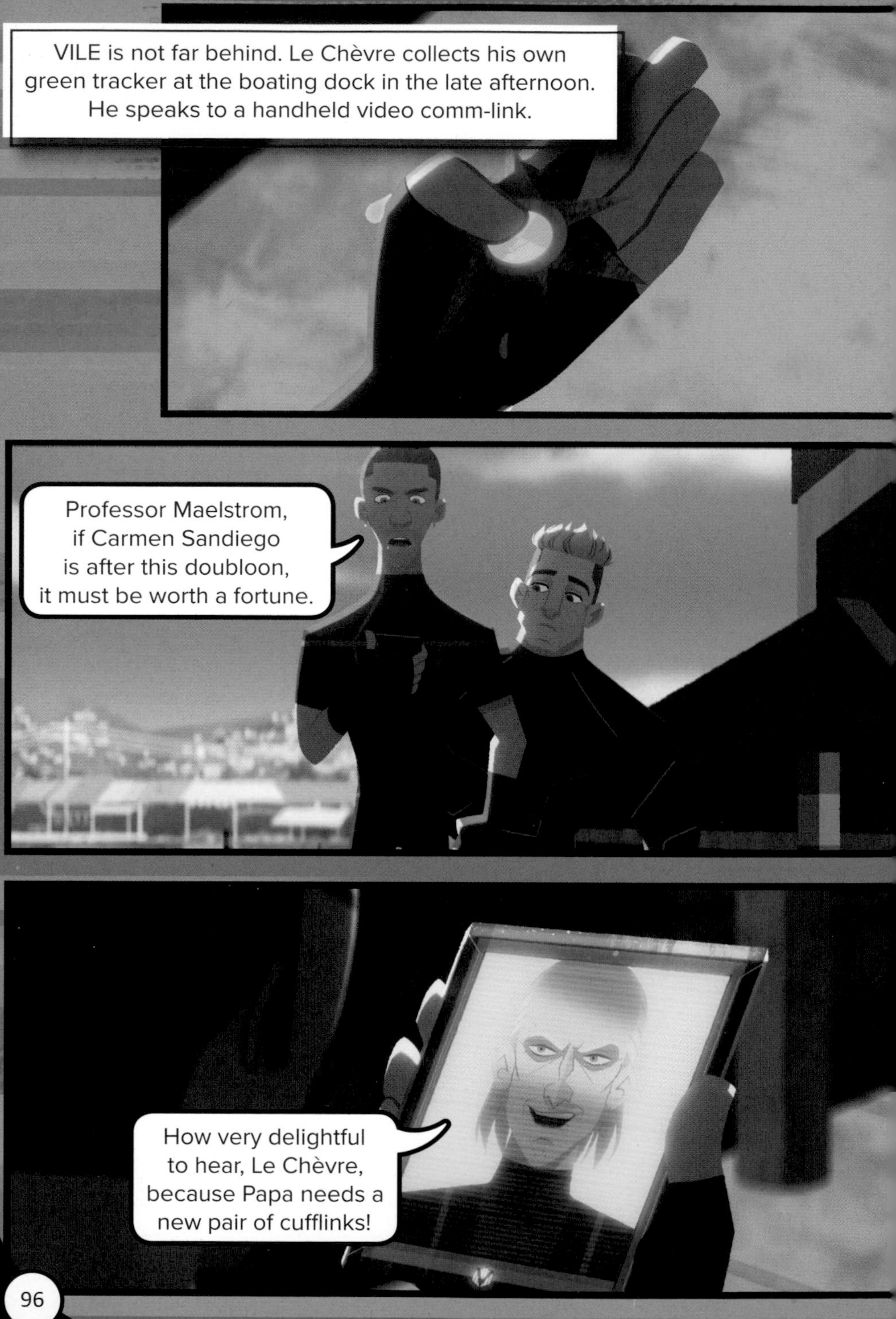
VILE is not far behind. Le Chèvre collects his own green tracker at the boating dock in the late afternoon. He speaks to a handheld video comm-link.
Professor Maelstrom, if Carmen Sandiego is after this doubloon, it must be worth a fortune.
How very delightful to hear, Le Chèvre, because Papa needs a new pair of cufflinks!

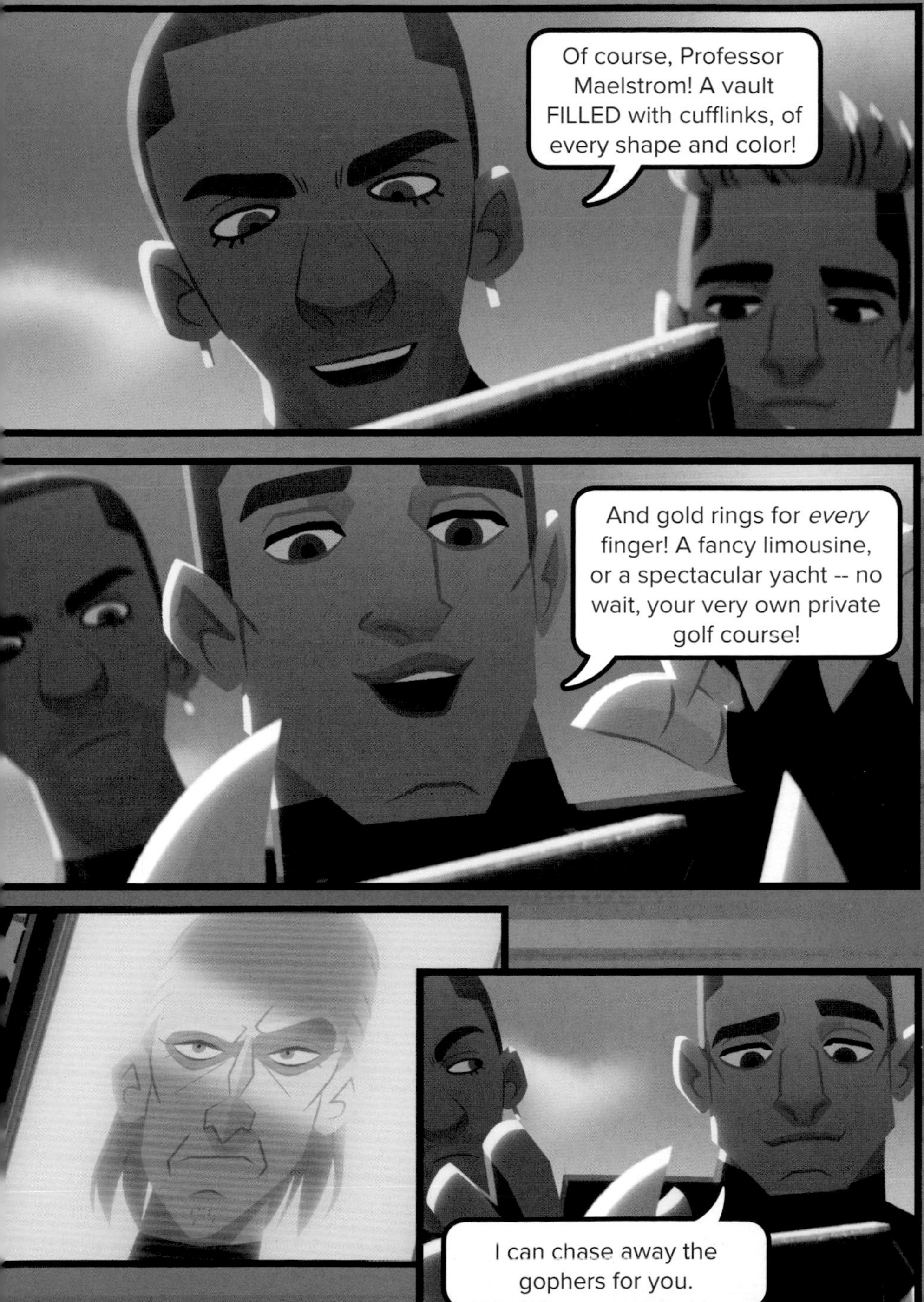
Of course, Professor Maelstrom! A vault FILLED with cufflinks, of every shape and color!
And gold rings for *every* finger! A fancy limousine, or a spectacular yacht -- no wait, your very own private golf course!
I can chase away the gophers for you.

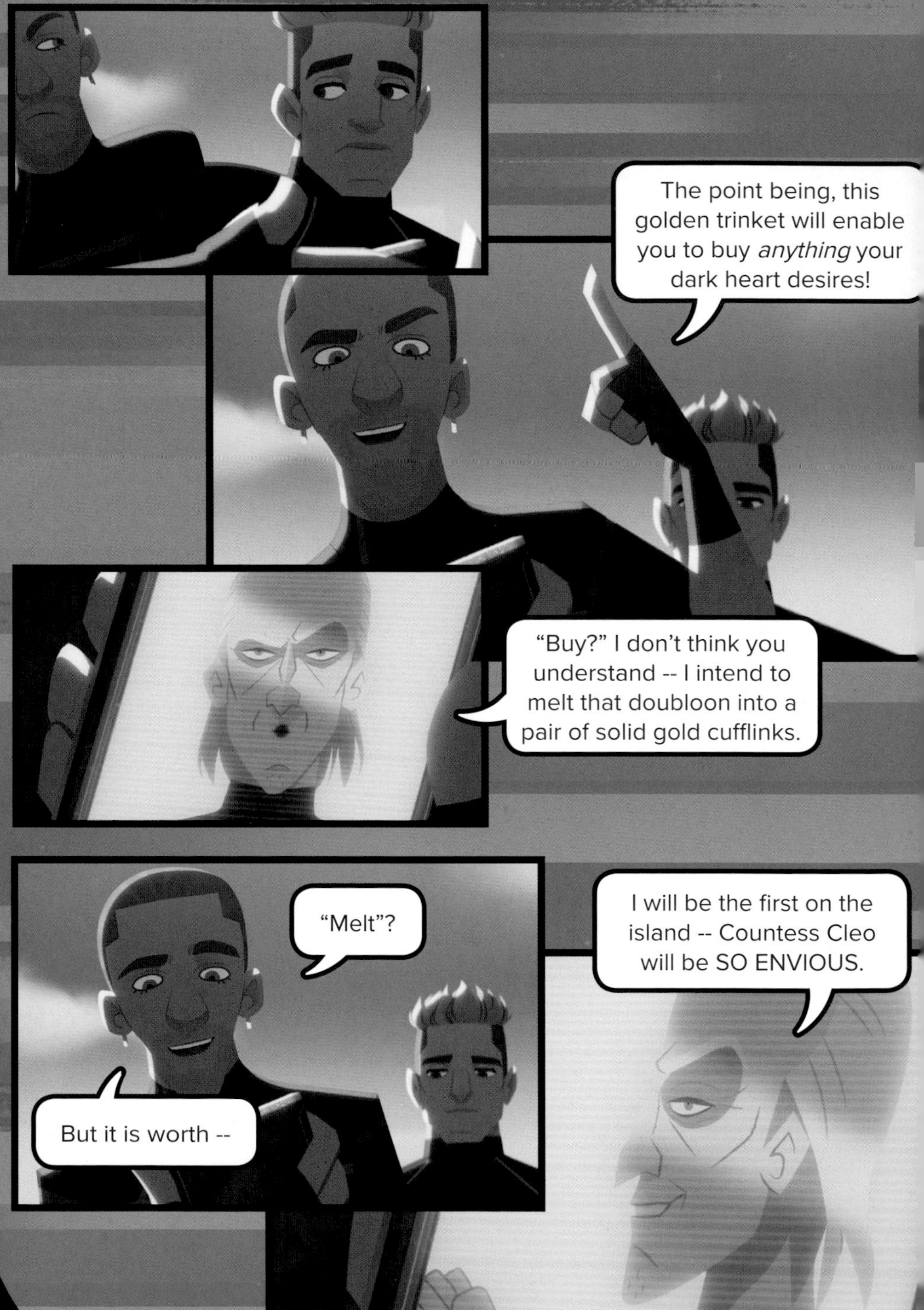
The point being, this golden trinket will enable you to buy *anything* your dark heart desires!
"Buy?" I don't think you understand -- I intend to melt that doubloon into a pair of solid gold cufflinks.
"Melt"?
But it is worth --
I will be the first on the island -- Countess Cleo will be SO ENVIOUS.

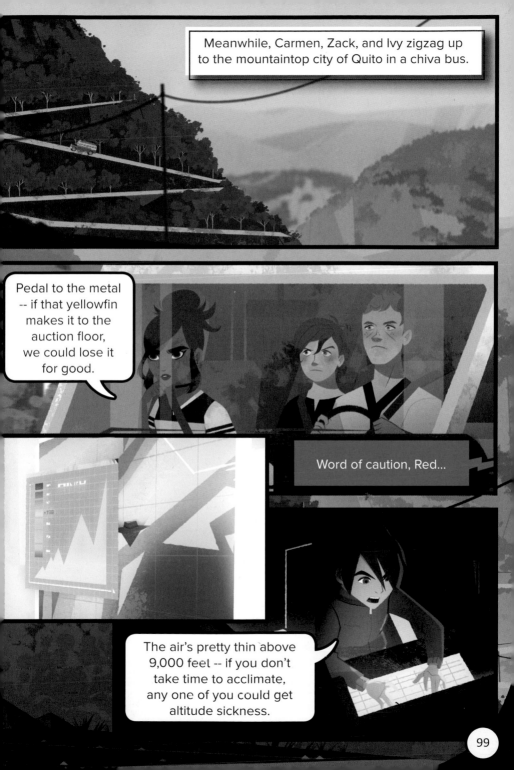

Meanwhile, Carmen, Zack, and Ivy zigzag up to the mountaintop city of Quito in a chiva bus.

Pedal to the metal -- if that yellowfin makes it to the auction floor, we could lose it for good.

Word of caution, Red...

The air's pretty thin above 9,000 feet -- if you don't take time to acclimate, any one of you could get altitude sickness.

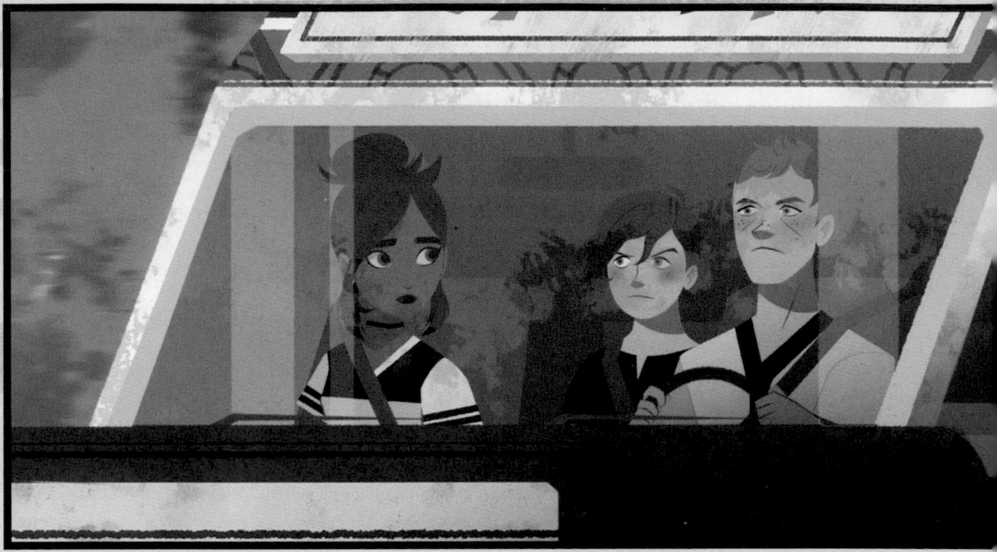

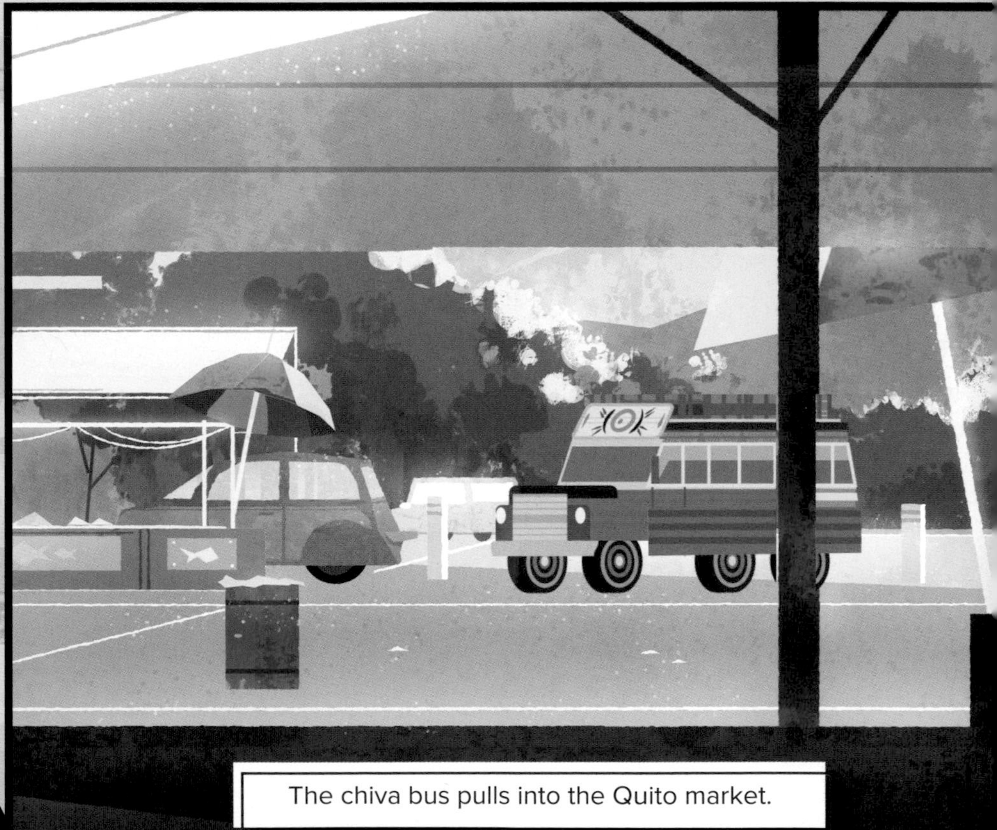
The chiva bus pulls into the Quito market.

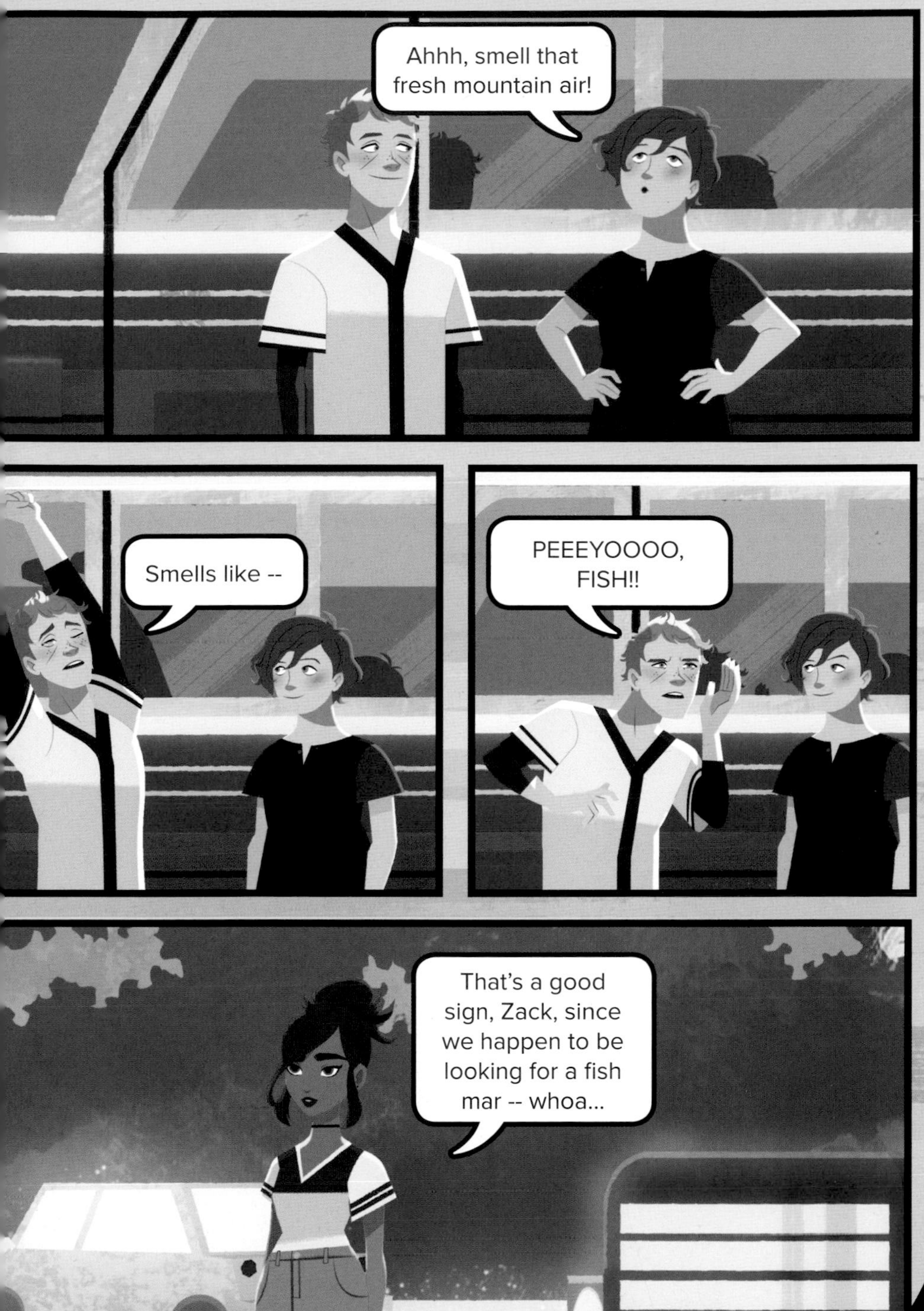
Ahhh, smell that fresh mountain air!
Smells like --
PEEEYOOOO, FISH!!
That's a good sign, Zack, since we happen to be looking for a fish mar -- whoa...

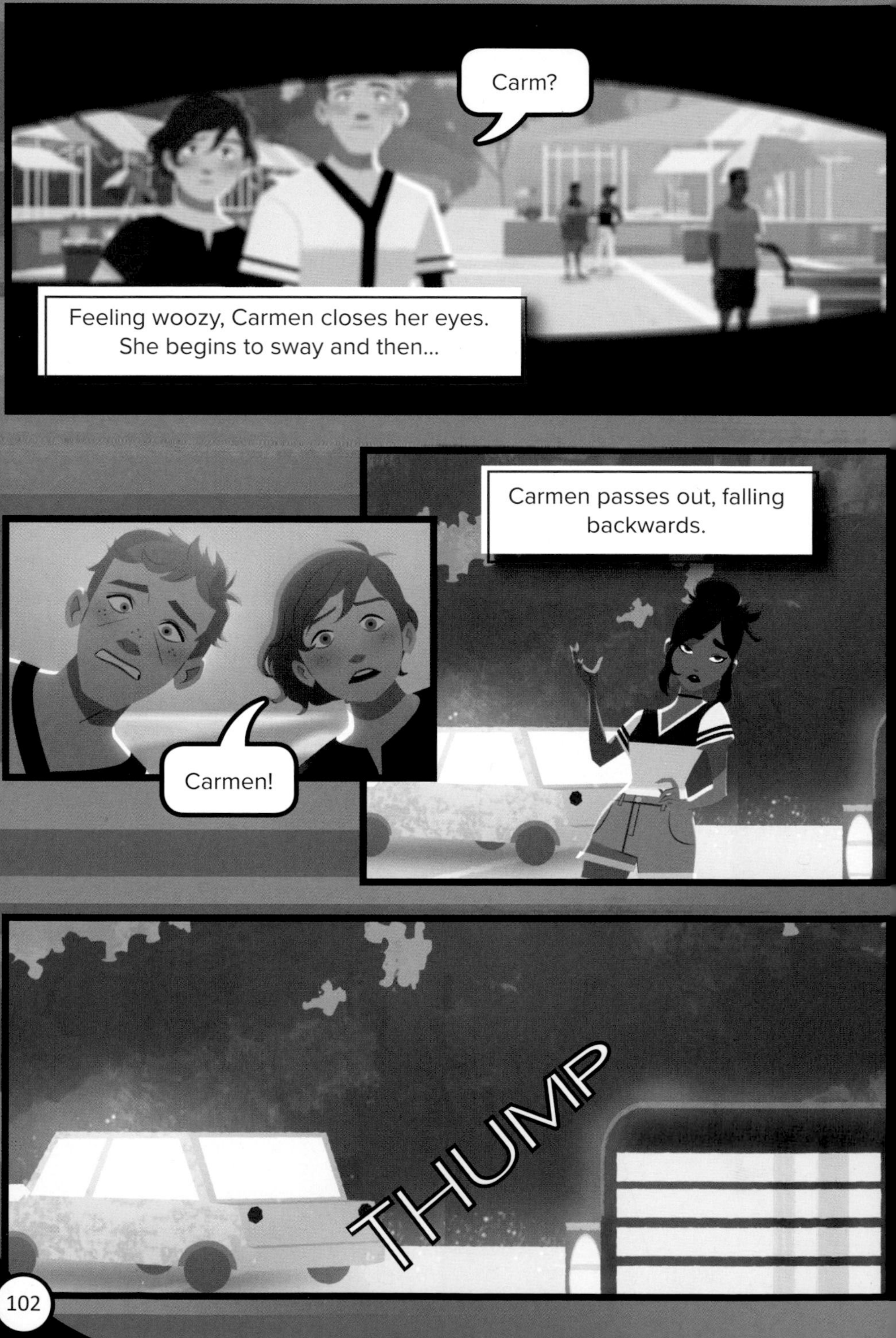
Carm?
Feeling woozy, Carmen closes her eyes. She begins to sway and then...
Carmen!
Carmen passes out, falling backwards.
THUMP

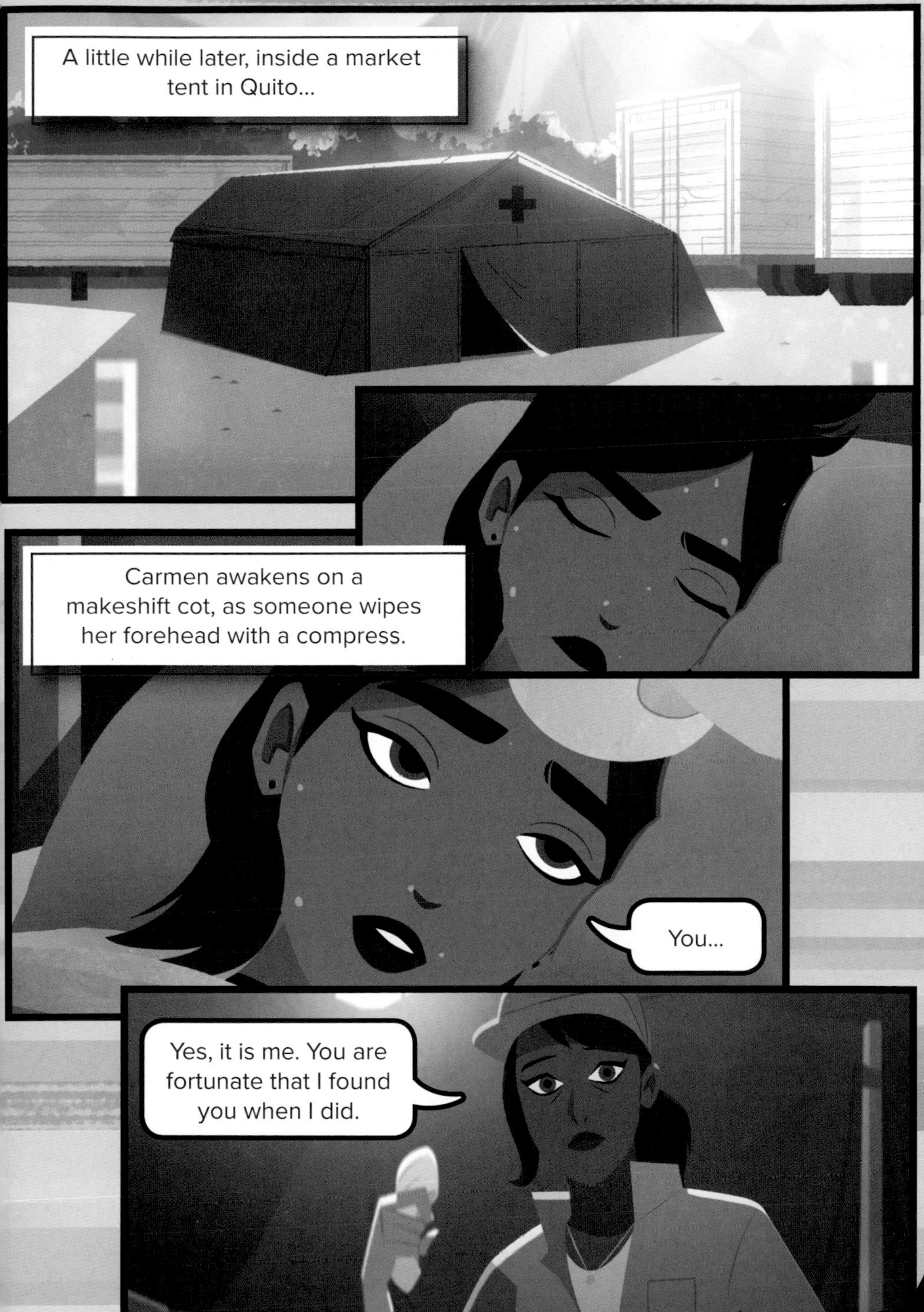
A little while later, inside a market tent in Quito...
Carmen awakens on a makeshift cot, as someone wipes her forehead with a compress.
You...
Yes, it is me. You are fortunate that I found you when I did.

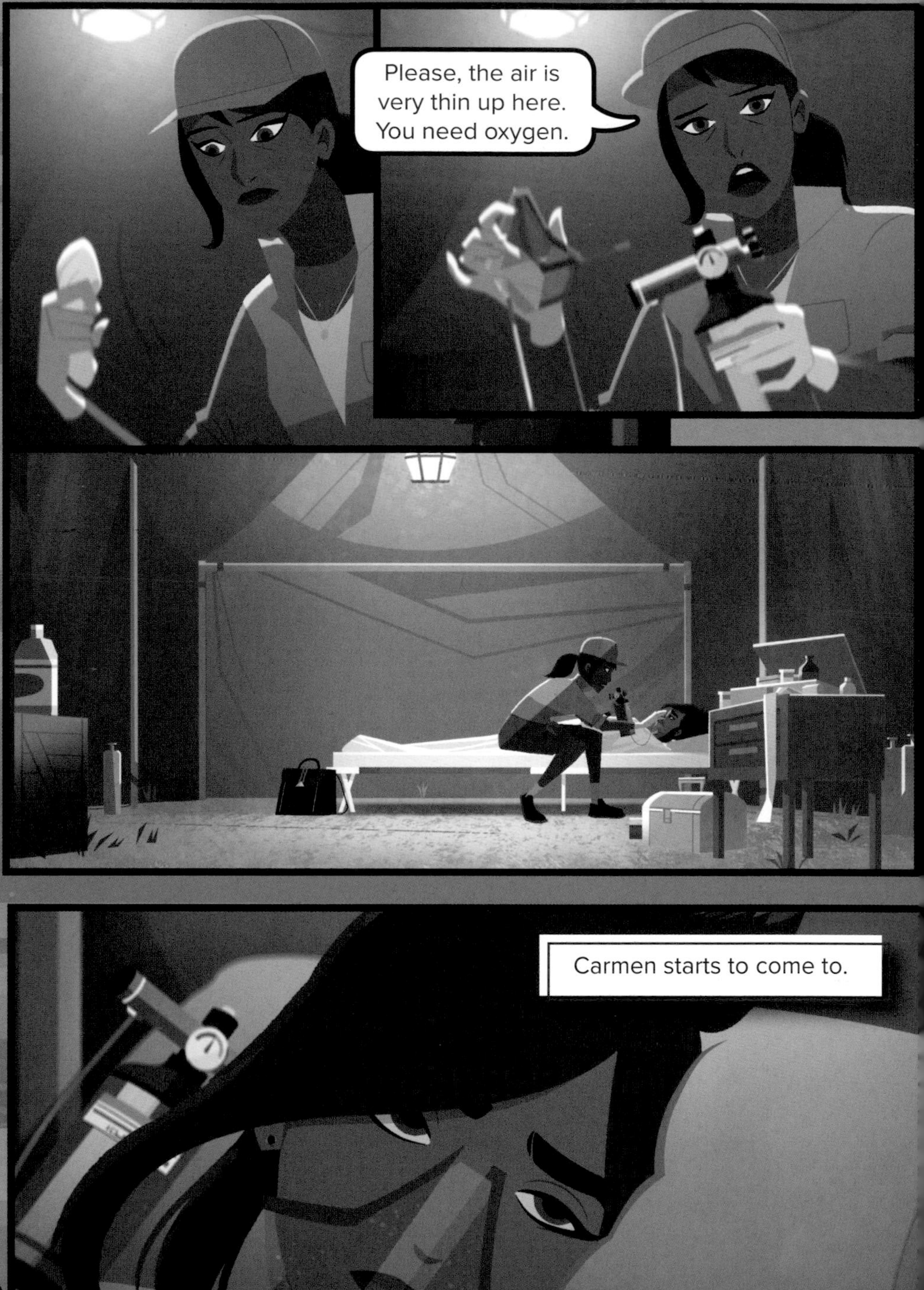
Please, the air is very thin up here. You need oxygen.
Carmen starts to come to.

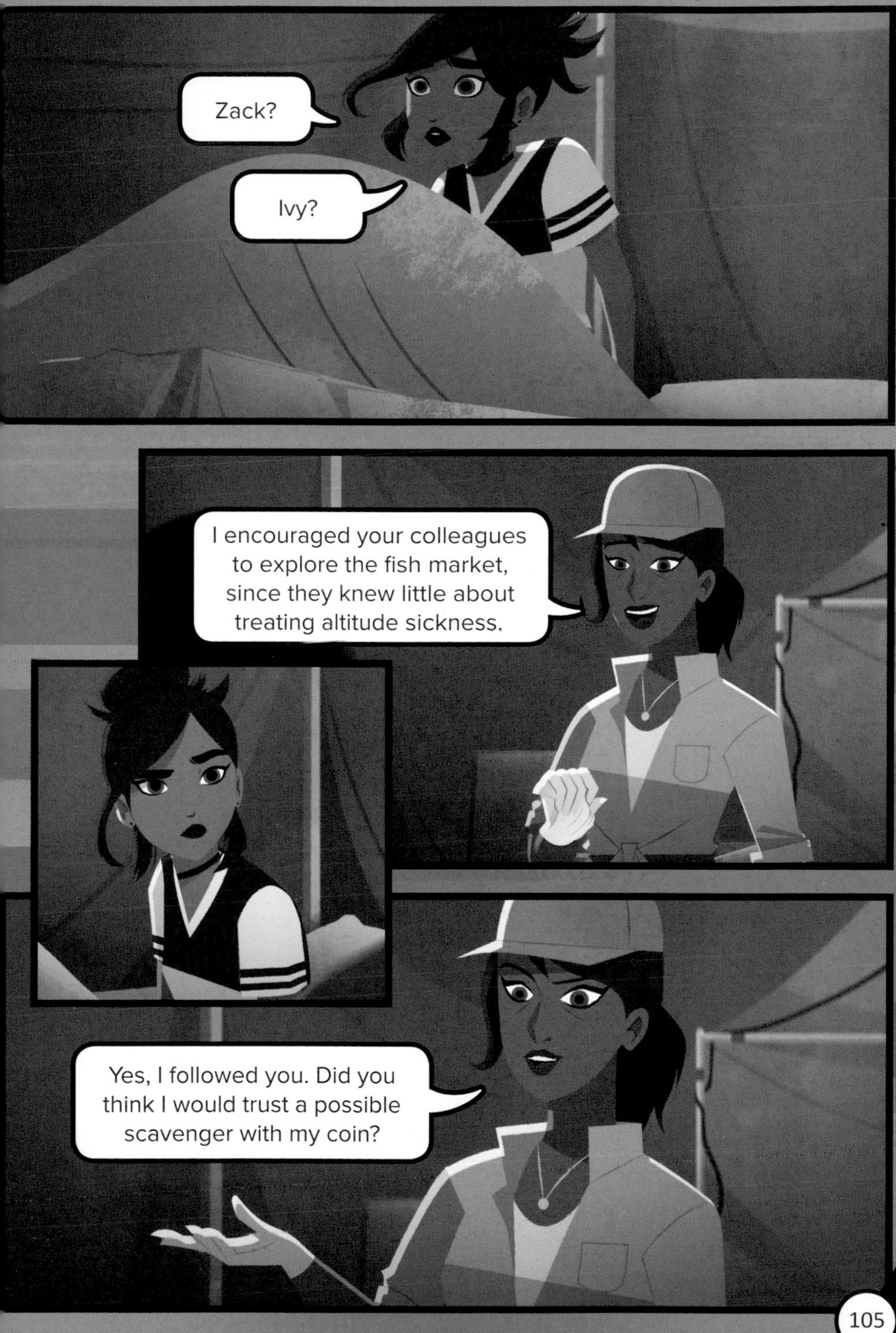
Zack?
Ivy?
I encouraged your colleagues to explore the fish market, since they knew little about treating altitude sickness.
Yes, I followed you. Did you think I would trust a possible scavenger with my coin?

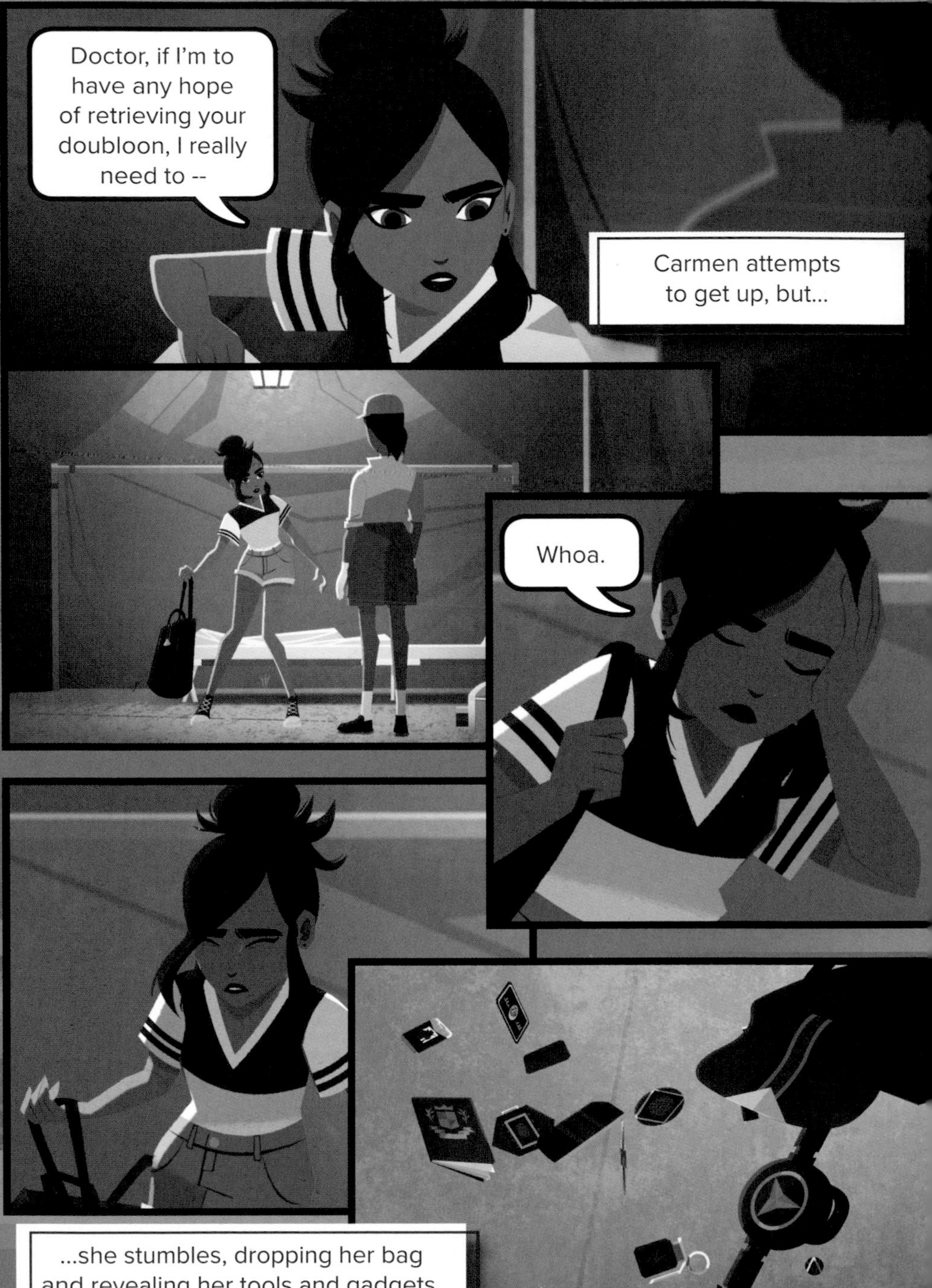
Doctor, if I'm to have any hope of retrieving your doubloon, I really need to --
Carmen attempts to get up, but...
Whoa.
...she stumbles, dropping her bag and revealing her tools and gadgets.

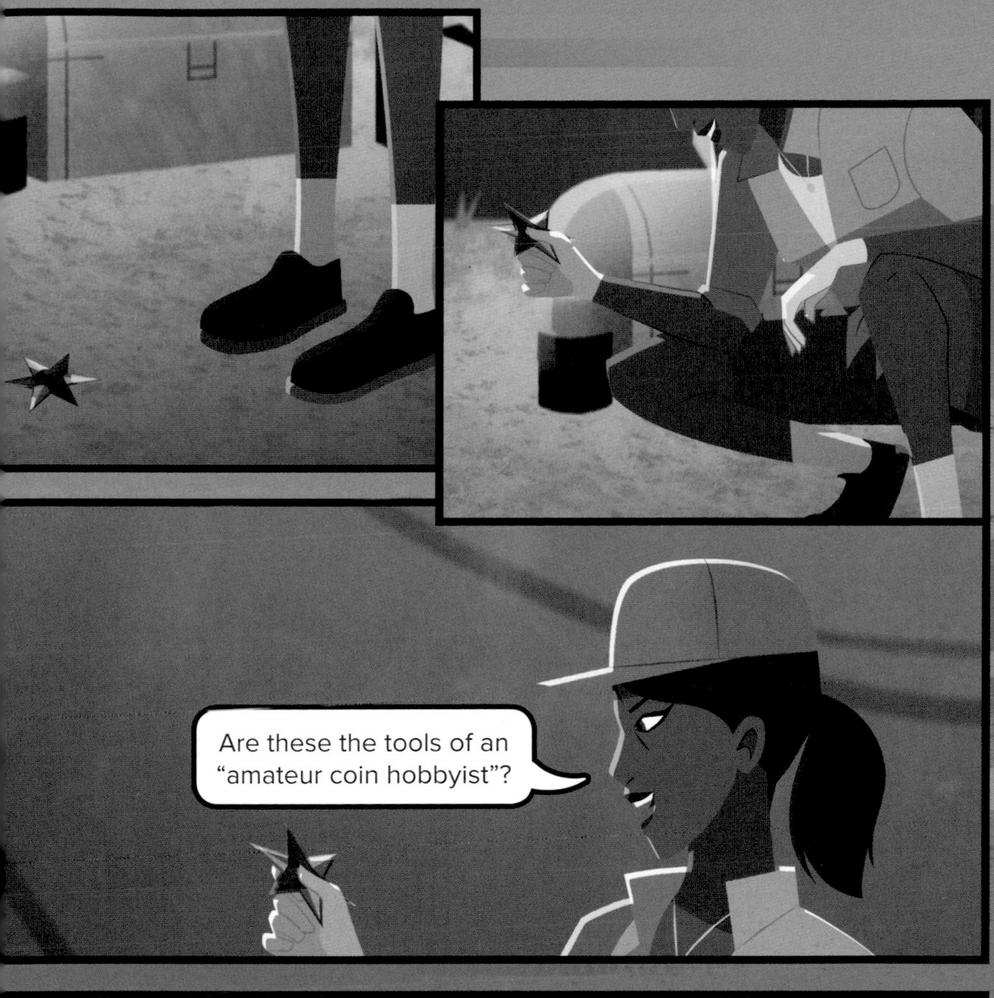
Are these the tools of an "amateur coin hobbyist"?
You helped me...

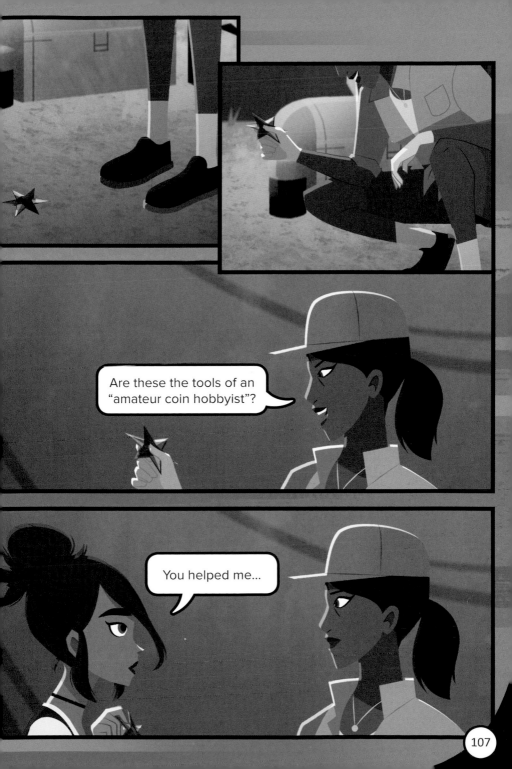

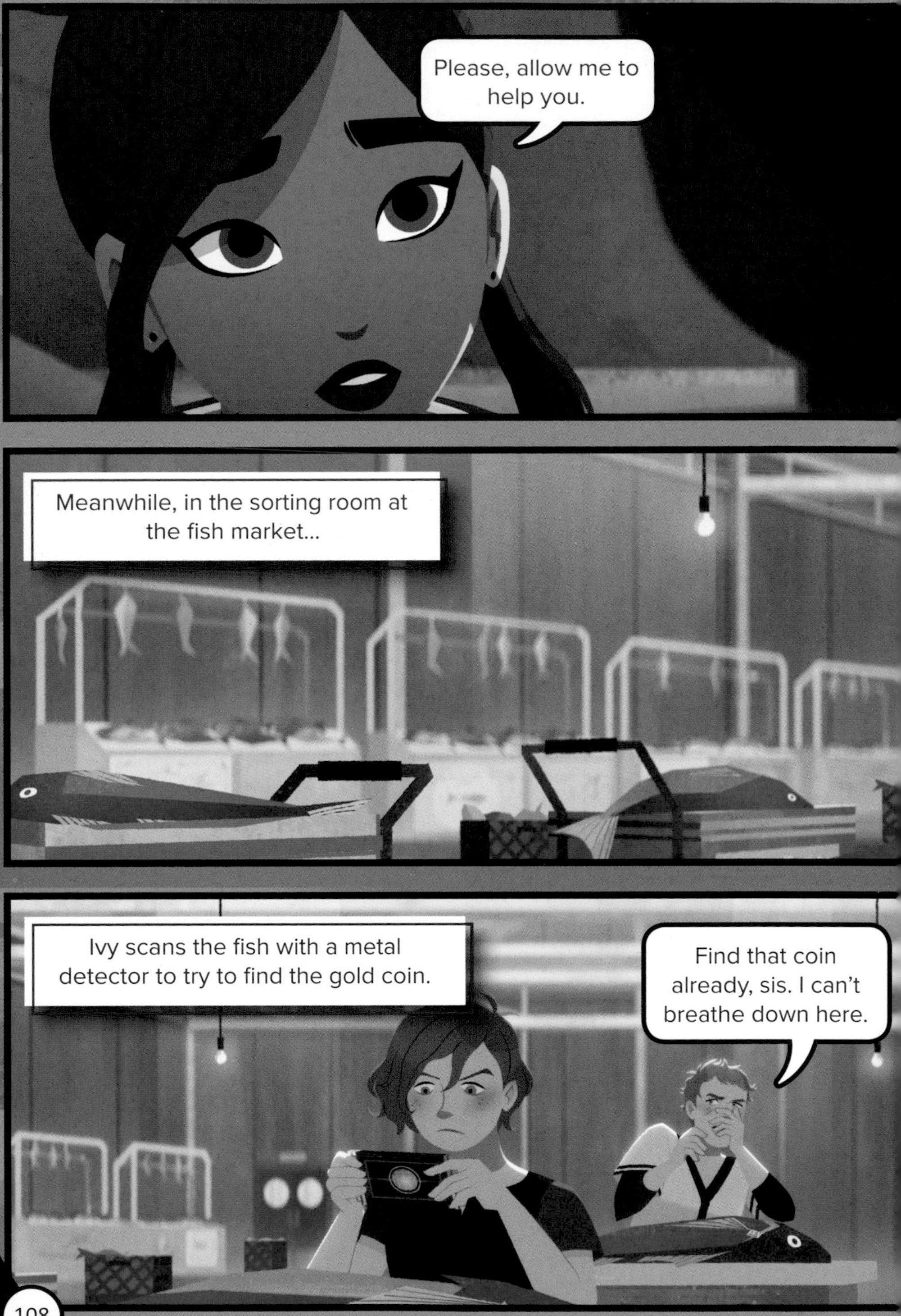
Please, allow me to help you.
Meanwhile, in the sorting room at the fish market...
Ivy scans the fish with a metal detector to try to find the gold coin.
Find that coin already, sis. I can't breathe down here.

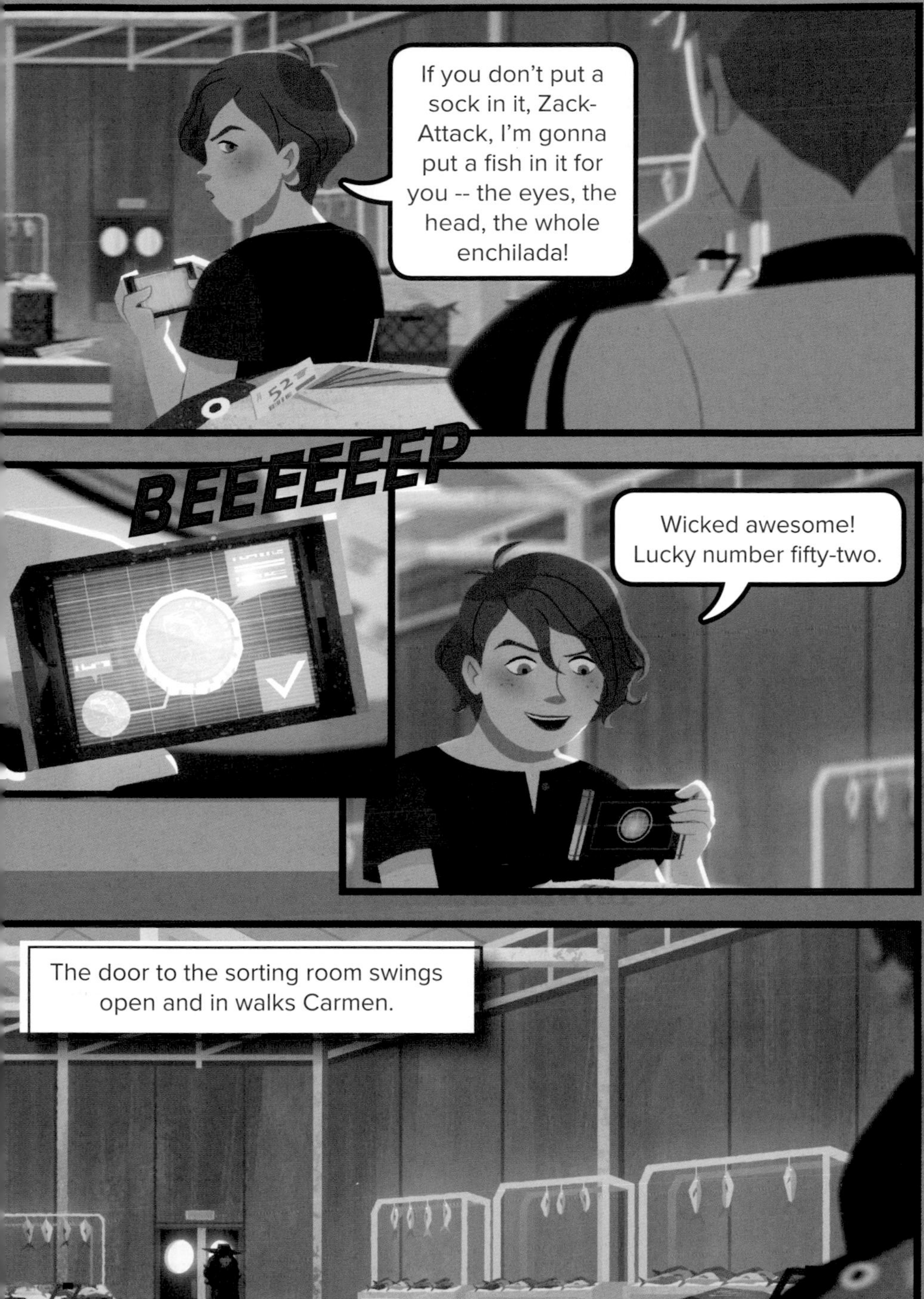
If you don't put a sock in it, Zack-Attack, I'm gonna put a fish in it for you -- the eyes, the head, the whole enchilada!
BEEEEEEEP
Wicked awesome! Lucky number fifty-two.
The door to the sorting room swings open and in walks Carmen.

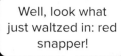

Well, look what just waltzed in: red snapper!

Don't be embarrassed, Carm: the smell of fish gets me woozy too.

Tell me you found it.

Yup! We've been scanning the tuna carts on deck for the auction floor first, to make sure it didn't get past us.

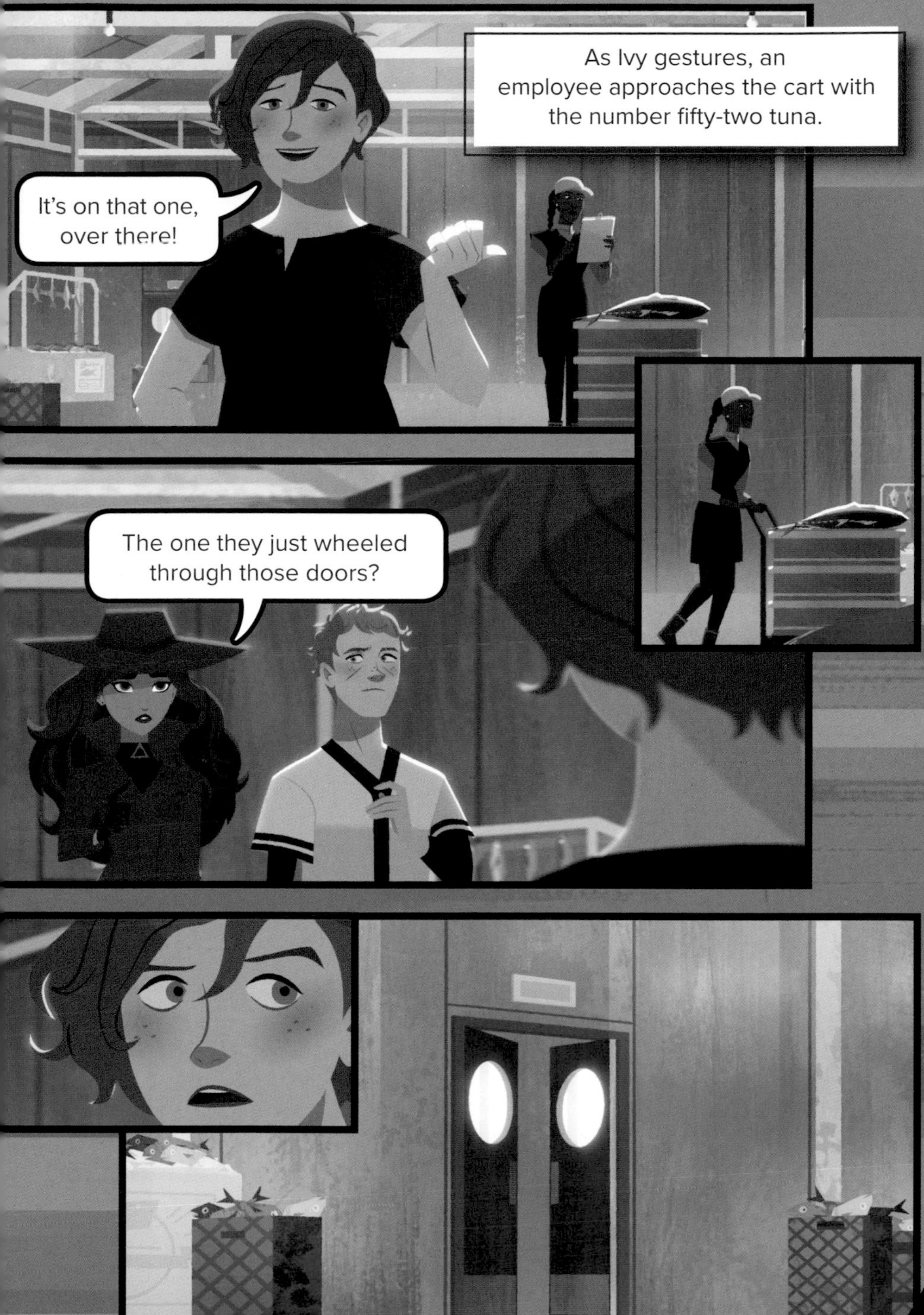
As Ivy gestures, an employee approaches the cart with the number fifty-two tuna.
It's on that one, over there!
The one they just wheeled through those doors?

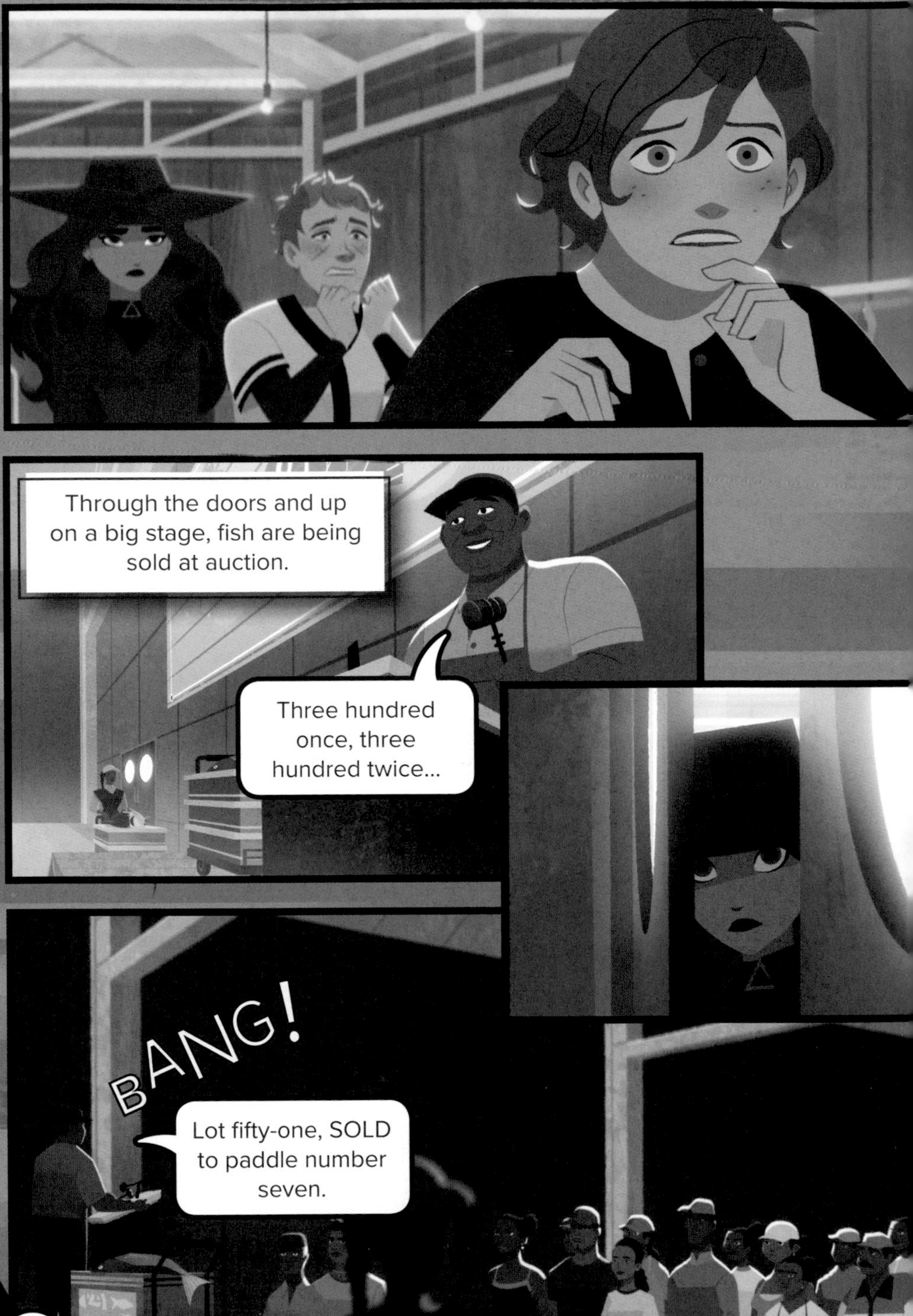
Through the doors and up on a big stage, fish are being sold at auction.
Three hundred once, three hundred twice...
BANG!
Lot fifty-one, SOLD to paddle number seven.

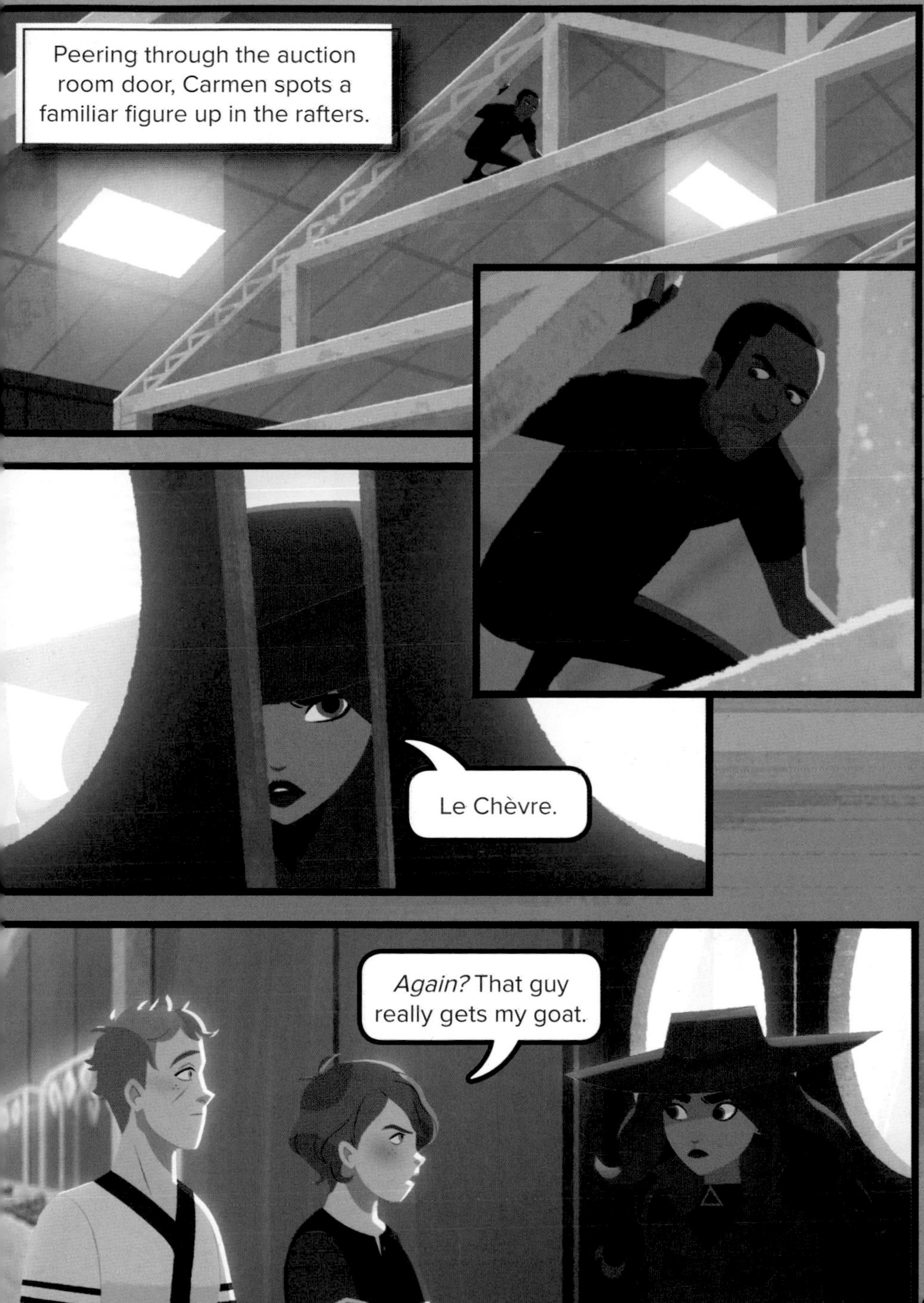
Peering through the auction room door, Carmen spots a familiar figure up in the rafters.
Le Chèvre.
Again? That guy really gets my goat.

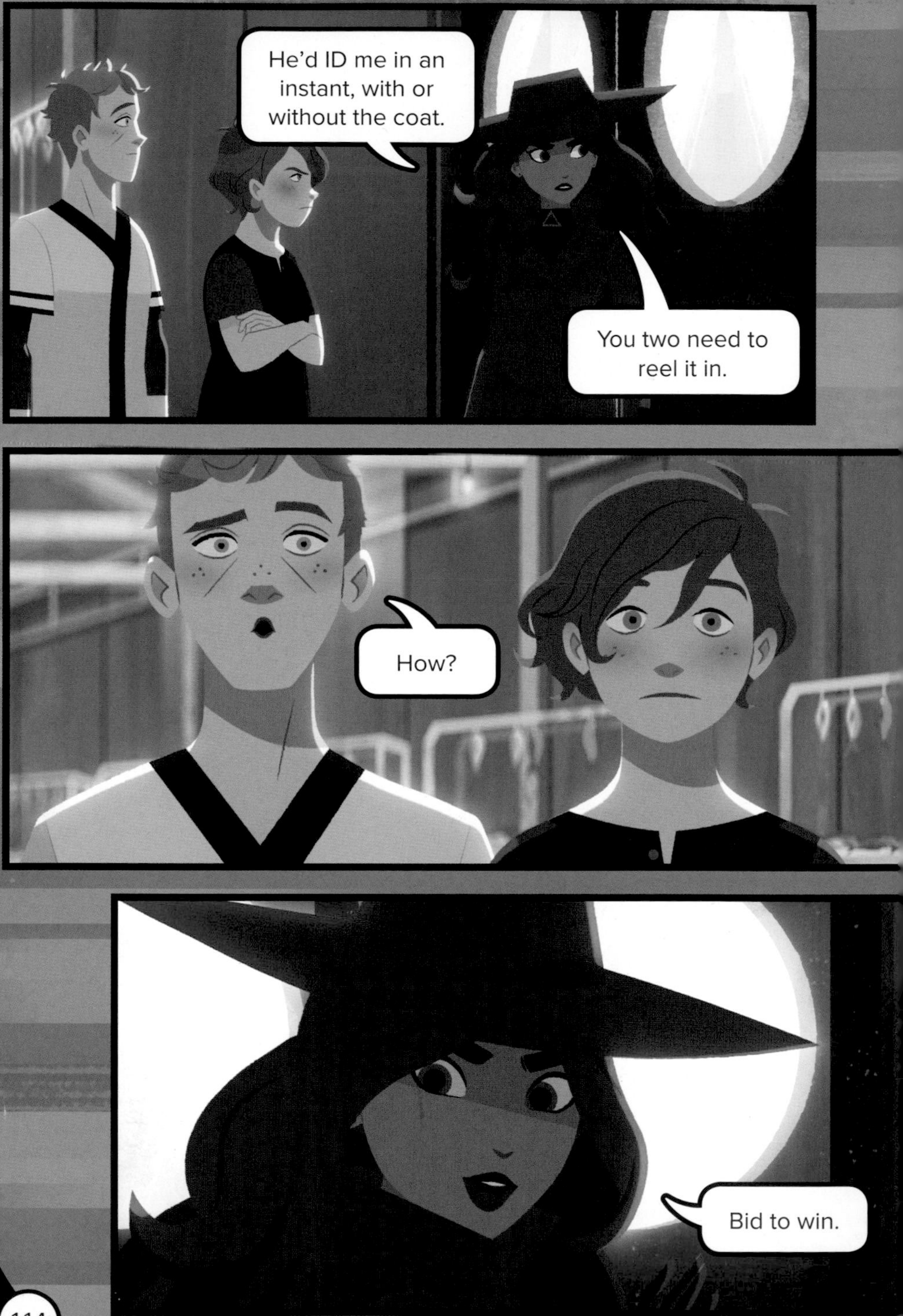
He'd ID me in an instant, with or without the coat.
You two need to reel it in.
How?
Bid to win.

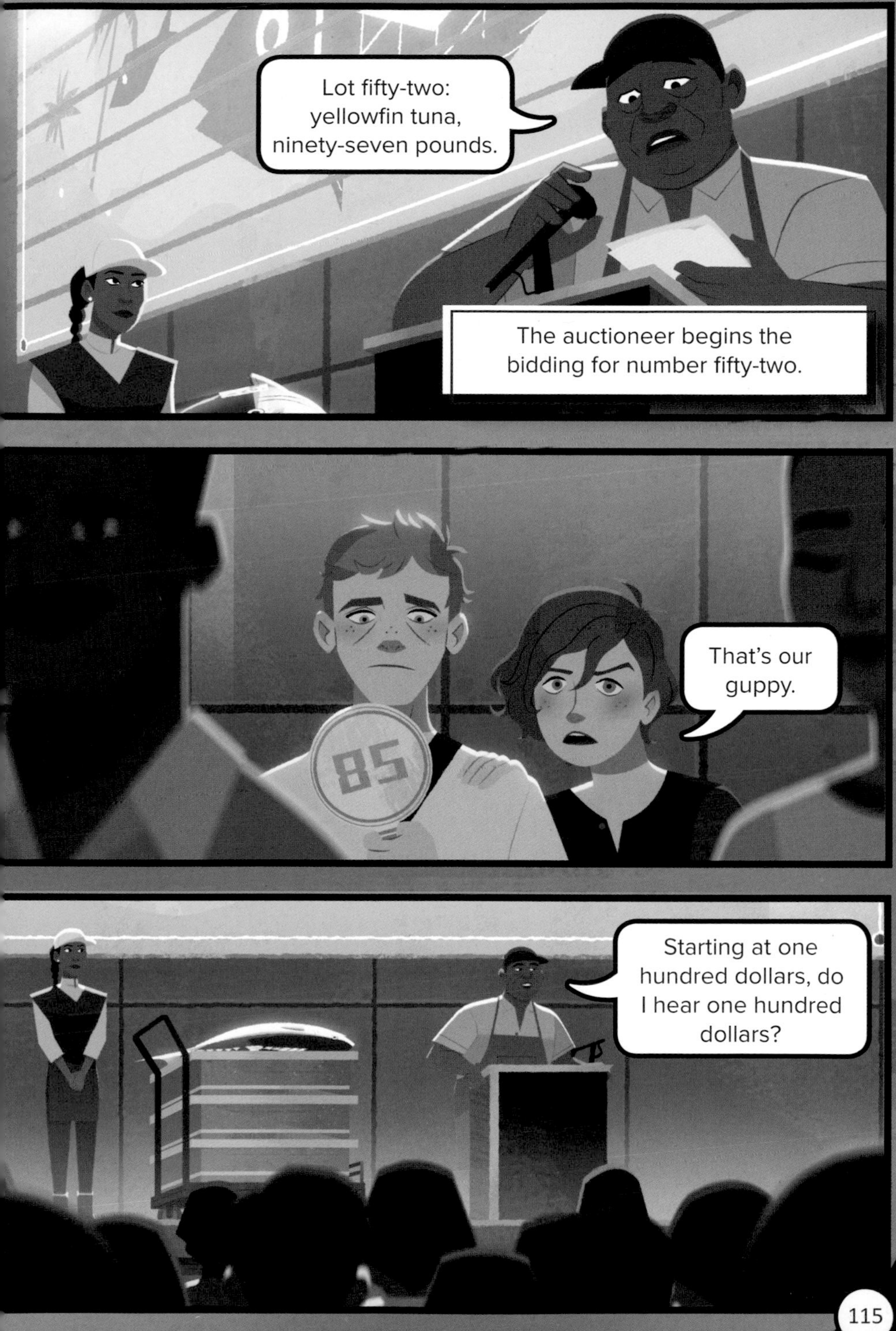

Lot fifty-two: yellowfin tuna, ninety-seven pounds.
The auctioneer begins the bidding for number fifty-two.
85
That's our guppy.
Starting at one hundred dollars, do I hear one hundred dollars?

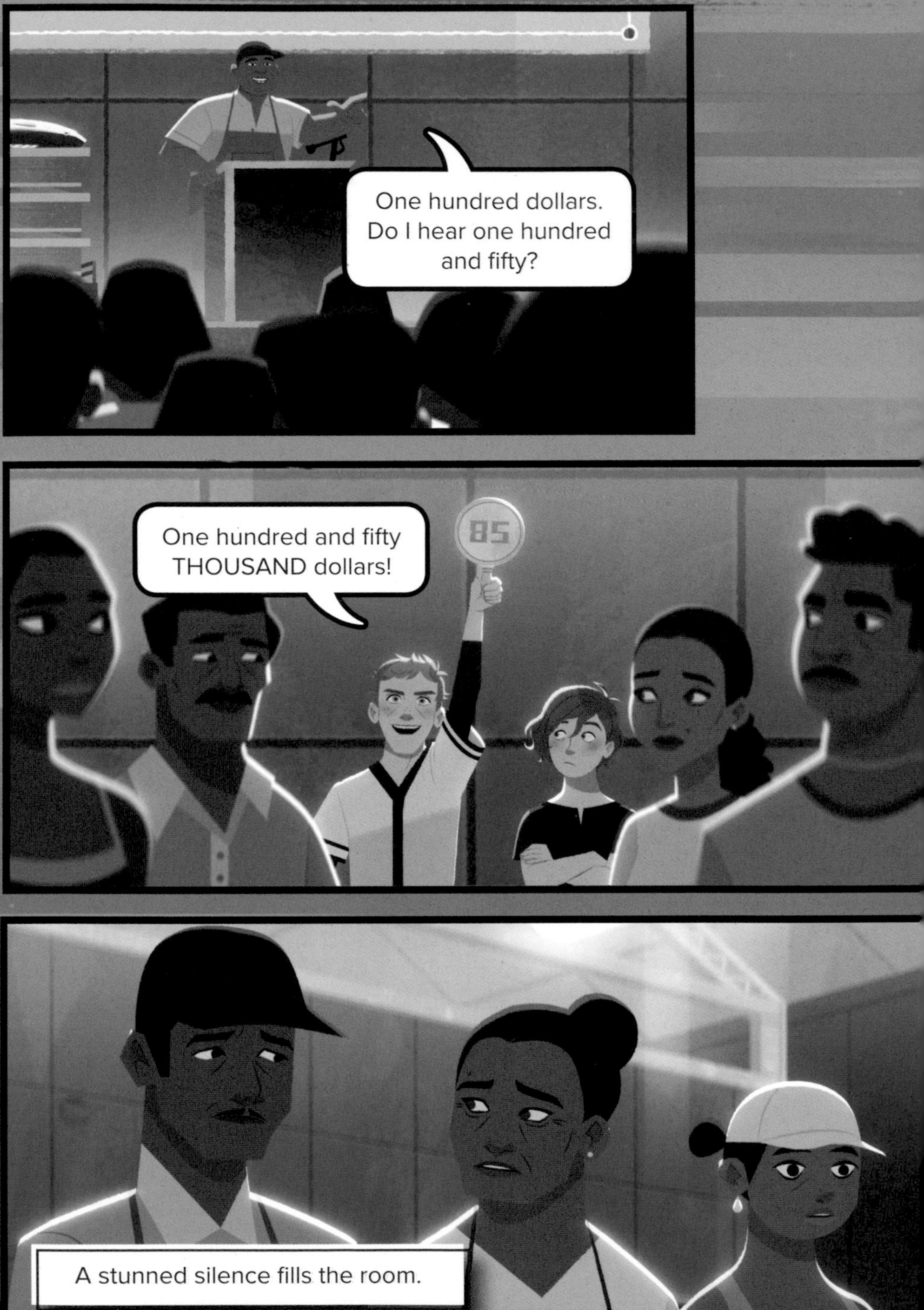

One hundred dollars. Do I hear one hundred and fifty?
One hundred and fifty THOUSAND dollars!
85
A stunned silence fills the room.

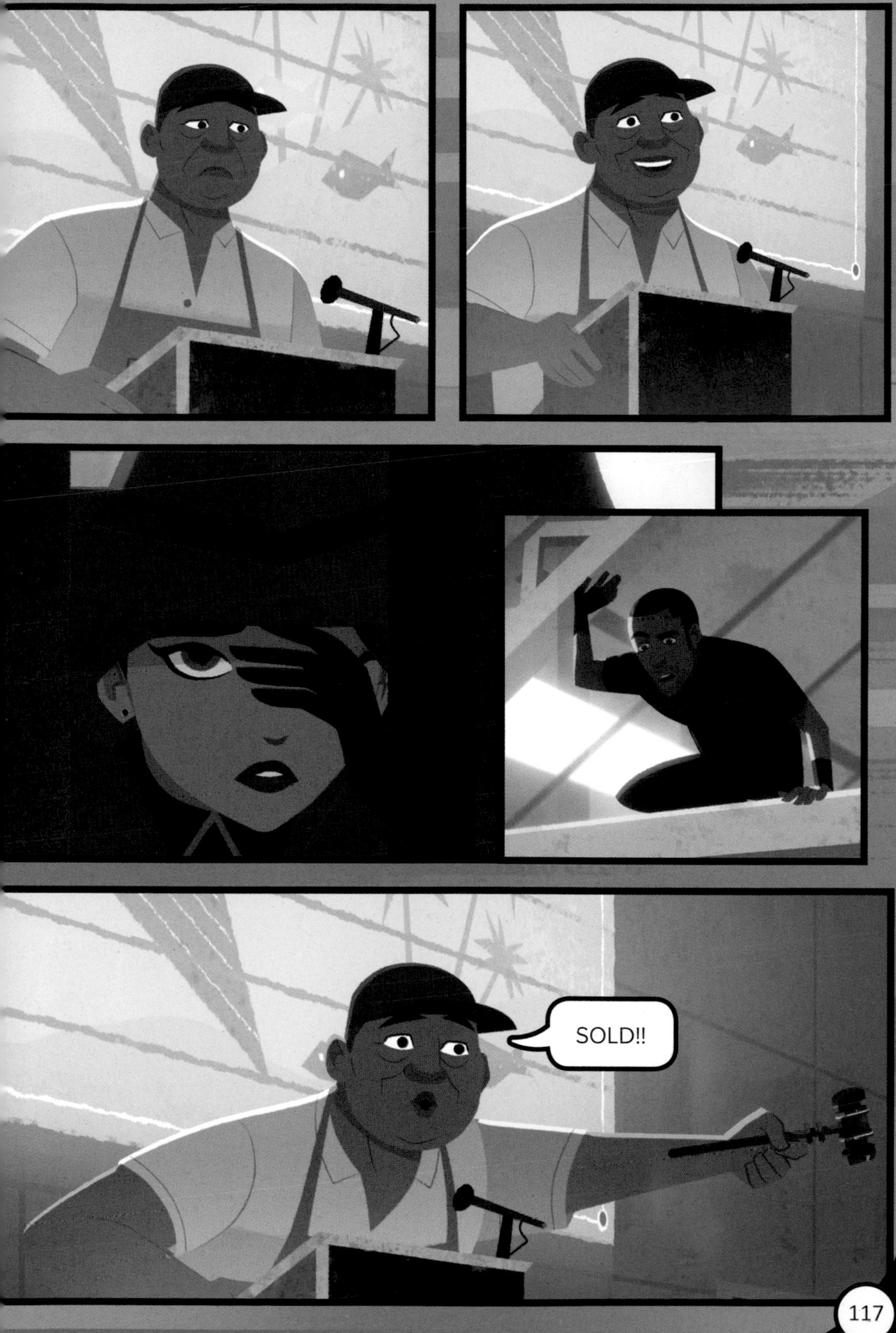
SOLD!!

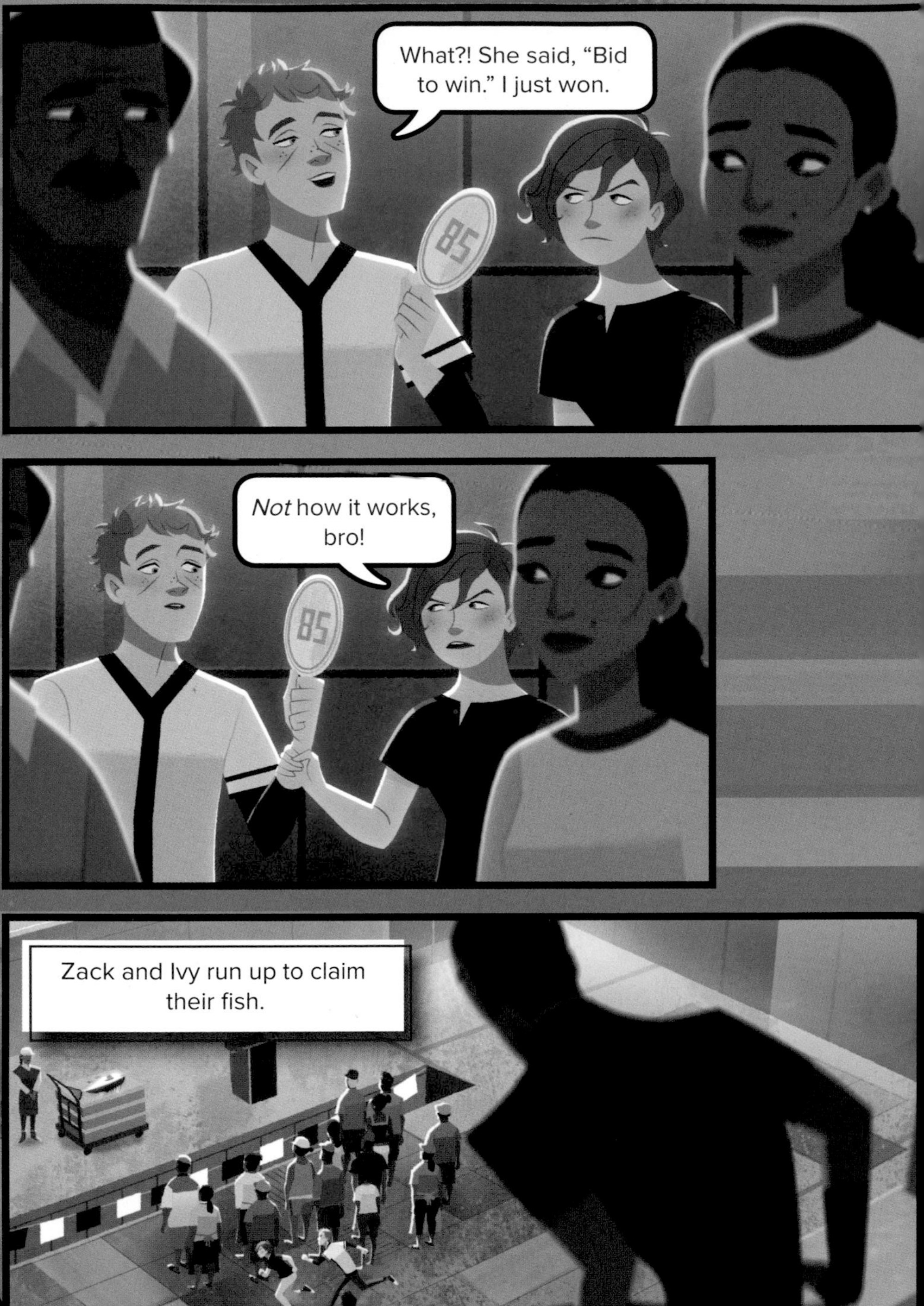
What?! She said, "Bid to win." I just won.
85
Not how it works, bro!
85
Zack and Ivy run up to claim their fish.

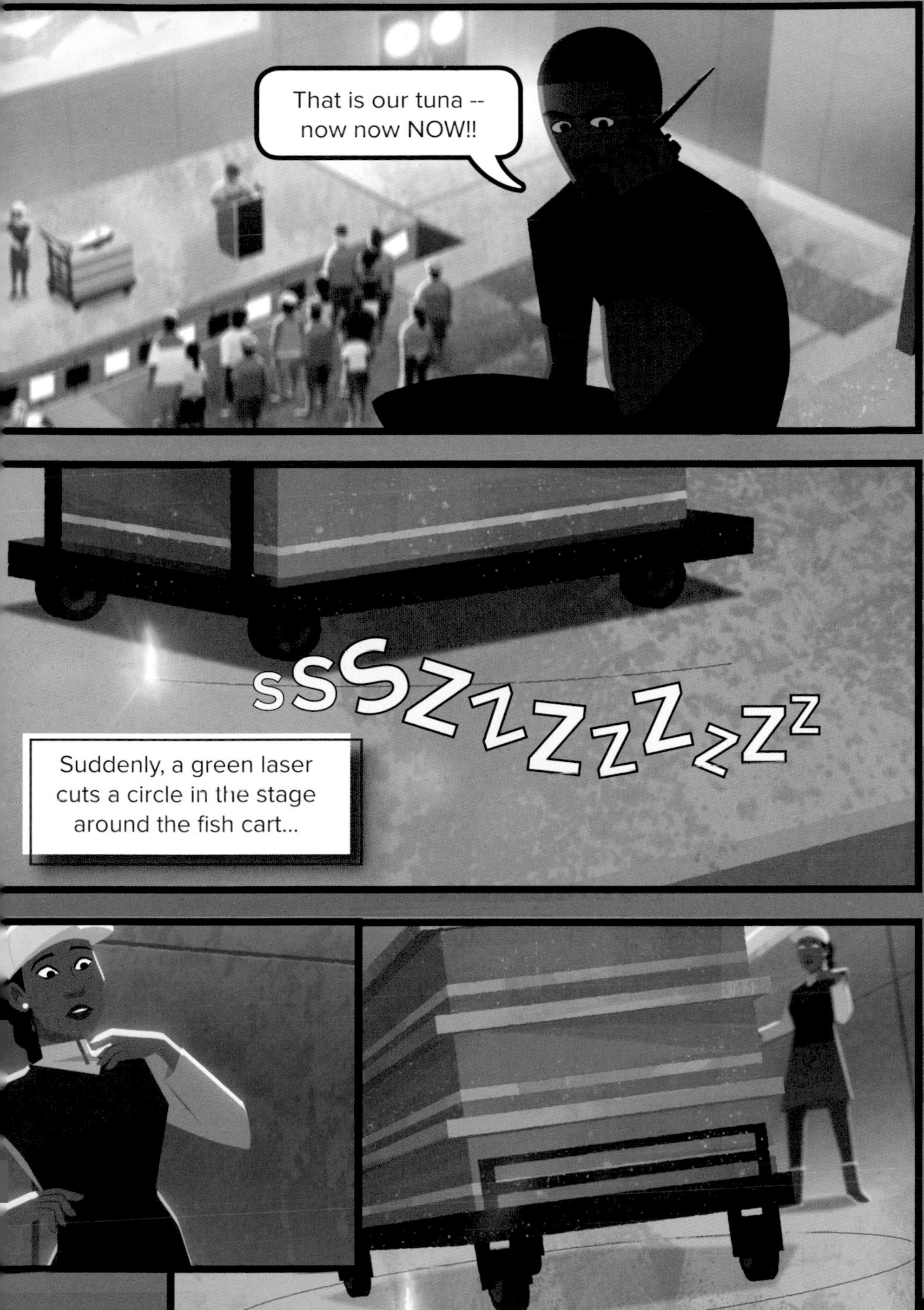
That is our tuna --
now now NOW!!
sSSZzzZzZzZz
Suddenly, a green laser
cuts a circle in the stage
around the fish cart...

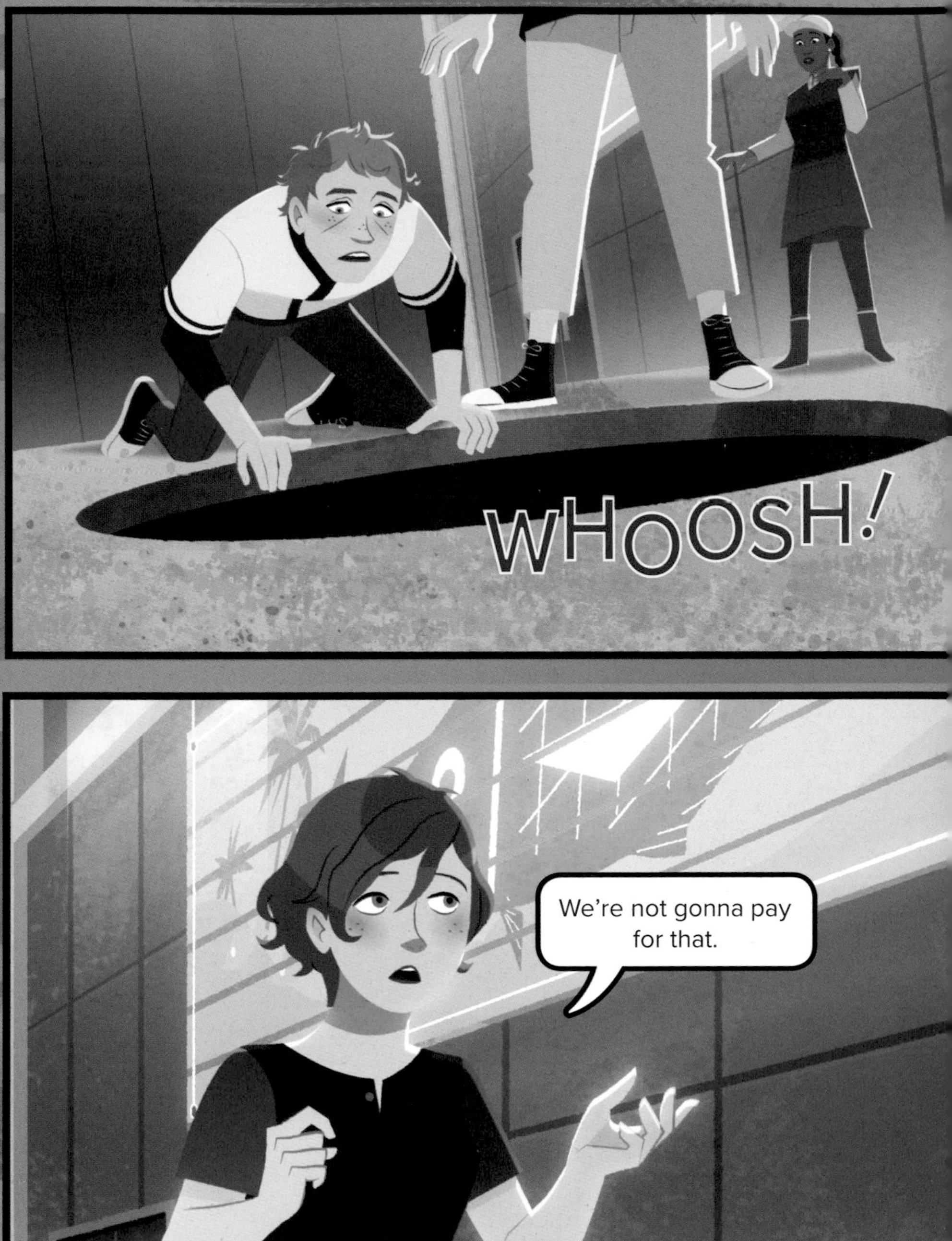
WHOOSH!
We're not gonna pay for that.

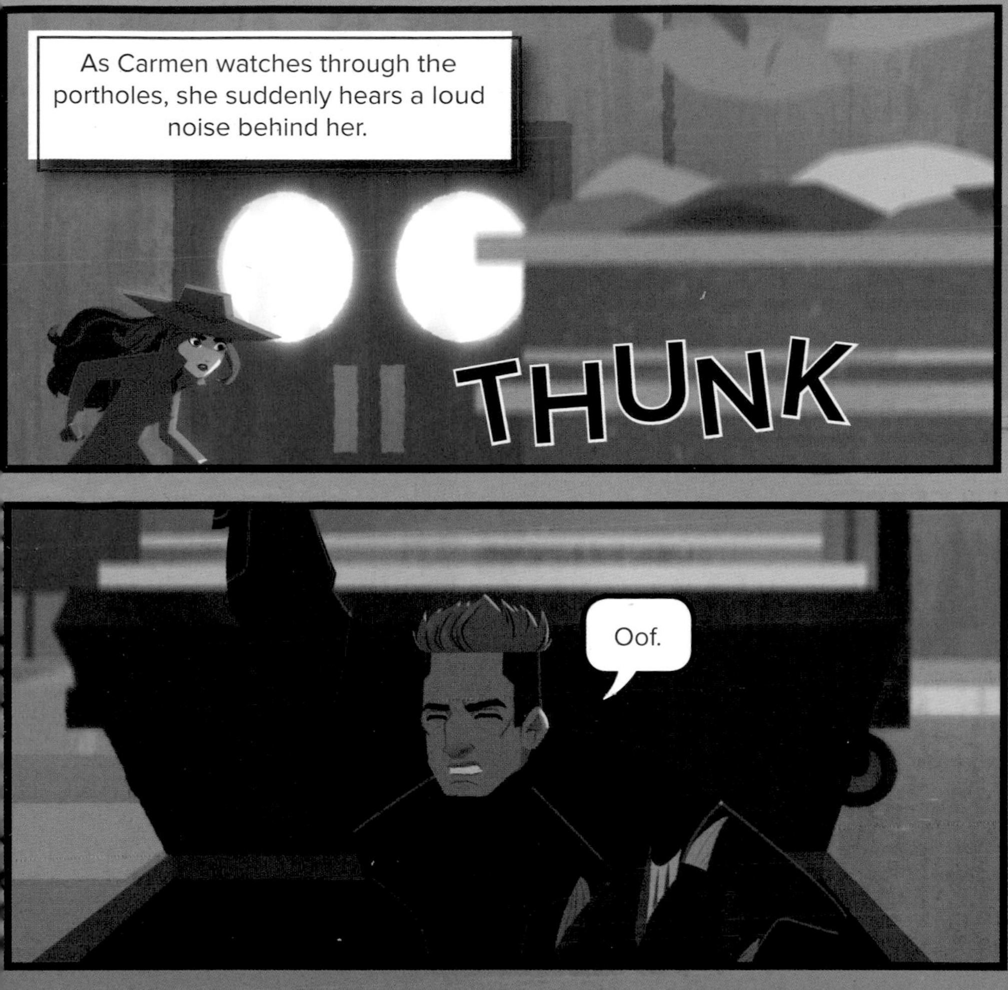
As Carmen watches through the portholes, she suddenly hears a loud noise behind her.
THUNK
Oof.
The human mole emerges through the floor and runs off with the tuna!

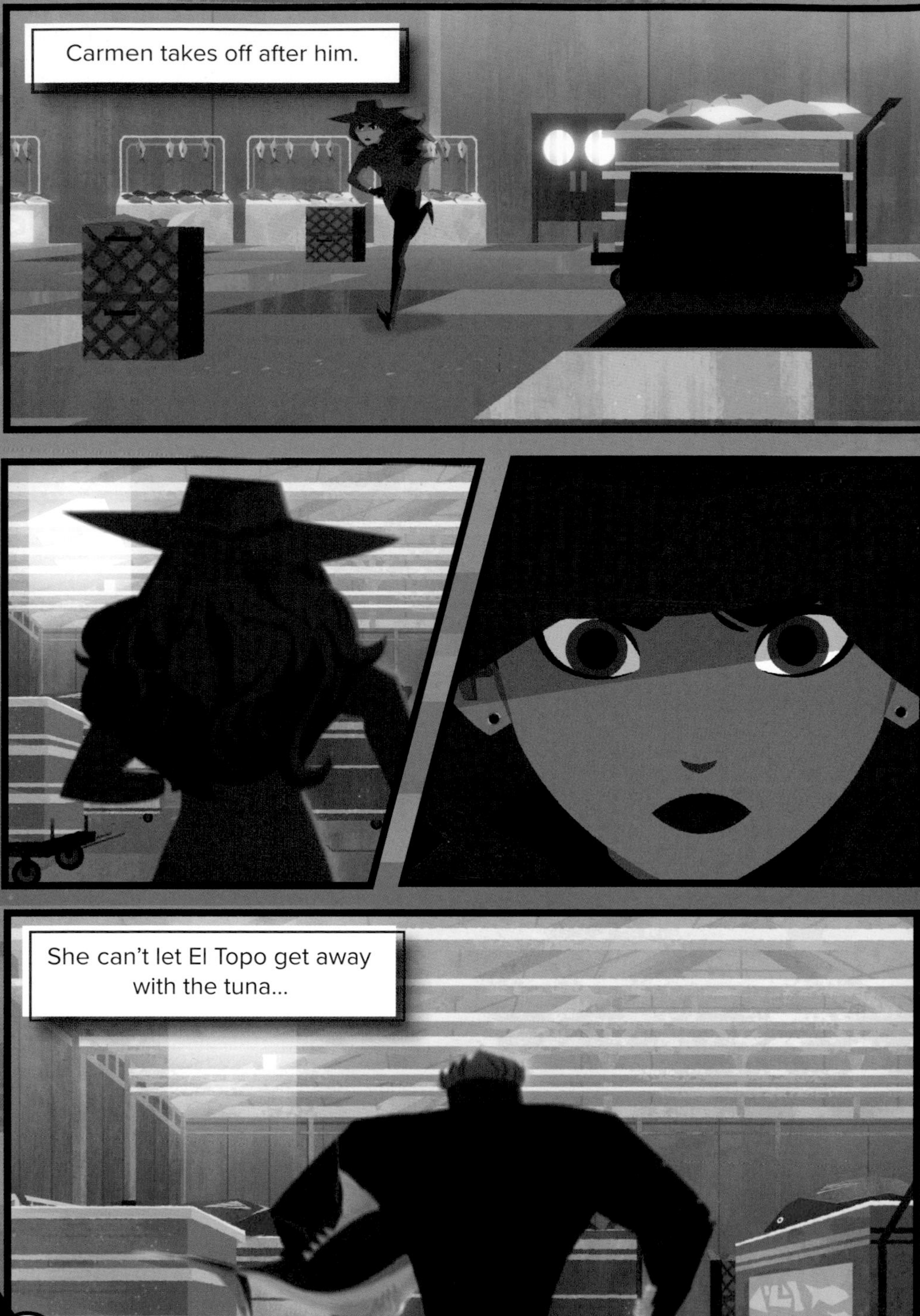
Carmen takes off after him.
She can't let El Topo get away with the tuna...

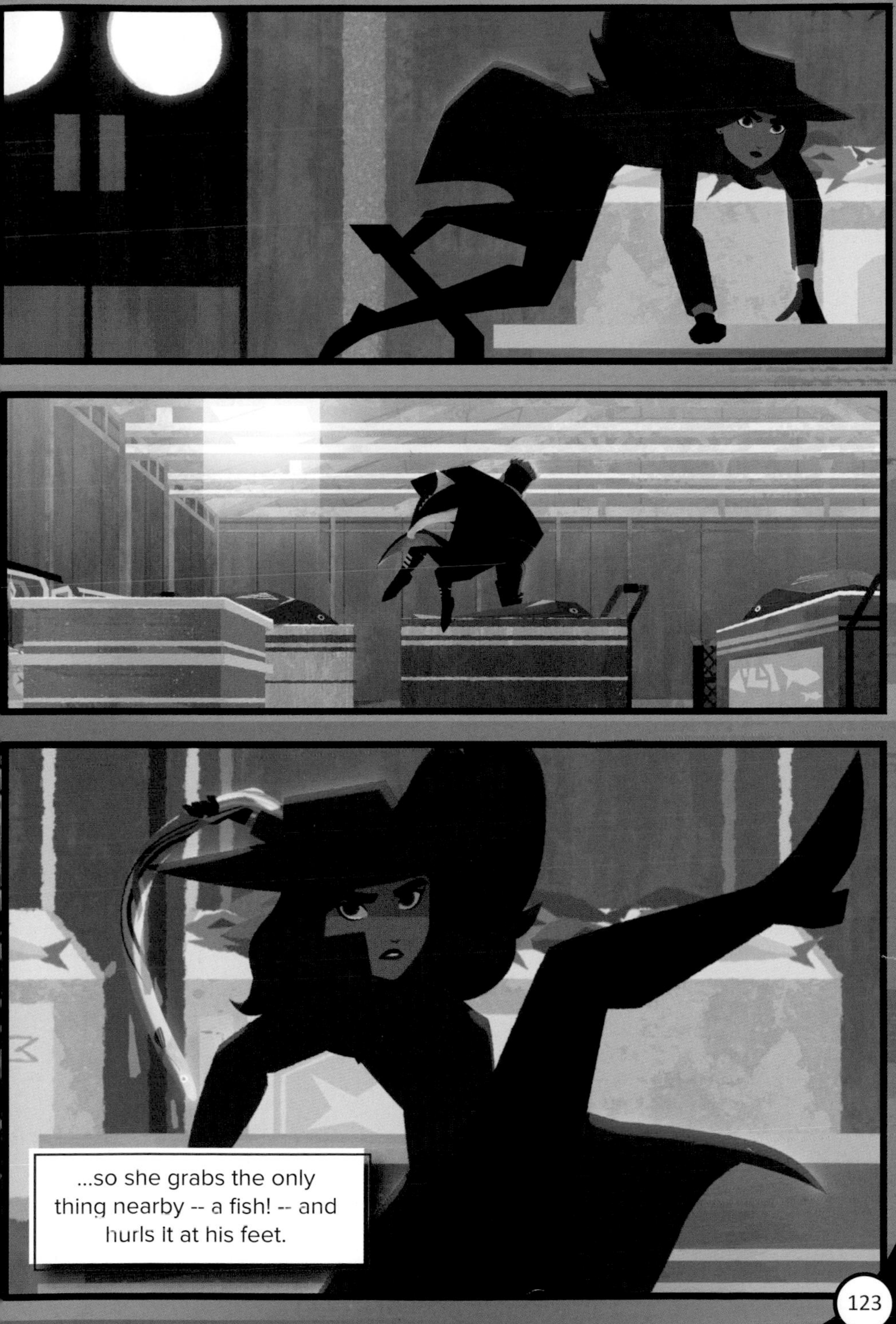
...so she grabs the only thing nearby -- a fish! -- and hurls it at his feet.

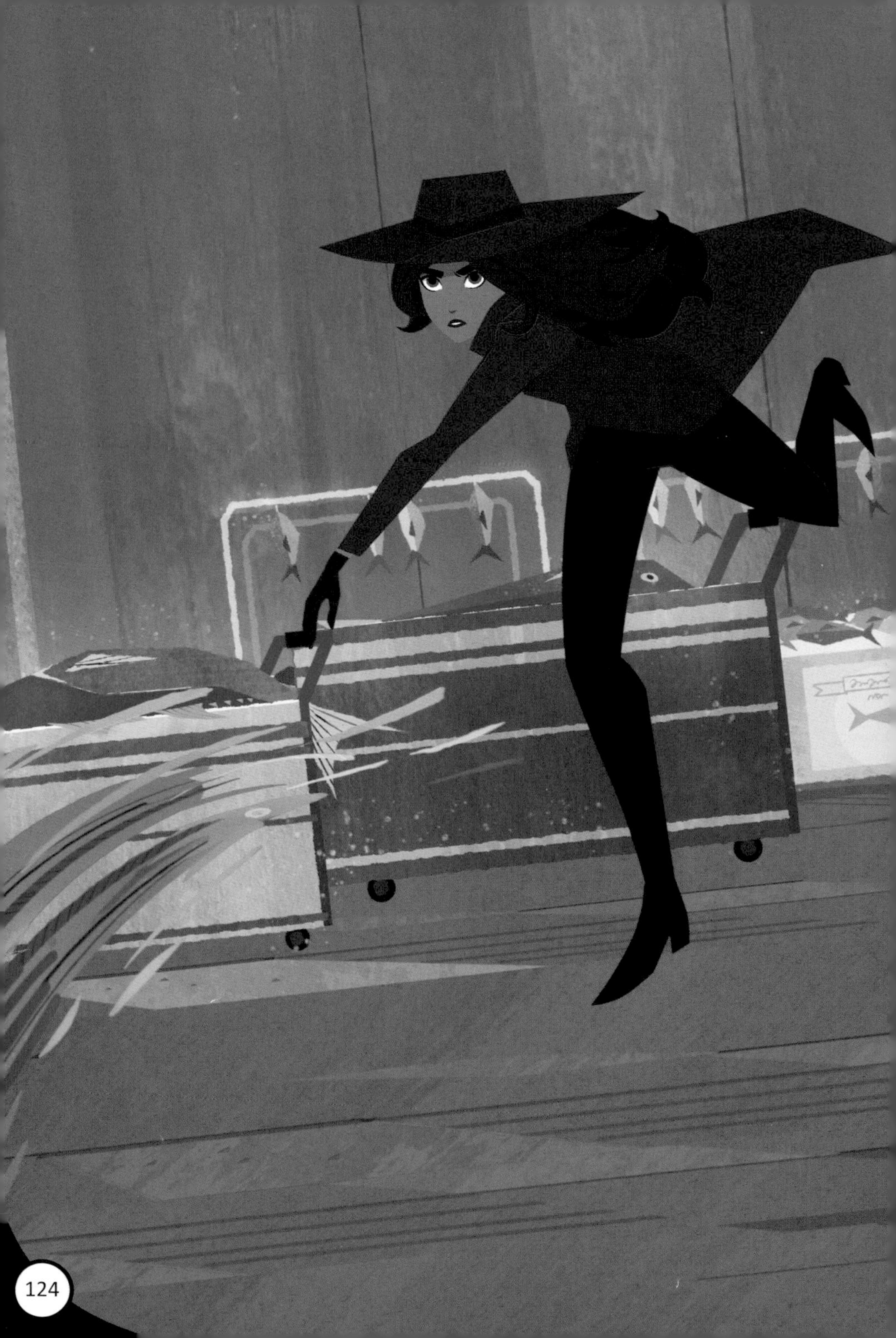

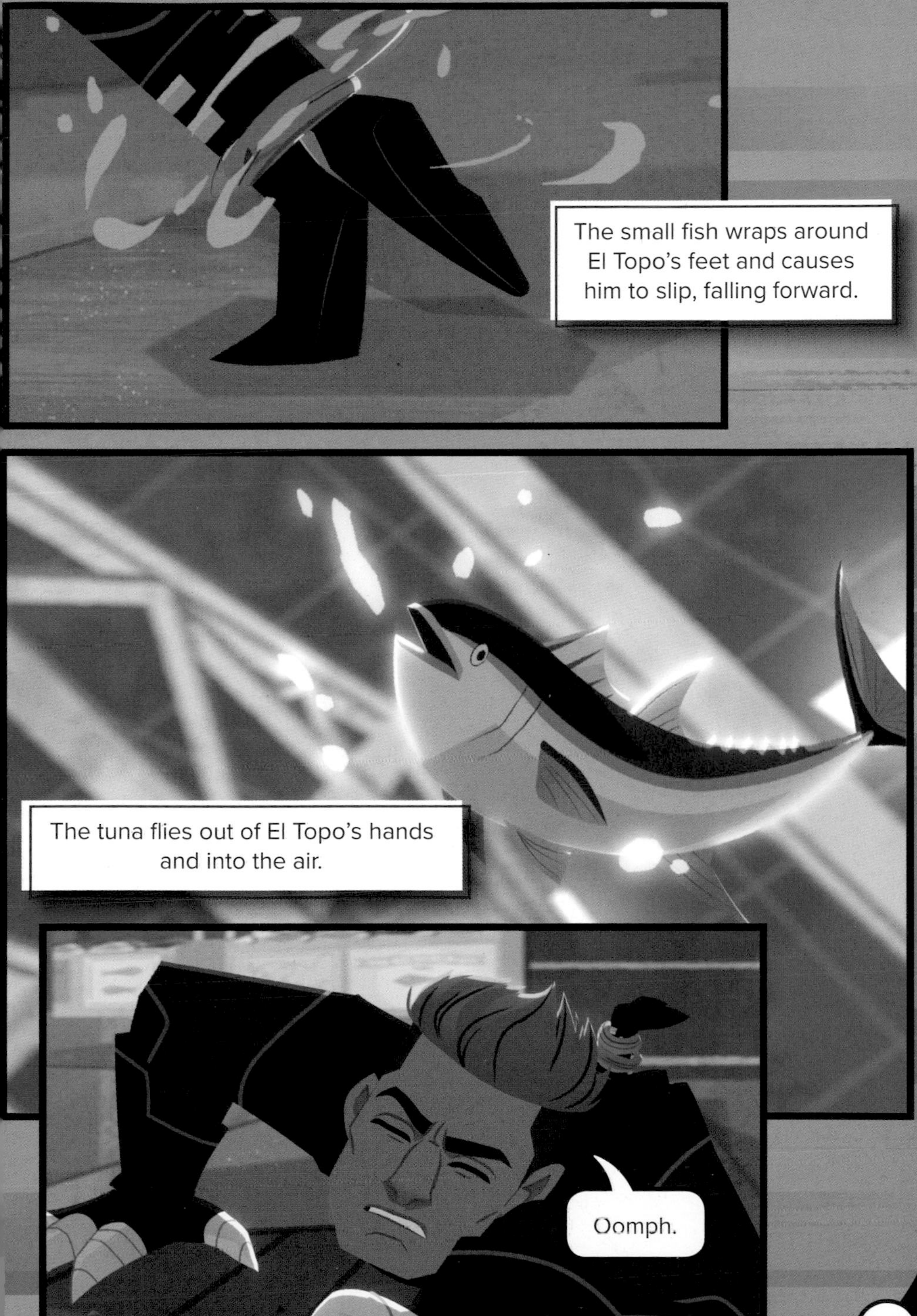

The small fish wraps around El Topo's feet and causes him to slip, falling forward.
The tuna flies out of El Topo's hands and into the air.
Oomph.

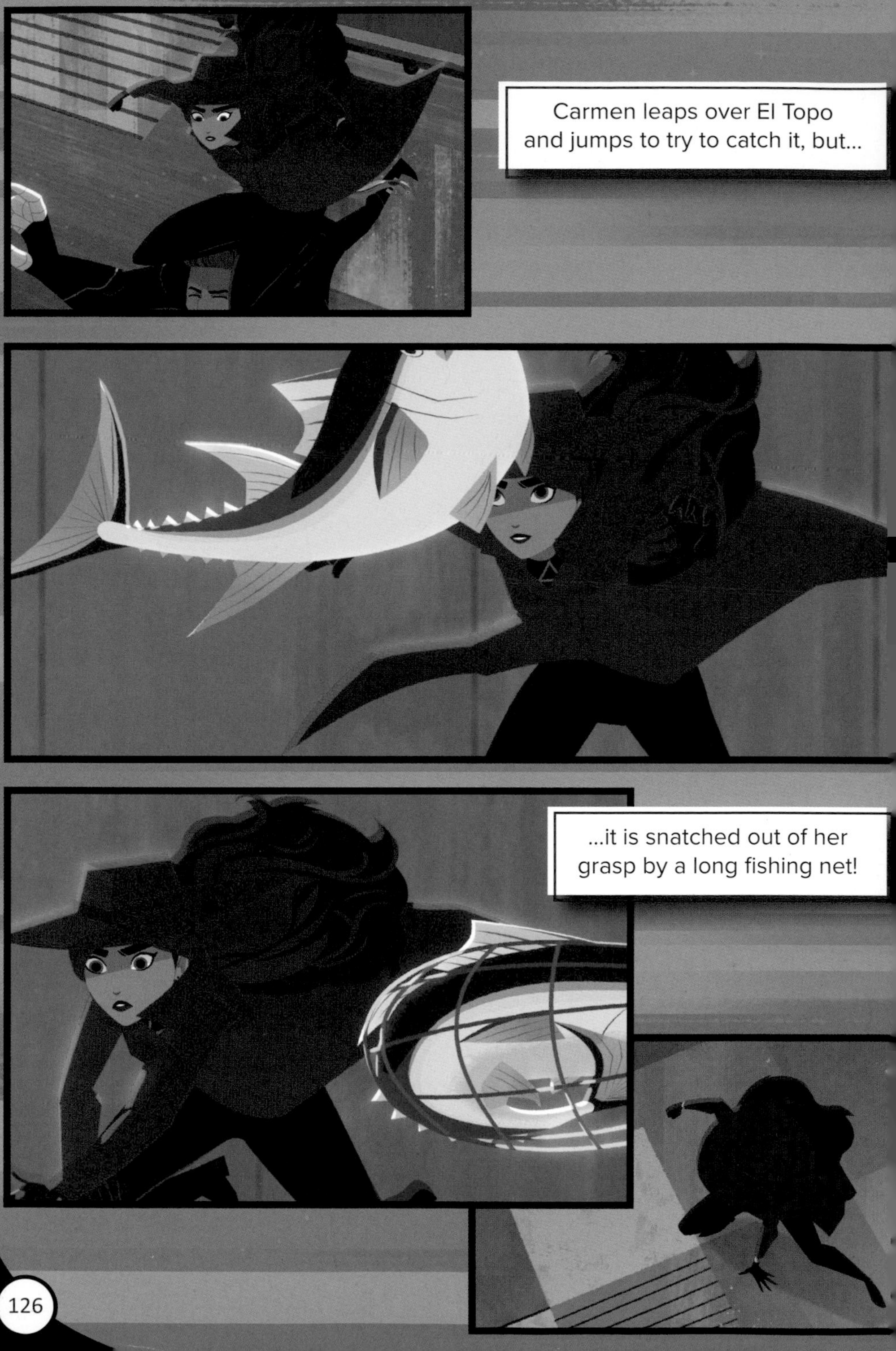
Carmen leaps over El Topo and jumps to try to catch it, but...
...it is snatched out of her grasp by a long fishing net!

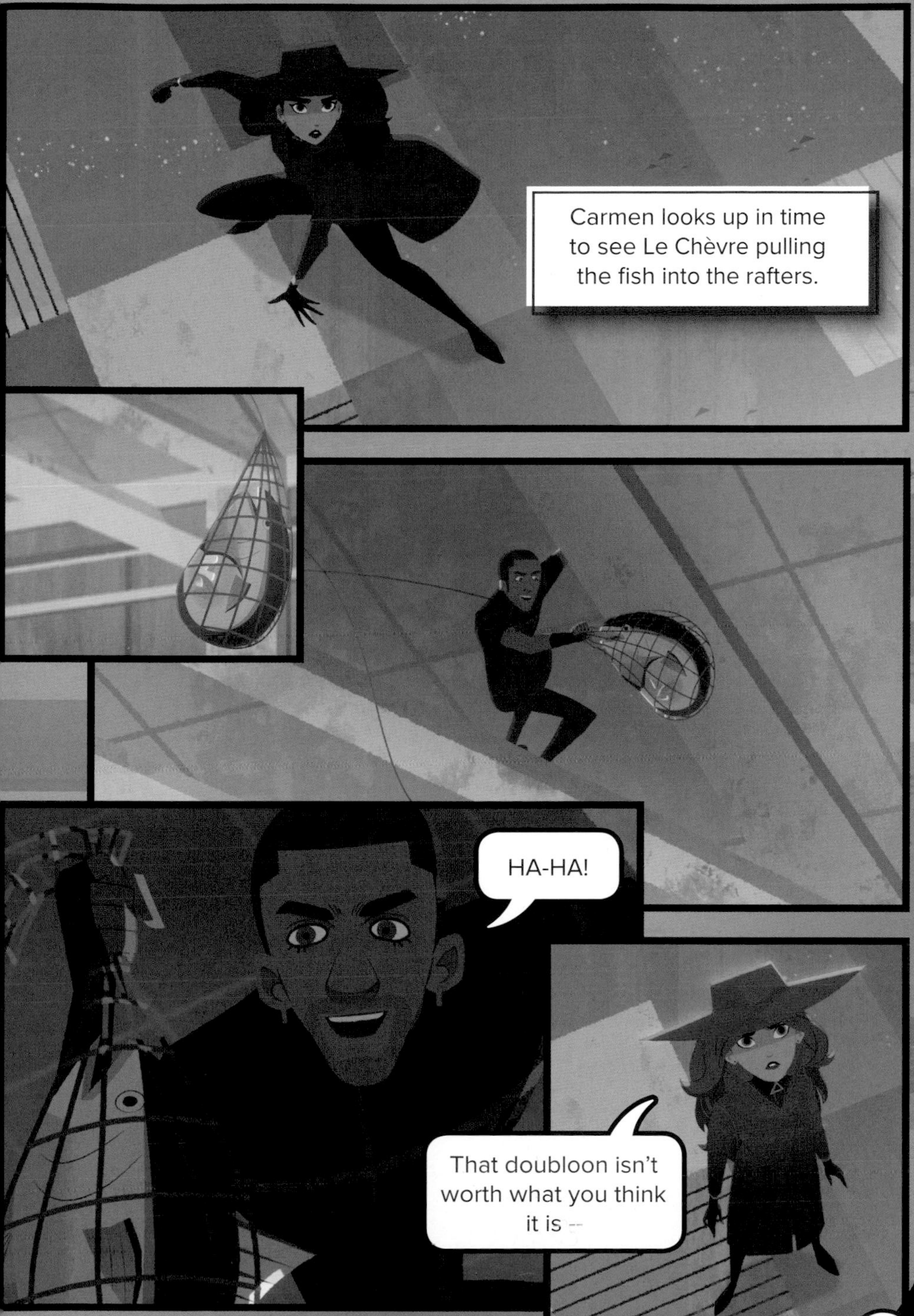
Carmen looks up in time to see Le Chèvre pulling the fish into the rafters.
HA-HA!
That doubloon isn't worth what you think it is --

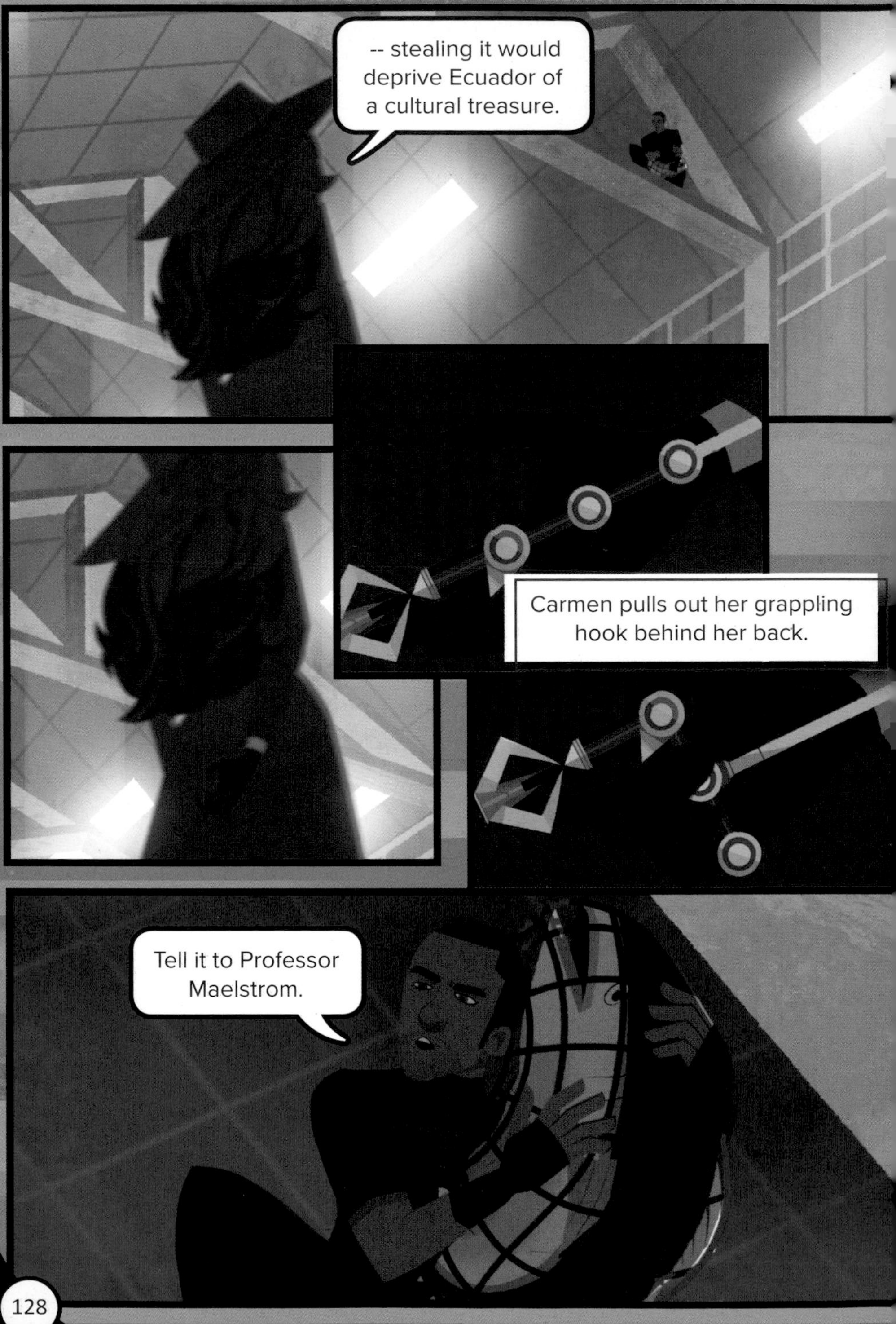
-- stealing it would deprive Ecuador of a cultural treasure.
Carmen pulls out her grappling hook behind her back.
Tell it to Professor Maelstrom.

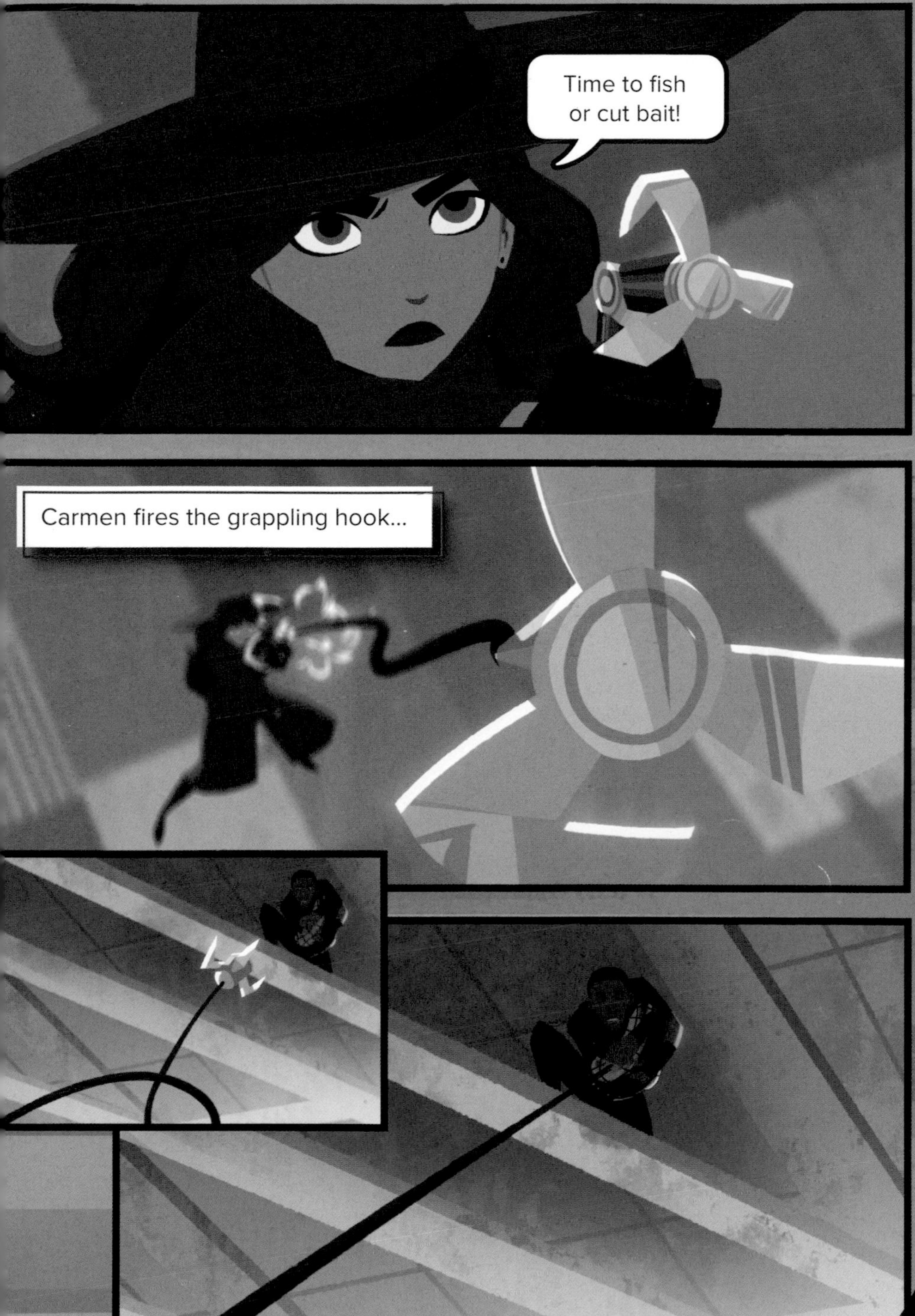
Time to fish or cut bait!
Carmen fires the grappling hook...

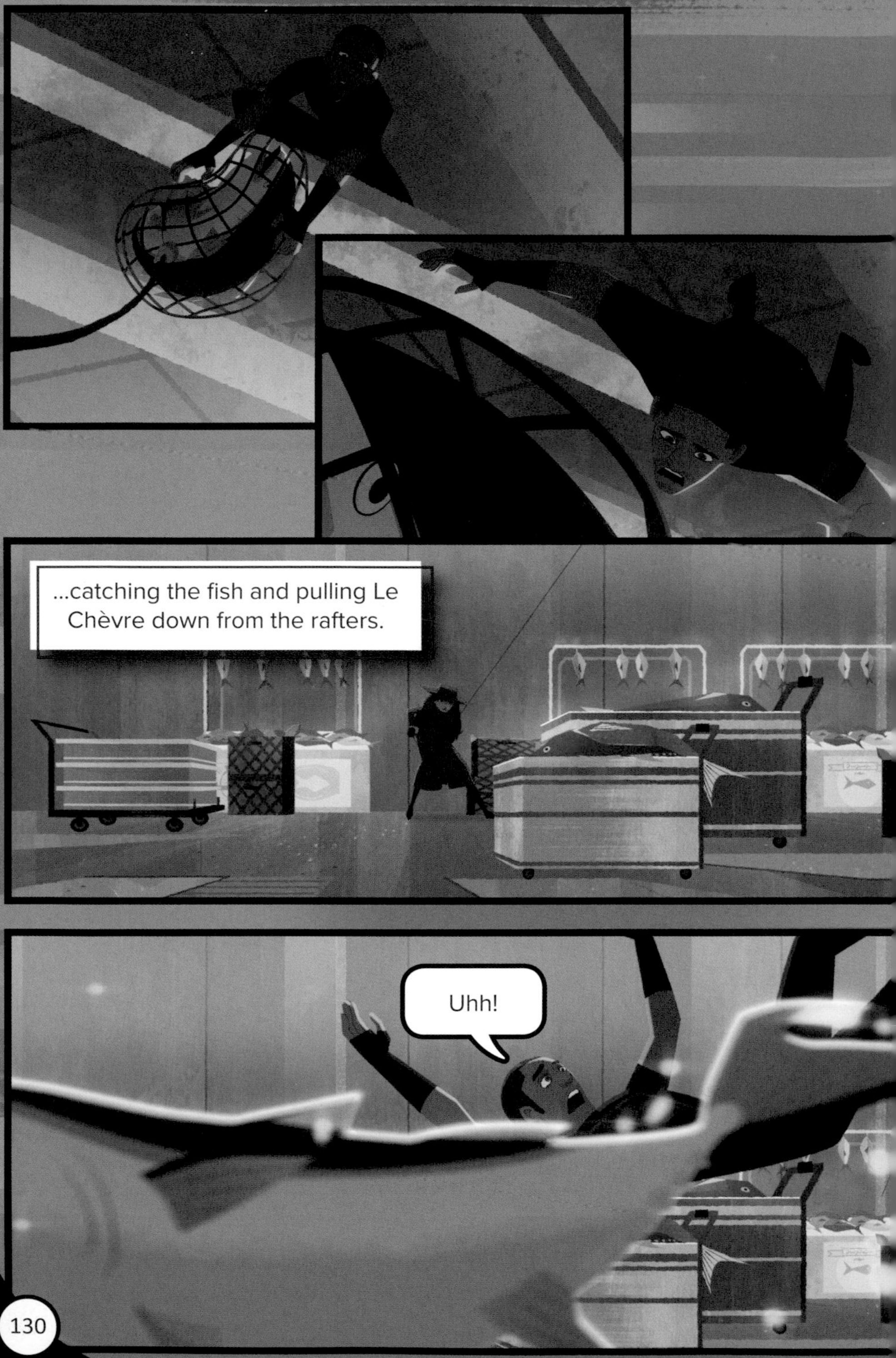
...catching the fish and pulling Le Chèvre down from the rafters.
Uhh!

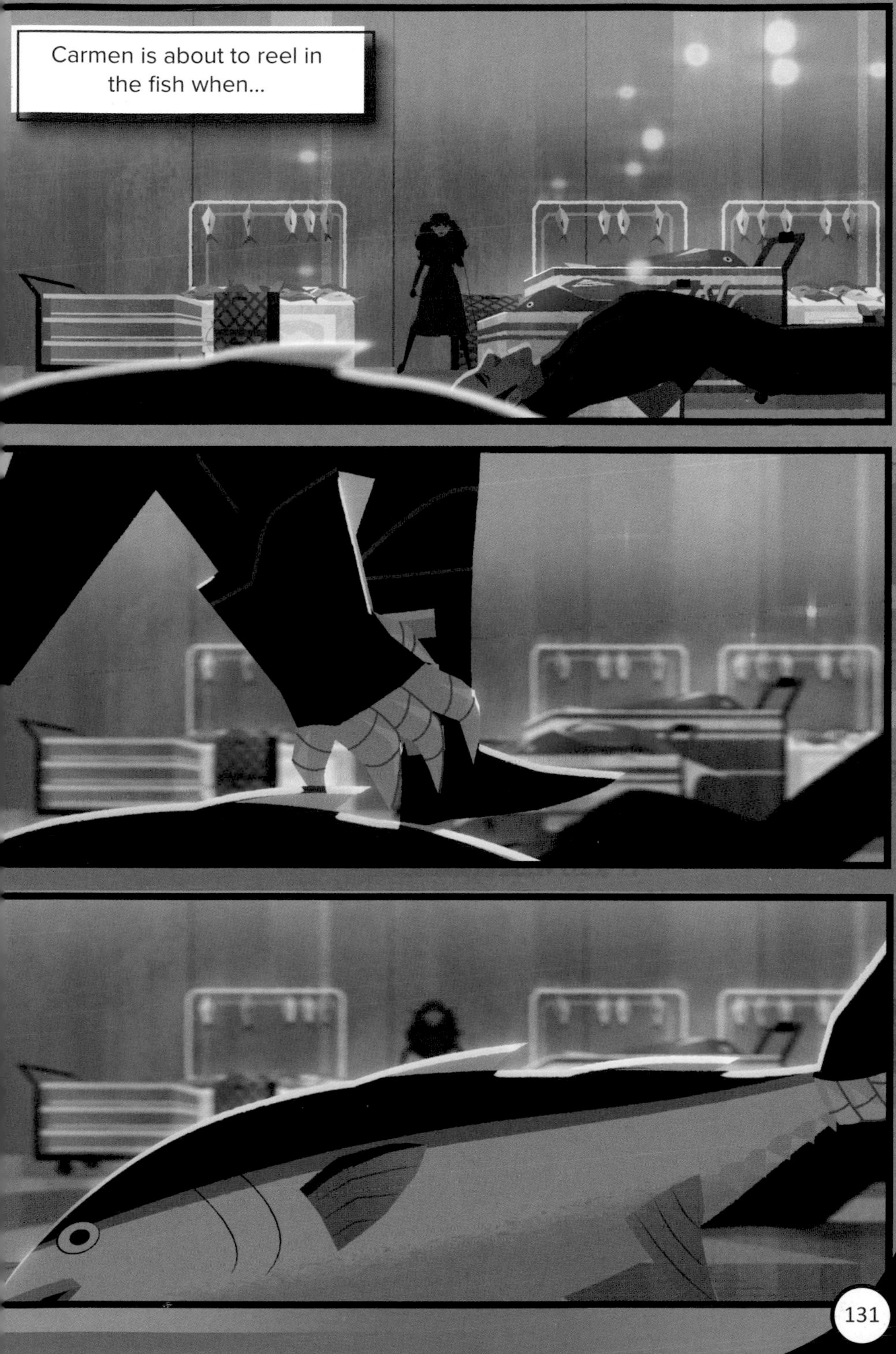
Carmen is about to reel in the fish when...

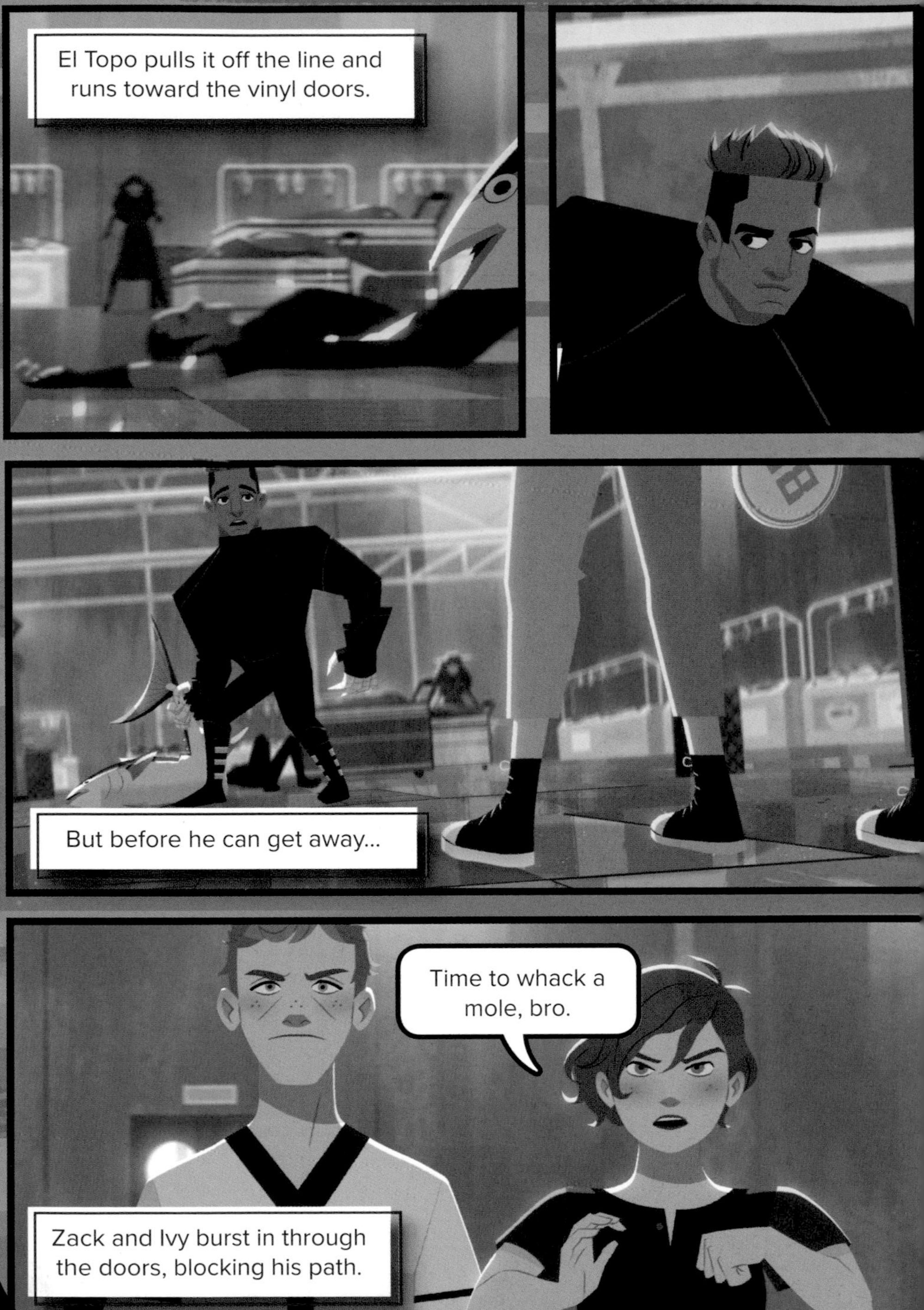
El Topo pulls it off the line and runs toward the vinyl doors.
But before he can get away...
Time to whack a mole, bro.
Zack and Ivy burst in through the doors, blocking his path.

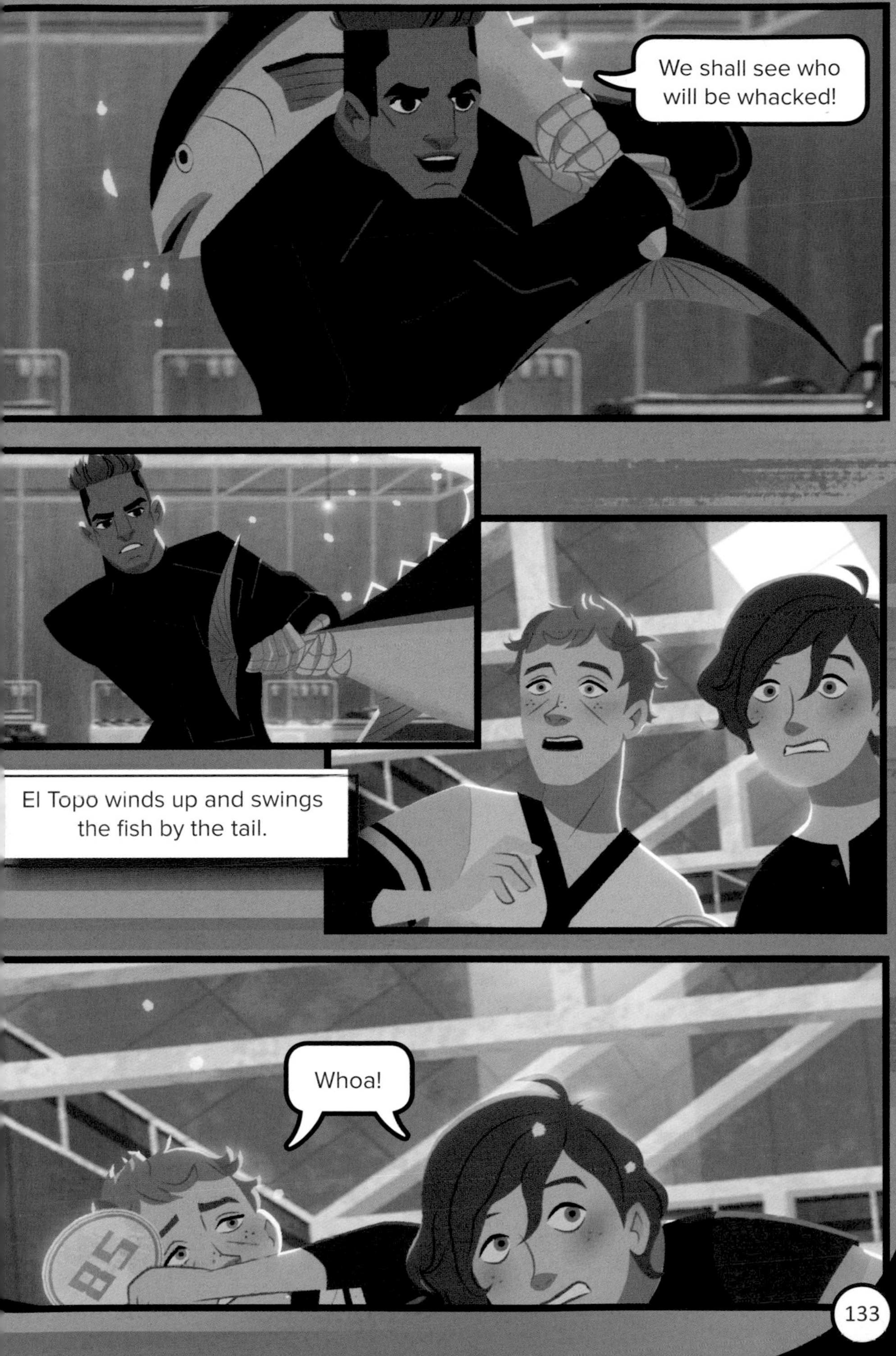
We shall see who will be whacked!
El Topo winds up and swings the fish by the tail.
Whoa!

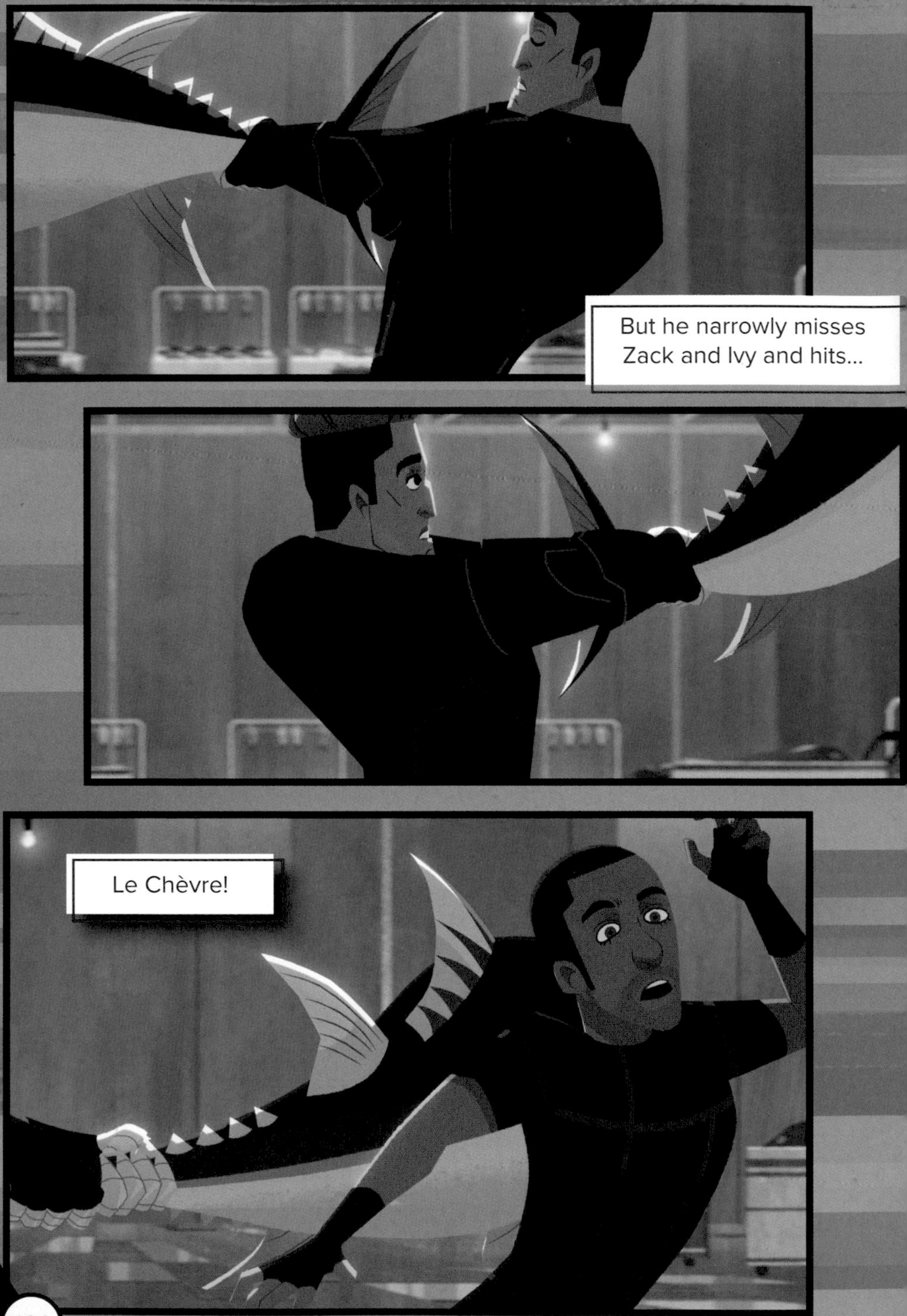
But he narrowly misses Zack and Ivy and hits…
Le Chèvre!

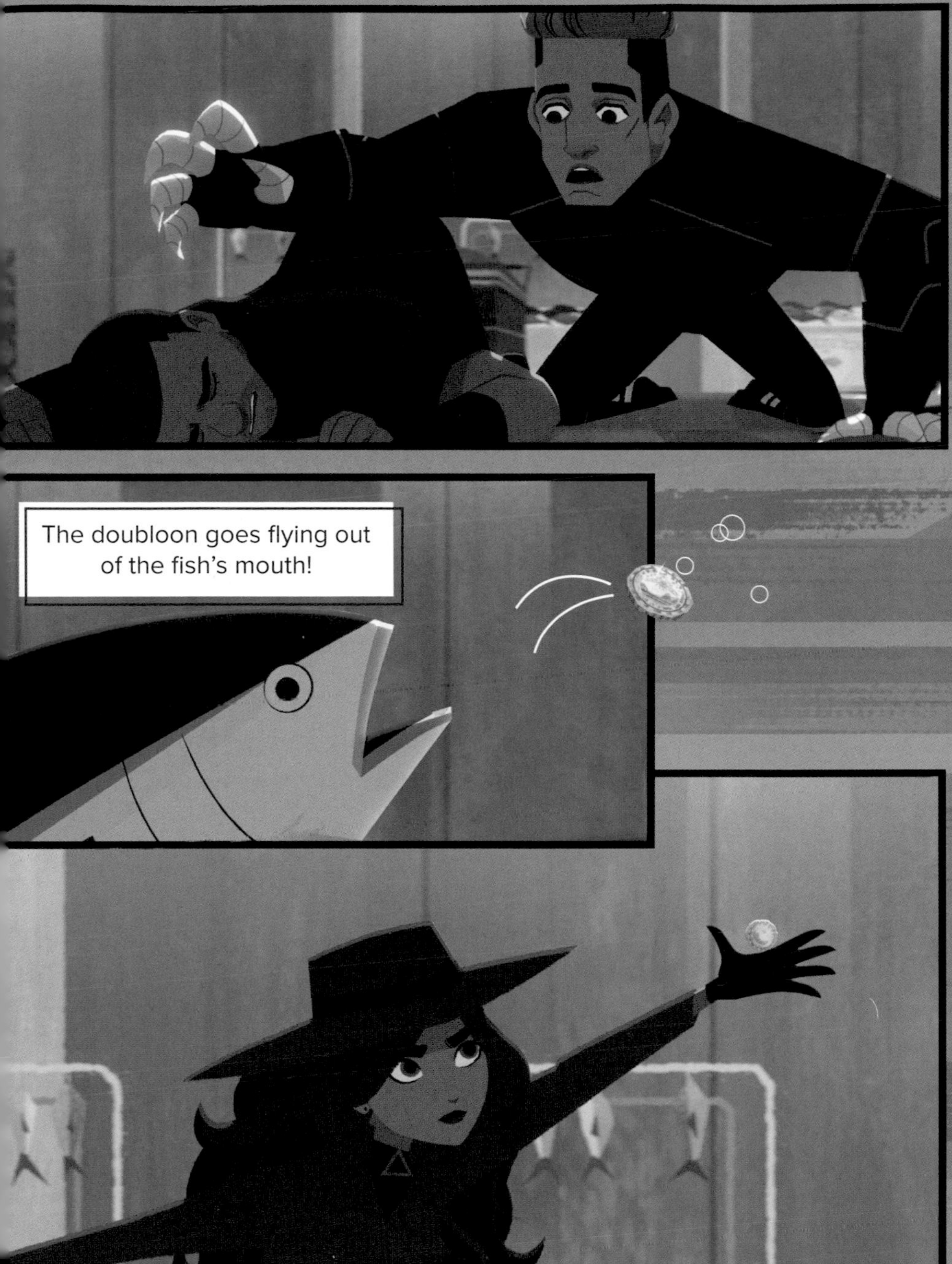
The doubloon goes flying out
of the fish's mouth!

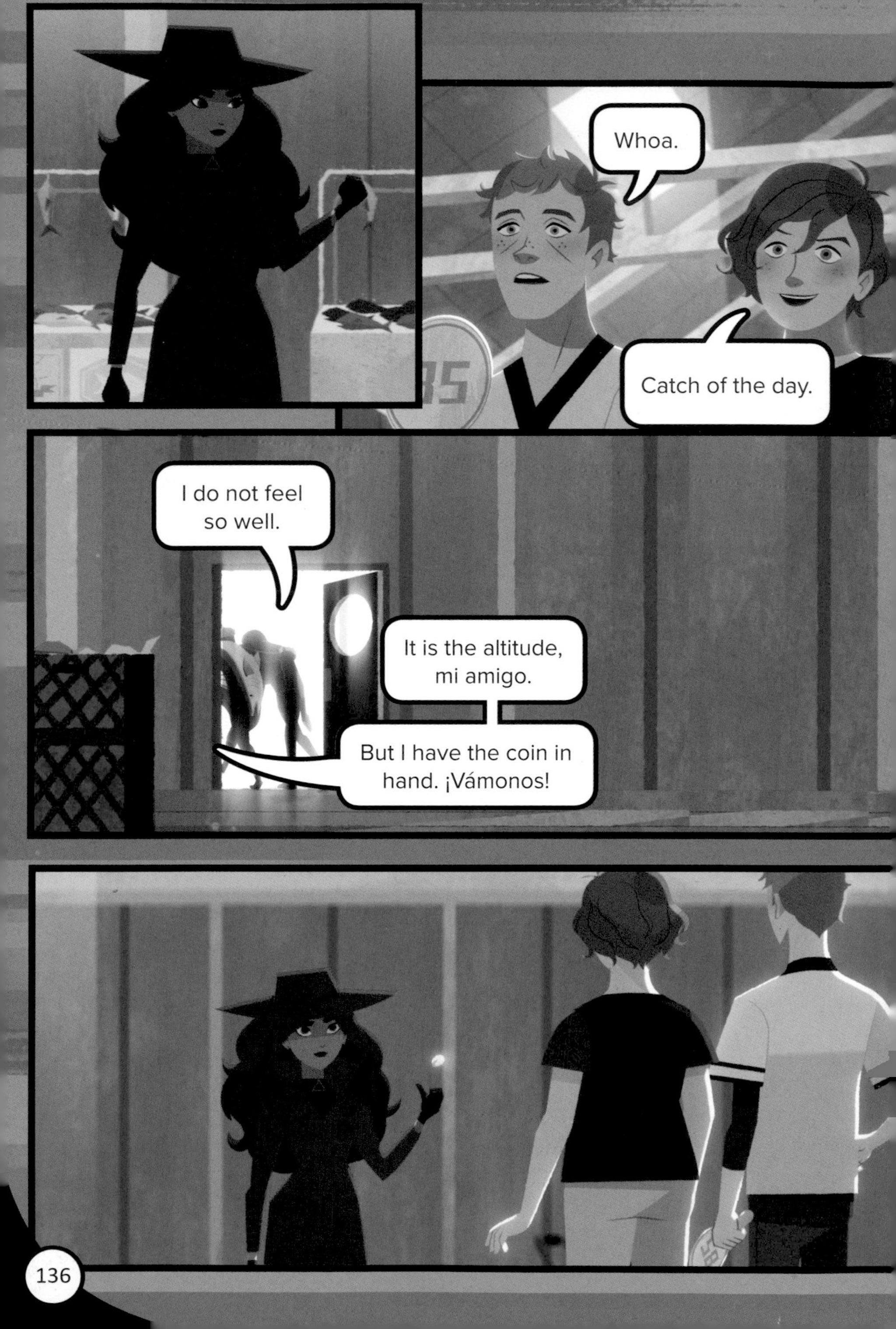
Whoa.
Catch of the day.
I do not feel so well.
It is the altitude, mi amigo.
But I have the coin in hand. ¡Vámonos!

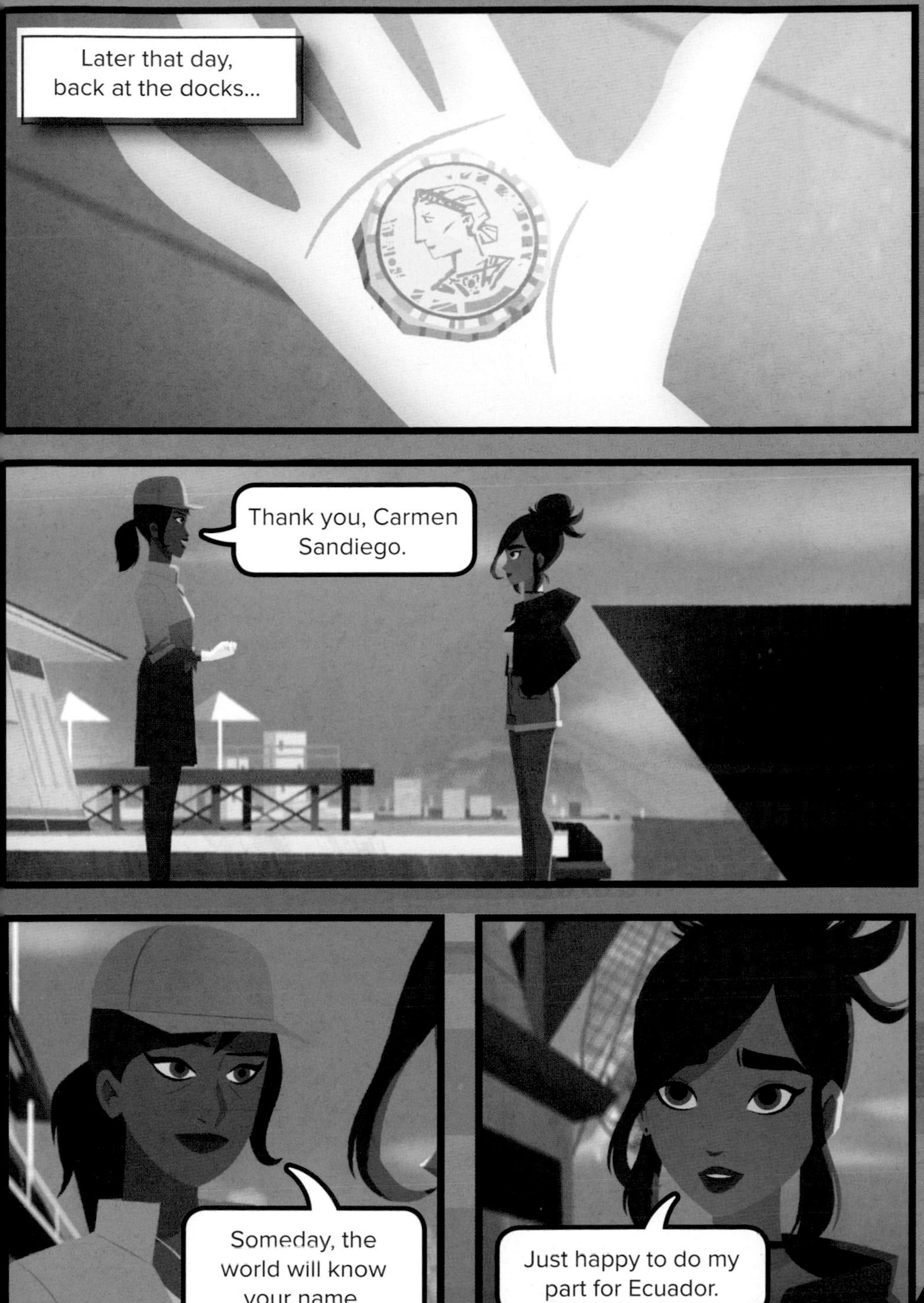
Later that day, back at the docks...
Thank you, Carmen Sandiego.
Someday, the world will know your name.
Just happy to do my part for Ecuador.

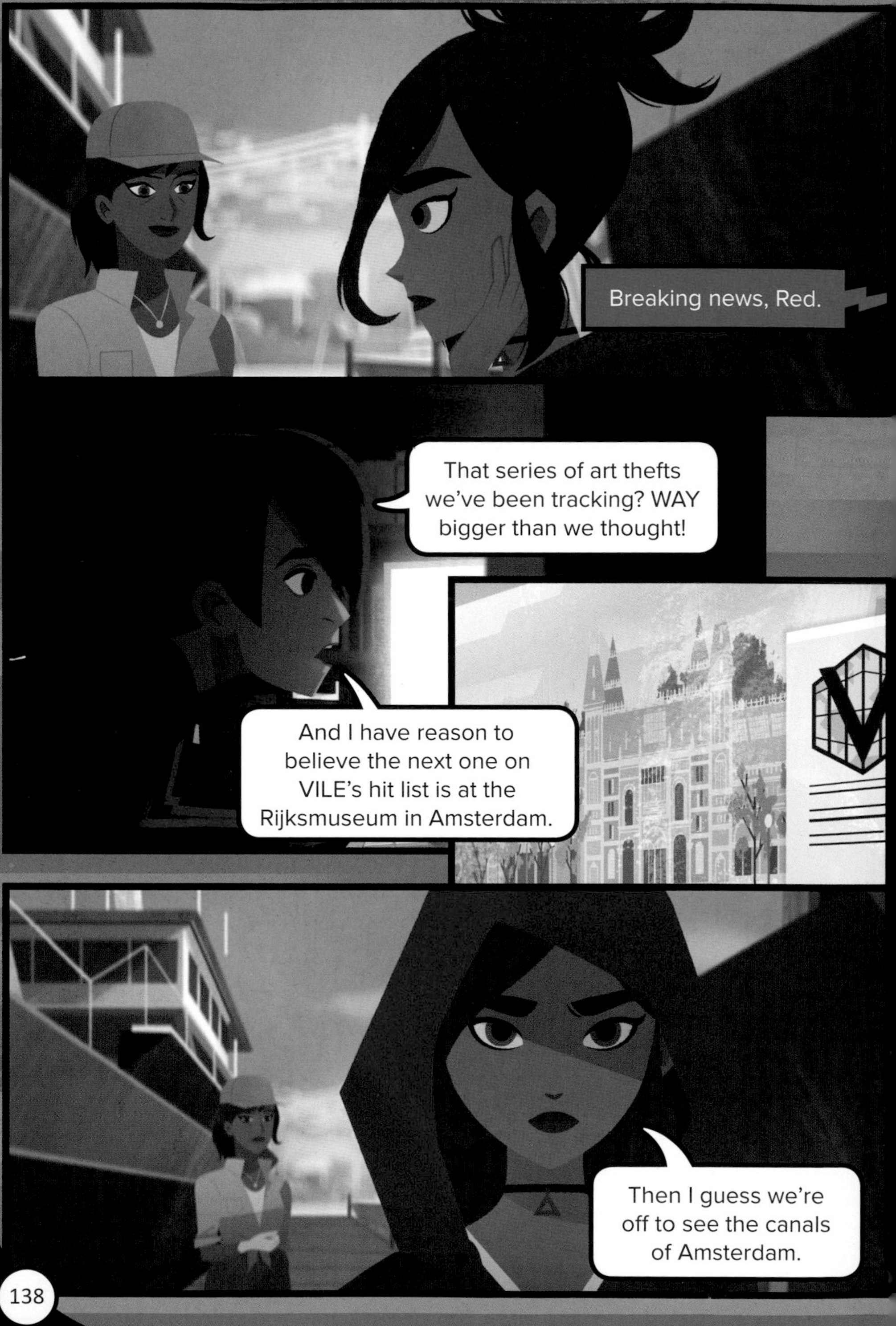
Breaking news, Red.
That series of art thefts we've been tracking? WAY bigger than we thought!
And I have reason to believe the next one on VILE's hit list is at the Rijksmuseum in Amsterdam.
Then I guess we're off to see the canals of Amsterdam.

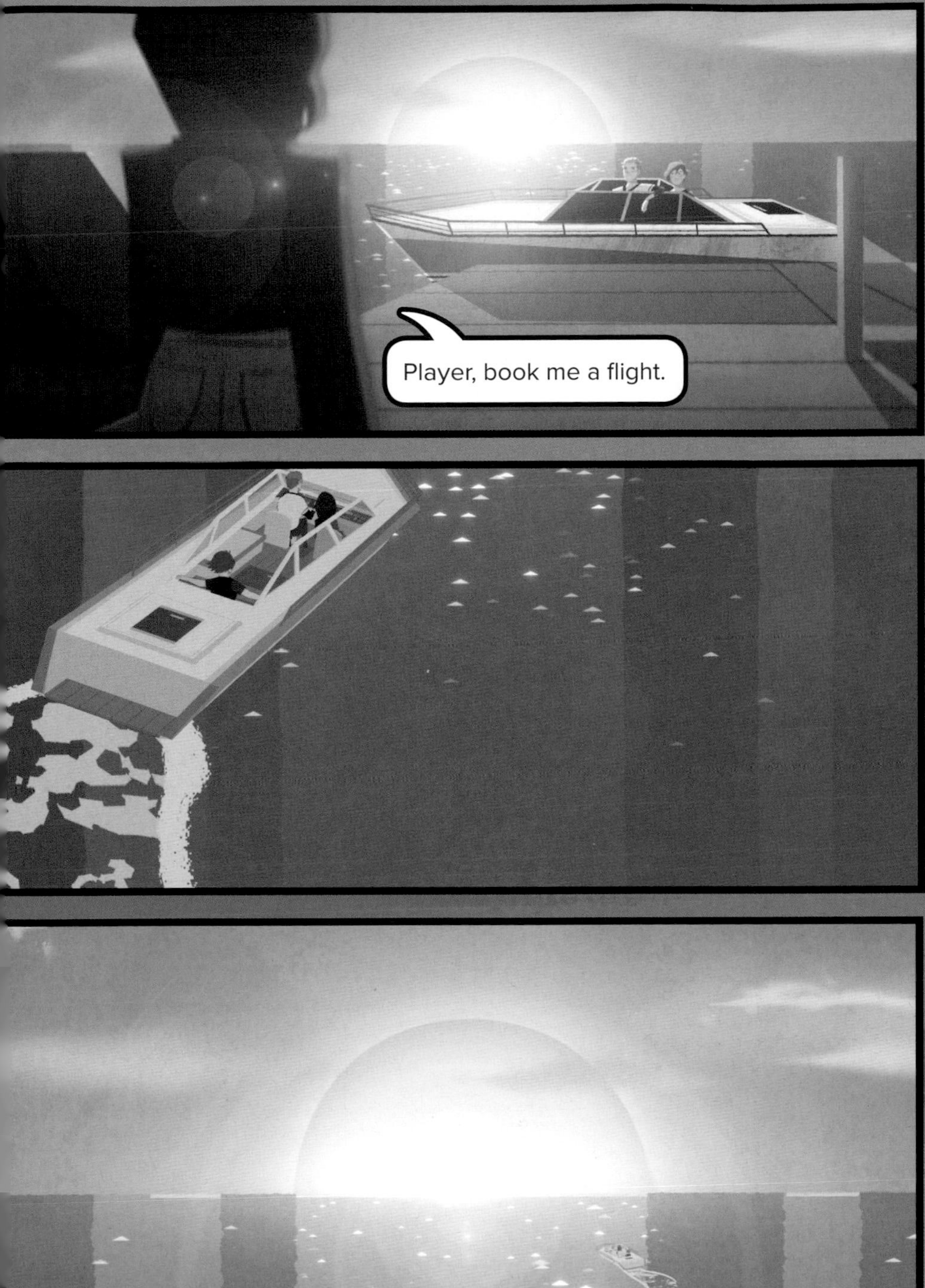
Player, book me a flight.

ECUADOR
DID YOU KNOW . . .

Capital: Quito

Population: 16.3 million people

Official Language: Spanish

Currency: US dollar

Government: Presidential republic

Climate: Tropical along the coast, becoming cooler inland at higher elevations; tropical in Amazonian jungle lowlands

History: The region was conquered first by the Inca and later by Spain. After fighting off the Spanish, Ecuador became an independent nation in 1830.

Flag:

FUN FACTS:

Quito is the world's second-highest capital city at 9,350 feet (2,850 meters) above sea level (after La Paz, Bolivia).

The Galápagos Islands are a territory of Ecuador, where Charles Darwin studied the adaptations of finches' beaks, which helped him develop his theory of evolution.

River dolphins swim in the Amazon -- an endangered species known for their pink color.

There is a monument in San Antonio de Pichincha commemorating the two-hundredth anniversary of the French Geodesic Mission to survey the equator, supposedly located on the equator, complete with a painted line for visitors to admire and take pictures with. Unfortunately, modern technology puts the actual location of the equator about 787 feet (240 meters) away from where the monument stands.

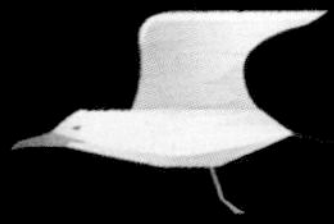

Birdwatching is a significant part of the tourism industry, with over 1,500 different species of birds in Ecuador.

The Galápagos Islands are also home to marine iguanas, the only seafaring lizard in the world, and the famous Galápagos giant tortoises, which can weigh up to 550 pounds and live over 100 years!

One of the most environmentally diverse countries in the world, Ecuador has coastal lowlands, the Andes Mountains, and a tropical rainforest inland toward the Amazon.

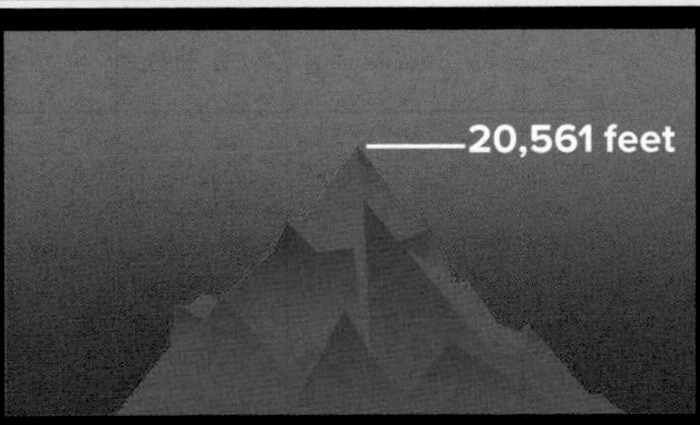
20,561 feet

Mount Chimborazo, at 20,561 feet (6,267 meters), is the highest point in Ecuador. Because the earth isn't a perfect sphere and is thicker around the equator, Mount Chimborazo is the point farthest from the center of the earth.

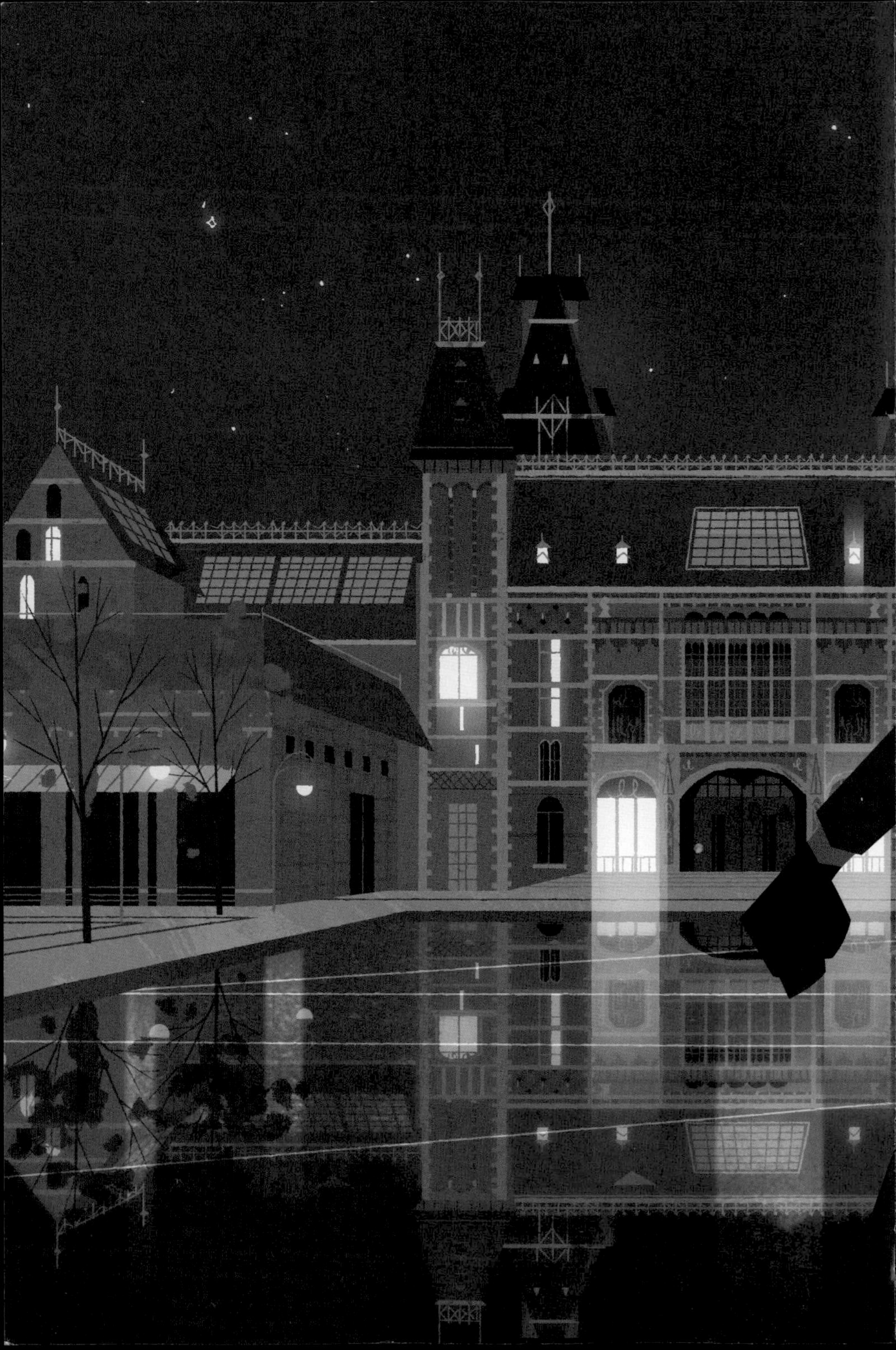

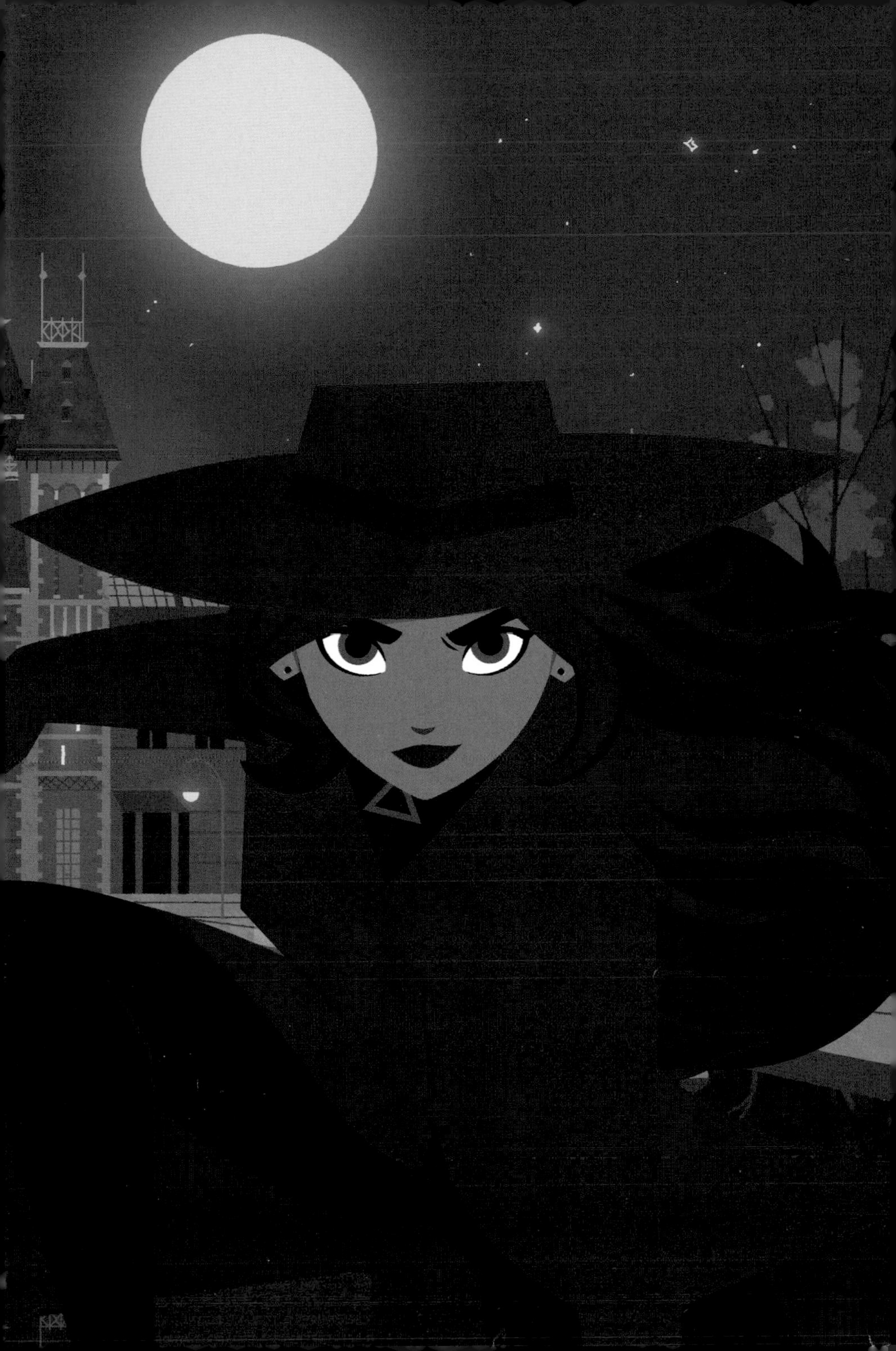

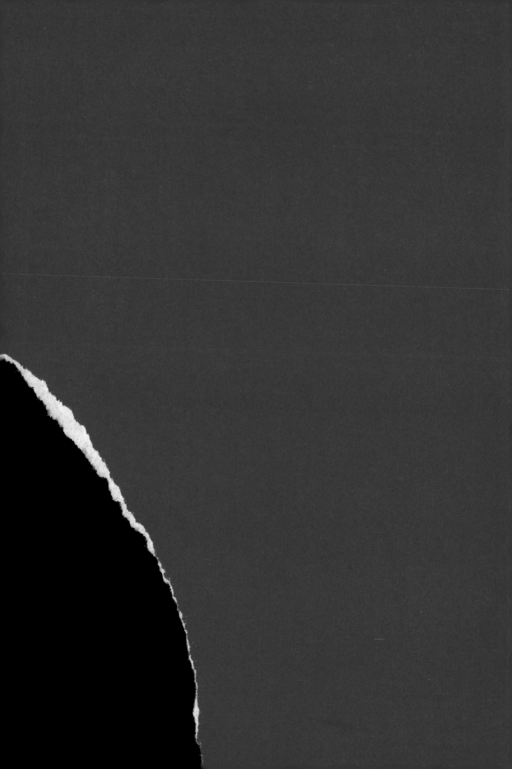